THE GYPSY LADY

"Maeve," he said.

Dear God, she cried out silently, *it cannot happen now. I cannot let him take me in his power again.* But she felt that sweetness in the core of her body and knew that he had seen her trembling.

"Maeve . . ." He was kneeling by her now; the kiss of his mouth on her palm was drawing her into him, as a leaf would be drawn helpless into the tunnel of the wind, and she took one last shuddering breath. . . .

And plunged on.

THIS WILLING PASSION

Patricia Cloud

THIS WILLING PASSION

PATRICIA CLOUD

BERKLEY BOOKS, NEW YORK

This Berkley book contains the complete
text of the original hardcover edition.
It has been completely reset in a type face
designed for easy reading, and was printed
from new film.

THIS WILLING PASSION

A Berkley Book / published by arrangement with
G. P. Putnam's Sons

PRINTING HISTORY
G. P. Putnam's Sons edition / May 1978
Berkley edition / September 1980

ISBN: 0-425-04650-8

A BERKLEY BOOK ® TM 757,375
Berkley Books are published by Berkley Publishing Corporation,
200 Madison Avenue, New York, New York 10016.
PRINTED IN THE UNITED STATES OF AMERICA

ACKNOWLEDGMENTS

1. The lines quoted on page 23 are excerpted from the poem "The Song of Crede" (anon.), translated from the Irish by Kuno Meyer, in *1,000 Years of Irish Poetry* (New York: Grosset & Dunlap Universal Library, 1962).

2. The lines quoted on page 99 are from A. C. Swinburne's poem *Atalanta in Calydon*.

3. The line quoted on page 144 is excerpted from the poem "Dark Rosaleen" (first version) by Owen Roe MacWard, translated from the Irish by James Clarence Mangan, in *1,000 Years of Irish Poetry*.

For

MILLET BAILEY

and

my grandfather,
HARRY W. ENGLISH

PROLOGUE

THE NEW YORK of 1870 had never seen an actress quite like her, this woman with green, fiery eyes in a dove-white face, with gleaming inky hair. She seemed to stand in an invisible wind.

And on that autumn evening when the first-act curtain fell in Daly's Theater on the tragedy of *Macbeth*, there was a strange stillness for an instant before the burst of wild applause.

Bernard O'Reilly, former Jesuit and escort to the well-dressed matron Mrs. Charles Patrick Dady, preserved a discreet silence. For he had known a similar dismay to hers when the theater manager had announced the name of Miss Fanny Davenport's replacement. Throughout the first act O'Reilly had been mouse-still, bemused despite himself by the actress' beauty and her power.

"The very devil of a thing," O'Reilly said unclerically to himself, stealing a glance at Mrs. Dady. Her lips were trembling. Beyond her, their irreverent young companion, Harold Schuyler, gave a little laugh and drawled, "I've never seen such a . . . racy interpretation of the play."

O'Reilly frowned, then reflected, *The boy doesn't know who she is*.

Mrs. Dady, recovering her poise, retorted coolly, "Nor I. I hardly know what the Judge would think of it." She gave the title its full, resounding capital; Judge Dady, a leading Shakespearean scholar, had been responsible some years

1

before for the erection of a statue to the Bard in New York's
Central Park. He was absent now only because a heavy cold
kept him to his bed.

O'Reilly smiled, asking in his cultivated voice, "Shall we
take a turn about the lobby?"

The poor woman is very pale, he thought, studying his
friend's face below the elaborate structure of graying hair.

Mrs. Dady called sharply to young Schuyler, "Come along,
Harold. I know you're dying to smoke." Preceding the men
up the aisle, she thought what a comfort Bernard O'Reilly
was—unostentatious, intellectual, refined. After the war he
had withdrawn from the Jesuits to devote himself to literature.

Mrs. Dady's reflections were interrupted by the sight of
smartly dressed acquaintances, and she nodded and smiled to
left and right. When they reached the teeming lobby, Mrs.
Dady exchanged a few words with Kate Chase Sprague, New
York's most modish woman, who was dressed tonight by the
city's own Mme. Demorest and not by Worth.

Mrs. Dady remarked to O'Reilly as they passed on, "I fear
the women mark the war merely by the absence of Worth."

A sad smile creased her companion's gentle face. "Indeed,
it seems so." The disastrous French defeat at Sedan in September had closed the famous fashion house of Worth in
Paris. O'Reilly blessed his friend's sharp intelligence and
looked about, remarking how untouched the splendid women
seemed . . . America's own conflict so soon forgotten!

A small gasp from Mrs. Dady made O'Reilly glance quickly
at her. "What is it?"

"Mrs. Morgan," she replied in a low voice, indicating with
a slight nod the portly woman in her sixties emerging from the
throng. "What must she be feeling?" Mrs. Dady asked. "Her
own son . . . and that other poor creature, destroyed by that
. . . woman."

"Oh, but surely now," O'Reilly protested, "that is not
quite—"

Mrs. Dady extended her gloved hand to Mrs. Morgan, who
she noticed was stouter than ever. How fortunate that bustles
were as small as they were!

"I beg your pardon," the foreigner murmured, stepping
aside for the box's other occupant to precede him, thinking,

There is a man with something on his mind.

"Quite all right." The other's voice was soft but deep. When they reached the smoking area, the tall, deep-voiced man offered his match-case to the foreigner. "Light?"

"I thank you." The foreigner, several inches shorter than his companion, held his cigar up to the proffered flame.

Puffing, he said, "Beautiful woman, the Lady Macbeth. Better actress than the Davenport as well. Hell to pay when the leading lady's up and around!" He grinned, proud of his use of the American phrases.

The tall man with the unusual eyes did not return his smile. "I imagine that . . . Miss Heron will not continue long upon the stage."

"Why, she was splendid! She gave the role a . . . you might say . . . sensual cast that has seldom been seen in my experience. Never, I should say."

But the speaker was dismayed at the effect of his remark. The tall man's face had frozen into an impassive mask; his eyes looked hard and cold.

Blurting out the first thing in his head, the foreigner said, "She has a most . . . uncommon air."

For the first time the tall, stern stranger smiled a slight smile. "She had a most uncommon story."

"Oh, I beg your pardon. You are acquainted with Miss Heron then?"

"You are a stranger to the country, it appears."

Puzzled, the other nodded.

The tall man was silent for an instant; then he said with an odd inflection, "I am Maeve Heron's husband."

Part I

BEQUEST OF FIRE

Chapter 1

"AND ALL this was . . . let me see . . . these eighteen years agone," the old Gypsy Thomas Rossar-Mescro said dreamily to his granddaughter Narilla. His eyes were black as pitch, and his face was the red of a winter apple; although he claimed years numbering more than a hundred, his thin hair was still sandy, not gray.

Thomas' granddaughter slapped her dark baby on its plump back and, hearing the small, awaited sound, shifted it back to her breast.

For a moment there was peaceful silence; they were sitting on the stairs of the Gypsy wagon-house. Scarlet curtains festooned its windows, and window shutters of bright green picked out with crimson panels adorned the wagon's sides. Between the let-down shafts of the wagon-house was the small curved flight of gilt and crimson stairs the two now occupied. Thomas was mending the broken bottom of a chair.

A gentle wind rustled in the summer leaves, and a far bird called rhythmically over Tullaghoe, in the country of Ireland.

"What were they like, the grand O'Neills?" Narilla asked suddenly. "And Shane, who was the man of my cousin Floure?"

Thomas was silent an instant, feeling the grateful absence of pain the summer heat granted his arthritic limbs, and let his memory wander backward. "Ah! The O'Neills," he murmured. "Well, I will tell you about them.

"For nearly six hundred years," old Thomas began, "the

7

Ui Neill, the fathers of the proud O'Neills who were the earls of Tyrone, ruled the green heart of Ireland.''

Narilla loved to hear her grandfather talking so, for he was a *posh ta posh*, half-Gypsy, half-*gorgio*, and was a man lettered beyond the other Gypsies.

"Among the distant forebears of Shane O'Neill were the Great O'Neill of the Fews and the hero Owen Roe O'Neill.

"Shane's father was an unhappy man called Phelim. His forefather had had to flee to England—I will not tell you the tangled web of wars and treason that sent him there, for it makes my old head ache!—but Phelim, with the love of Ireland in him, brought his family back to Tullaghoe in 1836.

"There were two boys, Shane and Arthur. Arthur was a winter-born, cold as that very season, but Shane . . . ah! Shane was March-born and wilder than the wind. I loved that boy. His hair looked like the black feathers of a wind-driven bird, and his eyes were as green as the sea that lashes the shore beyond Fermanagh! Just like Maeve.''

Old Thomas smiled and recalled himself to the story.

"They did say never a tinker or beast in Tullaghoe did not greet Shane with gladness or turn away from Arthur, his brother.''

"But what of Shane and Floure?'' Narilla asked with slight impatience.

"I am getting to that,'' Thomas replied with amiable reproach. "He met her the summer before he was sent down from Trinity College in Dublin.'' Thomas chuckled again. "What a racket there was in the city! It is said that Shane actually engaged in fisticuffs with his fine brother, Arthur, right before the Custom House, in the sight of the professors, and nearly knocked Arthur into the River Liffey!''

"But what of Floure?'' Narilla repeated.

"I will never forget that meeting,'' Thomas said. "That summer day when Shane O'Neill, the son of the Great House in Tullaghoe, first laid eyes on the grown-up Floure.''

That June day in 1843 young Shane O'Neill, lean and reckless in his dusty riding clothes, had cantered into the clearing where the wagon-house of Thomas Rossar-Mescro's family was resting.

When he sighted Shane, Thomas Rossar-Mescro raised his

weathered hand in greeting, calling out, "How are you?" in the Romany tongue.

"Splendid!" Shane replied. The boy seemed happy, indeed, to be back in Tullaghoe.

Thomas relinquished the chair on which he was working and stood up. "Will the young earl join me in a rum booze?"

Shane laughed. "Gladly." He followed as Thomas went to the rear of the wagon-house and took a pottery jug from the rack over the pan box. Thomas uncorked the jug with gusto and invited Shane to drink. It was poteen, not rum, and after a healthy swig Shane gasped a little.

Thomas drank, too, then motioned the young man back to the stairs. "Sit down and talk. Is all at peace in the Great House?"

Shane O'Neill threw himself full length on the sweet, trampled grass and lay a moment, silent, his hands clasped behind his handsome head. He sighed and answered, "Indeed, it is not, Thomas. I am always at war with Arthur, and now it is with my father."

Thomas shook his sandy head. Phelim O'Neill, he knew, had always favored Shane over Arthur. But of latter years the wildness of the younger son had been annoying the old man unceasingly.

"Is it because you have thrown in your lot with those young Papists preaching rebellion?"

Shane half rose in his surprise. "How did you come by that?" he asked, grinning.

"I have my ways."

Shane laughed. "It must have been Rosaleen in the kitchen. She has a tongue as long as the lough."

"Well, your young Ireland lads are all right with me," Thomas said easily. "I have no love for the lords in the castles. Aside, that is, from you," he amended, laughing.

Shane O'Neill looked up at Thomas with affection. "Thanks, my friend." He lay back again on the grass, listening to the wood sounds in the slow-rising wind. Something that might have been a hare rustled in the furze.

"I wish the hares well escaping the traps," Shane said drowsily.

"And I," Thomas agreed. How tender the boy always was over beasts! he reflected.

After a moment Shane remarked softly, "Peaceful, peaceful is it here this afternoon. Where are they all, Sacki and Reyna and the children?"

"Reyna's gone to see to an ailing cow, away beyond the Great House. As for Sacki and the children, whoever knows where they might be? They blow away like wind fellows in the mornings, and sometimes I do not see them until the night fires are burning."

Thomas' daughter-in-law, Reyna, like many of the Gypsy women, was far more remarkable than her husband, Sacki. "Ah, it is the Gypsy women and not the men," Thomas said, "that have caused the name of Gypsy to awaken wonder in your world. Sacki is shiftless; he is far too fond of making himself drunk on rum booze."

Thomas smiled. "Quiet it is, indeed, with all of them gone to their mischief."

No sooner had the words been spoken than the two were assailed, from the underbrush, by a hideous cacophony—the earsplitting cries of a captured fowl, footfalls crashing and a throaty young voice remonstrating with the bird.

Shane sat up on the grass, and Thomas dropped his chair. "What is that racket?" Thomas cried.

From the brush burst a wild-haired boy dressed in dusty breeches of corduroy and a wide-striped shirt; a pullet struggled in his grasp. His red-fired hair of the darkest brown was falling into his eyes, and he was laughing.

But Thomas Rossar-Mescro knew that this was not a boy, and glancing at Shane, who was staring, Thomas realized that Shane knew as well. His green gaze was taking in the swelling breasts under the many-colored upper garment, the narrow waist that curved out so sweetly. The girl shook back her tangled hair and laughed at the gazing men.

The gesture revealed all of her glowing face and let them see her dark, fiery eyes set slantwise in her soft little face with its short, impudent upper lip.

"What do you think you're doing, girl?" Thomas called out sternly.

"Taking myself a pet, from the big place beyond the hill," she answered pertly, and her voice was at once rough as a bramble and rich as honey.

Thomas avoided Shane's amused look. "Then you had better meet your benefactor," Thomas said. "For it is this young

man's fowl you have stolen. Don't you remember Shane
O'Neill?"

The girl's hot black eyes met Shane's green ones in surprise,
her winged brows ascending.

"This vixen is my granddaughter Floure," said Thomas
Rossar-Mescro ruefully.

Shane declared, gazing at her, "This cannot be, surely; this
cannot be the little girl who cried only last summer over the
trapped hare?"

Thomas heard his wonder, remembering how gently Shane
had taken the thin, childish body in his arms, comforting the
little thing Floure had been. Indeed the year's passage had
been a fairy miracle, thickening and firing her unruly hair
with foxlike redness, pushing out the full mouth into a softness that Thomas could see invited the pressure of Shane's
mouth now.

Thomas saw Shane's green eyes staring into the dark ones
of Floure Rossar-Mescro, careless of Thomas' frown, as if he
were drowning in those eyes.

"I knew that day," Thomas Rossar-Mescro said to Narilla,
"that all was lost. There is great suffering when a Gypsy
marries a *gorgio*. I know." The old man paused, remembering. "I knew that same terrible rage of love, more than
forty years before Shane met Floure. Ah, well!"

Thomas was silent awhile.

"Then what happened?" Narilla urged him.

"Oh, then, we had to give in to them. Shane and Floure
could not be stopped, for she had fallen as much in love with
him as he had with her. So it was I myself who united them;
Floure jumped the broomstick, and their wrists, like
everyone's, were pricked with Reyna's needle to mix their
blood. And their hands tied together after, signaling they
would not be two again."

But Narilla, who knew well this rite and had undergone it
herself, did not need reminding. Again she urged the old man,
"Tell me what happened after."

"After," Thomas said, "Shane came with us on the wagon.
I thought at first that he would be like a fish out of water,
away from his fine house and soft bed. But it was no time at
all before Reyna, even, hardly knew him from the Gypsies, he
learned so well." Thomas gave a reminiscent laugh.

"Why, he even bested Sacki at horse-trading! Where Sacki had to use tricks and herbs and all sort of devilment, Shane O'Neill had such a way with beasts that he could say a word in the horse's ear and the horse would follow him like a dog! Then, in the next town we came to, Shane would sell the horse for a fine price. He got such fine prices, indeed, that he was able to build a little store of money for himself and Floure. For all the good it did," he added somberly. "Ah, well, at least it helped keep him and the child Maeve after."

For a time his sorrowful memories seemed to overcome the old Gypsy. But then he resumed in a calmer tone that was still laced with sadness. "Yes, they were happy for a little time, until the birth of Maeve took Floure away."

The first few days of March, 1845, that month of winds and restlessness, had been lamb-mild in Fermanagh in the country of Ireland. But on this night, the seventh, young Shane O'Neill woke suddenly to hear the soughing of the leaves. The walls of the Gypsy tent where he slept with his even younger wife were whipped in a strengthening breeze.

Shane turned cautiously on the pallet, hoping that Floure still slept. But he saw that her night-colored eyes were opened wide, the coppery long lashes nearly curled into her winging brows with the width of her terrified stare. Helplessly she lay, as always, on her back, the convexity of her enormous abdomen in contrast with her childlike slenderness.

As cautiously as he himself had moved, Floure turned her head. Before she was able to mask it, Shane caught the look of animal fear on her soft face with its usually impudent upper lip. Seeing his wakeful stare, the brief lip trembled; Floure smiled uneasily.

A flood of excruciating tenderness washed him, lapping at his very limbs. Shane had never loved her so much as now, the moment of the terror's broadest shadow. If something happened, his mind cried out in silence, if he lost her! And Shane's warm tenderness chilled to desperation; a dread seemed to hover over the narrow body at his side, moving across the lustrous fox-colored hair, shading the tawny skin and brushing the red, impudent, small mouth he had tasted so often with exhilaration.

"Floure!" With great care he raised his lean body from the pallet and moved toward her; their bodies did not touch, but his slender hands lay upon her face and hair, light as a moth landing. "Beloved."

She kissed the hand that grazed her mouth and whispered, breathless, "It is time."

"My God!" he cried out. He leaped up to throw himself into breeches and shirt. "I'm going for the doctor."

"You will be cold," Floure said, speaking with difficulty. "And Reyna, my mother, will turn the doctor away, you know. Among the Romany birth is no great matter."

"It is of matter to me," Shane answered firmly. "Reyna will come to you now, and I will be back before I have gone!"

Floure gave him a tight smile that was more poignant than her tears. "I love you, I love you," he said softly, with one last downward glance.

"Shane!" Her cry arrested him, and he returned to her to kneel.

"Yes, yes, my love. What is it?"

Her upward look was one of naked worshiping. "Whatever . . . comes," she said hollowly, "I want you to know. . . ."

Shane waited, his hand upon her head, praying he would not fail her now, would not let the rending sob escape from his aching throat. He did not trust himself to speak.

"To know," she said at last, still with the same tight smile that made his body pain, "that you gave me . . . glory." She pronounced that strange word that had no counterpart in Romany. He kissed her face wildly, his tears escaping at last.

"You are all my glory," he answered softly. Then with a terrible reluctance he rose and said, "I must go, beloved. I will return soon, very soon."

It seemed to him a night and day and yet another night had gone before his feverish return, the chill sweat clammy on his thin-clad body, his teeth chattering with fright and cold, the sullen doctor in a rattling wagon behind him, as he galloped wildly.

When Shane saw them outside the tent—Floure's stony-faced mother, Reyna; her father, Sacki, sober for once, standing straight and tall with a terrible new stateliness; and her grandfather, Thomas Rossar-Mescro, looking back at him with compassion—he knew. He heard the wailing of a baby.

An awful lassitude came to Shane, and he was convinced that he would never weep again, for all weeping and aching had died in him when Floure had died.

"It is a girl child," Thomas Rossar-Mescro said. "She is beautiful." His old voice broke.

Astonished, Shane heard his own voice, cold and calm: "I will lie tonight in the tent with my wife and my child, the March wind's daughter. Do what you will tomorrow."

The three stood aside for Shane to stoop and enter.

"And when was it," Narilla asked, "that you first noticed the 'blackness' in Shane, that blackness that Maeve speaks of now?"

"Ah, yes, Thomas said to her. "Shane was born, I suppose, with a love of the drink, and it is destroying him now, the girl Maeve tells me."

"Poor Maeve." Narilla was still a moment; then she asked, "How did she come by that name?"

"Her father, Shane, named her for the warrior queen of Connaught, the famous woman from the *gorgios'* stories. He told me that she would always be cared for as befits a queen," Thomas said sadly. "We could only guess how they survived during the famine, for Shane would take no help from his father, even if it had been offered. Some said he did anything to keep his child alive—took to the highways, killing and robbing."

"I hardly remember the famine," Narilla said with wonder.

"You were so little. And we ourselves," the old man commented in a rueful manner, "were not particular either. It was only important to stay alive." He waved his old, thin hand as if to dismiss the horrors of that time; indeed, he did not like to remember those gaunt, black days, those days when they ate . . . well, anything! They had become brutes in order to live. But live they had, and so had Shane O'Neill and his daughter, Maeve Rossar-Mescro.

"The Gypsies' way of saying 'heron,' " Thomas murmured.

"What?"

"The *gorgios* call the *rossar-mescro* a heron. She still bears our name, you know. Floure and Shane had no wedding in the other world that could grant Maeve the name O'Neill for all that Shane calls her that these days."

And once again Thomas' remembering encompassed the years since Maeve's tumultuous birth—Phelim, master of the Great House, long dead; Arthur in Dublin with his stiff-faced wife and sons; and Shane O'Neill, skulking there in the Great House fallen to rack and ruin, alternately coddling and ignoring the girl Maeve, who most times was left to wander wild as a hare among the brushes and the furze.

Slim Maeve, the "March wind's daughter"!

Chapter 2

THERE WAS a ripple in the sun-warmed waters of the hidden stream; then, for an instant, a spreading blackness, like the fringes of a somber silken shawl, appeared on the surface. The darkness was a woman's hair, and as she rose from the water's depth, her face hidden in the sooty veil, the gentle sun of July lit her alabaster arms and shoulders, plashing from her rose-tipped breasts.

She gasped the mild air, shaking back her hair to show the insolent, classic face of Maeve Rossar-Mescro. Where usually her green gaze was fierce and arrogant, today it was calm and merry, the clear blue of the summer sky above her, unusually warm even for the month of July.

Careless of her nakedness, Maeve turned in a great splash to float on her back, the blue water pouring from her shapely breats, the flat, athletic belly and the long, slender legs. She closed her eyes to the sun and laughed softly, thinking of the sober words of Thomas Rossar-Mescro. He had called her changing as the wind and water, spoken to her as if she were a small child. Why, she was a woman already, even her body told her that! And she had never felt so sure. In October she would go with them in the *vardo*; nothing would stop her, nothing!

Suddenly she frowned; from far away she heard the hooves of horses. Surely no one knew this place, her secret stream. Then a nearer sound, a piping cry and a wingbeat like a giant whisper, erased her frown. Maeve raised herself, treading

16

water, shading her blue-green eyes with a slender hand, and looked up at the sky. She thought she saw the shadow of a bird, but its shape was like that of none that she had ever seen. How strange!

Maeve shivered a little in the rising wind; the day was not so warm, after all. And now the bird was gone. It was almost as if the shadowed creature had brought her some message she could not read. What did it mean?

The swimmer was transfixed. Then her white hand dropped from her brow, and with great reluctance she began to swim toward the shaded bank that enclosed the secret stream.

It was at that moment that she saw him, the tall young man with the delicate face, standing like a statue among the trees, staring at her as if he had never seen a woman.

He seemed as tall as the trees themselves, and he was very slender with a fragility of feature that seemed peculiar on a man. He was dressed in an open-necked shirt of white and costly-looking riding trousers tucked into polished boots. But in his eyes was an expression of bright gentleness that made her think of the old ways of Shane O'Neill, even the wisdom of Thomas Rossar-Mescro, in eyes many decades younger. The man's face had in it something humorous and tender; his thin lips were smiling now, smiling with delight to behold the vision in the stream.

She covered her breasts with her hands and called out angrily, "Who the devil are you? Why are you spying on me?"

The young man sobered at once and called back over the expanse of water, "I beg your pardon. I will leave you now."

Mollified, she reflected that his accent was alien to Tullaghoe; he sounded almost English. But now the cool water was chilling her skin; she crouched impatiently in its inadequate cover, waiting from him to leave.

But he had not moved from his position under the trees.

"Will you leave me now?" she cried with indignation. "I'm freezing."

He smiled again, and in spite of herself, Maeve warmed to the humor of his face; his eyes were crinkled almost shut with his broad smiling. "I think you are a fairy lady from the bogs," he returned boldly, backing away into the trees. "There's no other that could bear the cold waters of this stream, with nothing upon her but that gleaming you wear."

Maeve stared at the man and watched him turn and disappear into the trees. He had spoken like the singing verses in the books of her father, Shane O'Neill.

She felt a warmth begin to take her, chasing away the chill of the cooling water on her naked skin; mysteriously her veins heated with a kind of blue-white fire; she marveled at it.

Was it this, then, that had filled her father's blood and that of her dead mother, the Gypsy Floure?

Cautiously Maeve emerged from the water and padded to the small pile of clothing she had hidden behind a stone. After she dried herself swiftly with an old towel, she buttoned herself into her striped shirt and stepped into her trousers. Belting them tightly around her narrow waist, Maeve Rossar-Mescro peered into the trees. There was no sign of him now. Yet she had not heard him ride away; it occurred to her now that she had unconsciously missed a sound—the sound of horse's hooves fading along the road.

Where was he then? she questioned silently.

No matter; perhaps he was walking somewhere else in the thicket. And Maeve shook out her damp black hair and headed for the other path, which would take her back to the Great Place beyond the hill.

She wished now, though, that she had asked the stranger if he had seen the bird.

Michael Rathmullan watched with shamed excitement as the slim girl came dripping from the stream and began to dry her body with the ragged towel. God! He had never seen anything of such beauty in all his days. Perhaps this was the beginning—the beginning of his manhood and the end of the long sickness that had haunted him. He felt powerless to turn away his eyes. Michael Rathmullan almost exclaimed aloud; when she turned her head to shake out her hair, he got a clearer view of her enchanting face.

It was the color of a new white rose with the faintest touch of pink; the cheekbones were exquisitely modeled, austere and high, giving her the look of fierce passion and at the same time a childlike innocence. His gaze took in her slant eyes and small, full mouth. She was indeed a fairy woman from the bogs, with that calamitous beauty that drew at one, that drew so! Michael wondered then if she were real, if he were dreaming this.

But no, there was the history of human fineness on her face;
she had the chiseled features of one wellborn. Michael Rathmullan hesitated for what seemed an endless time; to keep on
spying in this fashion was villainous. She thought herself
alone. All that was honorable in him protested. Yet there was
in this encounter almost a fatefulness that filled him with a
wild hope: Perhaps this girl would be the cleansing anodyne
for his long, youthful sickness. He would be well again as
others were, a vital son with the power to fulfill his father's
dream. Even the image of Colin with the flaming hair had no
strength in this moment.

And his flesh, at once afire and chilling, called to him to
stay, called in a voice that could not be denied. So Michael
Rathmullan stood in the shadows, watching, watching, as she
covered her body with the strange striped shirt that looked
like the habit of a Romany and blotted out her loveliness with
the dusty trousers, belting them tightly around a waist of
almost incredible narrowness.

Stunned, Michael watched her disappear into the shadow of
the farther trees. A desolation such as he had never known
washed over him; it was as if the very sun had grown cold.

When Michael Rathmullan returned to the inn, his body
was possessed of a kind of weary languor. He regretted almost
to the point of aching ire his promise to pay a call upon Shane
O'Neill. He would, Michael resolved, send a message stating
he was indisposed. But no, it had to be endured some evening
before he left Tullaghoe, or there would be his father's irate
disapproval to be faced.

Therefore, with great reluctance, as the twilight fell,
Michael got up, washed and donned an elegant suit of fawn
color.

As his hired carriage wound around the lake road in the
falling dark, Michael thought they would never reach the
house. He wanted, in a fever, to arrive and dine, to leave, to
have done! At last he saw a very peculiar sight—a myriad of
sparks and spouts of flame in the near distance.

"What in the name of God is that?" he called to the driver,
and the man answered imperturbably, "A chimney's on fire.
There is always a fire in the house of O'Neill."

Michael was struck by the ambiguous beauty of the man's
reply and looked again at the bleak house ahead. Before the

carriage reached it, the fire had gone out; Michael was deposited at the door without being able to see clearly what manner of house it was, but he received an impression of great neglect. The hall door opened, and a slovenly old woman appeared.

Michael announced his name, almost asking about the fire. But the old woman appeared calm, smiling and motioning to Michael the way he was to go. He would probably never learn, Michael reflected with amusement, what became of the fiery chimney in the infernal house of O'Neill.

The woman showed him into a drawing room that had, like the façade, an appearance of disuse. By the cold hearth he saw a gentleman alone, and a gentleman, Michael felt, he was, despite the rather rusty look of his black clothes, the raffish angle of his cravat. He must, judged Michael, have once been a man of extraordinary handsomeness. Now his fine-boned face was soft with dissipation, and his bright-green eyes were dulled, the pupils shot with blood.

He drank, oh, yes, indeed, he drank! Michael thought.

"Welcome," said the man, "to the house of Shane O'Neill."

Michael Rathmullan bowed and took the extended hand, noting with shock that the nails were not quite clean. Yet the man's whole manner of receiving him, the ease of his motions and of the ensuing conversation, bespoke a man accustomed to living in the best society.

Shane put Michael at ease at once, for he was well acquainted with Michael's father.

Then from a doorway at the other end of the ruined room a young girl entered. In the shadows Michael did not at first see her features clearly; she was dressed in a shining, rather out-of-fashion gown of green, and her figure was proud and slight, her head held up and thrown back.

"My daughter, Maeve," said Shane O'Neill with pride. And as she came into the lamplight, Michael recognized the fairy figure from the stream.

Maeve came to the middle of the room and made a deliberate curtsy that a Paris dancing master would have approved. But the stunned Michael saw that in her, the gesture was a mockery, as if she had come to greet her father's guest reluctantly. Reluctantly, Michael marveled, as he himself had come to dine!

When she looked up at the visitor, Michael saw the astonishment on her face. But admirably she controlled her expression; a gleam of resentment shone from her oblique eyes, emerald-green with the reflection of her gown. She merely smiled and seated herself upon a sofa; it seemed as if she never intended to speak.

Shane O'Neill glanced at her with irritation; in recompense for her distant air, he began to chatter quickly to their guest.

At last Shane cried nervously, "Well! Well, will you come to dinner? Dinner's ready." He shot a baleful glance at his daughter, whose place it was to announce the meal.

But still silent, she preceded the men into a fine large dining room that bore also the musty look of the drawing room and the entrance hall. Standing at the end of the table was the same old woman who had opened the door; at each temple she wore, Michael noticed now, a thick bunch of coarse gray curly hair, in the fashion of thirty years ago. "You may serve, Maria," said Shane O'Neill, after an exasperated glance at the still-silent Maeve.

Maeve sat opposite Michael, and with the light of branches of wax candles glowing upon her, she seemed to him more fairylike than she had been by sunlight in the stream. He saw that at this moment her eyes had softened some and wore a look of faint amusement as they turned to him from time to time.

Michael Rathmullan could not have told for the life of him what he had drunk or eaten. In her presence he moved like a man asleep, answering Shane O'Neill's questions with replies of dreamy absence. All he could know was a burning chill of great excitement; *this then*, he thought, *is what men feel for women; this is what my father must have known when he first looked upon my mother*.

And this fairy woman was only a table width away. He determined to engage her in conversation and began to speak of books. A brightness grew in her glance for an instant, but suddenly, with the quickness of a winged thing, he saw her attention swim away.

He saw with a kind of amused irritation that she was testing him, offering him a challenge of their secret; determined not to show his helplessness, Michael made a chaffing remark.

Gratified, he heard her husky laugh, saw in her eyes a yearning loneliness as open as that of a child. And the paradox of her smote his senses as music would smite his ear; she was at once a passionate woman, he knew, as well as a longing child.

And once more Michael felt what he had felt on first beholding her—that once his fingers met her flesh and his mouth covered hers, there would be an end to his hateful desires. Yet his dual nature, even in the pounding of this alien yearning, made his reason do battle with his flesh.

Maeve seemed to sense the ambiguity in him, for in her green eyes he saw a look of disappointment, then a look of ironic sadness creeping. Michael's blue-gray eyes, bright with the pain of his warring reflections, held hers for an instant. Then his drumming resolve drowned out the sound of his fear. He looked at her beseechingly. She reddened and lowered her white lids over her eyes.

And he saw that Shane O'Neill realized what was happening and that Shane O'Neill approved. Exultantly Michael heard Shane say, when they were sipping their rather indifferent coffee, "Surely you will stay with us awhile? It is not fitting that the son of John Rathmullan should put up at the inn."

As he accepted with gracious thanks, Michael glanced sidelong at Maeve; he could not tell whether her gleaming eyes held joy or anger.

There was something in him, reflected Maeve, that exicted her and filled her, at the same time, with fear. What was it? Her father, with his unsubtle hints, obviously desired for them to marry. Yet there was something in the young man that dismayed her; the delicacy of his mind, which made him such a joy to talk with, his gentleness, which was so reassuring, yet seemed to her the very qualities, in their extreme degree, that made him not the same as other men.

Therefore, these several days she had avoided him. Shane stormed that she was remiss in her hospitality, leaving the young man without occupation. Neither he nor Shane O'Neill was a fisherman, the only sport remaining in this milder season, and there was little, Shane remarked, to do in Tullaghoe. She must help entertain their guest.

Nevertheless, Maeve continued to evade him, leaving early in the warm mornings on her mare and riding to the Rossar-Mescros', returning only in the dusk and meeting her father and Michael in the musty dining room.

She was surprised that Michael had not followed her on her expeditions to the *vardo*; reluctantly she admired his consideration.

This afternoon, however, she decided to risk another swim in the secret pool. Surely he would not follow, if he had not before. So it was with an easy mind she felt the embrace of the water on her marbly limbs; today, she knew with wonder, it was as it had never been before, so soft and warming that it felt like light. An odd new ache was gnawing at her core.

Floating on her back, Maeve suddenly recalled lines from her favorite verse:

> Great love of a man from another land
> Has come to me beyond all else. . . .
> He was a glorious flame, no boastful word fell from his lips,
> A slender mate for a maid's side.

She felt her pulses beat like the beating wings of the bird of shadows, wondering if it would return to her today.

Glancing at the bank then, she saw him, Michael Rathmullan. She gasped with shock: He stood naked, gazing at her with terrible hunger.

Hardly knowing what she did, Maeve stared back deliberately into his blue-gray eyes. And trembling with the boldness of her gesture, she beckoned him to join her in the water.

For a long moment he stood hesitantly, as if he were struggling with unbelief. Then, his firm flesh white as marble in the sighing shade, he strode to the edge of the water.

He swam toward her, close enough now to touch her. He stretched his reedy arms and grasped her shoulders. She came into his arms like one bemused; her closing eyes revealed her heavy, blue-veined lids. She raised her face for his kiss.

Michael leaned toward her, his mouth about to descend on hers, when suddenly he was taken with a dreadful shuddering. He withdrew, staring helplessly upon her sunlit face.

Puzzled, Maeve opened her eyes and looked at him; on Michael's face there was a look of purest desolation. Staring at a point beyond her at the green-gold trees, he began, to her horror, to weep.

"What is it?" she asked softly. "Michael, what is it?"

"I am not," he began, his words broken by a sob more terrible than his tears had been, "I am not . . . a man." His lean hand lay limply now on her wet shoulder, and his mouth was slack with self-disgust and sorrow.

"Not a man?" she repeated, uncomprehending. "What—what do you mean? Of course, you are a man."

With a look that blended pity and impatience, Michael said, "I am not a man who can love a woman."

With that he took his hand from her and began to swim away toward the bank with long, weary strokes. She watched his naked whiteness fading into the shadows. Then she swam back toward the wooded bank opposite. On the shore, as she dried her body and resumed her clothes, Maeve Rossar-Mescro knew at once the meaning of the shadowed bird. It was a symbol of the sorrow Michael was to bring, for despite his protestations and the cold realization of his words, Maeve felt her flesh aflame at the thought of his nearness and then the deadening cold of her frustration making lead of her strong young limbs.

She was unaware that there was another watcher in the wood: Shane O'Neill had seen it all from a distance, his drink-blurred sight not comprehending Michael's face or hearing their words. He knew only that the young man was a man of honor, who had stopped himself before he soiled Maeve. With a feeling of great joy, Shane knew that her future was assured.

The summer following, the houses of Rathmullan and O'Neill exulted in the marriage of Michael and Maeve. If Shane O'Neill noted in his son-in-law an excessive nervousness, he dismissed it as the natural timidity of so young a groom. He laughed with John Rathmullan at the pallor of the boy. John Rathmullan's disapproval struggled with relief; the boy was very young and must go on to finish his degree at Trinity. And yet, by God, he knew at last that Michael was a man, for his eagerness to marry had been touching.

It was the reaction of his daughter that puzzled Shane O'Neill. Her shy expectation, all that might become a bride of seventeen, was tempered by an alien emotion Shane could not quite read; she seemed to be possessed of some uncertainty, for all her eyes glowed when she looked upon the boy.

But Shane dismissed the thought as he had dismissed his thoughts of Michael's high tension. It was, after all, a solemn

step in their young and untouched lives! Then, all in an instant, his earlier doubts returned. Surely the two were
lingering beyond their time at the reception.

And that red-haired lad, keeping to himself, all in a corner
alone, tight-lipped, unsmiling. Who was he and what ailed
him now?

But Shane's anxious reflections were broken by the voice of
his friend, John Rathmullan. "Shane!"

He turned to encounter his friend, a grayed and stately
counterpart of Michael, smiling broadly upon him. And
gratified, beyond his friend, Shane caught the proud look of
Maeve; he was behaving well today, indeed, and she knew it.
He had only had a single glass of the bubbly. Maeve grinned
at him with conspiratorial affection.

"Your girl is about to leave," said John Rathmullan with
genial reproach. "Will you not kiss her in farewell?"

Shane moved to Maeve and clasped her in his arms; her
cheeks were glowing now, and her green eyes soft with unshed
tears, as she raised her face for his kiss.

Her father, near to weeping, watched her mount the stairs
and lean over to toss her white bouquet. There was a shrill,
laughing cry from the women. John Rathmullan's sister had
caught the bouquet.

Ah, God, Shane prayed in silence, *I ask you to take care of
her, my long-neglected darling . . . and tell me that I have not
done wrong to give her to this boy!*

They would, Michael said apologetically, now travel to a
spot near Dublin and stay the week at his cousin's estate. The
trip to Paris for which Michael longed would have to be postponed; he was, after all, still beholden to his father, who
would have to see him through Trinity and the lean days
following until he became established in the law.

Meanwhile, his father had found them a fine little house in
Dublin, where he hoped Maeve would be content.

That night in the great house the dazzled Maeve, who had
never been to such a place before, found that her luggage had
already been unpacked. A maid had laid out, in the dressing
room adjoining the bedchamber, a filmy alabaster gown and
floating wrapper that John's sister had had sent to her from
Paris. A pair of satin slippers were placed precisely below the
velvet-upholstered stool on which the garments lay. After
Maeve had bathed and changed into the ethereal garments,

she shyly entered the bridal chamber.

She noted with delight that a small round table had been arranged near a soft-curtained window, set with a light supper, flaming tapers and a silver ice bucket holding a chilled bottle of champagne. Two of the chamber's chairs, upholstered in gilt-printed crimson silk, were drawn up to the table. There were summer flowers everywhere.

Maeve gazed about the chamber, with its enormous rosewood bed made in the Gothic fashion, its headboard of pinnacles and arches and the green silk of its vaulted canopy. Surely nothing more wonderful could be found in Paris, she reflected. And Michael was to share it with her!

Maeve examined her own reflection in a great cheval glass with massive posts and found that her green eyes had an eager brightness she had never seen in them before; the filmy garments made a glory of her skin and gleaming hair, which fell loose now, falling to her waist.

She stood, exulting, listening to the summer silence of the vast estate, broken only by the plashing of the garden's fountain, drifting through the open windows on the cooling air. It was very strange. For an instant from nowhere came the image of the *vardo* of the Rossar-Mescros and her old resolve to join them. But she shook her head, as if to clear it of all but the magical present, for in a moment now Michael would enter, Michael would be hers. And she would know the mystery that Shane O'Neill had hinted of in his passionate union with her mother, Floure. Her own kisses and this soft flesh would soothe all of Michael's fear and still his weeping. Maeve trembled and grew warm and chill at once.

She heard the door of the other dressing room open. Michael Rathmullan stood here, his eyes apprehensive in his gentle face. He was wearing a magnificent storm-blue dressing gown of fine brocade over his deark wedding trousers. Dismayed, Maeve's first reflection was: *He has not undressed himself.* And she felt the roughness of anxiety bloom on her arms as she hugged herself with an awkward motion.

Without moving from the doorway, Michael asked, "Are you cold?" He smiled uneasily and moved then toward the long window as if to shut it.

"Cold? Oh, no. No!" Maeve cried, hearing her own voice tremble and break.

Michael came to her and held out his narrow long-fingered hand, taking her small white one. "Shall we have a glass?"

His social, evasive inquiry deepened her feeling of awkwardness and dismay.

"Yes." She nodded and, drawing her wrapper more closely around her slender body, followed him to the table. He had not looked at her directly, except for the first beseeching scrutiny of her face.

He pulled out a crimson chair for her and, when she was seated, uncorked the wine with a fumbling motion. Wincing at the small explosion, Maeve moved quickly aside as the cork shot past her ear.

The foaming liquid gushed onto the table. "Oh, dear!" Michael cried, and his voice shook. "I am sorry. Are you all right?"

She was touched at the true concern in him and smiled. "Of course I am," she answered gently in a teasing voice. "Pour me a glass."

His hands were shaking, she saw now, shaking almost uncontrollably. After taking the bottle from his hands, she poured a glass for each of them and replaced the bottle in the silver bucket.

Raising the glass, she said tenderly, "To us."

Michael raised his glass. Drinking, he blurted, "That was the salutation of the man you gave; I should have given it." He seemed tearful and agitated beyond anything Maeve had ever seen.

"What does it matter?" she asked consolingly; her tone appealed to him with softness.

He smiled again, that pitiful smile he had worn ever since he entered the chamber. And Maeve's fear grew with every moment.

Desperately he began to chatter, of the wedding and the journey, of the days to come at Trinity and of the house they would occupy.

Maeve made herself answer, keeping her rising panic in tight control.

At last, when the supper was eaten and the hour had grown late, it seemed the moment could be postponed no longer when they would lie together in the great canopied bed.

"Well?" Michael asked, his voice shaking. "Shall we?"

With a kind of pitying horror, Maeve reflected that he

might have been asking her for a waltz. He put out the lights and drew the curtains tightly before the windows.

In the smothering dark Maeve slipped off her frail wrapper and let it fall upon a chair. She drew back the silken coverlet and lay down. She could hear Michael's quick, agitated breath and the rustle of his abandoned clothes.

As soon as she moved near him and he put his tentative arms about her, she knew, from his soft, withdrawing flesh, that he would ever after turn from her desiring as he had that afternoon in the hidden pool of Tullaghoe.

Chapter 3

"YOU SEE, my dear, this testament has no validity."

Maeve Rathmullan heard her uncle Arthur's words as if from a great distance, feeling only a kind of despairing calm. She leaned back in her father's old, soiled velvet chair and stared into the crackling flames.

"Maeve," her uncle said sharply, "do you understand me?"

She looked at him then and answered coolly, "With great clarity and ease."

Her bookish, unaccented reply, not even coupled with the salutation "Uncle Arthur," which her kinsman thought proper, startled the rigid man sitting opposite. Arthur O'Neill looked keenly at his niece; almost three years had elasped since they had last met, at her wedding to Michael Rathmullan, and she seemed to have assumed a peculiar maturity for someone not yet twenty years.

Strange that the couple had had no issue; the thought fired him with curiosity. She certainly looked capable of bearing. Despite himself, Arthur O'Neill felt his gaze fall to her lush, ripened breasts, revealing their exquisite shape below the soft velvet of her black mourning gown; the heavy-lidded, disillusioned green eyes; and the sensuous rose-colored mouth with its brief, impudent upper lip.

"Your father, at the end," he resumed in a gentler voice, "was most unwell."

"You mean," she returned bluntly, "that he was in the final stages of alcoholism."

Arthur O'Neill frowned. The girl had an almost coarse way of putting things, he judged with disapproval. Ignoring her remark, he continued coldly. "Your father was the younger son, you know. Therefore, this house and all its lands are the property of my sons. But your own husband is an elder son," he added with a frosty smile, "and therefore, you need have no anxiety about material matters. The affairs of the Rathmullans are in perfect order. As their attorney I am well aware of that. And as your kindsman I feel it is no betrayal of professional confidence to make this known to Michael Rathmullan's wife."

Maeve moved restlessly in her chair. The preciseness of her uncle's words made her long to scream. She knew that her uncle found her calm demeanor shocking; her apparent lack of grief had raised more than one brow on the bare hill where Shane O'Neill had been laid to rest. Her grief was too deep and cold for tears; he throat ached with their unshed burden. It was as if she were mourning a ghost of one who long ago was lost to her.

Nettled by her silence, Arthur O'Neill went on in a cold voice. "Your aunt and I, of course, will sell this house, or what is left of it"—his sharp gray eyes took in with distaste the dusty room—"and make suitable provision for you. You must, of course, choose whatever furnishings and other knicknacks you want from the place."

"I want only this chair, and my father's books . . . and there are a few things that he saved that were my mother's."

Arthur O'Neill raised his thin white brows. What else could he expect, of course, from the child of a . . . tinker? She had made no mention at all of the ancestral treasures of the O'Neills . . . and not a word of thanks for his proffered bequest. Under the circumstances, he mused, more than generous.

"And the people?"

Again Arthur O'Neill was startled by her blunt, almost mannish way of expressing herself. The ill-mannered little . . . hoyden! Michael Rathmullan obviously gave her no discipline, no direction at all.

"What do you mean?" he replied huffily.

"What will happen to the people? Will provision be made for them, or will they be turned out to fend for themselves?

Some of them, you know, have been on the estate since you were a child."

Arthur O'Neill drew in his breath. Really, the girl was incorrigible! Restraining his rage, he replied, "The affairs of the estate and the disposition of the servants are entirely my affair."

Maeve Rathmullan stared at him, her lips parting with shock. Then she closed her lips, apparently framing a reply. He saw that her hands were grasping the arms of her chair so fiercely that the faint blue vessels in her marbly wrists protruded. At last she said, in a low, angry voice, "No, Uncle Arthur, the people today are more than your concern, one even wider than my own."

She rose and, without looking back, left the room, leaving the scandalized Arthur O'Neill alone before the fire.

"It may be true then," he whispered aloud, frowning. His son had brought him strange tales of Michael Rathmullan's companions at Trinity, a godless and raffish company that was often entertained, it was said, at the house of Maeve and Michael Rathmullan—those young outlaws and ingrates, the "Fenians." Maeve's friends more than Michael's! he wagered.

Arthur O'Neill sat for a long moment, frowning into the fire. And then he too rose and went to look for his wife. She was very uneasy, poor dear, in this disordered house and longed, he knew, to return as soon as possible to Dublin.

Glancing back at the ill-kempt room and the soiled velvet chair that Maeve had claimed, Arthur O'Neill had a sudden image of an afternoon so long ago by the populous Liffey, when he and his brother, Shane, had brawled over the question of his brother's rebellious companions.

In the misting new March night four quiet horsemen could be dimly seen along the steep banks of the Lough Neagh, the lake but a shining shadow by the hidden moon.

The spring moon emerged an instant from its edifice of cloud, lighting the faces of the riders to the fore. They were tall young men, grim-faced and strong; the fourth, who rode behind, was so small he seemed little more than a boy. There was a gleam of metal at the riders' belts. The smaller one behind was likewise armed but wore a voluminous cap, whereas the three before went bareheaded to meet the cold.

The riders' eyes were never still, darting here and there; their ears listened to every shadow in the windless night—for a footfall or rustling leaf, for the nicker or the soft percussion of another mount.

The moon hid itself again, and in the thick dark the riders slowed their horses. All at once, however, the heavy darkness moved with sound; beyond the next hill there were the muffled drums of two horses' hooves.

Where the path widened, the slender rider in the rear came abreast of the three tall men before.

"Get behind," one of the tall men snapped, drawing his pistol from his belt.

The boyish figure on the fourth mount stiffened with indignation but nevertheless obeyed, moving to its former position.

The first man waved the others into a thicket's shadow and, ignoring the protests of the second and third, said, "Get back. I will go to see."

The first man dismounted and crept forward on his soft-booted feet toward the brow of the hill. Dropping, he crawled over its gentle elevation, hidden in the tall grasses on the edge of the road.

The fourth rider heard then a soft call and seemed to recognize the names of O'Connell and Rathmullan. From the shelter of the thicket the fourth rider peered out. The first man was upright now, returning on foot between two other mounted men.

When they were abreast of the thicket, the fourth rider saw, amazed, the faces of Michael Rathmullan and his delicate companion, Colin O'Connell, with the flaming hair.

Neither man returned the greeting of the boyish rider. Michael Rathmullan's gentle face was stony with resentment.

It was then all of them heard the creaking of a heavy wagon.

The fourth rider, ignoring the two newcomers, moved toward the dismounted man. "This is my business now," the fourth rider said in a husky whisper and a kind of triumph. "It has the rattle of a tinker's wagon."

In latter years more and more of the *petulengro* went armed and, as all the riders were aware, were not averse to highway robbery. Therefore, the first rider put his hand upon the pistol he had replaced in his belt and shook his head.

"No," the small rider said urgently. "Stay. I will go to them."

At last, after a murmured conference with the others, the first rider nodded. And the other five watched the small horseman move forward over the hill and listened to the hoof-beats beyond the narrow bridge of gray stone, where by day the black-faced sheep were peaceably driven.

The swarthy driver of the wagon had a rifle at the ready. In the reappearing moon the small rider smiled at his surprise to hear the greeting, "*Koshti-sarla*, good evening," in Romany. The swarthy man returned the salute uncertainly.

And then the rider cried out in affectionate recognition, "Andres!"

The man lowered his weapon, grinning. He turned to speak to hidden listeners in the shadow of the wagon. "It's the pale one," the rider heard him say softly, "the child of Floure."

Then he turned back, still grinning, to the rider. "What do you mean," he asked, beginning to laugh, "going about like a fighter?"

"My uncle is driving out the people," the rider answered. "Did you not know?"

The tinker stared. "His own people," Andres repeated.

"It has not ended," said the small rider urgently, "the wrong that is done to the people, like the people of the Adare, so long ago, and to so many others. The Ulster custom means nothing to my uncle."

The rider had no need to explain the phrase; in Andres' sharp eyes was angry recognition. The custom that had protected the tenants for centuries, which gave a man an interest in his holding, let him stay as long as he paid his rent and let him sell his interest when he quit the land, indeed meant nothing to men like Arthur O'Neill. Andres could not forget how he had always hated the Gypsies.

Yet now he hesitated, protesting, "It is no quarrel of ours."

But now behind Andres the rider heard a stirring in the shadows of the wagon, and there appeared an ancient man who spoke out in a feeble voice, "How dare you say this is no quarrel of ours?"

"Thomas!" the rider cried and dismounted to run to the old man. *How frail he looks*, thought Maeve Rathmullan, and the tears came into her eyes.

"It is still the quarrel of the gentiles," Andres retorted sullenly.

"You are not *gorgio*, little snowball," said the old man, staring at the whiteness of Maeve's face. It hurt her heart to be called that old pet name again.

"What do you ask, child?" Thomas Rossar-Mescro inquired in his weak voice.

"Only that Andres let us pass without a quarrel," Maeve replied. "And without taking an excessive interest in our horses if we dismount and leave them unattended. We will need something to escape on." The Gypsy Andres laughed at this reference to the Gypsies' horse stealing.

"This is not only the business of the Fenians," Maeve added, "but also mine. For it is my uncle's men who have driven away the people who nourished me."

Thomas answered uneasily. "We cannot do anything, child. The rural police are after us. We must take the wagon on tonight. There are others coming."

"I know," Maeve said. "I saw the leaves." The tinkers, her father had told her long ago, always left a trail for the others to follow, and she had noted on the path an unusual number of dry leaves for such a windless night. "I understand." Maeve nodded.

Then she added, "The men will do you no harm. Just let us go in peace."

Two dark men unknown to Maeve were climbing from the wagon. Their brows were fierce. Andres held up his hand. Maeve noted with sadness that it was Thomas' grandson-in-law to whom they listened now, and not Thomas Rossar-Mescro.

"Let it be," Andres said to the other young men. "Let it be."

Muttering, they climbed back into the wagon.

Maeve smiled and raised a narrow hand to Andres and to Thomas. "Good luck," she said gently in the Romany tongue.

"Good luck to you as well," Thomas replied. He raised his withered hand in a salute of farewell. Andres clucked to the horse and took up the reins. The wagon began to roll away.

The small rider turned and passed the wagon to retrace her way over the brow of the low hill.

A sudden shot exploded. A loud volley came close after. Maeve could see the others now were leaping to the ground; four reached the shelter of the trees, but the fifth was hit and plummeted to the narrow road.

Maeve leaped from her mare and rolled down the hill into the bushes near the entrance to the closer bridge.

Someone scrambled out from the trees and crawled toward the figure on the road. Maeve heard Michael, her husband, crying out, "Oh, Colin, dear heaven, Colin!"

Sickened, she knew that Michael Rathmullan's first concern had been, not her, but the man who lay so still now on the road, his hair obscuring his delicate face. He must be dead, Maeve thought with a terrible coldness. She had never seen a man killed before, and she felt an overpowering nausea at the sight of Colin's body, with Michael leaning above him, sobbing.

Half-blinded by her dizziness and tears, Maeve Rathmullan saw them coming, then, the men who must be her uncle's agents. She wanted to rush out from her shelter to scream at them, to claw with her small, savage hands at the well-fed faces so terribly clear now by the uncovered light of the moon. She took her pistol from her belt. But at once she knew that if she fired, they would find her and the others. And other men would die as Colin had.

Maeve lowered the pistol, a long-barreled Army gun that Sean, one of the men, had carried in the American war; it was heavy in her small hand. She let it fall to the ground, suppressing the deep sobs that rose in her throat. Michael had disappeared, and Colin no longer lay dead on the narrow road. He must have carried the body away.

She closed her eyes to clear them of the blurring tears. There was a footfall very near, and she held her breath. Then, like a miracle, the footsteps faded; she heard the agents of Arthur O'Neill riding away.

"Maeve!" She heard the weak cry beyond her in the underbrush and crawled toward the sound of her name. "Maeve!" the cry came again. In the dimness she could see the long form of Michael, lying on the ground. He had been hit.

Maeve crawled nearer. Then, cautiously raising herself to

her knees, she ripped off her jacket and her shirt. With the shirt sleeve she bound a rude tourniquet as tightly as she could about the bleeding arm. She must, she reflected, get help for Michael. He was only here because of her, and Colin lay dead because of her! Where were the others?

They had agreed to ride their separate ways if anything went wrong; it was the Fenian method of surviving that had kept many a man from the gallows before this night.

Maeve lowered her head to Michael's breast. The weight of her black hair dislodged the full cap from her head, and the silken mass cascaded below her shoulders, brushing Michael's face.

With a sobbing breath she took his head to her breast, repeating his name. He gasped with pain, going quickly limp and leaden in her arms.

She gave out a soft cry and, stiff with terror, bent to hear his heart. There was a faint, slow thudding still; she sobbed out with relief. He had only fainted then. So great was Maeve's sudden release from fear she thought that she too would faint, and she dug her nails into her palms, clenching her teeth to try to stop the whirling in her head.

But then she almost shrieked aloud; in her desperate movements she had brushed against something cold and lifeless. It was the piteous body of Colin O'Connell. He lay farther away in the shadows on his back, his red hair streaming back like a dim fire, his face milk-white in the dappled moonglow.

Again Maeve felt that dreaded wave of weakness and fell into the dirt. She hardly heard in her moment of horror the melodious whistle—the signal of the Gypsies! Cautiously she edged toward the thicket's rim. The whistle came again, louder this time. They were there; they were there somewhere; her heart sang.

With a mighty effort Maeve rose to her knees and began to crawl out of the wooded shelter.

The whistling ceased; there was no one to be seen. Then all at once Maeve heard the rustle of the frosty grass and saw five Gypsies emerging from the dark. In their center was a majestic-looking young woman, wrapped in a bright heavy shawl, with a lovely face.

For one mad instant Maeve thought that the dead Reyna, her grandmother and the mother of Floure, had come to life again, but she realized that this was the young and sullen Narilla. The intervening years, though few, had brought to her a new stateliness; it was obvious that she now wore the dignity of Reyna like a splendid mantle.

"Narilla!" Maeve cried out and rose to stumble toward the older woman.

Narilla held up her broad, swarthy hand and called softly. "Hush, *posh ta posh* . . . come here. Come thou here."

Weeping to hear again Thomas' affectionate epithet, "half-and-half," Maeve ran toward the young woman. The woman took off her shawl and wrapped it around Maeve's body; it hung almost to the hems of her boyish trousers. "Hush, hush, child," Narilla said, calling Maeve "child" despite the few years that separated them. The dark men with her were frowning. Their eyes darted everywhere.

"These are Andres' brothers," Narilla said.

"We will be dead brothers for our pains," one of them grumbled to the woman Narilla.

"Be quiet," Narilla snapped. "Did her father not do countless kindnesses for the Rossar-Mescros?" Then she said softly to Maeve, "Where are your companions?"

Numbly the girl gestured toward the bushes. "Michael . . . my husband . . . wounded there," she gasped. "Hurry."

"Your man?" the majestic woman gasped and signed to the sullen brothers. They crawled into the underbrush, dragging out the wounded man.

"Come, get him to the wagon," Narilla ordered. The tallest of the young men paused, scowling. "Hear me," the woman repeated. "Do you wish to anger Andres? Get him to the wagon."

Skeptically, the tallest man, with the aid of his brothers, took up the bleeding Michael from the ground and bore him away into the dark.

"The wagon is there," said Narilla to Maeve. "Come." And she led the trembling Maeve across a field to a clump of trees where the friendly shape of the wagon could be faintly seen. A soft rain was falling now as the Gypsy Narilla moved with Maeve Rathmullan toward the wagon.

"Make room," she said brusquely to the children in the shadow and urged Maeve down onto a blanket in the rear.

Maeve lay down, sobbing, "Michael, save Michael."

"We will see to him," Narilla replied soothingly and

pressed Maeve to be still. In a moment the weeping woman felt a gentle touch upon her hair; opening her eyes, she saw the worn old face of Thomas Rossar-Mescro. When he was seen near in this fashion, his great age was all too evident; a myriad of wrinkles webbed his formerly smooth skin, which had been for so long like the skin of a winter apple. And his dark eyes were rheumy now and almost sightless.

"Oh, Thomas," Maeve whispered. "How I have always loved you, Thomas. You have given me the only love I ever really knew."

The old Gypsy screwed up his face in a vain attempt to stem his tears. But the moisture flooded his webbed cheeks, over his weak smile. "But what of your man, your husband, child?"

"No, Thomas, no! Only you," Maeve repeated desperately, feeling somehow that she must tell him now, must be sure that Thomas Rossar-Mescro knew the depth of her love and gratefulness.

"Only you," she said again. And Thomas Rossar-Mescro nodded, weeping, as he stroked her tangled hair.

"And you, little *posh ta posh*," he said in his broken voice, "have been all my joy since your mother with the fox's hair went to her sleep."

Maeve felt herself sliding into slumber. From far away she heard Narilla say to the brothers of Andres, "Lay him in the wagon here." And then Narilla called to one of the children, "Bring me my nettle. Is the pot boiling?" The child must have answered in the affirmative, for dimly again came the voice of Narilla. "Good."

Maeve fought with all her might against the sleep and raised her head. "No, no," said Thomas softly. "Rest, child."

But obdurately Maeve raised herself and watched Narilla at her tasks. The Gypsy moved to the side of the wagon, within Maeve's view, and plunged a handful of leaves into the bubbling water. After a time, lifting them out with a stick, Narilla took the leaves to the wagon. She would press them, Maeve knew then, to Michael's wounded arm, for Thomas and Shane had acquainted her with all manner of Gypsy lore and magic.

She lay down again and heard Narilla mutter, "The bleeding will soon cease."

Maeve heard then Andres' voice, rough with anxiety. "We

must go soon, we must go." And Narilla's answer.

She felt Thomas moving from her and heard him say in a stronger voice than he had yet used this night, "They will have to quit the country. You know what happened to the others. They found they were safe nowhere in Ireland, after all."

"And who will give them the gold for that?" Andres demanded.

"Look in the purse of the man, young Michael," Thomas said quietly. "He is a man of wealth and may have brought with him something. And I," he added in the same resolute manner, "have the rest."

"You will give your portion to them?" cried Andres.

"I will give my portion," repeated Thomas firmly, "to the child of Floure and her man, yes."

Maeve smiled in her half-sleep, hearing the Gypsies stamping out the fire, kicking its ring of concealing sticks into the field beyond, the bang of the kettle being replaced on the rack.

The rest to Maeve Rathmullan was a confusion of sounds and feelings. "Let us go then," someone said; she heard the word "Belfast" and then felt beneath her jouncing head the starting of the wagon.

In the light of the ringed moon Thomas gazed at the sleeping face of Maeve and murmured, "The child of Floure is with me for a little while. The child of Floure, my little vixen, and the youthful earl, the youthful 'earl of Tyrone.' "

The words came softly to Maeve like the words of a Gypsy air, and she fell at last into the blackness of a sleep, half dreaming, half remembering the early days in Dublin, of Michael and Colin.

Those three years more and gone, when Maeve and Michael had moved into the pretty little house near Trinity, she had for months lived on the hope that somehow all would come right. Surely, she reasoned, Michael's tenderness and consideration would one fine day become a desiring equal to hers.

But night after night her body burned as she lay beside him, listening to his quiet, even breath, waiting for the touch that never came.

The first year passed away so, and soon she realized there was one young man in particular whom Michael favored, his friend Colin O'Connell.

She said to Michael one afternoon, half-irritable, half-amused, "It is always 'Colin this' and 'Colin that.' When is your wife to meet this paragon?"

Michael blushed and made an evasive reply. It all seemed very strange. Her curiosity teased, Maeve kept on until at last Michael consented to invite Colin O'Connell to tea.

Maeve, in her long isolation in Dublin—broken only by an occasional visit from Michael's kind but conservative sister, Sheila, or from stiffer members of the Rathmullan clan—was so excited at the thought of company that she had made rather elaborate preparations.

She donned her most becoming dress for afternoon and arranged her hair according to the newest *Godey's Lady's Book*, in a short rolled bandeau and upon it a second bandeau turned back *à l'impératrice*, the two separated by small side combs. It would give her, said the *Book*, an "air of piquant coquetterie." She laughed at her own eagerness but nevertheless was very pleased when Michael commented favorably.

The entrance of Colin O'Connell, on the other hand, was an occasion for dismay. For apparently all her charm and powers of pleasing could not win the slightest warmth from Michael's boon companion.

He bowed over her hand in a Continental fashion, his thin lips not touching her flesh, and complimented her with such cold politeness that his flatteries sounded almost affronts. And it seemed to Maeve that Michael and Colin, conversing in her presence, were talking like utter strangers of very trivial things, as if something very important were left unsaid by necessity.

Maeve's heart sank, and the pretty room and shining tea things, the gleaming dress and French coiffure were suddenly pitful. What had she, after all, she thought darkly, to contribute to their conversation—a half-lettered girl from the wilds of Tullaghoe? And Colin had been to Europe on the Tour; his polite chatter glittered with the names of faraway places and treasures, as if he were determined to shut her out.

At last, to end her discomfort, she excused herself on the grounds of a headache. Avoiding Michael's disapproving eye, she left the room. Pausing irresolutely outside the door, she heard her husband cry out, "Really, Colin! You didn't have to be such a perfect bitch."

Shocked to the roots of her hair at Michael's use of the

female word, Maeve turned cold. She moved nearer to the
door. "My dear, it is a perfect farce. Why do you continue
it?"

That was Colin. After this there was a puzzling silence and
a smothered protest. Barely knowing what she did, she opened
the door soundlessly. Colin O'Connell was holding her
husband, Michael, in his arms. They were kissing each other.
Maeve hardly recalled how she got to her room or with what
strength she endured that night and the ones that followed.

She never told Michael what she had seen. But she never
asked Colin to tea again. And in the years ensuing nothing
was the same between them. Maeve found herself developing,
out of her shock and grief, a private haven of her own. She
turned more and more to books, finding in them the only
world she could value. Until she had met the students who
were Fenians. From these she drew her strength.

Maeve Rathmullan woke with a start. She could not judge
how long she had slept, but the light through the wagon's windows seemed that of early evening. *I must have slept the night
and day away!* she marveled. Beneath the wheels she felt the
uneven hardness of cobblestones.

And soon she heard Narilla saying in her ear, "We have
come to Belfast. It is time to make ready now."

Part II

THE STRANGER WINDS

Chapter 4

So SWIFT was the succession of events after the dazed Maeve's
waking that she found no time to question Narilla about their
destination. Indeed, her trust in Thomas Rossar-Mescro was
so strong that Maeve would have followed any of his bidding,
and she heard Thomas in Narilla's words.

Therefore, when the wagon drew up in a dark side street of
the city strange to her, Maeve made no protest as Narilla
thrust a little bundle into her hands. Narilla said quickly,
"Take this; it has some things of mine that may be of use.

"And this," Narilla added, handing Maeve a paper on
which could be made out, in Thomas' crabbed, literate hand,
a solitary name and address. "Guard this," Narilla said in the
same tense, hasty manner. "Thomas has friends everywhere,
and these people will help you in case of need."

Maeve folded the paper and put it in the pocket of her short
coat. "Gods!" Narilla cried. "Tuck up your hair under your
cap, child. You are to go aboard the ship as Michael's
younger brother. It is far better that you not reveal your true
self to the captain and the men."

With desperate quickness Maeve obeyed and, holding the
bundle under her arm, descended from the wagon to the cobblestones.

To her joyful surprise, Michael was on his feet, though he
looked deathly pale and leaned against Andres for support.
"Come," Andres said, "we must walk from here. The wagon
cannot be seen in the light."

Maeve nodded. Andres' dark eyes were bright with approval of her unquestioning submission. But she asked then, "Where is Thomas?"

"Here, my dearest child," Thomas answered, stepping from the shadows and clasping Maeve in his arms.

Suddenly her calm control gave way, and she burst into wild weeping. "Oh, Thomas, Thomas!" she cried. "How can there be a place for me away from you?"

"Hush now, little *posh ta posh*; there is a place. We will be together again by and by."

Andres pulled the clinging Maeve from Thomas, saying in a low, impatient voice, "There is no time. The *Falcon* is about to sail. Come."

His hard grasp bruised Maeve's resisting arm. "Good-bye, Thomas," she cried, half-turning, as she was urged along by Andres, to keep the beloved old man in sight as long as possible.

"But where are we going? What of—"

"Ask your man when you are on board," Andres replied tersely, and for the first time Maeve realized why he had become the leader of the Rossar-Mescros in these days of Thomas' failing. Andres wasted neither words nor motion, and his grim face commanded even the respect of herself, whose rebellious heart had always made her question and examine.

They were approaching the wharf, and in the deepening night Maeve could make out the high and brooding forms of several ships.

"The *Falcon* is only a merchant," Andres said, "but it was the first ship bound outward on this night."

"A merchant?" Maeve repeated. She had never been on any ship before, and the term meant nothing.

"A boat designed for cargo, not passengers," Andres said. "Now remember," he added quickly, "you are a lad. Keep your head down; stay in the dark as much as you can when we board. And do not speak."

They were mounting a wooden ramp that apparently connected the ship with the shore, and Maeve had an impression of bedlam on the lamplit deck—the rough voices of men crying out incomprehensible words and phrases, in alien accents and peculiar tongues. Obedient to Andres' orders, she hung back behind Michael and the Gypsy, keeping her eyes cast down, her face almost hidden by her voluminous cap.

When Andres half lifted her onto the deck, and she felt beneath her unaccustomed feet its rise and fall, Maeve knew a swift chill of terror. What were they doing here, she questioned wildly in silence, on this forbidding vessel bound for nowhere in the night?

She almost exclaimed aloud but, remembering Andres' warning, repressed her cry. Even a word, she knew, would give her away, for it would be uttered in the timbre of a woman's voice.

And she lowered her head again, standing away from the flickering lamplight of the bobbing flames in their cages of glass. Behind Andres and Michael she purposely lengthened her stride, so as to imitate more nearly the motions of a boy. The two before her paused; Andres had been hailed by a group of men who had been leaning on the rail. "I am the captain, Fingal Pearse," one said.

Dimly she was aware that the men were moving toward them, then that Andres had engaged the captain in low converse. So sheltering was the bill of Maeve's cap that she could not clearly see the man talking to Andres. She could see no higher than the middle button of his gaping shirt; it was worn carelessly open, though the night was chill.

But as he moved into the lantern light, Maeve perceived his form with clarity: He was evidently very tall, and the narrowness of his wide-belted waist swelled out and upward into a chest of apparent huge proportions. His tight dark breeches revealed loins as lithe and slender as a panther's and long, heavily muscled legs that were yet slim as well.

And to her own astonishment, in the midst of her uncertainty and fear, the untouched Maeve felt a path of fire spread out from her body's core into her arms and legs and belly, heating her neck and back and breasts and flaming to her very heart. She knew then, horrified, that these alien fires had risen in her merely from the contemplation of the stranger's half-seen form. A fluttering beat loudly in her ears.

And then she heard, though its strange wingbeat, the voice of Andres rise. "America! You were bound for Scotland."

"Take it or leave it." The captain's voice was cruel, almost growling; its owner, Maeve felt, sounded inflexible as steel. She shivered.

"We cannot touch Scotland on this voyage," said Pearse in

his metallic voice. "There are . . . certain considerations." A hint of dark humor glinted in the last words; again Maeve knew that loud fluttering of her pulses in her ears. "Make up your mind."

There was a muttered conference between Andres and Michael. Maeve caught, over the calling of the crew and the creaking of the great ropes, random words: "No choice. Six weeks, at least."

Then the captain mentioned a sum of money. There was a protest from Andres. Pearse replied, "It's little enough for a sick man and a child. The *Falcon* is not a nursery or a hospital. They would not be here at all if it were not for Thomas Rossar-Mescro."

Even in her anger—for Fingal Pearse was discussing them as if they were things, not people—Maeve realized with puzzlement that the captain was a lettered man. She had thought all seamen illiterate and rough.

"A doctor?" the captain barked, in reply to a quiet question from Michael. "There is one of sorts." And then, apparently to Andres, he said, "Well? I don't give a damn for anything but the money. Show it."

The callous declaration filled Maeve with a sick disgust. Again she felt that chill of apprehension that had struck her before. What kind of man were they being delivered to?

"Very well," she heard Andres reply. There was a sudden quickening along the decks, and the vessel echoed with the sounds of departure—terse, urgent calls and the heavy hurry of men's feet.

"Farewell," Andres said to Maeve, pressing her arm. "This Pearse—Thomas trusts him." He scribbled on a scrap of paper. "Take this New York address. They may still be there."

She nodded, afraid to reply.

Fingal Pearse was barking at a swarthy man to take them to their cabin. Maeve had still not seen the captain's face.

Michael's arm fell about her shoulder, and she tried to match her steps with his as they followed the man.

Maeve reflected with a sinking heart, *All from this hour is unknown and perilous*.

She pondered Andres' judgment of the captain, Fingal Pearse—"Thomas trusts him." That should be enough, yet

Maeve knew she hated the man named Fingal Pearse, and
nothing in her world would ever soften that hatred, despite
her body's first response to him.

The captain's peculiar given name was one that had endured in Ireland for a thousand years. The Vikings who had
sired the mothers' mothers of Fingal Pearse were feared as
ruthless and pagan invaders; the Norsemen were dubbed
"Finn-galls," "fair foreigners"; even in this year of 1865 the
country north of the Liffey was known as Fingall, "the land
of Norsemen." The surname Pearse had been bequeathed the
captain by his Irish father.

For centuries the kinsmen of his gilt-haired mother had
prospered on piracy; then the Vikings' daughter met and
loved the builder of sailing ships, Roger Pearse. But when he
grew to manhood, Fingal Pearse, scorning to join his modest
brothers in the family's shipyard, had taken to the sea. And
the tall man with gilded hair, whose pale eyes so strangely
mingled the coldness of the Vikings with the softer passions of
the Gaels, could best any man at the tasks of the sea. He could
climb a mast like a monkey; handling the massive ropes had
turned his arms into tools with the hardness of oak or metal.
There was no weapon he could not use with skill. The owners
of the ships that he commanded said among themselves that
he had been born too late, that Fingal Pearse should have
sailed when the Jolly Roger flew the seas.

Most hated, all respected him. Fingal Pearse had never
asked the shippers questions. It was one to him whether his
cargo was a hold of ivory or slaves; whatever merchandise
rode in the belly of a ship commanded by him, it was sure to
reach its harbor.

His men always judged him fair. But no one, it appeared,
knew anything about the private mind of Fingal Pearse. In
port he was as adept as any man at drinking and at whoring,
but no one of his crew had ever seen him drunk, nor had he
ever lost his head about a woman.

Once years before in Marseilles, when Fingal Pearse was
drinking with his second mate, the man—not long under
Pearse's command—had seen the captain's ice-blue eyes light
up a moment at the sight of a dark Arabian dancer.

The worse for drink, the mate blurted out to Fingal Pearse,

"You never speak of women, Captain! Have you not a wife somewhere, some woman who has your heart secured in some far port of the world?"

And Fingal Pearse had turned upon the mate, a sentimental Scot, a look of such cold hatred and resentment that the man quailed in its path. Pearse said no word but merely looked upon the second mate with his steely eyes, cold as a Norwegian fjord. And the baffled mate had asked no more thereafter.

Confiding in the first mate back on board, the Scot was told that there was one subject that could never be brought up with the captain, and that was the subject of a wife.

"They say," the first mate whispered to the feckless Scot, "that Fingal Pearse does not have feelings like other men, for all he is a good captain and fair to the crew. And spends," he added, grinning, "as much time as any man in the houses when we go ashore. My own opinion is a woman did him some terrible wrong. So when it comes to the matter of a wife, my friend, you'd better button your lip."

And the second mate afterward followed that advice, for he could not forget the murderous stare in the pallid eyes of the Norsemen's descendant, when asked that private question.

Andres had said the merchant vessel *Falcon* had not been designed for passengers, so it was with relieved surprise that Maeve examined their cabin when their swarthy escort lit the lanterns on either side of the door.

It looked like a relatively comfortable place. There was a wooden washstand with a washbowl and pitcher of water set into round holes at the top of the stand. A padded bench had drawers beneath; the drawers had peculiar fastenings, so that, Maeve reasoned, they would stay shut as the vessel heaved about. The floor was uncarpeted, but there was a chair and two bunks, one above the other, with curtains. Maeve thought wryly that the room was more immaculate than anything had ever been at Tullaghoe and that only in Dublin had she had better accommodations.

The seaman smiled at them. "It is the best cabin," he said proudly, "next to the captain's."

"It is quite satisfactory," Michael Rathmullan answered. His white face revealed his deep exhaustion, and he seemed, Maeve thought, to be repressing a grimace of pain.

"I am Juan," the dark man said; his dark eyes were kind. "Spanish for Sean," he added, and Michael smiled. "If you need my help, just ask for me."

"Thank you, Juan." Michael's reply appeared to come with terrible effort, and Maeve prayed that the man would leave them. The man's curious glances made her increasingly nervous.

At last they were alone. With a deep sigh of relief Maeve took off the constricting cap and shook out her heavy fall of black hair. She threw the cap upon the lower bed and went to Michael. His face had grown even whiter, and he sat limply in the chair, clutching his arm.

"The potion," he said in a weak voice. "In my pocket. Narilla gave it to me for the pain."

Obediently Maeve dipped into his near pocket, following his gesture, and removed a bottle of dark liquid. Looking helplessly about the cabin, she realized there was no spoon or glass.

"Never mind," Michael said in a gentle voice. "I'll take it from the bottle." He seemed unable to make the simple motion, so Maeve uncapped the bottle and tilted the potion to his lips.

Drinking, he soon lost the look of panic because, Maeve judged, of the promised relief of Narilla's mixture. "How do you feel?" she asked anxiously, touching his brow with her hand.

"Your hand is so cold"—he smiled—"that you will never be able to tell if I have a fever."

In truth, Maeve realized that she was cold all over—cold with the walk to the wharf and the wait on deck, almost freezing with the apprehension of the days that faced them.

She tried to smile, with the hope of reassuring Michael. Capping the bottle, she placed it on the washstand and sank down on the lower bunk opposite her husband.

"I am so tired," he said.

She rose, she took up her cap from the narrow bed and hung it on a hook over the washstand. Turning back the coverlet of the bunk, she said softly, "Come, come to bed now."

"There is so much to talk of," Michael protested, frowning.

"There will be weeks of time to talk. We will begin

tomorrow," Maeve replied with a tight smile. "Come now," she repeated.

"I am so tired," Michael said again, consenting to be led to the little bunk.

Maeve removed his coat and hung it on another hook by her cap. "Let me have your trousers," she said in a gentle, matter-of-fact tone.

"No, no, leave them," Michael answered, struggling to remove his boots. Maeve knelt down before him and with effort pulled them from his feet. He lay down with a sigh of relief so poignant that it sounded like a sob of agony. At once he fell into a deep, unstirring slumber.

Maeve stood a moment looking down at her husband. "What have I brought you to, Michael?" she whispered. "What have I brought you to, and Colin lying dead in the darkness and the mist, Colin whom you loved?"

Michael did not stir, and Maeve felt at last the release of the tears that she had held throughout the long walk to the *Falcon*, the interval of terror upon its heaving decks and these last dread moments of dissembling. Her narrow body shook with the force of her weeping. With an overpowering weariness, yet consoled, she undressed herself and washed, managing to climb to the little bunk above the sleeping Michael's.

The little bed surprised her with its clean softness; her body, aching with tension, relaxed utterly to its momentary ease. Yet her long sleep the night and day before had left her mind alert and wakeful, and as she lay wide-eyed, feeling the roll of the *Falcon*, she knew that sleep would be slow in coming.

She glanced about the cabin, still bright in the illumination of the lanterns that she had left burning for comfort. Suddenly she recalled the bundle Narilla had given her, which she had dropped carelessly into a corner of the cabin.

Cautiously she raised herself, and lightly climbed down. The bundle still lay in the corner of the cabin. Maeve took it up and unrolled it. The bright cover of flame-green silk, falling away with a whisper, revealed a many-colored shawl, a scarlet dress and a small silken pouch. Maeve pulled back the pouch's silken mouth and found within it a wooden comb and a pair of little golden earrings.

Exclaiming softly, Maeve took the pouch to her lips and kissed it, fresh tears spotting its smooth scarlet. Narilla had given her the only pair of earrings that she owned; Maeve remembered now the bare pierced earlobes of the other woman. And the shawl and gown that were her best, for these splendid garments must be that. The gifts touched the lonely Maeve with greater force than anything she had ever been given. The pathetic beauty of the few things meant more now than all the pretty gowns still hanging in her press in Dublin.

Remembering them, and the fullness of her days in the bustling city—comfortable and secure for all her loneliness— Maeve held the Gypsy's scarlet gown in her cold hands, the silent tears flooding her face. So much was gone, and no one knew what terrors lay ahead.

After a moment she replaced Narilla's gifts in the silk covering and thrust the bundle into one of the drawers of the padded bench. Her naked body was chilled and rough now with the cold; she climbed, trembling, to the bunk above Michael's, seeking the warmth of its coverlet. And this time she fell at once into uneasy sleep.

For five years now the wooden sailing vessels such as the *Falcon* had been giving way to steamers, which the *Falcon*'s weathered crew looked on, half with envy, half with contempt, as floating palaces that a woman could command. The accommodation of the *Falcon*'s crew was situated directly in the bows, the forecastle a dank area with room for little but their bunks, space to stow sea chests and the table at which they ate. They entered it down a forecastle scuttle and a steep ladder.

The forecastle's heat came from a stove with a funnel pipe that rose through the deck, and its covering was a cowl at the top to keep out some of the water.

It was a spartan existence, but Juan, the Spaniard, had known worse, in a house where ten people had slept to a room and meat was a rarely known delight.

He mused upon this now as he spooned the hearty stew that Henry Wong, the cook, had set before him and the other men. Juan took a swallow of his ale and remarked, "I think that fellow and the lad we took on are very queer . . . there's something crazy in the boy. Do you know he's never been on deck except at night?"

"Aye." The reply of McIntyre, the Scot, was brief and dour.

Nettled at this sparse response and with the Latin love of speech, Juan turned to the Portugee seaman at his other side. "You have seen him, Jorge?" Juan asked.

"*Si*," the Portuguese replied around a mouthful of stew. He swallowed and continued, taking up his mug of ale. "I think they are both *freiras*." He downed his drink.

"Fray-rahs?" repeated McIntyre, a glint of curiosity in his cold blue eyes.

"Sisters," the Portugee Jorge explained, grinning with contempt. "Nancy-boys. The lad has wrists like a bird, like a girl. He did not come on deck at all for a whole week, then only in the dark, always."

"Perhaps they are *vampiros*, vampires." Juan laughed, revealing tobacco-stained and broken teeth, but his black eyes were like a child's and bright with mischief.

"Idle chatter," McIntyre proclaimed sourly and, after scraping his bowl, took a pipe from his pocket and lit it, puffing slowly.

"Laugh you may, but the man Rathmullan, I tell you, will not be long upon the *Falcon*. And it will be a black day for the lad, vampire *or* nancy-boy, to land in the port of New York alone."

The two Latins turned in surprise at the sound of the indignant words. Seamus Corcoran, like McIntyre, was a silent man and rarely put in a word at the table.

"What do you mean, Corcoran?" The comely Jorge picked at his teeth, which were straight and white and perfect, as he leaned back lazily in his wooden chair.

"I mean," said Seamus Corcoran, "what Angus Hudson, the second mate—what calls himself a doctor—said to me after he was summoned to their cabin."

Amazement kept the others still: Corcoran had never said so many words, at one time together, since they had left Belfast. Apparently he enjoyed the sensation; he looked at the others with a kind of gloomy triumph, nodding his red head, waiting to be asked to continue.

The convivial Spaniard, Juan, prodded, "Tell us then, man, for the sake of the Virgin."

Snorting at this Papist reference, Corcoran replied, "The mate Angus Hudson, what calls himself a doctor, was summoned night before last by the lad himself to their cabin. The man Rathmullan was in great pain. When Hudson looked at his arm, he found someone had taken a bullet out of it, not many long days ago."

"Ah!" Jorge cried. "I knew that that was it."

"That *what* was it?" McIntyre cut in. "It is none of our affair what the man Rathmullan did. Enough of your chatter." The others looked at him curiously but did not comment. There fell an uneasy silence. They were thinking of the captain's change of route, the fact that they would not be landing at Scotland on this voyage. McIntyre colored, but he repeated stolidly, "Enough of your chatter."

"What's eating you, McIntyre?" Corcoran inquired in a teasing voice.

"Nothing's eating me at all." Indignantly the lean Scot pushed back his chair and stalked away from the table. He threw himself upon his bunk at the farther end of the forecastle and lay staring upward and sucking at this pipe.

"So what did Hudson find?" Jorge pressed the Irishman.

"He found the man Rathmullan's arm was almost rotten with infection. And that he had been taking into himself some kind of Gypsy potion which has done him no more good than a puff of wind."

"And how does the man fare now?" Juan asked with real concern, for he remembered the man's courtesy and the woe-begone look of the thin lad.

"Hudson did what he could, in truth," said Corcoran. "But the man is no doctor, whatever he calls himself. And he said to the captain in my hearing that the man will not be long upon the *Falcon*."

The facile emotions of Jorge and Juan had been aroused by the pathos of the dying Irishman and the lone boy.

"What will become then of the boy?" Juan asked Corcoran.

"The dear knows," said the Irishman, sighing. "It is a long way away indeed to find himself, in the country of America."

"*Sí*, you say true." The variable Juan's imaginings were already turning from the failing man above them to the country of America, which he had never seen.

"What are they like, these United States?" Juan asked Corcoran, who boasted of a cousin fighting in the American war.

"So large it is beyond imagining," Corcoran answered from his superior knowledge. "So big that you could set upon it Ireland and Scotland and England and Wales . . . aye, and

France and Italy and Spain . . . and still have lots of room.''

"But tell me of that king, the man Leen-*cón* . . . who set free the peasants," Juan said eagerly.

"He's not a king, you Spanish booby," Corcoran retorted, laughing. "He's the President. My cousin says he is a very great man."

"Then the people must love him," said Juan. "May he live long."

"Oh, he'll live long, all right," said Corcoran belching. "He's not so very old a man."

Contrary to the maxim that decreed the morning as the brightener of the troubled and the night as creator of imaginary woes, Maeve Rathmullan found the very opposite was so. She dreaded the gray light creeping through the round windows of their cabin, which Michael called portholes, for then she was imprisoned to the cabin. It was only after dark that she felt the return of hope; freed by the friendly, enveloping night, she could leave the confines of her cell and creep about the main deck, letting the cold sea wind refresh her grateful lungs.

They had been at sea three weeks, the Scot McIntyre had told her; it was April now, and the *Falcon* was scheduled to reach the port of New York near the month's end. It seemed a strange thing, to the country-bred Maeve, to mark the passage of days in this wilderness of water. For her there were no markers but the rising and setting of the sun, whereas in Tullaghoe the seasons had presented such sweet evidence; she recalled with a pang akin to a wounding of the flesh the wild crystal freshets of April over the hills of Tullaghoe.

But McIntyre had revealed that the sea provided its own shining markers of the seasons' change—the constellations in the skies above them, which he pointed out to her. With touched and grateful amusement, Maeve knew the dour Scot's friendliness sprang from his approval of her reticence, a closemouthed quality akin to his, little knowing that she kept silent from necessity and burned for speech.

With difficulty Maeve had found her sea legs against the constant tossing and pitching of the vessel; for her nightly expeditions in the spring winds she wore at first Michael's jacket buttoned high over her own. In this costume she had had the appearance of a beggar child, for the jacket was three times too large and made motion awkward.

Finally, the silent Corcoran had handed her, without comment, a soiled and bulky sweater of what had been ivory-colored yarn, and she wore it gratefully thereafter. Large as the sweater was, it was a more comfortable fit than Michael's jacket.

They hit heavy weather when the *Falcon* reached the North Atlantic, and Maeve cowered in fear when the ship jerked violently backward, forward, sideward; there was an incessant creaking and screaming, accompanied at regular intervals by the constant dull thudding of the massive seas which struck at all parts of the *Falcon*.

And there were nights when the wind was of such force—even at the times that the Scot and Corcoran called calm—that Maeve was confined to the stuffiness of the cabin in spite of the friendly dark.

The hours with Michael had brought them very near, Maeve thought with sorrow, now that it was too late. For she was aware from the first visit of Hudson, the mate, that Michael was bound to die, although the kindly mate had dissembled before them.

One gray afternoon when the rain was lashing at the portholes of their close space, Michael awoke from a feverish half-sleep. Without speaking he studied the restless Maeve from under lowered lids.

She was pacing the uncarpeted floor, moving now and then to the small round window to stare out at the blinding rain above the tossing waves.

He said her name, and at once with a start of guilt she turned to him and asked, "How are you, Michael, dear? Is there anything you want?"

He smiled with affection and answered weakly, "Come sit with me a moment and let us talk."

Maeve drew up the little wooden chair, but Michael made a motion with his slender hand and protested, "The bed. Sit upon the bunk with me, sweeting."

She was touched by his new habit of calling her pet names, something he had never done before. As if his love for Colin, unexpressed, must show itself to her. She knew that he was dying.

Maeve felt pain rise in her throat; she feared to speak, for her tears were close, so she merely nodded and sat down.

Michael's gentle eyes were almost unrecognizable, glazed as they were with fever, and Maeve knew once more a helpless rage.

He said weakly, "When you reach New York—"

"When *we* reach New York," she insisted, taking his hand.

But Michael said again, "When you reach New York, you must ask Thomas' friends how best to obtain the moneys that are mine. Do not write to my father; the authorities will be watching the mails. There were Fenians among us that night we killed two of your uncle's men. You would be brought back and imprisoned."

Maeve turned cold; she recalled with terrible clarity the sight of Mountjoy Prison in Dublin, with the barred circle in its yard, where the grim-faced Fenian conspirators prowled like caged animals.

"It is as well," said Michael, "that you are going to America. You will be safe, as James Stephens was so long ago in France." He managed a weak smile.

"Michael," she protested softly, "when we get to New York, we will go at once to a doctor, and you will be well again."

"Maeve, Maeve." He withdrew his hand, saying with tender reproach, "It's too late now for anything but truth."

She saw in his sorrowful look a terrible acquaintance with some shadowy place that he had come to know. For an instant she could see it, too, and a shuddering took her that she could not master.

"Maeve," he said again, this time more urgently, and she leaned forward, taking both his hands in hers.

"I tried to love you, you know," he said.

"Yes, Michael, I know. It is all right, all right, now." The tears burst at last and flooded her stricken face.

"You saw us that afternoon, Colin and me." It was a statement, not a question.

"Yes."

"And you never said a word," Michael whispered with wonder. "How kind you've always been."

With that his eyes began to close. His hands became quite still in hers. And when Maeve leaned forward to him, he had no more breath or motion.

Chapter 5

BURIAL AT SEA, Maeve learned with consternation, was always conducted by day; therefore, she, all shattered and discomposed by this desolation of her grief, would be forced to appear in that glaring brightness before all the crew. And worst of all, before the captain, whom she had managed to avoid these many weeks in artful ways.

The kindly Hudson, who had discovered the death of Michael when he came for his fruitless treatment, had conveyed all this to the stunned Maeve. Trying to comfort the lad, Hudson had questioned for the hundredth time why the boy always wore his cap, even indoors, and habitually stood away from the flickering light of the lanterns by the door. But the mate shrugged inwardly, having witnessed these strange phenomena for so many weeks. He said quietly to the boy that there was no alternative but to bury Michael Rathmullan at sea.

The clear-sighted Maeve shuddered, considering Hudson's unspoken implication—that it was not possible to preserve the body, even in the brisk spring weather, for the remainder of the voyage to America.

That night in the cabin that echoed with its emptiness, she lay awake on the bed above the one in which Michael had died. She did not sleep at all, and when the gray light crept into the space, she was still lying wakeful, stiff and aching with the tension of her nerves.

With the going of Michael, she knew, she was truly alone.

The mournful word echoed darkly in her mind, and weeping
at last, she found a little relief, although the word, shaped like
the very tears that flowed down her face upon the hands that
covered it, echoed again: "Alone."

It was not long before she heard the soft tapping at her
door, the clinging burr of McIntyre, saying, "It is time, lad; it
is time."

Exhausted, Maeve climbed down from the upper bed and
drew on her boy's trousers, belting them more tightly around
a waist that had grown narrower in these weeks aboard the
Falcon. Glancing in the glass, she was almost grateful for the
haggard thinness of her face, for it made her appear more
boyish, with its sharp new planes, than it had been with its
rose-white smoothness. Even her lips looked pale and thin.

Stuffing her hair under the battered cap with its great,
sheltering bill, Maeve gave herself a final glance. She prayed
the deception would carry through this day; the miracle of it
all these weeks had given her courage to endure.

She found her way with trembling limbs to the main deck,
where Hudson had told her the service would be held; he had
inquired gently what Michael's faith had been. When Maeve
had told him Catholic, the mate smiled wryly, saying, "It is a
pity that we have no priest, boy. But surely among all these
men there must be one wi' a Roman book of some description."

Even in her deep, pained grief Maeve could not help smiling
at the busy Hudson's researches among the men. He had come
back to report that oddly there was not among them all a
proper "Roman holy book," that even Juan's was in the
Spanish tongue, less than useless to a Rathmullan, that the
godless Jorge had not one at all and that all the other men
were either pagan creatures or Protestants, like himself and
Corcoran.

"But never mind, lad," Hudson concluded in a consoling
tone, "the captain is a man of glorious words when they are
needed. He will give your brother a proper send-off into the
waves."

Maeve felt a new and puzzled surprise: to imagine the
harsh and callous Pearse being a man of "glorious words"
was beyond her, just as Andres' assurance that "Thomas
trusts him" was less than sufficient to win her confidence.

As she reached the main deck now, she saw with dismay

that the captain and the entire crew were gathered there about
the canvas-wrapped bundle that had been Michael. Her first
thought was how ugly Michael's winding sheet appeared; she
would have given much to wrap him in a shroud of some
splendid color but, after long consideration, had sadly
decided she must keep her shawl. Subtracted from her
pathetic store of clothes, it would leave her with almost
nothing in America.

Then, seeing the eyes of the men upon her, Maeve recalled
her more immediate peril; she pulled the cap farther down
over her eyes and found a sheltered place behind Hudson to
conceal herself from the steely gaze of Fingal Pearse.

She still had not obtained a clear view of his face; in the
moment before she cast down her eyes and hid behind the
mate, she had a fleeting impression of ice-blue eyes and a fine-
boned, hard face like granite. All she could see now, as on
that first dim night, was the leanness of the captain's form; he
wore a dark-blue coat today she had not seen the first night
and even a dark cravat—Maeve supposed for the solemnity of
the occasion.

Despite herself, she warmed a little more to Fingal Pearse;
he seemed willing, in his curt fashion, to do a decent thing by
Michael, to pay a kind of honor to his passing.

It was then she heard the mate before her exclaim with surprise. He turned and said to her in a low voice, "Look, lad,
the captain has a holy book himself, and it must be Roman.
He has never been known to possess such a thing before."

Maeve peered at the volume in Pearse's long-fingered
hands; the book was of a green so dark it looked like the night
green of a shadowy forest, and she could make out dimly on
its spine gilt letters that appeared familiar. Surely they were
Gaelic. A melancholy gratitude softened the hardness of her
aching throat, and she tasted the healing salt of her own
weeping once more.

The day was unusually calm; the breeze upon the deck was
light, and the sun was silver behind small clouds, making a
kind of bright dusk of the air about them.

Fingal Pearse began to read from the green volume, and
Maeve heard with astonishment and delight a stately kindness
in the voice that had always sounded before like the growl of a
cruel buccaneer.

It was not the regular burial service he read now; she

recognized against the wind that carried away some of the words a prayer to Ireland that Michael had read to her:

". . . It was Thou that inspired its martyrs with courage to despise the power of tyranny and to sanctify the soil of Ireland and the soil of other lands with their blood.

". . . Thou art the Author of the finest, most beautiful, most wonderful and most glorious spectacles that ever God or angel looked down on. . . .

". . . in mountain cavern and forest glen . . . plundered and persecuted, and put to death in the thousands by pestilence and famine and hunger. . . .

". . . We were your 'chosen people' and you laid your hand heavily on us, and tried us as gold is tried in the crucible.

". . . and the fame of the Island of Saints increased before God and men."

She heard Fingal Pearse start then the Litany to St. Patrick and thrilled sadly to its slow measures:

"St. Patrick, glory of Ireland; St. Patrick, example of penance . . . St. Patrick, our powerful protector. . . .

"Beside me is the Hill of Knees—a small eminence where you spent some time in prayer, as you were wont—and where you left the impress of your knees on the green sward.

"And within view is Croach Patrick—a high mountain where you passed the Lent . . . conversing with God . . . communing with angels. . . .

". . . in your company and in the company of all the Saints of Ireland, the reward promised to all who fight the good fight and keep the faith. Amen."

The beauty of the words had brought to the suffering heart of Maeve a wondrous comfort. She listened, consoled, as Fingal Pearse concluded, "May the Lord have mercy upon the soul of Michael Rathmullan."

And he said the litany of the Irish saints, their names sounding to Maeve like sad silver bells on the rising wind from the sea:

"St. Malachy, patron of Armagh; St. Finnian, patron of Meath; St. Aedan, patron of Ferns; St. Finbarr, patron of Cork; St. Calain, patron of Down; St. Colman, patron of Dromore. . . ."

Then dimly came to Maeve the final blessing: "We commend thy body to the deep."

In her anxiety to hear the beauty of the comforting words,

Maeve had moved forward a little and stood apart, no longer hidden by the breadth of the mate Hudson.

Fingal Pearse gave the signal to his first mate to lower the body of Michael Rathmullan into the sea; as the slender burden fell from its canvas covering, the captain glanced a moment at the lad next to Hudson.

Something in the hands' fragility struck Fingal Pearse—he had never got a real look at the boy—and when a sudden gust of wind tore away the concealing cap from the narrow head, he almost expected the sight of a woman's hair escaping and flying like a dark banner in the precipitate gale.

Fingal Pearse looked at the slender, defiant woman standing before him on the windswept deck; there were loud exclamations from Juan and Jorge, but the others were silent.

The thin face and green eyes of Maeve Rathmullan plucked at the senses of Fingal Pearse, and something alien to his stony nature seemed to melt the hardness of his limbs and flicker in his cold eyes, silver-blue and piercing as the early winter sky. He had known the bodies of countless women; yet never until now had Fingal Pearse been so stricken by a woman's beauty. In that swift moment, then, the gold and silver of the words he had read over the body of Michael Rathmullan were his Irish childhood again; they were the color of the small white woman before him.

Maeve Rathmullan tried to read the light in Fingal Pearse's eyes. Then, trembling, she retrieved her boy's cap and fled to the safety of her cabin.

Reaching the familiar haven, Maeve slammed the door and leaned against it with a sobbing breath, trying to slow the beating of her heart, to collect the chaos of her thoughts.

Michael was gone from her forever—and now they knew her secret, all of them, these strangers who once had seemed so kind. But could they be trusted now, with a lone and unprotected woman in the middle of the sea? And what of Fingal Pearse?

Still trembling, Maeve sank down on the lower bunk. And all at once she realized that Fingal Pearse, the captain, was her greatest fear.

Even now in her confusion, Maeve's recalcitrant flesh was warming to the image of him as it had the first night she had boarded the *Falcon*; the childish, unawakened desire she had felt for Michael, all those years ago, now seemed like a flickering candle flame beside the heat of the sun.

She was recalling the gilded hair of Fingal Pearse, its strands almost silver around his ears, below the dark, peaked cap he wore; in the glare upon the deck that pallid hair had gleamed like the sun of early spring in Tullaghoe. And his eyes were the light blue of the morning sky in winter; looking at her, they had been at once piercing and ironic, demanding and cold.

She had felt their coolness wash away her body's grief, even as it mysteriously filled her veins with the blue-white heat of greater fire.

Most of all, the splendor of his form had deeply shaken her. The apparent strength of his limbs, though slender, seemed greater than she had ever seen in any man, even the steel-limbed knights of her beloved legends.

Maeve Rathmullan let the reflections flood her mind; her trembling ceased, and suddenly she was possessed of a hot, alien languor, then a total weariness.

What am I thinking of? she questioned sternly. *He is a man of no kindness; when he spoke to Andres of us that first night, we might have been boxes of merchandise to be thrown in the* Falcon*'s hold!*

I cannot face it now, she thought. *No more, no more!* And her exhausted body brought her instant sleep.

She dreamed then that she was swimming in a hidden pool, but it was not the cool, shady waters of the secret stream in Tullaghoe. It was a land so warm and bright that the sun shone like a million candle fires. And strangely, in the way of dreams, Maeve was a witness apart, watching the motions she performed.

There was a ripple in the sun-warmed waters of the hidden pool; then, for an instant, a spreading brightness, like strands of silver-touched black silk, appeared on the surface. The gleam was a woman's hair, Maeve's own, and as she rose from the water's depths, her face half-hidden in the glittering veil, the strong sun lit her arms and shoulders, plashing from her rose-tipped breasts.

Maeve gasped the burning air, shaking back the silken hair to reveal the passionate features of a woman older than she was; where her eyes had once been innocent and clear, this

woman's gaze was fierce and arrogant. The leashed wildness
of a woodland creature pulsated in her delicate nostrils.

And in her dream Maeve looked on her new self with
amazement.

Careless of her nakedness, the white woman who was
Maeve and not-Maeve turned in a great splash to float on her
back, the amber water pouring from her nipple-blooming
breasts, the flat, athletic belly and long, slender legs. She
closed her green eyes to the blazing sun, and Maeve saw that
her lids were colored with green and glimmered like the
phosphorescent bodies of the insects that darted at the pool.

But then a piping cry and small wingbeat came to her ears;
she raised herself, treading water, shading her green eyes with
a slender hand, and looked upward at the sky. At first she saw
only the shadow of a bird; then in a moment the bird itself. It
was a flaming blue with an orange breast, as if its very heart
were fire.

For only a moment the blue-winged bird with its fiery
breast hovered low above the pool, and the woman's heart
beat faster. It was almost as if the creature were bringing her a
silent message of joy. But as quickly as it had descended, the
bird soared on strong and pulsing wings higher and higher
into the summer sky of the mysterious country. And the
woman who was Maeve and not-Maeve followed the bird with
her eyes until it disappeared, its vivid color mingling with that
of the high air.

The swimmer was transfixed. Then her white hand dropped
slowly from her bow, and with great reluctance, she began to
swim toward the palm-lined sand enclosing the secret pool.

It was at that moment Maeve saw him; a man was standing
like a massive statue among the palms, staring at her as if she
were a wondrous vision.

The man was clad in a garment of scarlet and dark blue; his
accoutrements were of gold, those of a royal person. His
sensuous mouth was smiling with delight to behold her in the
pool.

And instead of covering herself in the amber water, turning
modestly away, Maeve stared deliberately into the alien's deep
eyes. For she knew that he had come, the one for whom she
had longed and waited. Trembling with the boldness of her
gesture, Maeve smiled and motioned to him.

For a long moment he stood hesitant, still devouring her

with his eyes. And then he began to unfasten his sword belt with its trappings of gems and gold. At last he threw off his dark-blue clothes and stood naked. To the woman in the water he looked like a prince from the land of sun, his firm flesh tawny in the sighing shade as he strode to the edge of the water.

Maeve woke abruptly, feeling the chill sweat upon her body, her heavy boy's clothes clinging roughly to her delicate skin.

Heavy-headed, she struggled up and threw off her jacket and trousers, then the boyish shirt. She was still in the spell of the strange dream.

The pool that was like and not like the pool where Michael had found her that afternoon; the bold woman who was like and unlike herself. And the man with the night-black hair! Who could he be? He was certainly not Fingal Pearse, she concluded with wry relief, and poor Michael had been brown-haired with blue-gray eyes. A bluebird, not a flying shadow, had heralded the dark man's coming. Did this mean, then, that he was destined to bring her the happiness she had been denied?

Perhaps she had, like so many of the Irish and the Romany, the Sight, and this was an omen!

"Nonsense," Maeve said aloud. And after moving to the washstand, she began to wash her sticky hands and face and body.

There was no royal savior; she herself was not an arrogant, free woman, passion-driven. She was penniless and alone, with poor prospects ahead. With this bald realization, she was conscious again of the harsh spray of ocean waves breaking on the windows of her prison.

As Henry Wong, the cook, left the forecastle with Maeve's tray, Jorge, the Portuguese, said, grinning, "So you have lost your place, Juan."

The Spaniard, shrugging, retorted, "It is all one to me. I have no desire to do the extra work." But his dark face was smoldering with resentment. No one but Wong and the middle-aged, ascetic Hudson had been allowed near the woman now these two weeks, Juan reflected.

"The *gringos* only trust each other," Juan said in a growling voice.

"And Henry Wong is a *gringo*?" Jorge retorted.

"Never mind," Juan returned irritably. "The captain is saving her for himself."

"Then she has been long in the saving." Jorge's melodious voice was ironic. "She has an unwilling look, to me."

I like it not. It is ill luck, having a woman aboard."

"Ill luck unless you are in her bed," Jorge twitted Juan.

"Ah," the other said contemptuously, "she is too thin for me. She is not enough of a *mujer*—a woman should be. . . ." Juan grinned and made curving gestures at his chest and narrow hips.

"She is *mulher* enough for me." Jorge's black eyes gleamed hotly. "I think it will not be long."

"What do you mean?"

"I think she is just the kind to get under the captain's skin . . . he is a strange man. And it would take a strange woman to unseat him."

Juan snorted with unbelief. "No woman can undo that man; once he is through with them, he is a man of stone."

The other did not answer.

In the weeks that followed the discovery of her secret, Maeve Rathmullan knew an even greater isolation than before. She rarely went on deck now, even in the nights, for she could feel the eyes of the men upon her. She no longer knew fear and reproached herself for her terrors. After all, the men were not pirates or barbarians, yet the heat of their repressed desiring filled her with an uneasy compassion. Like most of the true March-born, Maeve could sense the thoughts of the others.

No one indeed had occasion to visit her cabin except the old cook, Wong; she had grown so used to his impassive presence that he had become for her hardly more than a piece of furniture in the cabin. He never spoke or smiled, only studying her with his unreadable eyes, leaving her tray upon the table and silently going away.

The gentle mate Hudson had come now and then, to bring her a book to while away the time and chat with her in his thick, quiet burr; she had become quite fond of Mr. Hudson. There was almost something of Thomas in him.

About a week remained, he told her, before they reached the port of New York. And Maeve's dread deepened. These solitary weeks upon the *Falcon*, uncomfortable and desolate as they had been, were at least a known discomfort.

Kindly Hudson had told her all he knew of the country of America, "so it will not be completely strange to you, lass," he said, smiling. And Maeve warmed to him in gratitude.

She had still not had converse with the distant captain; sometimes she had seen him passing, on her rare excursions to the deck. He had never spoken, only nodding coolly, moving on about his business.

The odd dream she had known on the day of Michael's burial had almost ceased to haunt her, yet sometimes, unbidden, its vivid images came to her again, and Maeve colored with shame to remember the actions of the woman in the dream who was she and yet not she at all.

One afternoon as the voyage neared its end, the friendly Hudson brought her a basin of new rainwater. "It will be pleasant," he said, smiling, "to wash your bonny hair in. My own girl always loved rainwater for her hair."

Maeve was touched almost to the point of weeping by the gesture and took the basin from his weathered hands with thanks. "You have a daughter?" she asked gently. "In Scotland?"

"Aye," he answered in his economical manner and offered no more. Maeve did not press him, wondering again if this small mystery had anything to do with the fact that the ship had bypassed the port of Glasgow on this voyage.

What, she wondered, had Hudson to do with it all? Perhaps he himself was some kind of fugitive, like Michael and herself. If so, she concluded, then she would be safe, too, under such a closemouthed captain. Strange that it had not occurred to her before! She took a new comfort in the thought.

She thanked Hudson warmly again, and he went away. Taking out from the little silken pouch a sweet herbal soap that Narilla had included, Maeve washed out her hair. Sitting naked on the prickly cane-bottomed chair, she toweled the silky black thickness thoroughly and then began to comb it rhythmically, listening to the comforting rasp of the wooden comb that Narilla had given her.

When her hair was almost dry and gleaming brightly in the lanterns' light, Maeve decided she would try on the scarlet gown and many-colored shawl. She took the gown from its green cover, shook it out and slipped it over her head. To her delight, it seemed to fit almost perfectly. The thoughtful Narilla, whose figure was much fuller than hers, must have altered it for her.

Maeve fastened the gown and took up the varicolored shawl, arranging it around her shoulders. Then she went to the small looking glass. It was impossible to see all of herself at once, so first she examined her face and hair. She exclaimed with satisfaction; these isolated weeks, when she had healed a little from her grief and her appetite had been restored, had given back the face she knew.

Her black hair, fresh from its rainwater bath, fairly glittered with health, her skin again had its rose-white color and her green eyes shone. The color had come back to her mouth; it was no longer drawn in such a thin, tight line.

She moved back so she might have some perspective of the shawl and gown, noting that the vivid hues gave a wonderful value to her skin and hair and that the tight-waisted gown, although it was out of fashion, enhanced her shapely bosom, her tiny waist and the sweet, gradual swell of the hips below.

"Well!" she said aloud, feeling almost happy for the first time in weeks. "At least I will not be an eyesore when we reach America."

She grinned at herself in the glass. A light tapping at the door made her turn in surprise. It was not time for Henry Wong to bring her dinner, and Hudson had left her only a short while ago.

Puzzled, she opened the door a crack to peer out cautiously. She looked up into the shocked eyes of Fingal Pearse.

All her discomfort in his presence, even the memory of the dream that made her shy now with all men, dissolved in laughter.

"What are you laughing at?" he blurted. She was perversely glad to see that his cold poise had utterly deserted him.

"You looked so surprised," she answered boldly. "Did you think I never wore a gown?" She moved back a little to admit him.

His former impassivity returned. "I came," he said blandly, "to see how you fare. And to bring you this."

He held out to her a small, thin booklet of dark-brown leather. Questioningly she took the booklet from his hand and opened it.

"It's your passport," he said bluntly.

"But how—?"

Fingal Pearse smiled for the first time since she had known him, and the smile gave his face a warmth and youth she would never have suspected. "We have our methods. I have friends among the officials, but you never know."

"I am . . . I am beholden to you," she said shyly, regretting now the hostile feelings she had harbored toward this man.

"I owe it to Thomas Rossar-Mescro," he said carelessly, as if trying to cover the warmth that had crept into his address.

"Owe it?" She was conscious that his ice-blue gaze was flickering over her hair and face and gown, his admiration plain.

"Never mind." His distant coldness had returned, and she felt vaguely rebuffed.

"Nevertheless," she returned quietly, "I am beholden to you, Captain Pearse."

He nodded once, curtly, and replied in the same cool manner, "We will land in America in six more days . . . we should be touching there on the twenty-fifth of April. I trust your . . . garments will be adequate for the climate," he added stiffly. "Generally the spring comes late in New York, but there are mild days."

She was suddenly grateful for his concern, no matter how coldly expressed. "I trust so," she answered in kind, not smiling.

"Then I will leave you," he said, but something hot and bright gleamed in the inscrutable depths of his ice-blue eyes, and despite herself, Maeve felt a corresponding flood of heat in her own astonished body. She lifted her green eyes and stared into his cool, piercing ones.

But he turned on his heel and left her with great abruptness.

Hardly knowing what she thought, Maeve Rathmullan sat down on the nether bed, examining the dark-brown booklet in her hands. Then she stared at the half-open door, hearing the footsteps of Fingal Pearse fade off along the passageway.

On that same night Maeve woke with heart-stopping suddenness from an uneasy sleep; the door to her cabin was ajar, and in the dim light of the passageway she glimpsed the shadow of a tall man.

She felt a fluttering of terror in her very throat; fumbling below her pillow, she searched for the other treasure from Narilla's pouch—a sharp dagger of the kind that was common among the Romany.

The door widened; now in the lantern glow that shone in from the passage, she recognized the steely form and gilded hair of Fingal Pearse, the captain of the *Falcon*.

Maeve lay motionless, the dagger hidden in her trembling hand below the coverlet. Under her lowered lids, feigning sleep, she saw him draw near and stand above her, staring down at her with his strange, cold eyes. Then he leaned to her and kissed her hair, saying her name only once in a voice she barely recognized, it was so utterly foreign to the hard man she thought she knew, and expressing a sort of tender agony.

Still pretending sleep, Maeve waited. Still he stood above her, staring; she could feel his penetrating stare. Sidelong then, she saw him kneel down by the bed and again felt his strong hand upon her head in that uncharacteristic, gentle gesture.

A melting for an instant took her limbs, and the old fires he had set in her those many weeks ago burned once more in Maeve's being. From nowhere sang the memory of faraway words she had read long ago—"madness and blindness and astonishment of heart." She knew those weaknesses now, helpless under the touch of the man kneeling near her.

His hands, trembling, brushed her face, caressing her slender neck; he groaned, and she felt the hands descending from her throat to grasp her naked breasts with a hold that bruised and demanded.

In a moment all her melting froze; she knew a wild and overpowering anger. She was to him something only to be used, as he must have used countless other women in those red-lit houses of all the ports of the world. With a lightning motion, Maeve slid from Pearse's grasp and struck him in the hand with the little dagger.

He grunted with surprise. But then, to her horrified amazement, Fingal Pearse began to laugh. "Spitfire!" he said softly, still chuckling. "Little spitfire rebel!"

And careless of the wound that she could see had drawn blood, Pearse took the dragger from her protesting hold with such ease that she hardly felt it go. She heard the dagger clatter to the floor and once again felt his steely hands upon her, his hot, hard mouth on her cheek and brow and lips and throat. Her body knew a sweet amazement, fire and softness and a flowing light.

To her dismay he abruptly released her and stood up. He strode to the lanterns by the door and brightened them with a swift twist of his fingers. "Your virtue is safe with me," said Fingal Pearse with cool contempt, his back still to her.

Confused and perversely angered now by his actions, Maeve drew the coverlet up to her throat and stared at his back.

He wheeled, as abruptly as he had released her a few moments before, and asked in a hard voice, "What was this man Rathmullan to you?"

The question was the last she would have expected. But she controlled her astonishment and answered with dignity, "He was my husband."

"Your husband!" His bold ice-blue eyes were bright with contemptuous amusement. "No wonder you are unacquainted with the ways of men."

"I have no desire," she retorted with swift anger, "to be acquainted with the ways of . . . brutes. I know what sailors are."

Fingal Pearse's laughter rose harshly, cold as the sea spray battering again the windows of the cabin. "Young madam, you know nothing at all. But someday I will teach you."

"How dare you suggest I would marry a man like you?" she cried.

"I have not suggested marriage at all," Fingal Pearse replied smoothly. At her look of ire, his laughter rose again, and he moved toward the door. On the threshold, however, he turned and asked in a bland voice that annoyed her more than ever, "You did not say if your passport is in order—the age, the name?"

"The name must be changed," she snapped. He raised his brows, questioning.

"The name must be Maeve Rossar-Mescro."

"So that is who you are." His surprise was evident. "I would suggest, however, another name. A Gypsy name will not make you welcome in America."

"Heron, then," she agreed in a voice as bland as his, determined to hide from him her discomfort and confusion.

"Maeve Heron," he repeated, nodding. Picking up the

dark-brown booklet from the table, he said, "It will be seen to. I believe Hudson had the rest right."

Without looking back, he strode from the cabin.

Such a variety of emotions assailed the woman on the bed that she lay back weakly on her pillow, trying to straighten the disorder of her thoughts.

She could not forget the melting fire, the slow, shamed languorous joy she had known when the hard mouth of Fingal Pearse had met her own. A small voice cried out that something of her belonged to Fingal Pearse.

"No," Maeve whispered aloud. "No. I am Maeve Heron, and my body is my own, from this day forward. I will never let him touch me again. And in America we will never meet."

A little comforted, Maeve Heron went to sleep.

Chapter 6

MAEVE HERON'S initial sight of the port of New York in the country of America struck dread into her soul; the massive piles of warehouses lining the shores, in long and gloomy terraces, were all of them draped in deepest black. Maeve's green eyes followed the festoons of somber bunting, as far as she could see.

"Good God," Hudson, the mate, who stood at her side by the rail, cried out, "what is it?"

He squinted upward then at the mast of the neighboring packet; the American flag was flying at half-mast. And down the crowded quay, the standards of three steamships flew their nation's banner at the same mourning height.

"What does it mean?" Maeve asked, moving nearer to the kindly mate and drawing her varicolored shawl more closely about her shoulders. The American air, she noted, was thin and brisk and piercing, so much thinner than the soft air of Ireland that she could barely get her breath.

Hudson saw her shallow breathing and said with gentle reassurance, "You will soon be used to the air. All of us who come from northern islands feel it so."

"But, Mr. Hudson, what does it mean?" she persisted. "The flags and the horrible draperies of black?"

"It means someone of great import is dead," he replied. "There now, Corcoran has called out to see, there from the deck of the packet."

They saw the Irishman's weathered face grow pale under

74

his carroty hair. And Hudson moved down the deck, shouting to Corcoran, "Ho, lad, why are the flags half-masted?"

"Lincoln," they heard his cry faintly on the rising harbor wind. "Lincoln, the President, is dead."

Maeve Heron heard the shouted news with a chill of dismay. What a bad omen it was! she reflected. On the day of their landing, to know that that kindly man was dead. Michael, who had been so knowledgeable of the happenings in America, had told her something of the man Lincoln, and Hudson had added his information to her store.

"Ah"—Hudson sighed—"it is a sad and terrible thing. It does not bode well for this country, lass."

But seeing her woebegone face, the mate smiled in a reasssuring way and said, "It will be all right, lass. You will see."

Clutching her small bundle to her breast, Maeve was assailed with a feeling of utter desolation, and her ears ached from the rattle of carriages upon the cobblestones, the shouting of sailors and the harsh, impatient cries of the draymen on their carts.

"Oh, Mr. Hudson, I feel so very alone."

"There, lass, there now. You are not alone now at all. You know good and well I shall see you safely to your destination. It will all be fine now, won't it, when you are snug in the house of Thomas' friends?"

She nodded, not greatly consoled. For who knew, she reflected darkly, what the people would be like . . . and how she would maintain herself in this strange country with its knife-thin air? The voices of the men upon the quay were hard and sharp and piercing. It seemed to Maeve everyone was angry at each other, and she was stricken of a sudden with a longing for the soft voices of home.

"Come, lass," Hudson said again. "Do you not wish to bid the captain farewell?"

"No," Maeve said sullenly, turning away.

"Verra well," the mate said at last, after a shocked moment of silence. "Are you ready then?"

"I am ready," Maeve replied in a voice so subdued that Hudson could not hear her and turned. She nodded.

Fingal Pearse was nowhere to be seen. With Hudson's firm hand under her silk-clad elbow, Maeve descended slowly to the quay, covered with the produce of every country in the

world; barrels, sacks, boxes, hampers, bales and hogsheads
were piled in continuous elevations along the streets that led at
right angles from the port. Walking under the bowsprits of
the vessels that overhung the footway and fairly threatened
the warehouse walls with their invasion, Maeve and Hudson
passed, one after another, the slips where the different vessels
lay at anchor. Besides the standard of America, the ships flew
the flags of England and of France, of China, Africa and
Spain. The ways were thronged with sailors whose foreign
talk was a polyglot chaos of sound.

At last they reached the end of the street of jutting ships,
and the way broadened into a thoroughfare thick with
carriages, private broughams and commercial wagons. This
populous traffic seemed to Maeve to be proceeding with
almost dreamlike slowness, as if the horses' hooves and the
wheels of the conveyances were attuned to some funereal
rhythm. Vaguely she was aware the death of the President of
America was somehow connected with this phenomenon.

"Ah!" Hudson cried, grasping her elbow. "I see no public
carriage free, but there is a public bus now."

The "bus," Maeve saw, was a low-roofed four-wheeled
painted wagon drawn by two patient horses.

Approaching the bus, with Maeve following uncertainly
behind, the mate called out to the driver, "Ho, lad! D' ye go
up Broadway to Fourteenth Street?"

The driver, smiling at Hudson's nautical air and with a
curious, admiring glance at Maeve, called back, "Can't go up
Broadway now, my friend. It is closed to all traffic because of
the procession."

"Procession?"

"Where have you been, man? They are moving the body of
the President from City Hall this hour. I go only as far as that
by another way, if you care to see it. You will find another
way to Fourteenth Street from there. Are you coming or not?
If you are, step lively!"

Hudson said quickly to Maeve, "Shall we go then?"

She nodded, feeling a quickening of excitement, a strange
new liveliness of heart, distracted by the carriages and the
smartly dressed women clutching the black-clad arms of their
silk-hatted escorts.

The mate helped her aboard the bus and handed coins to the

friendly Irish teamster. Maeve had warmed to the sound of his familiar voice.

"What number do you seek in Fourteenth Street, miss?" he asked Maeve, his twinkling blue eyes taking in the unfashionable cut and brightness of her rustling gown and the many colors of her fringed shawl.

When she named it with a cautious half-smile, the teamster's amiable mouth, which had first grinned more broadly at the sound of her speech, twisted into a contemptuous grimace. Puzzled, Maeve tried to make out its meaning. But Hudson, who had missed the exchange, was urging her to take a seat before the entering passengers behind her occupied the space.

Maeve sat down next to Hudson; for a moment she puzzled still over the reaction of the teamster to her reply. Then, as the bus clattered slowly up a rough side street, she forgot the matter as she looked at the great parade of people along the thoroughfare.

Glimpsing Broadway to the east, as they proceeded slowly in a direction Hudson called uptown, Maeve exclaimed at the height of the buildings. Many were six or seven stories high.

"Ah!" Hudson replied, amused. "That is nothing. There are even higher buildings farther on."

Digesting this in silence, Maeve was uneasily aware that her clothes were terribly wrong; she looked theatrical, even, she reflected with horror, a little fast. For the other women on the bus were dressed in modest clothes of elegantly sober hues. The spreading skirts of bronzed browns and grays, of lavenders, and one ensemble of a delicate ocean-colored greenish gray that fairly made her mouth water filled Maeve with a pang of envy. She remembered the lovely dresses still hanging in the press of her bedroom in the little Dublin house.

Most of all, she felt the absence of a hat; no lady, Michael had often said, looked right without a hat. Her envious eyes returned to the wearer of the gray-green ensemble; the woman was possessed of a glorious head of auburn hair, drawn back in a great, polished chignon. And she wore tilted on her gleaming hair a small pancakelike chapeau of the same material as her jacketed gown, tied snugly beneath the chignon, with bronze-green ribbons streaming down her back, inches below her tiny waist.

Maeve sighed. It seemed a thousand years since she had

seen a *Godey's*! She imagined the pancake hat must be very new indeed, for several of the other women, who were wearing bonnet-style hats, were staring at the sea-colored lady as well.

But, Maeve reflected sadly, to dream of such finery was absurd. She might be faced—she *would* be faced—with the onerous task of earning her living in this huge place. It would be enough, she concluded, to survive. Poor Michael, as Hudson had reminded her, had been unthinking in his suggestion that she communicate with the Rathmullans. For to claim Michael's allowance might bring down upon her the wrath of the law, the immigration authorities. The little store of money in Narilla's silken pouch was all she could hope for at the moment.

Determinedly Maeve repressed her black reflections and turned her green gaze again to the passing streets, trying to enjoy as best she could her first sights of the splendors of New York.

The bus rattled to a halt, and the driver cried out to the passengers at large, "This is the end of the line! End of the line, folks! You can walk to the City Hall from here."

With a busy murmur, the crowd began to disembark. When they descended and began their short walk to the east, Maeve heard more clearly the medley of sounds that had come to her faintly through the closed windows of the public bus—the tramp of many hundreds of measured feet, the rhythmic clopping of slow-moving horses and the leisured, heavy roll of what sounded like a giant conveyance. The muffled beat of many drums and the dark-gray notes of Chopin's "Funeral March" grew louder and louder as Maeve and Hudson moved with the thickening crowds in the direction of City Hall.

Hudson led her to a slightly elevated portion of the emerald grass that fringed the wide thoroughfare of Broadway, south of City Hall. Hudson pointed out to Maeve its classical façade, flying four massive black-bordered banners, matching other banners waving from the roofs of buildings lining the great street, far, far uptown, as far as Maeve could see.

But it was the panoply of blue and sable splendor winding onto the wide way itself that made Maeve gasp and catch her breath; she had never seen anything of such solemn magnificence in all her days.

A double line of blue-clad soldiers, holding their glittering sabers just so at their trim and slender sides, were moving in a vast semicircle from City Hall and forming, as they marched slowly up Broadway, a rectangle of incredible precision, a human fence about the focal figure of the bier.

Fourteen ebony horses were, with precision equal to the soldiers', drawing the huge night-colored bier up Broadway through the pallid sun. The wheeled bier was festooned with garlands of gilt and fresh white flowers; above the gilt-trimmed coffin was raised a black canopy with tassels and turrets and plumes fit for any monarch, and at the four points of the bier around the coffin were softly furled flags with the stripes and stars Maeve had come to know as America's, with black-bordered banners matching those above City Hall.

Gently Hudson edged Maeve forward a little into the crowd so that she might see more clearly. As the bier passed them, Maeve's green gaze took in the single file of soldiers marching on either side of the bier. "The honor guard," Hudson explained in a soft voice, close to Maeve's ear. The third man in the nearer line of five, she noted, was of extraordinary handsomeness; his fine profile was almost that of a cameo. She saw that he was weeping, although he held his well-shaped mouth in tight control, and his soft, dark eyes never looked to left or right, but only straight ahead, in the approved military fashion. Yet in the glare Maeve could see plainly that his tanned face was wet with tears. Nevertheless, his upright carriage and measured step continued in flawless tempo.

A disturbing image flashed to Maeve; there was something so familiar in the dark-eyed blue-clad solidier. But then his stately grief and the weeping of the women, the clenched jaws of the watching men about her made Maeve feel faintly ashamed.

Her small concerns lost themselves an instant in the somber splendor of the pageant before her, the never-to-be-forgotten sight of the coffin on the bier.

And Maeve began to weep with the others, wishing that Michael could have had with them this last glimpse of the kind man he had so admired from his distance over the sea.

For a long moment Maeve and Hudson stood among the masses, watching the bier of Lincoln become smaller and smaller as it wound its royal way up the famous avenue.

Maeve and Mr. Hudson did not speak as they wended their way again to the west and found another rattling omnibus to take them "uptown."

The *Falcon*'s mate seemed overwhelmed by the pageant they had witnessed; Maeve herself was rendered silent even more by the ever-changing spectacle outside the windows—the hurly-burly of the industrial West Side, where commerce was beginning to disfigure the residential neighborhoods with brick and lumberyards, gashouses and distilleries, ironworks and warehouses. Even on this day of universal mourning, Maeve noticed that the noise was incessant.

Something of her discomfiture must have shown itself to the mate, for he said, raising his voice over the din, "There are far nicer things, lass, to the east of here. For instance"—he gestured, as they passed Tenth Street—"the A. T. Stewart's Store is just a block away there, a grand store indeed. And you will see the other stores, on Union Square—the famous Tiffany's and the Brentano Book Emporium."

She nodded, trying to smile, reflecting ungraciously that she would have little to spend in such splendid places.

The traffic slowed again, but at last the bus discharged them on Fourteenth Street. Maeve looked eastward at Hudson's direction, toward Union Square.

"Wallack's Theater is over there," Hudson said enthusiastically, "at Broadway and Thirteenth Street. The Union Square Theater, too. No doubt your friends will take you."

Maeve's heart lifted; perhaps there would be happy times! She might find all sorts of undreamed-of-splendors in the unceasing whirl of this wonderful place.

"The house of Thomas' acquaintance is but a step from here," said Hudson, gladdened by the expression on Maeve's face. "This must be it." He glanced up at a well-kept house of the new sort they called brownstone. "They must be people of substance," he said then in a tone of some surprise.

"Well, lass," Hudson went on a little nervously, for Maeve was staring up at the clean brown façade with sudden concern, "do not be dismayed now. Shall I come in with you?"

"No, no," she said hastily, feeling that she had imposed upon his good nature long enough. "I will be fine." But Maeve was filled with a chilling uncertainty; would she be "fine," indeed, and how would she be received by these people "of substance"?

"Oh, Mr. Hudson"—she turned to him, and her voice was trembling—"how can I thank you for being so kind?"

"Now, now, little lass," he returned soothingly and patted her with an awkward motion on her shoulder. "Are you sure I shouldn't come along?"

She shook her head, feeling a sudden wave of exhaustion. "No, no, thank you. I just . . . wanted you to know how grateful I am to you."

"That's all right, now. If anything should go . . . not quite as you expected," he amended hastily, struck by the look of fear in her green eyes, "just send a message to me at the *Falcon*. She will be at anchor here for several weeks. Do you understand me?"

"Yes, yes." Maeve nodded. Out of the corner of her eye, she glimpsed a cream-colored curtain above fall back into its place. Someone had been watching.

"Thank you," she said again. "Good-bye."

"Good-bye, lass, and all my luck to you," Hudson answered. With a friendly lift of his weathered hand, he had descended the stairs and was standing on the street.

"Good-bye," Maeve said again, faintly and with reluctance, for with the going of the mate went all that had been familiar in these lonely weeks at sea. She watched him for a moment disappearing around the corner. Then, squaring her shoulders, she mounted the remaining stairs and took the polished brass knocker firmly and tapped it several times.

The curtained door opened at once; a pretty maid in a black dress, an immaculate frilled cap of white and a filmy matching apron inquired in a strange accent, "Yes, miss? Whom do you wish to see?" There was an expression of avid curiosity on her smooth face, the color of rich coffee laced with heavy cream.

Maeve, who had never seen a mulatto woman before, stammered in reply, "Is . . . is this the home of the Barlows?"

To her amazement, the pretty maid burst into merry laughter. "Oh, miss," she said between giggles, "this is nobody's *home*."

Before Maeve could study this peculiar answer, a deep, harsh feminine voice called out from the dimness of the hall,

"What is it, Amelie? Who's there, what's the trouble?"

And Maeve caught a glimpse of the dazzling interior, the wide hall beyond the front doors that seemed to span the depth of the house, ending in an octagonal stairhall.

Here three dramatic jeweled glass windows apparently stretched two stories high. The domed stairhall was further embellished by a hand-carved staircase of what appeared to be polished oak. On the lower stairs Maeve saw now a buxom, handsome woman in an ornate gown of bronzed green; her bright-golden hair was dressed in a style Maeve had never seen—center-parted, drawn back behind her ears into a heavy chignon. Ribbons of the same material as her gown were tied in an intricate manner and knotted behind her left ear. Her earrings were enormous oval green stones, each on a delicate gold chain, dangling from her pierced and shapely ears. From this distance she looked like a queen, Maeve thought.

But as the woman descended the remaining stairs and hurried toward the door, Maeve noted the coarseness of her features, the unnatural vividness of her hair and a manner that was at once humorous and commanding. Her stateliness was as artificial as the color of her hair.

"Well," the woman repeated in her harsh voice, "what is it, Amelie?"

Grinning, the maid turned to the buxom woman and replied, "This . . . er, lady . . . is asking is this the home of the Barlows."

"Get out, you little bitch. There's nothing to laugh at."

Maeve could not believe her ears. In all her life she had never heard a woman speak so.

The blond woman, studying her shocked face, said more quietly, "There must be some mistake, girlie. Who sent you here? Did you come to tell our fortunes?" The woman's good-natured smile, revealing pristine dentures, took the sting from the last words. Nevertheless, Maeve felt a hot flood of ire; the epithet and the twitting reference to her clothes did not improve matters.

She said coldly, "I am Miss Maeve Heron. I was referred to the Barlows by Thomas Rossar-Mescro, who knows friends of theirs. I am from Tullaghoe in the County of Tyrone. That's in Ireland," she added sarcastically.

Immediately she regretted having told so much, but the woman's laughter reassured her; there had been nothing in the other's demeanor to reveal suspicion. "You needn't tell me *that*," the buxom woman retorted. "My own people came from Kerry. You have the mark of the bogs all over you."

Maeve wanted to cry out, *How dare you? I come from the O'Neills of Tyrone!* But she was inhibited by her own returning common sense, her anger soon abating. What, after all, would this common-looking woman know of the O'Neills, or care for that matter? And Maeve was in no position to choose her friends at this moment, she reflected with bitterness.

"Come in, girl, come in," the buxom woman said then with rough gentleness. Hesitantly Maeve stepped into the golden-lit hall, staring up at the jeweled windows.

"Come in, and I'll give you some tea . . . or something stronger, if you need it." The woman chuckled. "You came at a good time, after all. A little later would have been . . . awkward." And the woman gave a peculiar laugh.

Mystified, Maeve followed her down the splendid corridor into a parlor that was intimidating in its magnificence; a fine Persian carpet of enormous size covered most of the glossy floor, and the focal point of the chamber was a mahogany mantel that reached to the ceiling, inset with many mirrors and encrusted with colonettes.

"Sit down," the woman said brusquely and gestured to a settee upholstered in soft red velvet. She moved to the mantelpiece and pulled a brocade bell cord. Then she sat down opposite Maever in a chair upholstered in the same crimson velvet of the settee, gazing over the carven marble table that separated them. She spoke no further until another maid—this time a freckled girl with pale-blond hair that owned its color only to nature—entered. The woman gave orders for tea.

But she said to Maeve, with a twinkle, "Maybe you need a dollop of brandy?"

Maeve nodded, unable to speak for the confusion of her emotions. She bit her lip.

"Brandy," the big woman said brusquely to the maid, who withdrew.

"Never mind, girl," the buxom woman said more quietly than she had thus far spoken. "I saw the sailor with you; you just got off the boat, as we say around here. We'll talk."

The freckled maid with the pallid hair was already back and

setting a silver tray upon the table. Besides the tea things there was a handsome bright-blue decanter and two shining snifters.

"All right, Carrie," the big woman said carelessly to the maid, who was ready to serve them. "I'll take care of it." The maid disappeared.

The large woman got up with a grunt from her seat and went to the table to pour a generous dollop of brandy and hand it to Maeve.

Maeve nodded her thanks and sipped. She had never had brandy before, and tears formed in her eyes. She choked, coughing, but took another sip and in a moment felt easier.

"I'm Hallie McDermott," the woman said, smiling, and poured a glass of brandy for herself. She sat down again in the crimson chair. "And this is Hallie's place," she added.

"Hallie's place?" Maeve repeated.

"Yes," Hallie McDermott said, her coarse face twisted with amusement.

All at once it came to Maeve what the woman's words had meant. She started up from the settee and set down the snifter with a clicking sound on the marble.

"Careful, girlie!" Hallie McDermott said. "That's the best crystal in the house."

"I . . . I can't stay here, Miss McDermott," Maeve cried out.

"Hoity-toity," Hallie jeered. "She can't stay here, and she with nothing but the rags she stands up in and a tinker's bundle! Have you got any money?" The last words were matter-of-fact and brusque.

Maeve stared into Hallie McDermott's eyes; they were a faded, red-veined blue and gave her stare for stare. But the look in them was pitying.

"Not much," Maeve replied as bluntly as Hallie had spoken.

The other woman looked obscurely pleased. "Now we're getting somewhere. You're willing to talk a little sense, are you?"

Maeve nodded and sat down then, overcome with another wave of despairing exhaustion.

"Are you hungry?"

"Yes." Hallie moved again to the scarlet brocade tab and gave it two sharp, sudden tugs. When the blond maid reappeared with a steaming tray and set it before Maeve, she attacked the food with ravenous hunger. Hallie spoke no further until Maeve had finished. They were drinking coffee when Hallie McDermott demanded, "All right, who *are* you? You never came from a shack like the McDermotts, I'll be bound."

Maeve hesitated. Then she said with pride, "My father was an O'Neill of Tyrone."

There was a little silence, and then the other woman responded with an attempt at mockery, "It's a blueblood, is it, we have on our hands, descended from the Irish kings?" But Maeve could see that Hallie was impressed in spite of herself at the sound of the ancient name.

"And how did you come by a name like Heron?"

For an uneasy moment Maeve wondered how much she should tell the woman. In her position she might know anyone, everyone. Therefore, when she began to tell her story, it was with certain emendations.

"Why did you leave Ireland?" Hallie snapped.

Dismayed, Maeve fumbled for a reply. "Because of a . . . quarrel," she said at last in a low voice.

"A *quarrel* sent you over the sea, dressed like a Gypsy beggar, with nowhere to go? Bosh!"

Maeve was stubbornly silent. Hallie McDermott laughed her throaty laugh and said, "All right. You won't tell me, and I don't give a goddamn, girlie."

Maeve turned paler with shock to hear the profanity from a woman's mouth.

"You've got looks," Hallie went on blandly. "And brains. You could be a great success with me. I'd call you the Gypsy Princess. Jesus, Mary and Joseph!" Hallie ejaculated. "You'd drive them mad, you would, with that white skin and black hair. And those green Irish eyes." She grinned.

"What do you mean?"

"What do I *mean*? Why, girlie, I mean you should work here with me. You could make a fortune. There's nothing in the whole place as fetching as you."

Maeve was almost speechless. At last she spluttered, "Do you mean . . . mean you . . . that I should be a. . . ."

"An entertainer, dearie, an entertainer," Hallie replied, smiling.

Maeve repressed an angry reply; the woman, after all, had

not been unkind, had taken her in, at least for the moment. Quietly she answered, "I could never do that."

Hallie McDermott raised her sandy brows. "Well, you're a hundred kinds of a fool, my girl. You could have anything you wanted; you could be wearing emeralds in your ears"—Hallie flicked a pointed fingernail at one of the gleaming grass-green stones depending from her own—"and be wearing next year's dress now, instead of those Gypsy rags."

Maeve did not reply, turning her gaze away from the magnificent stones and the splendor of the bronze-green gown.

"So what are you going to do?" Hallie demanded. "Is there a man somewhere? There must have been one on the ship," she concluded wisely.

Maeve colored and lowered her eyes. Hallie laughed loudly. "So there *was*. And he has left you high and dry like this?"

Again the younger woman was silent.

Then she looked up at Hallie McDermott and asked in a cool, controlled tone, "Is there anything . . . else I could do here? Perhaps you need another . . servant?"

"I can always use a good maid. But Mother of God, what a waste! Is that what you want to do?"

"I have no choice," Maeve answered baldly. "I have got to make my way, you see."

Hallie McDermott sighed and said after a moment, "All right, girlie. I'll take you on. And just to show you my heart's in the right place," she added wryly, "you can work on the parlor floors. There are . . . duties above that you might find a little . . . hard to take."

"Thank you, Miss McDermott." Maeve rose, feeling numb with weariness.

"Nobody in town calls me Miss McDermott. It's Miss Hallie." Then she studied the younger women keenly. "You're dead beat, girl. I'll get Carrie to show you to your room. Why don't you get a little sleep before the . . . before the visits start? I won't need you tonight."

As the maid called Carrie led Maeve Heron from the parlor, Hallie McDermott wandered back to the marble table and poured herself another glass of brandy.

Now why, she asked herself ruefully, *am I taking such trouble with this one?* But while she took another sip of the rich liquor, feeling its grateful warmth upon her tongue, Hallie McDermott answered her own question: The girl Maeve Heron reminded her of the young McDermott girl who had come to this city, full of dreams, thirty years before.

Absently Hallie picked up the day's *Tribune* with its great black headline, THE CITY MOURNS, its drawing of the horse-drawn bier of the tall man from Illinois.

Hallie sighed, put down the paper and went to see if everything was ready for the evening's custom.

Chapter 7

MAEVE HERON had ever been vaguely aware that servants at Tullaghoe and in the houses of Dublin rose long before the sun to start the fires and begin their masters' breakfasts. But evidently this was not the way of Hallie McDermott's house, for when she woke the next morning, Maeve was surprised to see the clock hands pointing already to eight. Carrie was still asleep in the other bed, and there was hardly a sound in the house.

Maeve wondered when their work began; not soon, she concluded, eyeing the sleeping girl across from her, and lay back a moment on the pillow. Since the early evening before, she had not spoken to anyone; indeed, she had hardly seen anything at all in her exhausted climb to the fourth-floor rooms where the servants stayed. Almost unconscious with weariness, Maeve had thrown off her clothes and, after washing sketchily, had fallen into the little bed Carrie pointed out in the room they were to share.

It was with a feeling of unreal wonder now that Maeve looked at the pale, tousled hair of the young servant, spread out on the pillow of the other bed. Carrie had her back to Maeve, still deep in peaceful slumber.

Maeve realized that her own sleep had been so deep that she had not heard a sound during the night. Either the clients of Hallie McDermott's house were extraordinarily quiet, she reflected wryly, or she herself had been too tired to hear.

She rose quietly and padded to the window. Drawing aside the curtain a little, Maeve saw that the day was very bright. Then she turned back to her contemplation of the silent room. It was of unusual luxury for a servant's chamber, with dainty pale-blue coverlets that matched the brief window curtains and furniture that echoed in a less costly way the splendors below.

Maeve went silently in her bare feet to the pretty dresser and examined herself in the glass. This, too, was a touch of luxury she would not have expected in such a room—a fairly long oval looking glass that was very clear. Delightedly Maeve realized she could see almost all of herself in it; her white skin, still flushed with her long sleep, was petal-clear, and her green eyes looked bright. She took the wooden comb Narilla had given her from the pouch and began to comb her tangled hair.

It was then she noticed the brush on the dresser and looked at it with longing; how many months, it seemed, since she had had a brush for her hair! But the brush was Carrie's, after all, and to use another person's intimate things would be dreadful indeed.

Out of the corner of her eye, she saw another black-haired girl in a long white nightgown, combing her hair. Gasping, Maeve turned. It was she herself, reflected in a full-length mirror on the closet door!

A full-length mirror attached to the door—she had never seen such a thing, and certainly it did not belong in a servant's room. Was she to be only a maid after all . . . or did Hallie McDermott still have other plans for her?

Maeve stared at herself in the glass. On a sudden impulse, she lifted her white nightgown and examined her reflection. Blushing, she let her green gaze linger on her own naked body, noting its slender shapeliness, the soft, well-formed breasts, the waist of such incredible narrowness that swelled out with gradual sweetness to the rounded hips, the long, slender legs, and. . . .

Maeve blushed furiously, letting the gown fall back again to cover her dark-shadowed whiteness.

She glanced worriedly around; no, thank heaven, Carrie was still asleep! If she had been seen. . . . Maeve drew a breath of relief and went to the little hearth to warm some washing water.

Her motions, as stealthy as they were, must have awakened the other girl, for she heard a sleepy greeting from Carrie's bed.

"Good mornin'."

Maeve, squatting before the hearth, swiveled herself about and smiled. "Good morning."

"What are you doin'?" Carrie asked curiously.

"Heating some water to wash," Maeve answered, surprised at the drowsy question.

"Why, my Lord, Amelie does *that*," the blond girl said. "We're white, you know, even if we are the maids."

"I . . . I don't understand you." Maeve rose from her stooping position and looked at Carrie questioningly.

The other girl laughed and brushed back her pale-golden hair from her freckled, rather silly face.

"Lord ha' mercy, honey, don't you know *anything*?" Carrie asked with good-natured scorn, throwing back the blue coverlet and rising to stretch her arms above her head. "Where are you from?" she asked.

"I'm from Ireland," Maeve answered in a low voice, and of a sudden, with the very pronunciation of the name, there came to her such a lucid picture of the lough and the misty hills of Tullaghoe that she was overcome with a feeling of homesick desolation. She feared that she would start to weep.

"Well, I guess you don' know then," Carrie said gently. "How could you? But y'see, over here . . . well, Amelie gets up before we do. *Naturally*."

Maeve could not understand why it was "natural" for the pretty Amelie to get up before them; she supposed it had some connection with Lincoln and the black people but was afraid to exhibit further ignorance. So she kept silent.

But she did not want to seem unfriendly, so in a moment she said warmly, "We have a nice room."

"We sure do," Carrie agreed. "And we can *sleep* so late! That's one reason I came to work here. Why, even in those rich people's houses, the maids have to get up at six or seven in the *mornin'*."

"I suppose that's because people, er . . . sleep later here."

Maeve was assailed again by Carrie's whinnying laughter. "You have the funniest way of sayin' things. The girls don't never get up before dinnertime; that's when we change the sheets," she added matter-of-factly, "an' get things ready for later."

"Dinnertime?" Maeve repeated with surprise, passing over the reference to sheets. "In the evening?"

"No, *dinner*time, in the middle of the day. Lord, I wish I was pretty enough to do it. *You* are; I bet Miss Hallie told you that."

Maeve was torn between pity and disgust. She answered with an evasive question. "And where do you come from, Carrie?"

"Kentucky." The tow-haired girl was standing before the dresser now, brushing her long, light hair. "My pappy and my brothers was all killed in that war, that we had nothin' to do with at all, Ma said."

"What do you mean?"

"We didn't own no slaves or much of anything," Carrie explained indignantly. "One time they put my brother in jail for comin' home to tend the crops."

Carrie's people sounded so like the tenants of Adare that Maeve felt a warm, quick pity. No wonder the girl wanted to be a . . . wanted to be one of the "girls."

"So Ma and I couldn't run the place alone," Carrie continued calmly and without self-pity, twisting up her light hair into a neat knot. "She went to live with her cousin, and they got up the money to send me here so's I could maybe work in a factory. But that was too hard. An' then I heard about maid work bein' easier, and I come here. It's the nicest place I've ever been in my life. When I saw this room and they told me how much I'd be makin', why, I was just so happy I busted out cryin'."

Carrie turned to the listening Maeve and grinned. "Well, this ain't gettin' you dressed. I don' know where that Amelie is, she's suppose' to be bringin' your uniform."

The blond girl went to the door and, opening it, called out sharply, "Amelie! Where are you, girl?"

Again Maeve was mystified by the imperious tone of the tenant farmer's daughter. She supposed in the caste system of America the whites, no matter what class, considered themselves above the blacks. She vaguely remembered Michael's remarks on the subject, but he had been referring to the slaves.

Hearing an irritated reply from the hall, Maeve asked Carrie, "Isn't Amelie . . . free?"

"Free? Sure, they all are now, I guess. What do y'mean?"

"Well, when you speak to her—" Maeve stopped abruptly, giving it up. Things would be very uncomfortable indeed if she quarreled with Carrie, who shared her quarters.

But there was no time for further talk, for the pretty Amelie was entering, with a black dress and white cap and apron in her arms.

"Good morning, miss," she said grinning, in that accent of hers that sounded so Gallic to Maeve. Her smile revealed small white teeth of absolute perfection, and her creamy skin was as smooth as velvet. She studied Maeve with impudent curiosity sparkling in her great dark eyes. "These are your things."

She handed the black and white garments to Maeve, who noticed that another gown still lay over her arm, a dress that had been concealed by the uniform. It was a dress and jacket costume of a wonderful soft shade of blue-green, like the clear water of a tropical stream Maeve had seen a picture of in a book of Michael's.

"What is that?" she asked excitedly.

"Something Miss Hallie sent, which will have to be cut down for you. I am very skilled in these matters," Amelie added proudly in her careful speech. "But first, miss, try on the uniform."

Maeve hesitated in an agony of embarrassment. She was naked below her nightgown and would have to reveal herself to the others before she got into her underthings. And there was literally no place to go. Carrie laughed.

"What's the matter?"

The more sensitive Amelie understood at once and turned her dark eyes away as Maeve slipped on a petticoat under her gown, then hastily drew the gown over her head, covering her breasts with her bodice as quickly as possible.

The uniform fitted Maeve perfectly. But as she buttoned the neat black dress and was instructed by Amelie in the tying of the white cap, Maeve thought with cold despair, *I am a servant now.* And she recalled with what unthinking carelessness she had given gentle orders to the servants at Tullaghoe, to the little maid at the Dublin house where she lived with Michael.

Now they will order me, she reflected, and a shadow fell upon her face.

"Come, miss," said Amelie brightly, "take it off and let us look at the other."

"But what. . . ?"

"Miss Hallie is very particular," said Amelie with that peculiar pride that had so touched Maeve before. "Even the maids must look proper on their days off. This is the dress for you to wear when you go out."

"I see." Maeve felt a great obstruction in her throat and a moistening of the eyes. She was to have a dress, something new!

"It is not new," Amelie said then, smiling. For a moment Maeve had an eerie feeling that the pretty mulatto could read her thoughts.

"Well, I'm going," Carrie said in her sharp, nasal voice. Amelie did not answer, but Maeve smiled at her.

When the door closed, Amelie gave a sound of relief. "I am glad *that* one is gone," she remarked with frank distaste. Maeve did not answer, and the mulatto gave her a quick glance.

"You are wise not to quarrel," said Amelie and grinned. "No, the dress is not new. It is nearly three years old. And the *casaques*, the jackets, are not worn so fitted anymore, you know. Also, I think, if there were some braid sewn over the shoulders, just here, and around the hem of the *casaque*, we might approximate the newest fashion. So!"

Amelie illustrated with her slender coffee-colored fingers.

"Where did you learn all this?" Maeve cried, deeply interested.

"I belonged to one of the best dressmakers in New Orleans," said Amelie. "And oh, miss, how I wish I was there again! But I came here with my man. And now he is gone. So! I work here. And it is not bad."

Maeve's green look met the dark one of Amelie in the glass. Maeve smiled, thinking that Amelie, like the freckled Carrie, refused to linger in a self-pitying way on her misfortunes. Maeve resolved not to despair, to imitate as far as she could their resolute brightness.

"Ah!" Amelie said, with satisfaction. "You look very pretty, miss, in this color. I will soon have it done, and it will fit you to perfection.'' Amelie helped Maeve remove the dress.

"Miss,'' Amelie said then, "you came yesterday, from downtown. You saw the Liberator's procession, did you not?''

"Yes.''

"Oh!'' Amelie cried, "I would give anything to have seen. He was the hope, you know, of all my people.''

Maeve said gently, "I will tell you everything about it as soon as we have the time.'' When the other had gone, she reflected happily, *How glad I am she is free!* Then she again put on her uniform and went downstairs to report to Hallie McDermott.

With the adaptability of the March-born, Maeve Heron mastered her routines with an ease she had not thought possible. Her duties began at noon, when she was called upon to attend the "young ladies,'' as Hallie McDermott described the women in her employ. Later in the afternoons, when the visitors began to arrive, there were tea and drinks to serve. And in the evenings Maeve would spell Amelie at answering the door, a task she disliked more than any other.

The gentlemen who frequented Hallie's house were in general quiet and well behaved, and the names of some of them, she learned from the cynical Hallie, were those of the oldest families in New York, dignitaries from City Hall and men who had made their fortunes in Wall Street. Yet their scrutiny, which she could almost feel upon her hair and face and body, discomfited Maeve as deeply as those of the men on the *Falcon* after her secret had been revealed.

When she confided this to Amelie, the pretty mulatto shrugged her narrow shoulders and pronounced wisely, "Well, men are men. And exactly alike under their clothes.''

Maeve blushed, and suddenly her sleeping senses were wakened to a vivid image of the captain of the *Falcon*; she remembered with hot shame the lithe form and penetrating eyes of Fingal Pearse. Somehow she had not been able to tell anyone of him; the thought of confiding in the eager, man-crazy Carrie was distasteful. Amelie, for all her pride and prettiness, had the resigned sophistication of the Gallic mind toward matters of love and the matter-of-fact attitude Maeve had learned to associate with her race.

As for Hallie McDermott, her low opinion of the male sex was stated frequently and without equivocation.

"They're all a pack of fools . . . or swine," she said bluntly one afternoon when Maeve had brought her a glass of sherry. "They think they run the world. Run it, indeed! What runs the world is between a woman's legs."

Her red-threaded blue eyes twinkled up at the blushing Maeve. "Yes, men are fools," she repeated in a teasing voice. "And the women who give them what they want, and give it for nothing, are even bigger fools."

Maeve was aware that Hallie was still twitting her for her refusal to become one of the "young ladies." But she stood by without replying, having no wish to quarrel with the woman who had been so kind to her and who treated her with a gentleness she never showed the others.

That particular treatment had been noted and commented on throughout the house; the young ladies, from whom Maeve remained aloof but treated with great politeness, snickered. And the wise-eyed Amelie made a remark that Maeve had but imperfectly understood: "Women like Hallie are freaks of nature." And at once the pretty mulatto had closed her lips tightly, refusing to say more when Maeve tried to press her.

The friendship of Amelie and Maeve had grown warm; the inventive Amelie had made, from a scrap of the skirt of the blue-green ensemble and who knows what other ingredients, a smart little pancake of a hat in the latest mode. Maeve realized with utter delight that the hat was almost like the one she had seen on the head of the elegant woman in the bus, her first day in New York.

"Why are you so kind to me?" she demanded of Amelie.

"Because you are so kind to *me*," the creamy-skinned girl replied in her pert, careful speech. "You treat me like a white lady."

And this sunny afternoon in May, as she was strolling toward Union Square, Maeve herself felt like a lady again, in her carefully tended best gown, the jaunty pancake tied snugly over her black, geaming hair.

Amelie, whose talents included great skill in arranging coiffures, had done Maeve's hair for her outing. Exclaiming at the thick wealth of its shining darkness, a luxuriance that made superfluous the addition of false hair that so many ladies of fashion were using, Amelie had done Maeve's hair in her favorite manner. Deftly and with mysterious ease, Amelie presented Maeve with the finished product—a style smooth and simple in front, but the back hair a triumph of intricate, heavy, innumerable loops and coils that perfectly accomodated the pancake hat.

In her two previous visits to Union Square, Maeve Heron had paused an instant before the windows of the famous Tiffany's, gazing on its treasures as a child might; owning such things was beyond Maeve's imagining. She looked at them as she would have looked on museum artifacts, not as things to buy. And her visits to the stores, where salesladies looked as fine as noblewomen, were shadowed by the same feeling of unreality. Everything was beyond her purse.

But it was in Brentano's Book Emporium, oddly enough, that Maeve's hunger for possession gnawed at her. She had not realized before how much she longed for books; the memory of the library at Tullaghoe, the great room at Michael's cousin's, even the library of the little house in Dublin filled Maeve with terrible longing.

She walked smartly toward Brentano's now, playing a game: She was a fine lady whose carriage had deposited her at the entranceway of Brentano's.

This bright afternoon there were many gathered before its dignified façade; silk-hatted men in frock coats were staring at the display of notices on the bulletin boards. Maeve heard one say, "They caught Jeff Davis on the tenth, you know."

A high-nosed old woman was studying through her lorgnette the etchings in Brentano's windows. Her companion, a man in clerical garb with a sensitive face, said as Maeve passed, "That is the end of it, then, thank God." He nodded toward the man who had spoken of Jeff Davis. "Shall we go in, Mrs. Dady?"

The high-nosed woman, in a rustle of silk, moved ahead with a murmured reply and collided with Maeve.

She raised her lorgnette and studied Maeve in an insolent manner that ignited the younger woman's ire.

However, Maeve said coolly, "I beg your pardon," and moved ahead into the busy store. The scent of a faint perfume drifted to her from the woman, and she heard with a feeling of helpless anger the muttered words "New Irish" and a gentler reply from the high-nosed woman's escort.

But soon Maeve Heron put them out of mind, dazzled by the riches of the Literary Emporium. In the display of new books she handled reverently a book of poems by someone named Swinburne, *Atalanta in Calydon*. Neighboring it was a pile of *Poèmes saturniens* by a Paul Verlaine and *Drum-Taps* by someone with a very familiar name, a name she had heard at Hallie's, Walt Whitman.

Maeve was taken by the cover of a book called *Alice's Adventures in Wonderland*. The author's name was Lewis Carroll. Then she examined the title page of a novel, *Strathmore*. What a queer name the author had—a single word. Ouida. Curiously Maeve riffled its pages, then read a paragraph with utter disbelief. She put the book down and stared into the middle distance, in an agony of indecision. She could afford only one book, and which would it be? How she longed for them all, longed to say to an eager, respectful clerk, "Send them to my home."

Her hunger was so overpowering that an unspeakable solution occurred to Maeve Heron. She would buy one book and simply take another! She would *take* it. A scandalized voice inside her cried, *You are a thief*. But the hunger was too great to be withstood; looking cautiously about her, Maeve saw that the clerk's back was turned. The gentleman to her left had moved away in search of histories.

With a lightning motion Maeve slipped *Alice's Adventures in Wonderland* into the capacious carryall Amelie had lent her. Too late, Maeve sensed that someone was watching. The high-nosed matron with whom she had nearly collided outside was staring at her with contempt through a lorgnette. Defiantly Maeve took up the novel by the author with the strange single name and moved toward the clerk.

A man's voice, almost in her ear, arrested Maeve Heron's steps. In a hoarse stage whisper, the voice said, "I saw you, miss."

Transfixed with horror, Maeve stood beside the poetry display; she dared not turn. Her heart was beating so loudly she could hear it pounding in her ears like the wings of a great bird. A hand touched her arm. She turned at last to look up into the penetrating eyes of Fingal Pearse.

Maeve's first sensation was one of great relief, then came humiliation, a humiliation more complete for being witnessed by this man who still exercised his magic. It was unbearable to see the blend of pity and amusement on his handsome mouth, his pale-blue eyes gazing unblinkingly into hers.

Yet her incorrigible, unthinking flesh was being magnetized at this very moment, as it had been that first uneasy night on the deck of the *Falcon*. For a helpless instant she studied his regal features, trained to coolness by his years of long command, the steely leanness of his body, arrayed today in a gray suit of utmost elegance.

Even on the land he seemed to be balanced against the rolling of the sea, and the elegance of his clothes could not disguise the slender power of his muscularity or that rakish manner of a man who should be wearing the clothes of a buccaneer. On his gilded hair he was wearing a soft black slouch hat, but he swept it from his head in a mock-gallant fashion, grinning.

"Miss Heron," he said with ironic formality.

"How are you, Captain Pearse?" she replied coolly, staring with defiance into his ice-blue eyes; they had an unaccustomed twinkle at this moment.

"Give me the book," he said softly.

She raised her winglike brows, delicate slashes of darkness on the whiteness of her skin, and replied stiffly, "I don't know what you mean."

"Come now, Maeve," he whispered urgently. "No one is looking. Give it to me, and I will buy it for you—I'll buy both of them and whatever else you fancy."

Maeve Heron studied him, amazed. This was not the mocking man of that dreadful night in her cabin. She hesitated for a long moment and then, looking about her quickly, took the volume from her carryall and handed it to him.

"Thank you," he said grinning. "You might have got into trouble. Now what other literature do you see that I might purchase for you?"

"Why are you doing this?" she asked bluntly.

"To atone for other days . . . and nights," he said with heavy meaning.

She lowered her eyes, the thick black lashes curtaining her green gaze from him, and felt the hot color flood her face and neck.

"Come, Maeve," he said in a low, gentle voice that barely

carried to her, "I wish to atone for things I said and did. I have . . . thought of nothing but you these last weeks." It was as if the last words were uttered with reluctance.

She looked up at him then and saw in his blue stare a tenderness that amazed her, that softened his face into one that she barely recognized.

"I saw you reading this," he said in a conversational tone, picking up the Swinburne from the table of poetry.

He opened it and said softly, "Listen." He began to read:

> For winter's rains and ruins are over,
> And all the season of snows and sins;
> The days dividing lover and lover,
> The light that loses, the night that wins;
> And time remembered is grief forgotten.

Fingal Pearse closed the book and smiled.

She could not contain her astonishment; this was not the Fingal Pearse she had thought she knew.

"Shall I get this book for you?" he asked quietly.

She nodded, too full of confusion to speak, very aware of the thudding of her heart.

"Let us go then," he said and, putting on his hat, guided her lightly to the clerk and stood silent while the man wrapped their purchases.

"I must talk to you," said Fingal Pearse, as they emerged into the mild sun. "Shall we go in here?"

He indicated the broad white building at the end of the street and grinned. "It fancies itself a *château*," Pearse said with amiable mockery. Maeve looked up at its five tall stories, the French windows spanning its wide façade, and smiled.

"What place is it?" she asked.

"My hotel."

Fingal Pearse grinned more widely when he saw her stiffen. "Keep calm, your highness," he said softly. "There is a restaurant on its first floor . . . you see? I am only asking you to share a luncheon with me."

Maeve colored. "Thank you. I will."

But when he guided her into the place, she was but dimly aware of her surroundings, so overcome was she still by her sweet astonishment: This man was not the cold stranger of the

Falcon. This Fingal Pearse was polite and aware, his ice-blue eyes soft in their gaze as he examined her hair and face and hat and gown.

Attentive to her smallest preference, he ordered their meal with utmost care, and then said in a low voice, "I never knew until now how lovely you were."

Maeve looked into his piercing eyes without replying. She felt a flood of gratified warmth, a rising ease. To be in this place, with its soft lights and fresh flowers, was to be for a moment in the midst of her old life again, where instead of waiting, she had been waited upon, where she had been an O'Neill of Tyrone.

Silently repeating that name to herself, Maeve suddenly knew a stab of cold despair. It must have shown upon her face, for Fingal Pearse asked quickly, "What is it? What's wrong, Maeve?"

His quiet tone released her tears. He put down his goblet of pale wine and reached across the table. "Are you unhappy with your friends?"

"My friends!" To her horror, Maeve found herself weeping openly, felt the other diners staring.

"Come," Fingal Pearse said. "I will take you upstairs to my suite and have them serve our luncheon there. No," he said firmly when he saw her hesitation and dismay. "I assure you," he added, smiling, "my rooms are like a whole apartment; you will have the meal in my sitting room. It's all right, Maeve. We can't talk here. You must see that."

Subdued, she nodded and rose.

Fingal Pearse gave a quiet order to their curious waiter and gently led Maeve from the hotel dining room into the deep-carpeted lobby and took his keys from the clerk. With an awareness of something fateful in her actions, Maeve Heron preceded Fingal Pearse up the flight of soft-carpeted stairs.

The waiter had removed the luncheon dishes and left them with coffee and liqueur. The latter, which Fingal Pearse poured out for Maeve in a tiny glass, was sweet, unfamiliar and strong. With the first sip she felt its warm power and resolved to drink no more of it, for her head was swimming a little.

No wonder, she reflected wryly. A maid from a brothel, on her day off, was not often discovered stealing in a bookstore by a man she had thought never to see again—and then taken weeping to his rooms! Maeve leaned her black head, hatless now, against the plush of the high-backed chair and studied Fingal Pearse.

With apparent intentness, he was lighting a fragrant thin cigar, having gallantly asked her leave, and his sharp blue eyes were hooded for a moment by his strange heavy lids.

"Now then," he said with a sudden softness that startled her, "what was it that made you cry?"

She looked down at the tiny wineglass in her hand and hesitated. All the ancient, stubborn pride of the O'Neills and the wild majesty of Floure Rossar-Mescro rose in Maeve at once. She knew she could not tell him. Tell Fingal Pearse that she was a servant in a brothel—no. It was unspeakable. Maeve did not look at him but kept her green gaze on the little glass, which she carefully placed on the table at her side.

"Answer me," he said with brutal urgency.

Confused, Maeve at last looked into his strange, cold eyes; once again, somehow, they were in her little cabin on the *Falcon*, and she remembered that dreamlike night when he had entered while she pretended sleep.

Once again she saw it clearly, as he leaned to her and kissed her hair, saying her name in a voice barely recognizable, it was so drunk with feeling. And again she felt his steel-strong hand upon her hair, a terrible fire began to devour her. Now, as on that night, Maeve heard a far voice whisper to her, "madness and blindness and astonishment of heart."

I have had too much wine, she thought uneasily and looked away from him, unable to sustain his hard gaze another moment.

"Maeve," he said. With dismay, she knew a paining and an alien stir within her vitals at the sound of her name on his lips.

Dear God, she cried out silently, *it cannot happen now. I cannot let him take me in his power again.* But the sweetness in her core was unallayed; she felt an utter sickness of desire through the center of her body and knew that Fingal Pearse had seen her trembling.

"Maeve." He was kneeling by her chair now, and the fluid paining of her body strengthened when he took her hands in his and kissed their palms, murmuring soft words that she could not understand. But she knew that the drawing kiss of his hard mouth on her palms was drawing her to him, as a leaf or a plume would be drawn helpless into the tunnel of the wind, and she took a shuddering breath.

Now his hard hands were stroking her astonished limbs through the voluminous silk of her garments, and his proud head lowered to her knees; he was kissing her, kissing her again and again on her slender legs, and she could feel the heat of his breath through the cambric and silk of her clothes.

Dimly aware of what she did, Maeve Heron leaned suddenly to him and kissed his hair, her trembling hands stroking the back of his lean neck above the faultless collar. He gave a moaning cry, and his hold upon her tightened. Maeve cried out, her cry muffled in his clean, hay-scented golden hair, and thought despairingly, *I can stand no more*. She was in his power again, and something of her belonged to Fingal Pearse, as it had that eerie night in her little cabin on the *Falcon*.

She said no word when he raised his head from her lap and looked at her with the blue blaze of his eyes. He too, was silent; he rose and, still fixing her with his magnetic gaze, he took her hand and urged her upward from the chair, pulling her with a painful grasp.

Fingal Pearse held her close in his arms, and she was breathless in his bruising grasp, melting against the demanding hardness of him, knowing all the contours of his steellike body. Dizzily Maeve felt herself go soft and fluid everywhere; it was as if she no longer had the power to stand alone, but leaned upon his hardness, flowing to him, to him and around him.

She felt him shaking like a mighty tree bending to a gale; a sound of groaning joy, beseeching as the cry of a great animal, came from him, and his mouth parted over hers.

We cannot let each other go, she thought with wild, savage exultation; when at last his kiss was ended, he kept her so tightly clasped to his side that it was with difficulty that they could walk very slowly, toward the mysterious door that, opening now, revealed the bedchamber of Fingal Pearse.

From that moment nothing more was real to Maeve. The room was dim and large and filled with fragrance, and all of a sudden she began to know an awful fear throughout her trembling body. She felt the rough hands of Fingal Pearse curtly unfasten her clothes, heard the loud whisper of the falling silk, as if that were a feminine protest against his masculine hardness. Then Maeve was standing naked, her feet in the garment's silken midst like a blue pool on the floor.

Still feeling that strange dismay, she unpinned her hair, and her bare skin knew its soft impact on her shoulders and breasts; she listened to the hoarse breath of the tall stranger standing naked now before her.

Stunned, Maeve Heron sank down to the bed, to lift her white feet as delicately as a deer from the blue-green pool of her clothes and stared at the man before her. Her flesh turned cold; in the dim golden light he looked like an ancient Viking about to violate his captive, the breadth of his shoulders darkened by the sun, his arms full of a terrible power, neighboring the narrowness of his flanks, the heavy muscularity of his long legs. His narrow lips were curved into a triumphant smile, and his peculiar eyes were glazed with lust.

Hypnotized, Maeve saw the cruel man move toward her in the dimness; he was pushing her backward ungently. She fell onto the wideness of the bed, hearing his brief and shocking directions. His body was lowering to hers, and with a thrill of terror and anticipation, Maeve felt the beginning of a harsh, uncaring rhythm whose first touch was so hurtful that she nearly screamed from pain.

Horrified, she heard her own protesting words, her faint appeals to the creature above her, but now he was nothing but desire, and he was deaf to everything but the urgent tempo of his own implacable coursing.

The hard mouth of Fingal Pearse, buried in her soft neck, parted now, and she knew the piercing of his teeth in her delicate flesh. She cried out once more in protest and in pain, but he turned his head and covered her mouth with his own, devouring her chin and her lips and then both her cheeks with his widened mouth.

Then there was the slightest lessening of pain, and she felt a breaking and a flowing that alleviated a little the dreadful agony.

Maeve Heron lay helplessly, praying that it would end, thinking as she heard his relentless breathing, that this was not the love that she had dreamed. The blackness of despair flowed over her heart, and there was no more time, only her captive body waiting for release.

But soon there was a drastic quickening, and she could feel the hard form of Fingal Pearse begin to quake, as if he were a strong tree in a mighty gale, and when he gave his almost bestial cry, she knew that he had found his overpowering fulfillment. Strangely, something in her thrilled that her own body had given him so titantic an appeasement.

The light had changed. They must have slept, Maeve decided; her slowly opening eyes perceived a lavender grayness through the silken window hangings. She turned, breathing the musky scent of the man beside her.

Fingal Pearse was still asleep, his golden head pressing her shoulder; she could feel his hot breath upon her breast. Very lightly Maeve brushed aside the hay-scented hair and studied the sleeping face. How different he looked now!

Maeve breathed the clean, musky fragrance that was so distinctively his and lay very still beside him.

He stirred and opened his eyes, studying her.

"Forgive me," he said. "I wanted you too much . . . I was too. . . ."

She was abashed, not knowing how to answer.

He touched her face with his long-fingered hand, the first kindly touch he had bestowed since they had entered the chamber.

"Why didn't you tell me, Maeve?"

"Tell you?"

"That you were a virgin." He looked at her almost pityingly; his hard hand descended to her small head and rested there like a cap.

She colored and turned away. "It was a shame to Michael," she answered at last.

"Michael is dead," he said flatly, removing his hand.

Something in his tone struck Maeve with a chill of fear; he had reverted to the callous captain of the *Falcon*.

Thankful for the dimness, she rose softly from the wide bed and padded into the adjoining dressing room; motion was painful now, and when she thankfully found herself for a moment alone, she examined with dismay the evidence of her altered condition.

Freshening her body, Maeve reflected that all the magic was gone from the afternoon, the foolish, childish magic she had read into the character of the man Fingal Pearse. Why, he was no more than . . . the roughest pirate, who took a woman without pity, without caring.

She heard him call out, "Come here, Maeve, I want to talk

with you." And now in his coldness he sounded the way he had the night in her cabin on the *Falcon* when he declared that her virtue was "safe" with him.

Slowly she returned to the chamber and, sitting on the bed, covered herself with the sheet. His face was bland and smooth; whatever imagined tenderness had been there before had fled as quickly as the twilight gave way to dark. She trembled.

"What's the matter?" he asked in his ironic voice.

She did not reply, thinking coldly that he had said not one word of love; he had taken her, hurt her, made her helpless and said not a word of love. She felt a moistness gather at the ends of her closed eyes.

"Maeve," he said more kindly. She began to weep, and convulsive sobs shook her half-covered body.

"Maeve," he said again, with slow reluctance. "Maeve, none of this would have happened . . . had I known. You seemed to be a woman . . . whose body had . . . already known . . . love, as they call it."

She was chilled at his last words.

"But I am not the man to be your husband."

She heard the calm statement with a sick feeling. Could he mean that he was not going to marry her? She was speechless with shock.

"There is something in me," he said, reaching to stroke her naked body—and in spite of herself, she responded to his touch with trembling—"that cannot marry any woman, not even you."

She lay in frozen silence now, beyond speech, beyond tears.

"Maeve?" He said her name interrogatively, but still, she did not reply, continuing to lie beside him in that terrible calm silence.

"Maeve," he said again, "I am sorry. I will see that you are . . . provided for. You will have no more worry. But I am leaving the city tomorrow, to go to the West. I cannot stay long in one place, you see. It is not in me; it never has been. But I would like very much to see you when I return." He sounded almost beseeching; still, she did not answer.

"Say that you . . . can understand," he said in the same pleading tone and bent to kiss her face. She turned her head away.

Gently disengaging herself from his arms, Maeve Heron

rose from the wide bed and, after gathering up her clothes, moved into a shadow and began to dress herself.

"Maeve," he said again, but the silence was unbroken. "Let me, at least, see you to your friends'. You must let me know where to send . . . where to reach you," he amended, embarrassed.

When she did not answer, Fingal Pearse got up and threw a dressing gown around him, moving toward her with his lithe panther gait.

Maeve had lit a lamp and was arranging her hair in a simple chignon. *Anything*, she thought in desolation, *something neat enough to get me back to Hallie's without disgrace.*

Admiringly he watched her set the jaunty little pancake hat, retrieved from the sitting room, upon her glowing hair.

"Maeve," he said insistently, "at least take this from me." He handed her a purse heavy with gold pieces.

Proudly arrayed again, Maeve Heron stared up a moment into his eyes, then, smiling, took the purse from him and threw it with all her strength into his astonished face. He winced with surprise, and for an instant a look of cold rage glittered in his pale-blue eyes; then the pallid eyes became blank and neutral, the face expressionless.

After brushing past him, Maeve Heron walked quickly back to the sitting room, gathered up her books and carryall and disappeared through the door of his suite, leaving it slightly ajar.

In the deep-carpeted corridor, she felt the sudden moritification of an unescorted woman in an hotel—she, whose father had been an O'Neill of Tyrone, leaving a hotel alone like a . . . woman of the streets! Her face burned.

Then at the other end of the corridor she saw a discreetly lettered sign, LADIES' ENTRANCE, and drew a breath of relief. She would use those stairs and leave perhaps in the company of matrons who would take her for one of themselves.

But her humiliation, apparently, was not ended; emerging from a ladies' dressing parlor, Maeve encountered again, as if in a nightmare, the austere matron with whom she had collided before Brentano's. The starchy old woman was evidently descending to the restaurant. She recognized Maeve and raised her lorgnette to her cold gray eyes; she stared pointedly at Maeve's ringless left hand, uncovered by a glove, and then examined the very slight dishevelment of her hair.

The woman gave Maeve a look of disgust and contempt; Maeve returned her stare boldly, with a small half-smile that seemed to enrage the elegantly clad woman.

Maeve bowed mockingly and preceded the older woman down the stairs toward the ladies' entrance.

Pretending a dignity she was far from feeling, Maeve nodded civilly to an attendant, who opened the door, and stepped into the twilight of Fourteenth Street.

Dear God, she reflected, *it seems that everything is conspiring against me now*. A flashily dressed man with a huge handlebar mustache smiled at her and lifted his hat; she saw him from the corner of her eye. But as if he were invisible, she passed him expressionlessly and bit her lip to keep from crying.

She began the walk west, thankful that she would not have to pass the ring of idlers that she had sighted in her earlier walk surrounding the imposing statue of some American hero she did not know. And apparently her upright carriage discouraged further familiarities from passersby, for no one else approached her.

Maeve reached Hallie McDermott's brownstone with trembling relief; suddenly she was shaking with the exhaustion of the encounter with Fingal Pearse. *How strange*, she thought, *that Hallie's place is now almost like my home!*

And wearily she climbed the stoop and rang the bell. Amelie opened the door at once, saying, "I've been looking for you for the past hour. Miss Hallie is very disturbed that you are late."

"Late?" Maeve cried. "I didn't realize that I was that late."

"Quickly," Amelie said. "Let's do something with your hair. I . . . don't want her to see you like that." And with a few skilled touches Amelie had smoothed Maeve's glowing chignon. "There," she said with satisfaction.

"I don't understand what you mean . . ." Maeve began, but Amelie intervened quickly.

"Never mind that now," she said. "She's waiting for you in the big parlor . . . and mad as a wet hen, because it's almost time for the gentlemen to begin coming in. Go."

And with a gentle push Amelie urged Maeve in the direction of the imposing room in which Hallie McDermott had first given her tea.

Maeve was no longer intimidated by the sight of its ceiling-high mantel, and she walked familiarly upon the fine Persian carpet. But this evening the face of Hallie McDermott was not so reassuring; she was dressed magnificently as always, this hour in a gown of glowing red with a sheen of gold, and wonderful rubies depended from her ears below the intricate puffs of brassy hair.

Hallie McDermott did not smile. She asked brusquely when Maeve entered, "Where the hell have you been? I saw you when you went out, and your hair was different. You've been to bed with a man, you little fool, you've. . . ." She broke into obscenities that left Maeve scarlet with blushing. "And you didn't get a penny, I'll be bound," Hallie concluded coarsely.

Maeve stood silent before the angry woman. Her silence seemed to enrage Hallie McDermott, for the latter cried out, "Answer me, you little fool! You've been with a man, haven't you?"

Gathering her wits, Maeve replied calmly, "They have freed the slaves in America, I am told. I was out on my afternoon off; I was not aware that my personal life concerns you."

Hallie McDermott was trembling with ire. She rose from her chair and crossed to Maeve in three long strides. She raised her strong, rather weathered hand and fetched Maeve a brutal slap upon the cheek.

Maeve gasped with shock and then, weakened by this attack and the overwhelming events of the afternoon, began to cry. Her sobs shook her slender body.

Hallie McDermott's face changed and crumpled. She took Maeve in her arms and pressed the girl to her jutting breasts. "Maeve, child," said Hallie softly, "little Maeve." And stroking Maeve's slender back, Hallie McDermott began to kiss the younger woman's wet cheeks. "Ah, Maeve," the big woman was crooning in a strange, seductive voice that the girl barely recognized, "don't you see, my dear? Don't you see?"

Maeve stiffened in Hallie's gasp and tried to draw away. Suddenly she did see, very clearly, the source of Hallie's anger. Maeve remembered Amelie's remark about the big woman, that she was a "freak of nature," recalled Hallie's contemptuous opinions of all men. And Maeve knew then that she would have to leave this house somehow; she could stay no longer. For Hallie McDermott would never let her be.

Dissembling, Maeve relaxed a trifle in Hallie's arms and said, "I'm sorry." She cast about in her mind for some reassurance that would make the woman release her. "I'm sorry I was late," she said, "but you are wrong. I was with no man."

Hallie's grasp loosened, but she kept her strong hands on Maeve's arms. She moved back and stared into Maeve's face. "My dear, you don't have to be a maid here, you know."

Chilled, Maeve waited.

"You can be my little . . . pet." Hallie smiled, her red-veined blue eyes staring into Maeve's green ones.

"But the other girls," Maeve protested, on a sudden inspiration, "would be very jealous. There would be trouble."

"I run this place," Hallie said stubbornly. "There will be no trouble."

"Let us," Maeve stammered, "let us not change anything for now. I am . . . not sure that. . . ."

"Of course, you are not, my sweet one," Hallie said indulgently. "These things take time."

Maeve looked into the hard eyes, repressing a shiver. She had made a terrible error, she realized now; there had been in her evasive replies a tacit consent.

"Things are going to be very different now," Hallie McDermott went on in a tender voice. But her hand rested lightly now about Maeve's shoulders, in an almost motherly gesture. "We'll move you from that awful little room," she added, smiling. "And for tonight, just rest. I don't want to see you down here, exposed to all those. . . ." Hallie laughed.

Maeve nodded, thinking desperately, *How am I going to escape her? If I am sequestered somewhere in the house, I will never meet anyone who will take me away from here!* For she was convinced that her escape lay in the clientele of Hallie's place; there was surely no one else to aid her, and sometime, somehow, there would be a kind man to help.

Amelie was waiting in her room when Maeve reached the upper floor. "What did she say?" Amelie whispered as Maeve entered and closed the door.

"Oh, Amelie, Amelie!" Maeve's control broke at last, and she began to cry, the tears gushing down her face, careless that they were staining the front of her one good dress and that the lovely little hat was pushed all awry on her disheveled hair.

"Now, now," said Amelie in a soothing way, "now, now." Gently she removed the smart hat from Maeve's head and set it, with her carryall and books, upon the dresser.

"We will get you comfortable," Amelie added quietly, "and then you can tell me all about it."

"But you have to be downstairs," Maeve replied worriedly between her sobbing breaths.

"No, Maria is at the door for now; Miss Hallie said I was to help you rest." Amelie's voice was carefully bland, yet Maeve could hear in her words the unexpressed irony of the Southerner.

But Maeve submitted in weary silence as Amelie unfastened her gown and drew it over her head, took the pins from her hair and let it fall about her bare shoulders. There were tiny bruises upon Maeve's upper arms, where Fingal Pearse in his unheeding passion had held her like a vise, but Amelie, if she noticed, made no comment. However, when Maeve caught sight of the petallike marks in the long pier glass, her white skin flushed red.

"Sit down," Amelie said calmly, "and tell me everything."

Maeve sank onto a small, straight pillowed chair and looked up at the pretty mulatto.

"She . . . she wants to . . . make me her . . . pet." Maeve said at last.

"Ah." Amelie raised her graceful brows a trifle and blandly went to the press to hang Maeve's gown and jacket.

Shocked almost speechless by Amelie's matter-of-fact reception of her news, Maeve stared. Then after a long moment she asked in a trembling voice, quivering on the edge of hysteria, "Is that all you have to say . . . 'ah'?"

Amelie turned and smiled sadly at the other young woman. "My dear, she has had other pets, you know. She tried to make one of me, but that is not my way."

"Nor is it mine," Maeve retorted angrily. "But how did you evade her?"

Amelie closed the door of the press; laughing, she sat down on Maeve's bed. "I know a good many things," she replied. "And I told her if she did not leave me alone I would send Christmas cards to the wives of all her best clients, signed with her name."

In spite of her agitation and weariness, Maeve's spirits rose. She began to laugh, and her laughter rose into a hysterical giggle that threatened to overcome her. The tears were running down her cheeks.

"Stop it!" Amelie cried. "You will make yourself sick." But the shrill laughter could not be curbed; Maeve felt herself losing control. Abruptly the pretty mulatto rose from the bed and moved to Maeve; she slapped her smartly on both cheeks. Startled, Maeve heard her uncontrolled laughter die, and she drew a rasping breath of relief.

"I've never been slapped so often in one day," she said ruefully.

"I'm sorry, but it was the only way I knew." After an instant Amelie asked, "What do you mean . . . so often?"

Maeve told her then of the interview with Hallie McDermott and of the older woman's blow.

"And was it true, what she said?" Amelie asked. "Was there a man somewhere?"

Maeve hesitated.

"I know there was," Amelie said wisely. "Else how could you have changed your hair . . . or why?" Se grinned, and her even teeth were dazzling white in her *café au lait* face.

"Yes," Maeve admitted, "there was."

"He is no doubt a *bâtard*," Amelie remarked with her Gallic casualness.

"As a matter of fact, he is," Maeve said, smiling for the first time, feeling a great relief in talking to this worldy-wise girl who seemed beyond surprise or shock, who never reproached or questioned. "I *do* like you so much, Amelie."

"And I you." Amelie grinned at Maeve. "But something will have to be done about Miss Hallie."

Maeve's heart sank. "I know. But what?"

"I think," Amelie said with judicious slowness, "that you must contrive somehow to meet the gentlemen. One of them may help you."

Delighted to hear her own thoughts repeated to her, Maeve said eagerly, "Yes. I have felt that, too. But how?"

Amelie frowned, thinking deeply. "Ah, it is a problem. If I should play sick, and you replace me, opening the door . . . but *non, non*. That has several disadvantages. Miss Hallie could easily replace you. And sometimes the gentlemen do not really look at the maid opening the door. But if you were in one of the *rooms*. . . ."

Maeve turned cold with horror. "You mean . . . replace one

of the . . . young ladies, the 'entertainers'?" she cried.

"Not *really*. You see, if you were there, you could throw yourself on a gentleman's mercy and tell him your story. There are those who would not . . . take advantage."

Maeve looked skeptical and commented, "That is quite a chance to take."

Amelie laughed, "Yes, I would say so, too. But there is one—and he is coming here tonight. He has an especial appointment with the Creole, Anne-Marie. He loves dark women."

"Who is that?"

"Harley Blaine, the actor."

"Harley Blaine!" The name of the famous Shakespearean actor had long been known to Maeve; she had seen him perform once in Dublin. "But why do you think he . . . why, is he such a man? Are you sure?"

Amelie nodded sagely. "Indeed I am. Once, when he visited a new young lady—and she was very young indeed—who was hesitant to . . . perform, she told me he gave her money and went away and called her a poor child. She didn't have to . . . do anything at all!"

Maeve colored at this frank expression, but she felt a surge of wild hope rising. "Do you think I could do it?"

"Of course you could! I will arrange it with Anne-Marie. Of course, if there is much money changing hands—and with him, there will be; he is very generous—you would have to give it to Anne-Marie. She will think it a splendid joke, to make money without working for it." Amelie laughed merrily.

"Naturally I will give her whatever is . . . given me." Maeve felt a sudden coldness of fear. What if Harley Blaine were not so noble as Amelie had painted him?

Amelie saw the reluctance on the other's white face, and she said, "You will be all right, I know. He will never be able to resist you. He was born when the sun was in the *lion*, you see; he is fatherly and generous."

"The lee-ON?" repeated Maeve. "Oh, the lion! You are referring to some astrological thing then?" Maeve's distaste was barely disguised.

"Ah, you scoff," Amelie cried, "but you yourself were born in *mars*, the March, *non*?"

"How did you know?"

"Oh, that is very easy: You are fluid, lovely, helpless, sensitive, a true March-born. *Oui*?"

Maeve grinned, impressed in spite of herself. "You must tell me more of this."

"Not now, my friend! I myself am a Capricorn and have all the common sense of the Goat. And my common sense tells me now we must hurry. I will go to see Anne-Marie, and we will arrange for you to be in her room when M. Blaine arives for his engagement."

"But what if Hallie . . .?"

"Miss Hallie will believe that you are lying down with a bad headache and have begged not to be disturbed." Amelie grinned widely. "She is so fond of you she will obey such a request."

"I believe it might succeed." Maeve's hopes were rising every moment.

"Of course it will. I will go now. And good luck."

Smiling, Amelie left Maeve's small chamber and softly closed the door.

Maeve's heart was in her mouth; the hour for Harley Blaine's visit had almost come. It lacked but a few minutes of eleven. And he was meticulous, Amelie had said, about appearing on time. "A result, no doubt," Amelie had remarked, grinning, "of his actor's training."

Seeing Maeve's pale, frightened face, Amelie had added softly, "Cheer up, *amie*. All will go well, I am certain. And you will be free of this place forever. When you are rich and married, you will send for me to be your personal attendant. And we shall both be very happy then, *non*?"

Trying to smile at Amelie's sallies, Maeve Heron had submitted to the pretty maid's attentions to her clothes and hair. But after the other had gone, Maeve undressed again and donned a chemise; the gown of flesh-colored chiffon, with its matching peignoir, was all but transparent. Amelie had said, with a wicked little smile, that it would do no harm to let Harley Blaine know how beautiful she was, but Maeve could not endure the thought of appearing almost naked before this stranger.

Now her hands were icy-cold, and she was trembling in every limb. The softness of the alien chiffon, redolent of Anne-Marie's heavy scent, was light as thistledown swirling about her satin-slippered feet as she moved nervously across the velvety carpet. Yet the softness of the garments was like a fragile manacle, the cloying scent of corruption.

To distract herself from her gloomy thoughts, Maeve studied the chamber; a fortune, she reflected, must have gone into this house. There were great looking glasses everywhere, even, she had discovered with distaste, below the canopy of the huge four-poster bed with it silken coverlet. Everything was the color of pampered flesh and young roses. Apparently the Creole Anne-Marie was about to become a favorite of Hallie's—Amelie had told Maeve that this was the Creole's favorite color.

The globed lamps were rose color as well, and a bowl of pale-pink roses bloomed upon one of the marble tables. The air was heavy with their odor and with that other aroma that had filled Maeve with such sick distaste—a shut-in aura, as of dried flowers closed for years in an ancient chest.

Maeve shivered. She studied her reflection in a tall pier glass. *How pale I am!* she thought and felt a chill of apprehension. What if Harley Blaine were not the "gentleman" Amelie claimed? What if he . . . forced himself upon her?

"I would die," she said aloud. "I would die."

She found it increasingly hard to breathe in the shut air of the great pink room with its scent of stale roses.

And suddenly, as she had heard it was with drowning men, the past assailed her, but it was not so much at first pictures that she saw, but precious scents filling her nostrils—the smell of Tullaghoe's green hills in the winds of spring; the pungent smoke from the fire of the Rossar-Mescros, beside their bright-painted wagon; the rain-scent flowers of April in the garden of the house of Shane O'Neill.

Maeve breathed the ghostly aromas with gratified amazement, and then the pictures came: Old Thomas' weathered face, red as a winter apple, smiling, as he called her teasing, "little *posh ta posh*," the Romany word for those born half gentile, half Gypsy.

And there was her father, Shane, with his glass of wine, sitting afternoon upon afternoon in the dusty library, among his memories of Floure. And the shamed face of Michael on their bridal night.

His canvas-shrouded body upon the deck of the *Falcon*, and the captain, Fingal Pearse of the blue eyes like ice and

morning-colored hair, his thin mouth saying the names of the
Irish saints the day that Michael's body was given to the sea.

Fingal Pearse! The name smote Maeve like a blow, and she
felt an aching in her throat of unshed tears as she stood
staring absently into the great mirror.

"Never again," she vowed. "Never again will I let a man
assume such power over me."

Maeve wandered to a damask-covered chair before the
fireplace. She sank down upon its softness, glancing at the
marble table set for two, with its silver bucket of champagne,
its dainty foods. To contemplate them now, in her state of apprehension, set Maeve's head to spinning with her nausea.

For a fleeting instant, and astonished at her own empathy,
Maeve could feel as the others might; she could agree a
moment with the cynical advice of Hallie: "A woman is a fool
to give away such power." And for that brief time Maeve
Heron knew what it was to be as the other women were.

She realized with horror that she was thinking like a . . . she
could not repeat the word, not even here, in silence, to herself.
But what, she marveled, had given her such understanding of
those so foreign to herself? It was almost as if she could play a
part, any part. And Harley Blaine was an actor.

A new idea came to Maeve, and she was filled with a new
hope. What if . . . but no, that was too foolish a notion to
contemplate at all.

And the hopelessness of everything overcame her. She put
her face into her hands and wept.

A light tapping on the door arrested her. He was here then,
the stranger. And she was at his mercy. Maeve did not raise
her face from her sheltering hands.

She heard the door opening softly and a deep, amused
voice, a voice with such beauty and resonance that for a
moment it fairly hypnotized her, saying, "You are not very
welcoming, Anne-Marie."

There was a pause, and then the voice said, "You are not
Anne-Marie." Maeve raised her head then and met the
twinkling eyes of Harley Blaine.

"You are a nymph from the Forest of Arden. And to find
you here is sacrilege."

Chapter 8

"AND THERE she was, my boy, in Hallie's sporting house." So perfect was Harley Blaine's control over his famous voice that his declaration, hardly more than a stage whisper, reached the ears of Lester Wallack with clarity. No one else in the austere dining room of the Union Club had heard a syllable.

Lester Wallack took a sip of port and drew on his fragrant cigar. For a moment he watched its smoke curling upward in the bright air of early October, but soon his flashing black eyes returned to his companion, for Harley Blaine was speaking again. And Lester Wallack was curious about the little Heron.

He had wondered more than once how it had all begun. First the girl had appeared as dresser to Irene Marsden, the second leading lady in Wallack's company; later in the summer, suddenly, Blaine had asked him to engage her in a very minor, nonspeaking role.

"And there she was," Harley Blaine repeated, dropping his voice ever so slightly, forcing his companion to lean forward in his chair to catch the words. A trick, Lester Wallack reflected, that particularly delighted the ladies. "A vision," Blaine said, "delicate and woebegone in those borrowed draperies the color of . . . pale flesh." Blaine's tawny eyes gleamed; he paused a moment and took a sip of his wine before continuing.

"Then, my friend, her incredible story—too incredible"— Blaine twinkled at Wallack—"to be anything but true!

Pleading with me to take her away from that place. Jove, a line from a bad melodrama! And proud as Lucifer, saying she wanted to support herself through her own efforts. Throwing herself on my mercy, as it were. I'll tell you, it gave me pause. It has *given* me pause, these last months.''

Cynically Lester Wallack raised his black brows and smoothed his heavy, walruslike mustache to hide his incipient smile.

"You need not look like that, my boy," Blaine said wryly and began to laugh. "Surely you don't think I'd slander myself this way, and admit my unsuccess, if it were not so? Ah, but you . . . you are too much of a free spirit to understand how this girl has . . . entangled me."

Wallack smiled and studied Blaine indulgently. The two men could have not been more unlike; both matinee idols at the pinnacle of their careers, Wallack and Blaine were as dissimilar as air and fire. Nature had been good to Wallack; his hair was raven-color, and his dark eyes gleamed. He was possessed of a fine figure and superb carriage, one of the handsomest men of his time.

But onstage he was fascinating without passion, a man of cool resource and action, light as a bubble with the cynical levity of the man of the world.

Harley Blaine, on the other hand, was all fiery emotion; it smoldered in the very color of his red-gold hair and flickered in his tawny, catlike eyes. Quite as tall and as commanding as Wallack, Blaine's physique was an even more striking one—the breadth of his shoulders and the extraordinary leanness of his flanks had caused more than one smitten woman to liken him to a lion.

"You are too romantic, Harley," Wallack drawled. "What is she, after all, this pretty little . . . Gypsy, did you say?"

"Her mother was an Irish Gypsy, her father an O'Neill of Tyrone."

" 'An O'Neill of Tyrone,' " Wallack repeated in a mocking way. "You have assumed your protégée's very inflections as you tell me of her fantasies."

Offended, Blaine did not reply.

After a moment Wallack asked in a more genial manner, "She is not related to Matilda, is she?"

"To Matilda Heron! Never." Blaine's reply was not flattering to the absent lady, but he sounded a little mollified.

"Why 'never,' with such emphasis?" Wallack teased his friend.

"Great Scott, man, look at them! Maeve with her look of a . . . fairy creature, and Matilda with that broad, bovine face of hers."

"Really, Harley," Wallack retorted with offense. "Your infatuation is interfering with your judgment." When Blaine made no reply, Lester Wallack queried bluntly, "What are you going to do? What is Marianne's view of all this—this kindness toward your protégée?"

"That is all she is, God help me." Blaine sighed. "And Marianne knows it; she knows everything."

Wallack was diplomatically silent; indeed, the wife of Harley Blaine seemed to have eyes in the back of her head and managed to know things before anyone else. He did not envy Harley Blaine.

"But I have a feeling, Lester," Blaine said now, squinting at the glowing end of his own cigar, "that Maeve Heron has the gift." Seeing Wallack's black brows ascend again, in amused question, Harley Blaine brought his large palm down with force upon the mahogany table.

"I tell you, Lester," he repeated, "she has the gift. And that, I think, is what is disturbing Marianne now, more than any other factor." Harley Blaine's narrow, well-shaped mouth curved in a wry smile. "Marianne's getting a little long in the tooth for Rosalind. And think, man, think what a Rosalind Maeve Heron would make!"

Aloud Wallack did not agree or disagree. But he was thinking that in truth, the lithe dark girl Harley had so impetuously adopted would make a very good Rosalind indeed. There was something about her, Wallack admitted silently, something about Maeve Heron's elusive loveliness that magnetized him.

But as a manager, Wallack amended to himself. Not as a man. No, he was not besotted, like Harley Blaine. And Lester Wallack looked with pity at the dreamy eyes of Harley Blaine, gazing into the sunny middle distance.

The long makeshift dressing room for minor female players was, as always, empty when Maeve Heron entered this late-October evening. She was the first to arrive, and had been since the beginning; the solitude was glorious, the little in-

terval before the more blasé of her sisters rushed in to array
themselves as the pages, attendants, "et cetera" of *As You
Like It*.

Maeve lit the lamps, surveying the protracted table before
the rectangular looking glass. She noted with pleasure that the
autumn air, during her brisk walk from the boarding-house
on Sixteenth Street, had colored her face becomingly. Maeve
removed her smart pancake hat—Amelie had covered it for
her with a dark bronze-green for the new season—and hung it
by its ribbon on a hook in the space allotted to her street
clothes.

With care she removed and hung her dark-green skirt and
jacket below the hat, reflecting how glad she would be when
there was enough money to buy a dress from a store.
However, the little suit was quite presentable, tailored with
skill by Amelie, who was a frequent visitor at the boardinghouse on her afternoons off from Hallie's.

When Maeve protested that she could not afford to pay
Amelie for her services, the dark girl had laughed and replied,
"You are my . . . how do you say? . . . investment! I am
making you beautiful to marry a rich man, and then you will
take care of me!"

Maeve was amused at Amelie's Capricornian frankness but
was not deceived; a deep friendship had grown up between the
two, and Amelie received Maeve's small successes with
delight. She had, as a matter of fact, presented Maeve with
two luxurious neckties that Maeve had seen in *Godey's*—one
of dark-green silk, the ends embroidered lavishly with gold
braid and trimmed with bronze lace; the other one of cherry-
colored silk, spotted with gold bugle beads, meant to be worn
with an ivory-colored shirtwaist.

Maeve had not asked Amelie how she acquired these expensive articles but felt uneasily that one of the young ladies
at Hallie McDermott's might have furnished them without
knowing. Nevertheless, Maeve wore them with an air and
dismissed the matter of their origin from her mind.

After all, she consoled herself silently, *my grandfather
Sacki was one of the most skilled bandits in Ireland*. And indeed, Shane O'Neill had told her boastingly of his own horse
thefts in the days of Floure.

Now Maeve untied the dark-green necktie and, after folding
it tenderly, placed it in her drawstring purse. She took off her

shirt and hung it over the jacket. Clad only in her petticoats and chemise, Maeve went to the costume alcove and drew aside its curtains.

With a sigh she donned the plain brown gown and simple headdress of an attendant to the lady Celia. Later Maeve would wear, as page, the doublet and hose of that role, Lester Wallack having judged her long-legged slenderness appropriate to the part.

Maeve could not help thinking of the rich russet leather jerkin, pert plumed hat and shining hose worn by Miss LeClaire for the role of Rosalind.

Yet as she seated herself before the glass and began to paint her cheeks and lips and eyes, Maeve reflected that she had not been so full of joy since Tullaghoe. As then, every day now was a new adventure; even with few funds, the sprawling city was a place of magic, each byway and side street holding fresh excitement.

And Harley Blaine—Maeve smiled, blending the rouge into a natural flush upon her satiny cheeks. Harley Blaine had been the greatest miracle of all. Ever since that unforgettable first night, when she as an impostor had received him in the room of Anne-Marie, Maeve Heron had been waiting for the inevitable, the moment when his endless-seeming patience would come to an end and he would make the demand that all men made. But the moment had not yet come. It seemed too good to be true.

Maeve, her makeup completed, put away her paints and stared into the glass, remembering the night they had met in the house of Hallie McDermott.

"This is sacrilege," she had heard that bell-like voice declaiming. Removing her sheltering hands from her tear-wet face, Maeve Heron looked up at the man in the doorway. He was one of the most dazzlingly handsome men she had ever seen; he was well over six feet in height, with shoulders of unusual breadth and flanks so lean and athletic his body resembled that of the king of beasts.

Lionlike, too, were the tawny red-gold color of his hair which swept back from a high forehead, and the proud, willful expression of his face. He was studying her with twinkling eyes.

"Who on earth *are* you?" Harley Blaine asked, lowering

his voice in the subtle way that had so often captured Maeve's imagination when she had heard it from the stage. Harley Blaine closed the door softly and came slowly into the room, not approaching her, but standing near the door and staring.

Maeve rose and pulled her draperies about herself, as if to ward off a chill, for all the close chamber was so warm and heavy with the scent of roses.

"I am one of the maids, Mr. Blaine," she said with quiet matter-of-factness. "I am here to ask you to help me."

"Help you?" Harley Blaine smiled, studying her keenly. "Well, this is most intriguing." He sighted the bucket of wine on the round marble table and asked courteously, "Will you have a glass?"

Maeve, dazzled at his appearance and intimidated by his offer to serve her, could only nod.

"Sit down, my dear," he said genially. "I promise I will not bite you at all." Harley Blaine laughed his deep, easy laugh and with grace uncorked the bottle.

Maeve winced a trifle with her nervousness and at the small explosion. She sat down on the edge of one of the elegant chairs.

"There now." Harley Blaine poured a thin goblet three-quarters full and held it out to her. She took the glass with trembling hands and held it, not drinking.

He poured himself a glass and said in the same genial voice, "I will not propose anything so banal as a toast. Drink up."

She obeyed, taking a timid sip of the champagne. It tickled her nostrils, and she sneezed. The absurdity of it, even in the midst of her discomfort, struck Maeve with force. She began to laugh, a hearty, unfeminine laugh, and all at once her embarrassment evaporated.

Harley Blaine's deep laughter joined hers. He said, "I like that. You do not neigh or giggle or whinny, like so many females. As a matter of fact, your speech . . . your bearing are hardly those of a servant. You move exquisitely. Who are you?" he demanded, smiling. "And what on earth are you doing in this house?"

Maeve studied his kind face. And there was something open and accepting in his gaze that reassured her. She leaned back in the silken chair and began to tell him, speaking with a frankness she had not know since the days of Shane, her father, and of Thomas Rossar-Mescro.

Harley Blaine listened without interruption. Once he paused to light a slim cigar; once to pour another glass of wine for them. But in the main he was silent; his handsome face revealed his fascination.

When she concluded, "It was the only way we knew to . . . help me find another life," he replied softly, "I see. Yes, I see." For a long moment he puffed thoughtfully at his cigar. Maeve knew a quick unease. What was he thinking? What would he do?

"A Gypsy's child," he said at last, and his tawny look flickered over Maeve's gleaming night-black hair, the delicate planes of her pale-rose face. The feline eyes lingered for a moment on her small, round lips, interrogatively parted as she waited. Harley Blaine smiled.

"This is the most fantastic story I have ever heard," he commented. "So fantastic"—he chuckled—"that it would make a terrible play."

"Then you don't believe me?" Maeve asked coldly, trying to keep her voice steady.

"Of course, I believe you, my dear. No one could make up such a story! But why did your friend . . . refer you to me?"

Maeve colored and looked down at her hands twisted together in her lap. "You are known as someone who is very . . . kind," she answered in a low voice. "And far too popular with women," Maeve added impudently, "to have to take advantage of someone like me." She met his eyes, grinning.

His quick laughter reassured her. "Splendid," he said, setting down his wineglass on the marble table. "And what is it you want of me?"

"A job," Maeve said promptly. "Just a job, Mr. Blaine. They told me you have . . . great influence with the managers. Anything. A maid's position, a . . . dresser perhaps?" She looked at him hopefully, her eyes alight.

"Have you ever thought of pursuing a career on the stage?" he asked her, as if she had not spoken.

She hesitated. Then resignedly she said, "No, oh, no. I could not . . . think of it."

"Why not? I have told you that you move exquisitely; your speech is uniquely good, especially for an Irishwoman"—he held up his shapely hand, stemming an indignant reply she was apparently about to make—"and you are one of the most beautiful young women I have ever seen in my life. You have imagination and independence and courage. Do you realize what could have happened to you here, with one of the other . . . clients of this place?''

She nodded, subdued.

"You see, little one, more than all your other attributes—your beauty and charm and grace and delicacy—you have luck, Maeve Heron. I think you will always have luck." Harley Blaine smiled widely. "Is it something bequeathed to you by the small people of your country who hide in the bogs?''

Maeve grinned back. "You know my country then," she said warmly.

"Oh, yes. There was a time when I was younger—" Blaine stopped abruptly. "But no matter. I have the strangest feeling, Maeve Heron, that you have the gift.''

"The gift'?" she repeated.

"The actor's gift. Now listen to me. Since I am a fool and have always been a fool, I am suddenly possessed of a very far-fetched idea.''

She leaned forward eagerly, waiting for him to go on.

"I think," Harley Blaine said slowly, "that you might make an actress of yourself. Are you willing to work very hard, to listen to every word I say about the profession of acting, to do whatever must be done to advance yourself?''

Ah, she thought, *here it comes*. And Maeve waited.

"Are you?''

"That depends," she said with dry caution.

Harley Blaine laughed. "Oh, no, my dear, I am not talking about your going to bed with me . . . or anyone else. I am talking about hard work and apprenticeship.''

She flushed. "Yes," she said after a moment. "I am willing. But it sounds too good to be true. Do you think that I—''

"We are going to see," Blaine said firmly. "We are going to work and wait and see. First of all, the second leading lady can be induced to take you on as her dresser. The first leading lady is Marianne LeClaire. You have heard of her?''

"Of course.''

"Miss LeClaire is my wife. And she is a very difficult lady indeed. I would suggest that when you present yourself to Irene Marsden tomorrow—''

"Tomorrow!" Maeve gasped.

"Tomorrow," Blaine went on, unheeding, "at three o'clock in the afternoon at the theater, that you make yourself, if possible, a little . . . plainer."

Maeve smiled. "I understand."

"Good. And stay out of my wife's way. I have said that she is a difficult lady; this is putting it as civilly and as mildly as possible." Blaine's voice was wry. "And later, who knows? There may be more interesting work for you to do."

He stemmed her effusive thanks.

"And my dear," he said, rising, putting out his cigar in a little silver dish upon the marble table, "do not be too trustful of me."

She raised her black brows in question.

"My interest in you is not so altruistic as it may appear," he said bluntly. "After all, you are the most beautiful woman I have ever seen."

Maeve, before the mirror, woke from her reverie smiling. Yes, he had actually warned her, this generous and impulsive man. Yet, up to this very moment, nothing had ever occurred between them that was in the least improper. What a mystery he was!

He was different, indeed, from any man she had ever known. Harley Blaine was as sensitive as Michael had been, yet had none of Michael's hesitant delicacy, for Blaine was certainly a man in every sense of the word.

Yet for all that and his protestations of a sinister character, Blaine had not yet tried to make love to her.

Whatever the reason, Maeve concluded, examining her reflection in the glass and finding it satisfactory, she was grateful. And she had not even thought of Fingal Pearse for weeks!

Not until this moment, she amended darkly, feeling the old stab of pain to remember. A light tapping at the door broke in upon her reflections.

"Come in," she called out and turning, saw the manager, Lester Wallack. His massive figure filled the narrow doorway.

Wallack smiled. "Good evening," he said. "You're quite the early bird." There was approval in his tone.

Maeve nodded, returning his smile. She waited. For she was aware that Lester Wallack did not visit the dressing room of the minor players without an excellent reason.

"How well do you know Phebe?" he asked bluntly.

Maeve's heart leaped. She had been understudying Jenny Pyne in the role of Phebe, the shepherdess, and was letter-perfect in the part. But Jenny, as Harley Blaine had remarked, had never missed a performance; it was his contention that she would play if she had to crawl onstage.

Maeve controlled her excitement and answered simply, "Perfectly well." Then she asked, "What's happened? Has something happened to Jenny?"

"She injured her ankle very badly just this afternoon. She wanted to go on, but the doctor is adamant. She must stay off her feet for several days at least. Can you do it?"

Maeve's heart was thudding loudly in her ears. She managed to answer with a measure of calm, "Of course."

Wallack's black, snapping eyes held a look of reluctant admiration. "I hope so," he said with some skepticism. "Well, you'd better come along to Jenny's dressing room and let them fit you out."

With a blend of terror and exhilaration roiling within her, Maeve rose from the dressing table, gathered up her street clothes and followed Lester Wallack to the room that Jenny shared with the young actress who played Audrey, the "country wench."

Miss Henrietta Plum, the wardrobe mistress, was holding Jenny's shepherdess costume in her plump arms. She smiled at Maeve. Maeve, who had always liked Miss Plum and delighted in her absurd name and wizened, comical appearance, grinned back warmly.

"Well, my dear, get out of that awful dress and into this. Quickly, now, there's a good child; I am certain it's a mile too big in the waist. You have a waist like a willow wand."

Maeve took the dress from Miss Plum. Lester Wallack had closed the door and left them; Maeve hastily undid the brown dress with Miss Plum's aid and stood patiently as the wardrobe woman removed her headdress and took the brown dress off her. Slipping the blue and white shepherdess gown over Maeve's slimness, Henrietta Plum made a complacent little sound.

"I knew it," she said smugly. "I can tell without your even trying it on." Maeve felt the woman's gentle fingers fastening the gown and pulling at the waist. "Just so," mumbled

Henrietta Plum, her mouth full of pins.

As Miss Plum pinned the waist of the gown, Maeve was suddenly assailed with panic. She couldn't remember a word of Phebe's part now; not a word. Nausea took her, and she swallowed noisily, trembling.

"There now, child," said Henrietta Plum in a soft, soothing voice. "If you need to be sick, be sick right now. Do you?"

Maeve shook her head, not trusting herself to speak.

"I've seen them like this, night after night, for years," said Henrietta Plum matter-of-factly. "You're scared to death."

Maeve nodded, still trembling. Her hands felt icy cold and almost numb with terror.

Miss Plum chuckled. "It's better so. All the good ones are afraid. Why, Miss LeClaire is like a mad child on opening night. And Mr. Blaine often loses his dinner."

"Mr. Blaine?" Maeve cried, unbelieving. Already some of her fear was lessening; her hands felt a little warmer, and the dreadful nausea was going.

"That's right." Miss Plum nodded with satisfaction. "Now then, off with this and let me get to work. What a blessing you were so early!"

When the wardrobe woman had removed the gown, Maeve found that she was shivering again.

"Put this on." Miss Plum handed her a makeup-stained dressing gown of Jenny's. Maeve obeyed and sat down before the dressing table, rubbing her small hands together, feeling miserable once more. "You'll be fine," said Henrietta Plum. "Why don't I get them to bring you a cup of tea?"

"Oh, yes, yes," Maeve said gratefully, her voice emerging almost in a croak. She cleared her throat and laughed nervously.

When the woman had gone, Maeve sat quite still for a moment. She began to repeat to herself the opening words of Phebe's first speech, to Silvius the shepherd:

> I would not be thy executioner:
> I fly thee, for I would not injure thee.
> Thou tell'st me there is murder in my eye. . . .

As she went on, she felt her voice grow stronger, and the

memory of the words returned. But now her poor hands were freezing again! She rubbed them together hard, feeling them tingle as the numbness fled.

It was going to be all right, she repeated to herself in silent desperation. It would have to be all right.

"I would not be thy executioner . . ." Maeve repeated, and took up the blue ribbon she would wear as Phebe, the shepherdess.

The callboy raised a thin, fisted hand, about to knock on Harley Blaine's door. Then, hearing the famous voice issuing from behind Miss Marianne LeClaire's door, the callboy hurried down the corridor and raised his fist once more, preparing to tap for the ten-minute warning. But an arresting phrase from behind the door gave the callboy pause; he heard Harley Blaine urging, "Modulate your voice, my dear; you can be heard at least in Philadelphia."

The callboy grinned and lowered his hand. He leaned a little toward the door. They were at it again, he thought with glee, and this time he wasn't going to miss a word. He glanced around him. All clear. And the callboy settled in to listen.

"You are not exactly silent," he heard Marianne LeClaire declaim in her husky soprano.

"What is it you are accusing me of?" the voice of Harley Blaine demanded. "Do you imagine that I inflicted her injury on Jenny so that Miss Heron might play?"

"*Miss Heron!*" The reply of Marianne LeClaire was mocking and scornful. "Listen to the man! As if I didn't know what you and that little whore are up to!"

"You are quite wrong, Marianne." There was a melancholy humor in Blaine's retort. "We are up to nothing at all."

"If that's so, it's even worse." Marianne LeClaire's husky voice had risen almost to a shriek. "Then you are . . . courting her as if you intend to marry."

"You are ridiculous, my dear, perfectly ridiculous. I have taken an interest in the child—"

"Child!" screamed Marianne LeClaire. "Why, you. . . ."

The callboy, catching sight of Miss LeClaire's approaching dresser, had begun to knock on the door. "Mr. Blaine," he called smartly, "Miss LeClaire. Ten minutes. Ten minutes, Mr. Blaine."

But the callboy saw that he had not been quick enough. Marianne LeClaire's Irish dresser glared at him and said, "Do you mind if I pass? What do you think you're doing there indeed? Spying on your betters! You ought to be ashamed, you should."

And the dresser flounced past the callboy into Marianne LeClaire's dressing room.

Stumping away, the callboy reflected bitterly, *Betters, is it? Why,* he had heard fishwives in Billingsgate Market, back at home, speak softer than the great Marianne LeClaire. *Betters, was it!*

To Maeve Heron, it seemed no time at all had elapsed between her donning the altered gown and the horrifying moment when, with Silvius, the shepherd, Phebe entered the painted forest under the dazzling light.

Maeve was at once assailed by the brightness that cast the audience into a yawning black beyond them, into a mere knobbed dimness—the knobs were heads, she realized sickly; heads of people staring—the brightness' heat and her own body's terrible cold; the voice of Silvius as if from a great way off, "Sweet Phebe, do not scorn me; do not, Phebe . . ." and then, after what seemed only an instant, the words that were her cue: " . . . will you sterner be/Than he that dies and lives by bloody drops?"

Maeve Heron heard a woman's voice reply—surely it could not be her own! So silvery and full and carrying was it!—yes, she heard herself replying:

> I would not be thy executioner;
> I fly thee, for I would not injure thee. Thou tell'st
>   me there is murder in mine eye:
> 'Tis pretty, sure, and very probable,
> That eyes, that are the frail'st and softest things,
> Who shut their coward gates on atomies,
> Should be call'd tyrants, butchers, murderers!
> Now do I frown on thee with all my heart. . . .

And there was no more room for thought, only for the astonishing sound of her own voice that seemed another woman's voice; the motions that appeared to be those of a beautiful stranger.

Become the shepherdess Phebe, in her blue and white, the woman who had been Maeve Heron sweetly pleaded with the shepherd Silvius.

Major William Morgan listened to the lovely woman say, "Dead shepherd, now I find they saw of might,/'Who ever loved that loved not at first sight?'"

He gave a sharp exhalation of held breath, so vehement that Mrs. Charles Patrick Dady, seated to his right, glanced sharply at him. What ailed the boy? Not once, since the character named Phebe had come onstage, had William moved or even seemed to breathe, Mrs. Dady reflected with unease.

William's cameolike profile, with its nose of perfect aquilinity, its firm, thin lips, was still turned straight ahead; his great, soft dark eyes, so melting for a man's in Mrs. Dady's estimation, had not left the slender figure in blue and white. Usually young ladies looked that way at *him*!

Mrs. Charles Patrick Dady glanced then at William's mother, next to her; the stout Senator's wife, with half-lowered lids, seemed to be almost asleep. Ah, they had dined too well before the play! Mrs. Dady thought with amusement.

Well, she's a pretty little chit, Mrs. Dady mused, looking again at the shepherdess. *Haven't I seen her somewhere before? How could I, though?* she questioned. *Where would I have met a common little actress*?

Mrs. Dady stole another side glance at her young companion, William Morgan. She thought indulgently, *All these young men run after actresses—what harm is in it, after all? Poor boy, he deserved amusement, now he was home from that horrible war!*

The striking man with the morning-colored hair and ice-blue eyes who was ahead of the Morgans and Mrs. Dady stared transfixed at the stage. The first words of the shepherdess echoed in his mind. "I would not be thy executioner:/I fly thee, for I would not injure thee." A cold emptiness of regret assailed him. Now he heard Phebe say in her bell-like silvery voice, " . . . . I have more cause to hate him than to love him:/For what had he to do to chide at me?"

And Fingal Pearse felt that Maeve was speaking the words to him, of him; that unaccustomed emptiness chilled his vitals again, but only for a moment. No woman meant that much, not even this quicksilver creature in her white, ruffled bodice and blue-striped skirt, crying now as the act ended, ''Go with me, Silvius.''

Part III

INTO THE GOLDEN HOUSES

Chapter 9

MAJOR WILLIAM MORGAN, USA, was grateful for the fact that Father Bernard O'Reilly shared escort duties with himself this evening. For in the interval following the third-act curtain William Morgan was hard put to follow the conversation of his mother and her friend, Mrs. Dady.

He could still hear that plaintive voice, saying before the curtain's fall, "Go with me, Silvius." William Morgan was very glad that hers had been the final voice in the scene; since her first appearance, he had been almost hypnotized by her grace and beauty, bemused by the whiteness of her neck and bosom above the white, ruffled bodice. So white, he reflected now, it was almost impossible to discern where the snowy flesh left off and the garment began. The glittering blackness of the shepherdess' heavy hair, the bewitching eyes that seemed now blue, now green, then almost lilac; the impudent, small, roselike mouth—all these had shaken William Morgan to his depths. His very flesh responded.

Recalling himself to the present, William Morgan heard O'Reilly speak to him. "I beg your pardon?" Morgan replied in a slow, dreamlike fashion.

"The President's parole of Alexander Stephens," O'Reilly said. "I fear the ladies take a sterner view of it than I."

William Morgan answered absently, "I'm afraid I have been inattentive." The alert Mrs. Dady had turned her head a little as if to listen to William's reply. "I was thinking of . . . the play."

William Morgan saw Mrs. Dady's fine mouth curl in a teasing smile. "The *play,* my dear boy?" she asked chaffingly. "The performance seems to have impressed you greatly. I notice you could not stop looking at the shepherdess."

William Morgan colored slightly and bit his lip, raising a slender hand to his dark-brown cavalry mustache. He smoothed it to conceal his grimace of irritation. *Damn the woman,* he thought, glancing at his mother. Mrs. Dady still thought of him as a child playing upon her lawn, for the friendship of Mrs. Dady and his mother was one of long standing.

He answered casually, "She is a very pretty young lady," and the genial O'Reilly added, "A very fine actress, too."

" 'Young lady'!" Mrs. Morgan repeated, scandalized. "I have never heard actresses referred to as 'ladies' before." Her plump face was indignant; she pursed up her mouth in a comical fashion that made William Morgan laugh despite his annoyance.

"I have seen her somewhere before," said Mrs. Dady. "Somewhere last spring. Now, how irritating that is, not to remember!"

"Perhaps in another play," said William Morgan.

"No, no. It was not in the theater at all. Oh, well, I daresay it will come to me. It makes no matter. The Judge and Mr. Badeau are talking of the propriety of giving General Grant a public reception, my dear," said Mrs. Dady, addressing Mrs. Morgan. "The Judge wants a hundred gentlemen to meet the general on horseback. Could we count on you, William?"

Charles Patrick Dady, the Judge, was the only person of Mrs. Dady's acquaintance who escaped her caustic wit. Her love for him was so colored by hero worship that his every utterance was repeated by Mrs. Dady like holy writ. The Judge, an habitué of the Shakespearean theater, had been prevented from attending tonight by an urgent business appointment, and William Morgan was not sorry. The Judge's eyes were even sharper than his wife's.

William Morgan smiled and made an evasive reply. Mrs. Dady stared at him keenly. Then, suddenly, she remarked in a sharp, excited voice, "I know now where it was!"

"Where what was?" Mrs. Morgan's amiable, slow voice was puzzled.

"Where I saw that young person, the one who acted

Phebe," Mrs. Dady said impatiently. "And, my dear, it was *most* improper," she added, lowering her voice, glancing at O'Reilly and William.

"You forget, my dear Mrs. Dady," the Jesuit teased, "that William here is an officer of the U.S. Army and that I myself am a former one." O'Reilly had served as chaplain to the 69th Regiment. "We can hardly be shocked by impropriety."

Mrs. Morgan and Mrs. Dady looked at the Jesuit with surprise. "Really, Bernard!" the latter cried, tapping his arm with her folded fan. "You are becoming very worldly indeed."

"You say," William Morgan addressed Mrs. Dady, "that there was something improper. What was it, Mrs. Dady?"

"William!" Mrs. Morgan's plump face revealed her dismay. The boy was usually so gallant and . . . tractable. "Don't take that tone with Mrs. Dady!"

"I beg your pardon." William Morgan's handsome face reddened with embarrassment. "It is just that I cannot imagine such a lovely lady in any . . . improper situation."

Bernard O'Reilly studied the younger man with compassion. Mrs. Dady laughed her tinkling laugh and said, "Why, William, I do believe you are smitten with this young person."

William Morgan felt that if the woman said "young person" once more, he would be forced to turn on his heel and walk away to prevent himself from striking her. "What," he pursued in a calmer tone, "was the impropriety?"

Nettled, Mrs. Dady snapped, "I saw her trying to steal a book in Brentano's, but she was prevented by her . . . paramour. Later I saw her coming unescorted from a hotel."

William Morgan felt a strange sickness in his stomach pit. "It seems more a case for pity than condemnation," he said to Mrs. Dady bluntly, all pretense at courtesy gone.

"William, you are . . . not yourself this evening," his mother protested, sounding near tears.

The young officer took his mother's hand. "I think she deserves our compassion," he said stubbornly.

"*I* think we have discussed this matter long enough," Mrs. Charles Patrick Dady declared. "It is almost time for the curtain. After all, the young woman is only an actress, and we all know what they are."

Mrs. Morgan raised her heavy brows, a trifle jarred by Mrs.

Dady's plainness of speech. Her friend, Mrs. Morgan thought, was far more circumspect in the presence of the Judge! Nevertheless, she made an assenting murmur and said, "Let us speak no more of it."

But as the ladies preceded their escorts from the lobby and began their descent down the aisle, Mrs. Morgan glanced back at William. There was something in her son's face she had never remarked before. And Mrs. Morgan knew with certainty that the matter was far from ended. Alas, it had just begun.

Maeve Heron fairly floated to her dressing room, the praises of her fellow players loud in her ears. She tingled with the memory of the applause, as if she had taken wine. How wondrous it had been! The generous actor who had played Silvius, after bowing with her to the audience, had given her a gentle shove forward so she might enjoy a tribute of her own. And to Maeve's joy and astonishment, the applause had sounded deafening—almost as enthusiastic, she judged with a delighted shiver, as that accorded to Marianne LeClaire herself.

Winifred Reynolds, who played Audrey, was already seated at the dressing table when Maeve hurried into the dressing room.

"Congratulations," Winifred said flatly, a tinge of her country-wench accent still coloring her low, lazy voice. There was no warmth, only a perfunctory civility, in the word.

The generous-hearted Maeve was a little pained by the tone of Winifred's greeting, but when she caught the twinkling glance of Henrietta Plum in the glass, she realized that she was experiencing the first envy she had known.

As if reading her mind, Miss Plum grinned and murmured, "The first . . . but not the last."

"Why, Miss Plum," Maeve cried, smiling, "I believe to my soul you have the Sight."

"What was that remark, Henny?" Winifred asked sharply.

"Nothing, my dear, nothing at all; my dentures are paining me, that's all." Miss Plum's wrinkled face was bland. To Maeve she added, "In Liverpool we didn't call it the Sight, dearie."

It had not escaped Winifred's notice that Miss Plum moved first to help Maeve remove the constricting blue ribbon from her glittering curls of coal-black hair and begin to undo the white ruffled bodice.

"Could you give me a hand here, Henny?" Winifred demanded in an aggrieved way.

"Oh, please," said Maeve, "do help Winifred, Miss Plum. I can handle the rest."

But Maeve saw that she had only made the situation worse; it was as if she had expected Miss Plum to wait for her permission. To make amends, she asked Winifred, "How is Jenny? Have you had further word?"

"She'll be laid up for quite a while," Winifred replied sullenly. "That's good news for *you*, at any rate."

Maeve was shocked at the other actress' malice, but she was silent. Nothing, she resolved, nothing was going to mar her unbelievable triumph!

As she scooped out cold cream and spread it over her face, eradicating the bright-pink cheeks and doe eyes of Phebe, Maeve saw that her eyes were glowing brilliantly with the excitement of the night.

The dressing room, which had been such a short time before a cage of terror, had been transformed now into a welcoming little home. And to think she had never known how it could be! Her previous experience of the stage had been nothing but the unobtrusive, nonspeaking roles; she had always been in the background, unnoticeable. But now!

Maeve longed for Winifred to be gone, so she might speak her heart to Henrietta Plum. For she knew with a glad knowing that the old woman wished her well; it had shone from her twinkling eyes the moment Maeve had entered the little cubicle.

At last, Winifred rose from the table and put on her street clothes. With a curt good-night, she was gone.

"Well!" Henrietta Plum sighed loudly, with a comical effect, and sank down in the chair vacated by Winifred. "Alone at last!" she declaimed, in the style of a melodrama's villain, and Maeve laughed her hearty laugh, an infectious sound in the echoing space.

"You were magnificent, my dear!" Henrietta Plum beamed up at Maeve, who had risen and was buttoning her blouse. The old woman watched her step into her green skirt and tie the smart little necktie Amelie had given her.

"Thank you." Maeve smiled gratefully at Miss Plum, her

cheeks, innocent of makeup now, glowing almost as brightly as they had in the makeup of Phebe. "Thank you."

"My dear, may I give you a word of advice?" Miss Plum asked softly.

"Of course."

"Be careful; be careful of Miss LeClaire."

Maeve raised her brows in question, puzzled at the seriousness of the old woman's warning. "But why?"

"You are going to go far," said Henrietta Plum soberly. "And Miss LeClaire is a jealous woman. There is no more malicious creature on earth than an aging star."

"But how could I threaten someone as famous and beautiful as that?" Maeve cried.

"Come now, Maeve Heron. You are twenty years younger, a hundred times better-looking . . . and who knows? Someday you may be a better actress."

"Oh, surely not! Why, I—"

"Ah!" Henrietta Plum made a face of disgust. "I am a prattling old fool. Enjoy your triumph, and never mind me. Enjoy your wonderful night!" After a moment she chuckled and asked, "Is there no gentleman to help you celebrate?"

"I fear not," Maeve said quietly, tying the ribbons of her pancake hat. "There. I'm ready now, I suppose. Good night, Miss Plum. And thank you—thank you for all your kindness."

"Call me Henny. All the others do. Well!" the old woman ejaculated. "At least Mr. Blaine has had the good sense to stay away."

Maeve colored deeply. There was a quick knock, and the watchman poked his head into the cubicle. "A gentleman to see Miss Heron," he announced.

"Ah, you see?" Henrietta Plum grinned.

"I can't imagine who . . ." Maeve began. But she stopped abruptly and stared at the opening door. Fingal Pearse was standing on the threshold.

Marianne LeClaire paused a deliberate instant on the threshold of the supper room; her irritated husband, Harley Blaine, a step behind her, knew this habit of old and paused in time to preserve his own graceful bearing. The two actors in his wake were not so fortunate; one almost collided with Blaine, giving a little grunt of surprise.

Miss LeClaire, without seeming to notice, noted well the turning heads and murmurs of the diners already seated. She smiled a gracious smile and moved on, permitting her husband and their two companions to move on again as well.

She was a striking picture; for all her forty years, she had kept a surprising look of youth, and if her auburn hair owed its vividness to art and not to nature, few were the wiser. Her gown annoyed the women; those with red hair did not generally have the temerity to wear scarlet. The gown was from the 1865 collection of Worth, a luxurious creation with a tightly fitted waist and an elegant train. It was made of silk, cut low over Marianne LeClaire's generous bosom, with tiny caplike sleeves showing off her plump arms; the wide skirt of the gown featured elaborate V-shaped appliqués of black silk lace. In her flaming hair and on her soft neck, Marianne LeClaire wore ornaments of vivid rubies.

The dining room was wide and glittering; lights played upon a central fountain whose murmur mingled with the discreet bubble of low voices, the chiming collision of silver with fragile china. The diners followed with their eyes the progress of Marianne LeClaire and her train.

An obsequious, grinning waiter seated the four at a big table beside one of the narrow windows shut against the autumn chill; they were screened by tall palms in great carven tubs. Harley Blaine, from obscure malice, had chosen the table, for he realized that his vivid wife had come here to be stared at, and this location irritated her very much.

Blaine spoke to the waiter in unaccented, perfect French; the waiter bowed and withdrew.

There was an awkward little silence. With relief, Harley Blaine sighted the massive figure of Lester Wallack at the door. Wallack's snapping eyes lighted upon them, and with a smile he strode toward their table.

"Marianne, my dear," said Lester Wallack with a bow to the flame-haired woman. He raised her white-gloved hand to his and kissed it lightly. "You were magnificent, as always."

Marianne LeClaire accepted this tribute with aplomb and shot a side glance at her husband. "How nice that you are joining us," she said in her rich, controlled voice.

As Wallack seated himself, and the waiter returned, Blaine commented casually, "It went well tonight, didn't it, Les?"

The dark manager glanced at Harley Blaine with

amusement, knowing full well he was referring to the performance of Maeve Heron.

And some devil in Wallack, prompted perhaps by his recent difficulties with the imperious leading lady, made him declare, "The Heron woman is excellent. It would not surprise me to see her mentioned in the papers tomorrow."

The two actors looked uneasily at Marianne LeClaire; her sensuous mouth had taken on a sullen cast, and her blue eyes were cold. "She's a pretty enough little thing," said Marianne LeClaire in an indulgent, purring voice, "but surely you exaggerate her ability, Lester."

"I do not at all," Lester Wallack replied, and Harley Blaine made no attempt to conceal his delighted smile. "I can see her as Ophelia in our next production."

"Ophelia!" cried Marianne LeClaire, and Blaine saw her pale with anger. She ignored his proffered goblet of champagne and went on in a low voice "I thought I had made it clear to you, Lester, that I have not yet decided which role I choose to play."

"There is quite a span between Ophelia and Gertrude, my dear," Lester Wallack commented. His tone was silky but bore an undernote of subtle malice that did not escape Marianne LeClaire.

"Are you telling me that I am too old to play Ophelia, Lester?" Miss LeClaire's reply had the threatening rhythm of a cat's tail that metronomed the cat's intent to pounce.

"Why, Marianne, how could you think such a thing?" Lester Wallack parried. "I have told you before—only you have the glamor . . . the womanly appeal to give to the part of Gertrude. Any little ingenue can perform a creditable Ophelia."

Harley Blaine repressed an irreverent snort. Surely, he reflected, this was too thick, even for someone as vain as Marianne!

But to his astonishment, Marianne LeClaire rose to the bait at once. "You are such a darling," she purred, leaning to Lester Wallack to touch his massive hand with her plump one, now gloveless and insinuating upon his hard flesh. Wallack smiled and made himself submit to her touch. "I *have* been such a naughty girl," she added with unattractive coyness. "*So* naughty not to make my decision before. Very well," she concluded with the air of one bestowing a royal favor, "I will be a good girl and play your old Gertrude for you, Lester.''

''Marvelous!'' Wallack exclaimed. ''I had feared we might not come to terms. And you know I could not do without you.''

Harley Blaine reflected wryly that Marianne LeClaire could not easily do without Lester Wallack either; he was permissive beyond reason with Marianne LeClaire. But it had occurred to Harley Blaine more than once in recent days that Lester Wallack's patience might soon come to an end. And then the Blaine-LeClaire act, he thought sourly, would be seeking another manager.

''Marvelous,'' Lester Wallack repeated. ''I knew I could count on you, my dear lady.'' Again he kissed her hand.

''On one condition,'' she said in a small, coy voice.

''Condition?'' the manager reiterated, a look of stubbornness coming over his handsome face.

''Yes. On the condition that someone else play Ophelia. Not this young Heron.''

''Why do you make this condition?'' Wallack demanded. ''No one makes conditions for me; I am the manager of Wallack's, let me remind you.''

''Very well. Then I shall not play Gertrude or any other part for you, my dear Lester.'' Marianne LeClaire rose in a flurry of silk and lace, gathering up her gloves and little back-beaded reticule from the table.

''Marianne,'' protested Harley Blaine. ''Everyone is looking at you.''

Everyone *always* looks at me!'' Marianne LeClaire said royally. ''You need not see me home, Harley. I shall find my way myself.'' And she flounced away from the sequestered table. The four men stood in silence, watching her majestic exit toward the doorway.

''I had better go with her,'' said Harley Blaine in resignation. ''Good night, Lester. George, Harold.'' Blaine nodded to the others and followed his splendid wife.

On the threshold of the dining room, Marianne LeClaire's impetuous progress was almost arrested by Maeve Heron and Fingal Pearse.

The party consisting of William Morgan and his mother, Mrs. Dady and the Jesuit Bernard O'Reilly had gone unnoticed by Marianne LeClaire's; except for the envious glances of the matrons at the actress' figure and gown, the austere four had been more discreet in their scrutiny than the other diners.

Father Bernard O'Reilly, unable to help overhearing the exchanges between Miss LeClaire and Wallack, had reflected in his absent worldliness how childlike were the creatures of the stage. The ladies had affected not to hear, and William Morgan noticed hardly anything at all. He was queasy with desire.

His head was swimming with the vision of Maeve Heron, her milk-white skin, the blooming quality of her little mouth and the peculiar changeable eyes that seemed to him to alter with the changing stage light—from blue that matched the stripes of her skirt to sea green to an indescribable lavender. He had never seen such a woman before, anywhere, in all his journeys. William Morgan, like most young men of his class, had made the Grand Tour, but nowhere in Europe, even among the lustrous-eyed women of Spain or the pert, stylish Parisiennes, had he encountered such enchantment. And the pampered young ladies of his set seemed now to William Morgan like so many identical dolls, lacquered without, empty within. All the other women dimmed in his mind.

For the young Maeve Heron had had a quality of fire and feeling new to William Morgan. Now, as he gave an absent order to the waiter, Morgan was amazed at his own poetic thoughts. Well, he reflected wryly, he had never been much of a soldier; a book was more his line. His mother could never understand, for he had been three times decorated for bravery in the war, yet the memory of it seemed to William Morgan like a nightmare play in which another man had performed, in his name, feats of horror that ironically earned him rewards.

And just as William Morgan had learned, in that time of savagery, to appear to attend where mentally he did no such thing. Morgan had carried over the habit into civilian life. No one apparently, but Bernard O'Reilly, knew tonight how far away he was!

Morgan was touched by the indulgent fondness that made the Jesuit relieve him of attention to the ladies—O'Reilly chattered on, with such charm and continuity that neither Mrs. Morgan nor Mrs. Dady noticed William Morgan's abstracted air.

It was only when he heard, as if from a great distance, the

powerful voice of Lester Wallack saying, "The Heron woman is excellent. It would not surprise me to see her mentioned in the papers tomorrow," that Morgan came to attention. Perhaps, he thought with rising excitement, Schuyler's friend could help him find out something tonight. . . .

Dimly he heard, above the babbling of voices around him, O'Reilly gently chaffing the ladies over fashions, saw, from the corner of his eye, the bright-colored Marianne LeClaire sweep past.

But then an exclamation from Mrs. Dady brought William Morgan forcibly into the present once more. "Well!" Mrs. Dady said in a low, scandalized voice. "I hardly thought that *here*, of all places. . . ."

Morgan followed the line of her stare and saw, in the doorway, moving slightly aside for the exit of Blaine and Marianne LeClaire, the young actress Maeve Heron. William Morgan drew in his breath sharply and with care kept his face bland. She was lovelier than ever. What an Irishness there was about her, with that milky skin and the black, black lashes; the wildness of her air! To kiss that skin would be. . . .

"Good heavens!" Mrs. Dady said. "Are they admitting people in street clothes these days? I should have thought. . . ."

"No doubt," said Mrs. Morgan in her apologetic fashion, "it was an impromptu visit."

Mrs. Dady snorted. "Nonsense, Fanny! There *are* standards, heaven help us."

But William Morgan hardly heard what the women were saying; as Maeve Heron moved nearer, Morgan thought, in exaltation, how her flesh glowed like silk before a candle flame, it was so fragile and transparent. For all the young actress' striking looks, he noted, there was nothing remotely vulgar in her. She bore herself with dignity, and William Morgan knew that the other women recognized in Maeve Heron a quality alien to themselves. Therein lay their resentment. The repressed mischief of the green, slanting eyes, the lips' defiant tilt, not quite smiling, marked her as more than an idle lady of fashion.

Morgan's heart turned over with pity when he remembered Mrs. Dady's report of the theft in Brentano's. Suddenly he knew he wanted to give this woman everything.

But then he saw the man who followed her, a man as striking in his way as Maeve Heron was in hers. The man was

tall and hollow-faced and reckless-looking; for all his elegance, he had a faint air of lawlessness. It was as if the pair
had brought into the gaslit room a wind of wider places that
stirred the dark trees beyond the long, sheltering windows.

William Morgan felt an unaccustomed anger rising in him-
self; he longed to challenge the man with the cold blue eyes.
Openly now, careless of his mother's worried glances,
William Morgan watched the pair while they were seated.

The peculiar eyes of the blond man that seemed so strange
to softness became softer, Morgan saw, when the man looked
at Maeve Heron. Yet to Morgan's irrational delight, the
beautiful young woman did not seem to respond in a like
manner to the blond man.

Their waiter wheeled in a bottle of wine nested in a silvery
bucket; there was a hollow pop, a foam, a reverent pouring.
The man and woman raised their glasses.

From nowhere there came to the watching Morgan a line
from a poem he loved, "For there was lightning in my
blood." Quite by accident the green eyes of the Heron woman
then met William Morgan's. She looked modestly away. But
Morgan's blood was pounding in his veins.

So taken aback was she by the appearance of Fingal Pearse
that Maeve could not gather her wits to protest when he led
her to a carriage. "You must let me stand you a little supper,"
he said genially, staring down into her startled eyes.

She was dismayed to feel the undiminished power of that
cold blue look; it pierced her as he had once pierced her very
body. A sweet pain arose in her, and she silently protested,
Never, never will he have me in his power!

Nevertheless, Maeve submitted, preceding him timidly into
the glittering supper room, feeling out of place among the
elegant evening dress of its patrons.

"I am not dressed," she protested softly to Pearse.

"What does it matter?" he answered casually. "You're
lovelier than any of them, Maeve."

Despite herself, she warmed to his words. No sooner than
he said them, however, she met a new unease. The dazzling
Marianne LeClaire was almost upon her.

Maeve moved slightly aside to permit the splendid woman
to pass. Miss LeClaire did not greet her at all. The younger

woman's green look devoured the exquisite Worth creation, the leading lady's rudeness almost forgotten in the contemplation of her splendor.

Harley Blaine, on the heels of Marianne LeClaire, said with formal geniality, "Congratulations, Miss Heron! You were very good tonight."

Before she had a chance to thank him, Blaine, after a curious glance at Fingal Pearse, had hurried away.

When they were seated and the waiter had departed, Fingal Pearse smiled at Maeve and commented softly, "I like your dress much more than that eyesore we just passed."

"Eyesore! Surely you cannot mean Marianne LeClaire," Maeve answered with amazement.

"Indeed I do. M. Worth never meant that gown to be worn by her."

Maeve raised her brows and retorted in a teasing way, "You know a great deal of women, Captain Pearse . . . of women and even their clothes."

"Yes." His reply was cool. "I know more about them, I daresay, than any other man."

His effrontery silenced her, and she did not speak during the ceremonious opening of the wine and the filling of glasses. She recalled his brutal ineptness with her.

"You have changed, Maeve," said Fingal Pearse. "If anything, you are more beautiful."

Maeve felt a sudden need to conquer the anger roiling within her. She turned her head slightly and met the eyes of an extraordinarily handsome man who was gazing fixedly at her. Maeve knew somehow that he had been looking at her since she entered, for he had not moved at all when her eyes met his. Again that feeling of the familiar teased her.

Where, she wondered, had she seen those eyes before? She had seen him, she was convinced. Modestly Maeve turned her gaze from him. He had aroused something warm and new within her.

Evasively she answered Fingal Pearse, "And you, Captain? Where have you been keeping yourself? I thought the *Falcon* would have sailed long since."

"The *Falcon* sailed without me. I have been out West, seeking a treasure that they said had sunk with the wreck of a steamboat."

"And did you find your treasure?" she asked lightly.

"Not that one; there was plenty of gold, for those who knew where to find it."

"And you did?"

"Yes, my greedy little Maeve, I did." He laughed at her haughty expression.

"I have no interest in your gold, Captain Pearse, or indeed in you," she added coldly.

"Come now, Maeve," he said cajolingly, "how can you talk like this, after all that happened between us?"

"You are coarse to refer to that at all," she protested, and her voice trembled. To her horror, a vivid picture of his brutal nakedness had flashed before her inner vision.

He might have read her thought, for his eyes warmed and flickered, staring into hers until she had to turn away.

This time she glimpsed the other diners at the table of the young man who was staring, the dark, handsome man with the liquid eyes. There was a distinguished-looking priest of middle age, with a wise and humorous face, and there were also two matrons, elegantly dressed. One was very stout, with a rather foolish, good-natured face; the other had the air of a bird of prey. She was the woman with the lorgnette who had seen Maeve's furtive action in Brentano's . . . and had later met her on the stairway of Fingal Pearse's hotel.

Maeve Heron blushed crimson. Pearse asked, in a half-jocular, half-tender tone, "Is this sweet color all for me?"

Maeve was forming a tart reply when she saw the manager, Lester Wallack, approaching their table.

"Miss Heron," he greeted her with courtesy, "I hope I am not intruding."

"Not at all," she answered, hearing with delighted surprise the poise with which she spoke. "Mr. Wallack, Captain Pearse."

Pearse rose, with a neutral expression, extending his hand. "Mr. Wallack," he said calmly, "I have admired you in both the roles of actor and manager."

"Thank you, Captain Pearse. If I may . . . join you for only a moment?"

"Of course."

Maeve heard all this with rising excitement. As always, Lester Wallack never made a meaningless visit or overture, and he obviously had something to say.

"Miss Heron," Wallack turned to her without preamble, "you were splendid tonight. How would you like to play Ophelia in our next production?"

For an instant Maeve was speechless with astonishment. Then she answered in a rush, "I would love it, Mr. Wallack. I would love it!"

"Your enthusiasm does me good." Wallack laughed. "You would bring to your work the same élan." Then he remarked abruptly, "I must leave you now." He rose, and Pearse rose with him. "Captain Pearse," Wallack said perfunctorily; more warmly: "Miss Heron." And he was gone.

For a moment there was silence.

Then Fingal Pearse said, "Well, Maeve, I suppose your answer, then, is no."

"My answer?"

"To my invitation, not yet given." She studied him, puzzled; when she did not reply, he went on, "To come with me to Europe."

He had still not mentioned marriage; Fingal Pearse was just the same, Maeve thought with a blend of hurt and irritation. But with a quickly beating heart and exhilaration bubbling in her like wine, Maeve realized all at once that she did not need anyone now! She would be as proud as the daughter of Shane O'Neill had been taught to be, as wildly free as her Gypsy mother, Floure.

"My answer, then, *is* no," she said to Fingal Pearse, smiling. Not the faintest doubt assailed her, for all his magnetism. For he had brought her nothing but humiliation and despair, insult, pain and longing.

So in her new strength Maeve Heron barely heard the cajoling protest of Fingal Pearse.

Chapter 10

MARIANNE LECLAIRE, presenting her high-nosed profile to Harley Blaine, had preserved a stony silence for the fifteen blocks between the hotel and their fashionable Italianate house facing Gramercy Park.

When the carriage drew up before its elegant red-brick facade, laced with cast-iron porches and balconies, Blaine handed his wife down in silence and followed her up the stoop to their oaken door.

Blaine murmured a greeting to the pleasant-faced little maid who opened to them, hoping that the storm would not break until they were alone. Thankfully he noted that his irate wife was already sweeping up the stairs to the second floor and he followed without stopping to remove his outer garments.

The maid stood staring after them; there was something in the air, and she did not make her customary inquiry, "Will there be anything else, sir?" for he seemed in a state tonight.

The lamps were alight in Marianne LeClaire's ornate bedchamber, which was divided from Harley Blaine's by her capacious dressing room. She entered quickly, slamming the carven door in his disconcerted face. Blaine stood by the door for an instant and heard her slam and lock the communicating door between their bedrooms.

He tapped tentatively, calling in a low voice, "Marianne." There was no answer. He tapped a trifle louder and raised his voice a half note, repeating his wife's name. "Let me in."

"Be damned to you!" he heard her throaty reply.

"Lower your voice," Blaine retorted. "Do you want the servants to hear it all? I've got to talk to you." When she did not answer, Harley Blaine began to bang upon the closed door and repeated in a stronger voice, "Let me in, I say. I will break this damned door down, Marianne, believe me."

He waited. There was the rasping sound of a bolt being withdrawn and the door opened wide. Marianne LeClaire stood on the threshold, her florid face livid and worn by the light of the lamps.

"If you think I am going to let you in my bed, after what you have done. . . ."

"You flatter yourself, my dear," said Harley Blaine coolly. "This is merely business. You had better let me in, for we are going to have a talk if I have to tie you in a chair to accomplish it."

Her hard blue eyes flickered with something like fear; she moved aside to let him enter, waving her white hand in a mockery of welcome.

"You give me little choice," she returned. "That is a pretty speech indeed, you . . . you adulterous bastard."

Harley Blaine closed the door softly and smiled an unpleasant smile. "Your language is quite pretty, too, my lady." With consummate skill, Blaine gave the final word such a poisonous value that Marianne LeClaire's face was flooded crimson with renewed anger.

"What do you want?"

"I want you to sit down and listen to me," he said in a steely voice. "And turn down some of those cursed lamps; we are not onstage now." Blaine glanced with distaste about the room, a garish expanse of red and gold. Its satins and brocades, Blaine reflected, smothered him. With an irritated exclamation he strode to a window and threw it open, taking deep, grateful breaths of the chill October air.

"Do you want to give me the grippe?" she shrieked and slammed the window.

Blaine opened it again, growling, "Put on a shawl then. I cannot breathe in this . . . harlot room."

"If anyone knows what harlots' rooms are like, it would be you," she spat. "And as for shawls, I leave them to your little . . . immigrant. Does she serve you potatoes under glass?"

"That is enough!" Harley Blaine thundered, and on his face Marianne LeClaire saw such a look of maddened rage that she sank into a chair, intimidated.

"Now," he said, more quietly, sitting down upon the canopied, satin-covered bed, "we had better discuss some business. Before," he added sourly, "we have no business left to discuss."

"What in hell do you mean?"

"I mean that you have gone too far with Lester Wallack. He has taken more from you than any other manager ever took from an actress." Stemming her indignant reply, Blaine held up his hand. "Wait. Be quiet. Yes, even an actress of your standing. You will play Gertrude, or he will find another leading lady."

"Not while that . . . bog-trotting bitch plays Ophelia," she answered viciously.

Harley Blaine controlled himself with effort. "How I itch to strangle you," he said at last.

"Oh, that would be very convenient, wouldn't it, my dear? Then you could wallow in her bed without interruption, couldn't you?"

"I have told you that there is nothing between us."

"What kind of fool do you take me for? Why else would you be pushing her career? Do you imagine for a moment that I believe you—that you would lift a hand for any woman who hadn't spread her legs for you?"

He sprang up from the bed. "God damn you!" he shouted. "You belong in Hallie's place, with your filthy tongue!"

Marianne LeClaire's red mouth widened into a mocking smile. "So you do go there, you . . . you devil."

Harley Blaine bit his lip. He struggled to bring himself under control and answered in a quieter tone, "Marianne, all this will serve no purpose. We have not been Romeo and Juliet for a very long time. What is relevant here is that your career—and mine—are in the balance. You have got to be more sensible. Do you want to lose it all, this house, those jewels, the dresses by Worth?"

Suddenly she rose and screamed, "*That* for Worth!" And before his astonished gaze, Marianne LeClaire began to rip at the low-cut bodice of the exquisite gown, tearing it from her body. The bodice fell, revealing her pendulous, blue-veined breasts.

"Stop it!"

"I'll stop it when you stop running after whores!" Marianne LeClaire ripped savagely at the waistline of the Worth gown. It fell in a crimson pool about her feet, and she stood before Harley Blaine naked, wearing only a narrow garter, black stockings and scarlet shoes.

"Am I not whore enough?" she shrieked and moved toward Harley Blaine, grinding her body against his. With distaste he breathed her cloying scent, and the aroma of her aging flesh assailed him. Her dyed hair rasped against his face.

A sudden image of the pearly flesh of Maeve Heron smote the husband of Marianne LeClaire. "Stop it," he said in a hushed voice. "Stop it, Marianne. You've got to come to your senses."

She stepped back and looked up at him, her flushed face piteous under her disheveled hair. "Am I not enough?" she cried.

He turned away. "Marianne, Marianne," he said hollowly. "This cannot continue."

"What do you mean?" she screamed, a fresh paroxysm of rage overpowering her.

"I want to marry Maeve Heron," he said bluntly. "If she will have me."

"Marry! Marry!" Marianne LeClaire was maddened with her anger. Looking about the room, her blue eyes fell upon a great perfume decanter on her dresser. She ran to the dresser and picked up the massive bottle in her hands, hurling it with all her might at the head of Harley Blaine.

It struck him with a thud on his forehead, the force of the blow dislodging the glass topper from the vial; he grunted and bellowed out his disgust; he was drenched in the hated, costly scent of Marianne LeClaire.

"I will never be clean of it," he muttered in an aggrieved fashion. "I will never be clean of your filthy scent. Or of you," he added coldly, as the blood trickled from the cut on his brow. "Not until you are dead"—his voice rose to a shout—"you flabby old harridan."

He strode to the door and opened it. Without bothering to lower his powerful voice, Harley Blaine shouted again, "I long to see you dead, you bitch!"

Careless of the chill upon her quivering flesh, Marianne

LeClaire snatched up a vase from the table by her bed and flung it at the departing figure of her husband.

To her disappointment, it encountered only the closing door.

In the corridor below, the maid and her friend, the cook, moved back into the shadows until they heard Harley Blaine's door slam shut above them.

When Maeve Heron arrived at the theater the following evening she was greeted by Henrietta Plum; the excited old woman was bearing three newspapers in her arms.

"Look!" cried Henrietta Plum, displaying the New York *Times*, the New York *Tribune* and the New York *Mercury*. "They have written about you in all three!"

Unbelieving, Maeve took the papers and sat down before the dressing table to devour them with her eyes; she was too excited to remove her gloves and fumbled at the pages.

"Here, let me." Miss Plum found the relevant page in the *Times* and read over Maeve's shoulder, " . . . a fresh and lovely new face . . . in the role of Phebe. . . ." The *Tribune*'s reviewer referred to Maeve's "gifts," declaring he hoped to see her in more demanding roles. And the *Mercury* spoke of her "exciting talent."

Maeve read and reread the reviews. Finally, she laid the papers down upon the table and leaned back, her glowing eyes meeting Henrietta Plum's glance in the light-splashed looking glass.

"Oh, Henny!" she cried. "Mr. Wallack has asked me to play Ophelia when they open *Hamlet* in November!"

"No!" Miss Plum leaned forward and embraced Maeve, kissing her on the cheek. "Why, that's . . that's marvelous, my dear! Can you . . . do you know the part?"

"Like the back of my hand," Maeve retorted, grinning. "I have known the play for years—my father fairly inundated me in Shakespeare as a child. And I have given it a great deal of attention lately, even before this happened!" She chuckled. "I have always found it wise to be prepared."

A knock sounded on the door, and the callboy entered, almost obscured by an enormous bunch of red-tipped white roses. "What is this?" Maeve asked.

"Ah! It is beginning," Henrietta Plum declared with satisfaction, relieving the boy of the massive bouquet. She placed it gently on the table and searched among the green-wrapped stems for the card.

"Here we are," she exclaimed in triumph, removing the stiff white florist's card from its minute envelope. "Major William Morgan, USA," Henrietta read. "William Morgan! Why, do you know who he is?"

"No," Maeve replied, taking the card from the old woman's hand, examining the graceful black strokes of William Morgan's script, like the sweep of gulls' wings on the stark white cardboard.

"He's the son of Senator Morgan . . . and was in the honor guard, my dear, in the procession of the President last spring!"

The honor guard, Maeve repeated to herself. Of course! That was where she had seen the handsome young man who had stared at her last night. The memory of her first day in America returned to Maeve. The beautiful young officer, the man with the large, dreaming eyes! And the eyes had been full of tears for the dead man Lincoln. The same eyes that had stared at her last night. How strange it was. And there was yet another memory that teased her. What?

"What does he . . . look like?" she asked Henrietta Plum.

The latter described him. "Have you not seen his picture in the papers?" she asked Maeve.

Maeve shook her head. He was the same, then, she reflected. "I have seen him," she said softly to Henrietta Plum.

"Oh, really, where?"

Maeve described to Henrietta the scene of the night before. And then she asked, "Who were the people with him, do you suppose? A priest . . . and two older ladies. One looked like . . . a kind of hawk." Maeve shuddered.

Henrietta laughed. "Oh, that could only be Mrs. Dady!" she cried. Henrietta Plum was an avid reader of the society pages.

"So his mother," Maeve said in a considering voice, "is the one who looked . . . rather silly, but not so bad. A fat lady with a great deal of hair."

"That's the one," Henrietta said. "Why do you ask, my dear?"

"Oh, no reason." Maeve shrugged and turned away. How could she tell Henrietta of her encounters with Mrs. Dady? The thought was horrifying.

"I think you like him," Henrietta said teasingly.

"He had a very . . . interesting face," Maeve answered coolly.

" 'Interesting,' is it?" cried Miss Plum. "They are one of the richest families in New York. He is the nephew of the governor."

But it was not those attributes that made William Morgan so interesting, Maeve reflected. There was something in his eyes, something so proud, yet worshiping, that she warmed to the thought of him. He was not a man, she judged, who would offer anything but marriage. And he would be tender.

Maeve's expression was thoughtful, and Henrietta studied her curiously as she helped the actress into her blue and white gown.

She was winding the blue ribbon into Maeve's black hair when another knock, this one perfunctory and quick, arrested the motions of Henrietta Plum. She gave the ribbon a tentative twist, then went to the door.

Harley Blaine, already arrayed in the flowing black wig and tunic and hose of the Duke, entered smiling. He did not remove his plumed forester's hat with its cocked brim that, drawn low over one eye, almost concealed a bandage on his brow below the bangs of the wig.

"Could I have a word with you, Miss Heron? he asked courteously. As if to compensate for not removing his hat, Blaine jestingly touched the brim, peasant-fashion, with a gesture of rustic respect.

Maeve smiled. "Will you excuse us, Henny?" Harley Blaine asked softly.

"Of course," Miss Plum replied; Maeve could not read her carefully bland expression as the dresser left them alone.

"Well, Maeve," Harley Blaine began in a bluff, nervous fashion. He stood uneasily before her, as if he did not quite know how to begin.

"Won't you sit down, Mr. Blaine?" She felt his deep unease and wanted, in her kindhearted fashion, to allay it.

He did so, but he still did not speak, merely staring at her soft face about the low-cut whiteness of her blouse. Then his tawny eyes lit upon the roses.

"An admirer?" he asked casually.

"Yes," she answered softly, wishing he would come to the point of his visit, for his unexpected presence was making her very nervous now. He had never been more than kindly and civil to her, particularly in the confines of the theater.

"Maeve," he said abruptly, paling, "I love you."

She was shocked into speechlessness. True, he had told her that evening at Hallie's—but oh, so lightly—that his interest in her was not wholly altrusitic. Yet in all these months he had never approached her in such a fashion; he had seemed to make almost a point of avoiding her.

Finally, she summoned her wits and said with gentle slowness, "Nothing has . . . prepared me for this. Why, you have never even . . . hinted of such feelings for me."

The contrast between Maeve's calmness and fresh beauty and the ugliness of the night before almost unmanned Blaine now. He colored like a schoolboy.

Taking a deep breath, he replied softly, "I know that. I know that this . . . declaration, my dear, comes as a complete surprise. I have longed for you from the first moment that we met. But there was in you a rare and beautiful quality that made my feeling different from any I have ever known before. I have longed to touch you, but have dared not; I have not wanted to . . . spoil things, you see."

"But why do you say this to me now?" she protested. "You are a married man."

"I am on the point of correcting that mistake," he said. There was a faint rustling movement in the corridor.

"What do you mean?" Maeve inquired.

"I may not be married to her much longer," Blaine replied in a firm tone. "Oh, Maeve, Maeve, I had to tell you of my feelings, no matter how you receive them. I. . . ."

He rose and bent over her, pulling her to her feet. He lowered his head, with its great plumed hat, and kissed her hard on the mouth. She struggled in his grasp.

A slight noise at the doorway startled her. Maeve looked up and met the contemptuous stare of Marianne LeClaire's dresser.

"Harley," she said in a whisper. Blaine turned and said to the woman coolly, "Well, Grace? And have you forgotten how to knock?"

Ignoring his sarcasm, the woman glared at him malevolently and replied with mock respectfulness, "Miss LeClaire is asking after you, sir."

"Very well." Harley Blaine, with enormous self-possession, said to Maeve, "We will talk of this again." And he followed the dresser, Grace, from the cubicle of Maeve Heron.

The woman turned at the doorway and gave Maeve one last look of utter hatred.

It was a week later when, on an afternoon of driving rain, Maeve told the intently listening Amelie all that had been occurring. Major William Morgan, she related, had sent her every day another bouquet of exquisite roses, each more beautiful and costly than the last—American Beauties of a vivid fuchsia that almost sang of color, roses the color of sunrise, tiny, pale-pink ones the hue of delicate flesh and some of an indescribable ivory shade that Maeve had never seen before.

Her little boardinghouse room was massed today with the red-tipped white roses like those Morgan had sent the first night.

Amelie commented, sipping the tea that Maeve had made on a small gas ring in the corner, "This Morgan is very enamored of you, my friend. And you say that he has not presented himself at the theater? How *drôle* that is!"

"It is *drôle* indeed," Maeve retorted, smiling affectionately at her pretty friend. "The fact that he does not come fascinates me."

"That, no doubt, is his intention then," Amelie judged. "Ah, well, I do not understand these Yankee men, for all they are the same under their trousers."

Maeve blushed crimson at Amelie's matter-of-factness, and the other laughed. Maeve hoped they were not all like Pearse.

After a small, companionable silence Amelie declared, "How well it all goes! You will soon be rich and famous. Even Hallie McDermott talks of your success to come."

"How is she?"

"She is splendid now; Anne-Marie is consoling her for your absence," Amelie commented wickedly.

Maeve, though shocked, could not help laughing at Amelie's mischievous expression. "Amelie," she said eagerly, "if things . . . do go well and I am able to move from here, will you come to live with me and take care of things?"

The other turned shining brown eyes on Maeve and cried,

"Oh, above all else would I like that! What a splendid maid I should make for you!"

"Not a maid," Maeve protested. "A companion and friend; a housekeeper, if you wish."

"You are too kind," said Amelie, setting down her cup and saucer on the room's one small table and taking Maeve's white hand in hers. "I can do many things for you, make you wonderful clothes. Here, for example."

Amelie picked up a fashion paper lying at the other end of the table. "You comprehend, this gown for day—its lines and draperies are wonderful indeed, but *mon Dieu*, the drabness of the colors! For you I can make a gown, imitating this one so, but where the brown pleated bib and apron trim this sad ecru color, I shall make a bib and sleeve trim, and the apron effect below, in the most wonderful shade of heliotrope; the gown proper will be the palest lavender-blue. Ah, lovely!"

Amelie's pretty face glowed with her enthusiasm. "Ah! You see the tiny little fitted waist, the emphasis of the bosom, to make you look a little fuller. And the elaborate drapery behind. Your waist will not seem three inches wide!"

Maeve smiled at her friend's infectious gaiety. "Very well, you are very kind and dear. But this time," she said firmly, "you must let me pay you for your work. I can afford it now. My salary will soon be three times what it is now. And oh, Amelie, what fun we can have then! I will move from here and take a little flat somewhere nearby. And then you can leave that wretched place and live with me. Are you willing to take the chance?"

"Take the chance! What chance have I at Hallie's? I will bless the day where there is only you to look after."

"I will have another woman to do the hardest work," Maeve said. "I want you to have a little rest . . . a little enjoyment for a change. Your life has been so hard."

Amelie shrugged, grinning. "So. But you are so good, Maeve."

Embarrassed, Maeve sought for another topic. "I have been most uneasy," she said, "since that evening that Harley Blaine. . . ."

"That one!" Amelie exclaimed. "There is going to be trouble from him . . . and I thought he would be only kind. What a fool I was!"

"But, Amelie, had it not been for you . . . and meeting Harley Blaine . . . none of this would have happened. It is just that I am uneasy about Miss LeClaire. It mystifies me that she has been so courteous since that night."

"She is up to no good, you may be certain," Amelie said wisely, nodding her sleek head. "Be very careful, Maeve."

"I have been," Maeve assured her. "I have avoided Harley Blaine wherever possible, except at actual rehearsals."

"The opening night is soon, yes? Shall we go over your lines again?"

Maeve had at first protested when Amelie had offered to cue her in her part. But she soon realized that the other girl was thrilled at this oblique contact with the glamorous world of the stage. Amelie read amazingly well. Her mistress in New Orleans, she said, had taught her to read long ago, in defiance of the law that prohibited teaching blacks that skill.

"All right." Maeve rose and retrieved the small, leather-bound book that contained the play of *Hamlet*. "Let us run over the third act, then, the first scene where Ophelia encounters Hamlet." She gave the book to Amelie.

As they read, Maeve felt the poignant irony of the lines:

> My lord, I have remembrances of yours,
> That I have longed long to re-deliver;
> I pray you, now receive them.

After Hamlet's answer, "No, not I;/I never gave you aught," Maeve's voice trembled as she replied:

> My honour'd lord, you know right well you did;
> And with them, words of so sweet breath composed
> As made the things more rich: their perfume lost,
> Take these again; for to the noble mind
> Rich gifts wax poor when givers prove unkind.
> There, my lord.

Sharp and unbidden came the memory of Fingal Pearse —his lean height, his mocking face and the penetrating quality of his ice-blue eyes under the random lock of sun-colored hair that frequently slipped down over his brow. Maeve remembered the jewels he had brought her the night of the supper after her first performance of Phebe. She had refused them.

Her reading was so absent and mechanical, to the end of the scene, that Amelie remarked it, saying, "I think, Maeve, that with your so adventuresome life, you are keeping something else from me. I think that not only Harley Blaine and this young Morgan run after you. There is another, isn't there? One you never told me about."

Maeve colored faintly and nodded. "Someday perhaps I will . . . when the memory is not so new." She smiled sadly.

But the indomitable Amelie was looking out the window. "See!" she cried, with delight. "The rain has gone, and the sun is coming again. Let us go out, then, and buy the lavender and heliotrope materials. And I will make you the wonderful gown!"

"Amelie, you are impossible!" Maeve said in a warm, teasing voice. "I must do something for *you*. All right, let us go out then, and I will buy you a trifle. Later it will be something better, I promise."

"I will be very glad when you are rich," Amelie said frankly.

Laughing again at her friend's Capricornian greed, Maeve donned her hat and cloak and followed Amelie from the little room into the burgeoning sunlight.

For days, Harley Blaine felt that he moved on thinnest ice. Waiting for the storm to break, he forced himself to be calm and treated his wife with the utmost courtesy. To his surprise, she had made no mention at all of the incident in Maeve's dressing room; on the contrary, Marianne LaClaire was the soul of graciousness at rehearsals of the new production, which had begun four days ago.

She no longer balked at playing Gertrude; her professional demeanor impressed Lester Wallack deeply, and the manager remarked one afternoon in a quiet aside to Blaine, "I was worried sick for a while. And then when you appeared with that cut on your forehead—" Wallack raised his black brows, smiling an ironic smile.

"I told you how that occurred, Les."

"And I still do not believe you. But what happened? Have you put a spell on her?"

Blaine smiled with a complacency he was far from feeling.

"It's all a matter of experience, old boy. Just a matter of experience. You have to know how to treat them."

But a sick apprehension gnawed at Harley Blaine below his self-possessed exterior. She was plotting something; he knew it. He had seen her like this before. And so he waited for her to make her move.

It came during the second week of rehearsal. The actors were still rehearsing in their street clothes, the time for costumes not having yet arrived.

Harley Blaine almost liked his wife again that day—she had a fresh look she had not worn for many a month, and her simple, costly gown, with its biblike decoration of pleated brown velvet and its soft back draperies that minimized the size of her wait, was very becoming. The ecru of the gown contrasted agreeably with the vivid auburn of her hair, which she wore dressed plainly today.

And her rehearsal was letter-perfect; they had reached the last scene of the play, when the sensuous Queen Gertrude drank from the poisoned cup and died.

At the end of the play, Lester Wallack called out, "That was splendid! But, Hamlet, there is just one thing . . . in the 'I die, Horatio' passage . . . may I show you what I mean?"

"Of course," Blaine gave his usual good-natured answer.

The other players patiently arranged themselves on chairs about the stage.

"And, Harley, I'd like to run over the scene with Ophelia now, if you don't mind." He turned from the lit semicircle of the stage and peered out into the darkened theater. "Miss Heron!" he called. "Are you there?"

Maeve's soft reply came from the dimness, and Harley Blaine saw her approaching the stage and moving gracefully up the stairs.

To his amused horror, Harley Blaine realized that Maeve Heron was wearing a duplicate of the gown so proudly displayed by Marianne LeClaire. But where Miss LeClaire's dress was brown, Maeve's was a wonderful shade of heliotrope that gave a remarkable value to her eyes; where Miss LeClaire's gown was a quiet, almost drab ecru, Maeve's garment was a delicate lavender-blue.

For a split second the cast watched the two women encounter each other. Maeve Heron blushed crimson with mortification; Marianne LeClaire, though she did not change expression, shot Maeve a malevolent look from her hot blue eyes.

Harley Blaine knew that this was more than a social trifle, involved with women's vanity. Marianne, he reflected, no doubt judged that Maeve Heron had done this on purpose to ridicule her. But looking at the younger woman's uneasy face, he was convinced that this was not so.

When the run-throughs were ended and the others had dispersed, Harley Blaine found himself onstage with Marianne LeClaire.

Looking about slyly to make certain they were unheard, his wife addressed him in a loud stage whisper which had an edge of steel. "You've wondered why I've been so quiet, haven't you?"

Harley Blaine nodded and stared into her bright-blue eyes, sickened by the cold hatred he read there.

"You and your mistress have gone too far. I will not be the butt of your jesting. I am going to ruin you, Harley, ruin you both. I have someone gathering evidence at this very moment, against you and that . . . peasant bitch. I'm going to divorce you, my dear, and I will end up with everything you own."

"What do you mean?" he cried.

Marianne LeClaire merely laughed in answer and moved away out of the light into the dimness.

Harley Blaine stood alone, staring down at the makeshift flagon from which the king poured the deadly wine—the wine meant for Hamlet that Gertrude drank by mistake. Blaine felt his heartbeat quicken, and he trembled.

Then, with an unpleasant feeling that he was being observed, Harley Blaine left the echoing stage.

Chapter 11

JENNY PYNE, the original Phebe, continued indisposed, so it was understood that Maeve Heron would play the part until the opening of *Hamlet*.

This evening in early November, the customary flowers had arrived from Major William Morgan, but this time they were anemones; vivid and perfect in flaming scarlet and royal purple, they were a splash of brightness in Maeve's dressing room. As she admired them, removing with cold cream the face of Phebe, the shepherdess, Maeve Heron wondered again about the melancholy, handsome young officer with that pleasing dash.

Why, she repeated silently, had he not come to the theater to seek her out? And was it cleverness, or merely a self-effacing temper, that kept him away? For she had to admit to herself that his continued absence titillated her until she was actually eager for his appearance. Perhaps it was, as the worldly Amelie had said, a device to arouse Maeve's interest.

So it was with some excitement, when she was leaving the theater, that Maeve heard a quiet, well-bred voice calling her name.

"Miss Heron."

He stepped then from the little passageway beside the rear stairs, his gray slouch hat in his hand. William Morgan was faultlessly attired in civilian clothes. His suit of gray fitted him with excellence; his white ruffled shirt was pristine and dazzling, set off by a wide black cravat with a fine cameo stickpin. He took her breath away.

"Major Morgan?" Maeve's reply was only half-interrogative, for there was no mistaking the aquiline face and the sensitive eyes of profound darkness.

Maeve smiled at him and added softly, "I have not been given the opportunity to thank you for the masses of wonderful flowers. Had you sent an address with them, I would have written you."

He was silent, staring. "That's very thoughtful of you," he said then a little stiffly. His tone was so conventional that a less aware woman might have been put off by it. But the delicately tuned Maeve knew at once that his courtesy masked extreme emotion. She admired his control.

Suddenly Major William Morgan laughed and said, "It is kind of you not to remark on the banality of my 'rough soldier's speech.' "

Maeve's delighted laughter answered his. She recognized the phrase from *Henry V* and savored its aptness. It was strange, she reflected, for a "rough soldier" to have sent such poetic flowers. The paradox titillated her the more; a man reared in conventional society was not generally so imaginative. She felt a tender excitement sharper than her first reaction to Pearse.

"But don't let's stand here," he said firmly. "Will you have supper with me?"

She hesitated, remembering the ill-fated luncheon with Fingal Pearse. But observing this man's gentle manners and stately appearance, Maeve answered, "I'd be happy to."

William Morgan's face lighted with a brilliant smile that made him look much younger and even more attractive than before.

He donned his gray slouch hat again, presenting Maeve with his arm. Lightly she placed her fingers on his sleeve and walked with him to the curb, where a hansom cab was waiting. William Morgan handed her in so carefully that he made her feel like some precious object cradled in velvet against jarring.

Morgan sat down beside her and said to the cabman in a voice accustomed to command, "Drive slowly." In an obliging manner the hansom driver nodded, clucked to his patient dappled horse, and they began to rattle away.

"Your flowers . . ." Maeve began.

"Would you mind if . . ." Morgan burst out simultaneously.

They stopped speaking and smiled at each other in a friendly fashion.

"I beg your pardon," he said.

"Not at all."

"You were about to say?"

"Only that your flowers have been invariably wonderful. And tonight the anemones . . ." Maeve's voice trailed off.

"Were different?" He smiled. "For a reason. This was the night I could no longer play my game and stay away."

Maeve was silent a moment, reflecting that it had been cleverness, after all. The vividness of the brighter flowers, to his subtle mind, evidently symbolized the growing heat of his feelings. What a delight this man was . . . and what an almost grotesque contrast was the arrogant Fingal Pearse!

Misreading her stillness, William Morgan's tone became serious. "Have I been . . . too presumptuous?"

"No," Maeve murmured, finding to her surprise that she meant it. Again a soft thrill lapped her body. "What was it you were going to say?"

Morgan stared down at her with his sensuous eyes, at the startling swoop of her black, winglike brows above her glowing eyes, the faint pinkness the brisk air had brought to her white face above the dark fur-trimmed pelisse. "You are not cold?" he asked.

She shook her head. It was mild for November.

Smiling, he continued to look in her eyes and admitted, "I have quite forgotten." She heard the unspoken phrase "in your nearness," warmed even more by his honesty, his unabashed feeling. It made him seem so . . . caring, for all his air of worldiness and his overpowering virility.

He must have sensed her growing warmth, for his color changed, and he said, exhilarated, "I remember now! I was going to ask your permission to drive you through the park before we dine. Do you have any objection?"

"None at all," she said with the childlike frankness that filled him with delight. "Do you mean the Central Park? I have never seen it before!"

"Never seen it! Your friends have neglected you, I fear."

"My . . . friends are not so numerous. I am new to the city, you see."

"And the country?" he inquired with gentleness, smiling down at her like an old friend.

"Ah, then you knew that," she said with an uncertain inflection.

"Certainly not through your *speech*, Miss Heron," he said hastily. "But there is a great deal of Ireland in your face and hair and manner."

The rather poetic declaration touched Maeve; how easy and good he made her feel! And to think that they were strangers, really. Yet he moved her . . . as a man.

Again it seemed that he had almost read her mind, for he said in an apologetic fashion, "I fear I may offend you by my . . . personal remarks."

"You do not offend me at all, Major Morgan. I like you very much." Maeve said with sincerity.

He was so struck with her words that for several long blocks William Morgan could find nothing to say; he stole admiring glances at her now and again or conscientiously pointed out certain buildings along the Fifth Avenue as they proceeded uptown.

"Driver, you may go a little faster," he ordered then, saying to Maeve, "I fear you may take cold."

She smiled at him, remarking upon his consideration, and the hansom rolled on at a somewhat smarter pace.

Soon they sighted the dark mass of the park, and Maeve exclaimed with surprise and delight, "Why, it is a veritable forest in the midst of the city!"

William Morgan grinned to witness her wholehearted enjoyment. "We must drive here by day, and then I can show it to you properly. Perhaps . . . tomorrow?" he asked eagerly.

She nodded. "Yes, tomorrow morning. I would like that."

"Just once around the lake," Morgan said to the driver and then explained to Maeve, "It is an immense and wonderful place. These curving driveways go all the way to One hundred and second Street, more than forty blocks from here. Tomorrow I shall show you the Mall and the ramble . . . and the Bethesda Fountain. There are even some deer and cranes!"

Maeve inhaled the leaf-scented air with delight, enjoying

the view of dark massed trees under the bright moon. Now it was her turn to smile at Morgan's boyish words.

"You love this place," she said softly.

"Yes."

"I can understand—it is so fresh, and wild . . . and beautiful." Suddenly she was sick for Ireland, for the hills of Tullaghoe; something green and wet and free in the air of the wood about her plucked at Maeve's senses. She sighed.

"Are you homesick?" Morgan asked.

"You amaze me." She stared up at him, feeling a melting warmth again.

"What do you mean?"

"This is the tenth time, at least, that you have read my thoughts tonight. Who are you, Major Morgan . . . a sorcerer disguised as a soldier?"

Her teasing voice was so seductive that William Morgan made a half-stifled sound, almost a moaning, and turned his head away.

"What's the matter?" she asked with real concern.

He turned back to her, and she could see that he was struggling for control. His dark eyes lingered on her mouth, and in them was a look of great yearning. "There is so much, Miss Heron, that I long to say to you, and are not . . . not as yet . . . that—"

Morgan stopped abruptly. "I think," he said in a wry tone, "that we had better go on to supper. We can visit the park more properly by sunlight."

"Very well," Maeve knew a peculiar disappointment. She would have liked to go on driving with him alone in the autumn night. She realized she wanted William Morgan to touch her and was almost frightened at the thought.

Throughout the pleasant dinner at a smart restaurant Maeve Heron, with cautious pride, took care to speak lightly and appear unconcerned. Never would another man humiliate her, she resolved. But in Morgan she felt a steady undercurrent of strong and tender desire.

When, delivering her at her door, he kissed her hand, Maeve could not repress an inner trembling at the touch of his lips on her flesh. And afterward, as he raised his dark eyes and held her look unswervingly, she wondered if he were the man in her dream on the *Falcon*, the prince from the land of the sun to whom that abandoned dream-Maeve had beckoned.

True to his word, William Morgan appeared early the next morning to show her "properly" through the park; daily afterward he brought her small but costly gifts that she could accept with propriety—gossamer handkerchiefs embroidered by Belgian nuns, of such frailty that it seemed a breath could tear them; chocolates so expensive that their boxes could have contained gems; and flowers, always wonderful flowers. Apparently he took great pains to send the rarest blooms he could find. Maeve's feeling for him, it seemed to her, was deepening almost every day.

And on the opening night of *Hamlet*, Maeve was almost overcome with the bouquet delivered to her now-private dressing room: rosemary and pansies, a single daisy, columbines and something, she reflected, that must be fennel.

"Henny!" she cried. "Look here! There are Ophelia's flowers from the fourth act—rosemary 'for remembrance'; pansies 'for thoughts'; 'fennel for you, and columbines: there's rue for you. . . . There's a daisy.' " Maeve quoted delightedly from her fourth-act mad scene.

"He is a most considerate gentleman," Henrietta Plum declared, nodding her grizzled head. "But there's a note, my dear. You have not read it."

Maeve unfolded the note and read, in William Morgan's graceful script, "I wish the pansies were amethysts and the daisy made of pearls. Will you tell me you will marry me, so I may be allowed to give you the jewels you deserve?"

She colored and turned away a little from the curious gaze of Henrietta Plum.

"What does he say?" Henrietta asked shamelessly.

"He wants to marry me, Henny."

"Why, my dear! And what will you tell him?"

"I don't know yet, Henny. I just don't know." Maeve stared at her reflection in the glass, strange to herself in the golden wig of Ophelia. Ophelia! Nothing else must occupy her now.

And suddenly she faced, in all its terrible enormity, the hour to come—when she would move into the flooding light to play the most important role of her stage life thus far. The terror she had known stepping into the part of Phebe was a mild anxiety compared to this night's fear!

Her teeth actually began to chatter.

Henrietta Plum clucked in sympathy, "My dear!" and with her worn hands chafed Maeve's icy hands between them.

"Henny, I am so afraid," Maeve said in a whisper she barely recognized as her own; her throat was so tight that the sound emerged as only an asthmatic croak.

"I must get out of this room!" Maeve cried, in a stronger voice. "Even if it's only for a minute."

"But, my dear child," Henrietta protested, "you know how cold and drafty it is out there—you could take cold and lose your voice. Besides, you've heard Mr. Wallack say. . . ."

"I know, I know," Maeve returned impatiently. Indeed, all the actors knew by heart the strictures of Lester Wallack on opening-night decorum. Wallack, an easygoing man in small matters, was for some reason obsessed with the idea that all the players, leading and minor, should not stir from their dressing rooms before the first-act curtain. Whether it was a superstitious fancy or a measure to give Wallack a sense of security to calm his own nerves, no one seemed to know. But the order was universally obeyed.

"Henny, Henny, I shall go mad!" Maeve cried. The tears gathered in her wide, heavily made-up eyes.

"Oh, dear, oh, dear." Henrietta Plum made a moaning sound and dabbed ineffectually at Maeve's eyes with a rouge-stained cloth. "You will ruin your makeup!"

"Just for a moment," Maeve said, wheedling. "I will be very careful; I won't let anyone see me."

"But where will you go? You can't wander in the corridors."

A sudden idea took Maeve, and she said, with relief, "Why, the prop room, of course! There shouldn't be anyone there before the first scene. In any case, Robert is my friend; he wouldn't give me away."

"Henrietta agreed silently that Robert Allen, the property man, was so devoted a slave of Maeve's that he would tell any lie for her. "Oh, dear. Very well," she said at last. "But do not be gone long; I will be in an agony of nerves until you get back. It's like—like an omen, somehow, to break the tradition."

"Nonsense, Henny!" Maeve laughed and rose. "Here," she said, "if it will comfort you I'll wrap this scarf around my throat."

"It doesn't comfort me much," Henrietta grumbled. She went to the door. Turning, she hissed conspiratorially, "All's clear. Quickly now!"

Maeve slipped through the door into the deserted corridor and, taking a grateful breath of the cold, musty air, hurried toward the prop room. On its threshold she stopped and took one last look about her. There was no one in sight, but she fancied she heard the rustling of a gown.

Attributing the fancy to nerves, Maeve shook her head impatiently and entered the unheated property room. The air was quite chill, but invigorating. Nervously Maeve wandered to the long table and surveyed the various props that would be used in the play, arranged with perfect order by the meticulous Robert; each item used earlier in the play was nearer to the door, those in the later scenes at the end of the long table near the window.

Glorying in the refreshing cold and the welcome silence, Maeve felt her terror vanishing and her pulses slow. She walked slowly, taking deep breaths, to the other end of the property table and stood admiring the colorful simulated gems of the flagons used in the final scene. One, in keeping with Gertrude's splendid velvet gown of vivid hues, was studded with imitation sapphires, rubies and amethysts.

Maeve paused before it, suddenly at ease with herself. She recalled the flowers William Morgan had sent and his urgent, poetic little note. Maeve's mouth relaxed into a smile.

Rubies, sapphires, amethysts. Maeve's smile grew wider. William Morgan had written, "I wish the pansies were amethysts."

How romantic he was! A flowing excitement, stronger than she had ever felt before, flooded Maeve all at once, making her skin feel tingly and new. Could she trust him, after all, to be as tender in intimacy as he was now? What if, in the privacy of the marriage bed, he turned to the brute that every man was, according to the cynical Amelie?

Maeve Heron knew that she could not face the question now. Absently she picked up the flagon that held the deadly wine of the last scene and turned it in her hands.

It was cold in the room, she realized in a moment, and perhaps it would be a good idea to return to the dressing room. Henny said the draft might injure her voice.

But somehow it was colder now than it had been before. How strange! Maeve was replacing the flagon with great care in its place when she heard the faint rustling sound again. Mother of God, could there be mice? She hurried toward the door.

Maeve was furtively peering about the corridor again, about to close the prop-room door without a sound, when she hard a footstep behind her.

Grace Macon, the dresser of Marianne LeClaire, was staring hard at Maeve, with an expression of triumphant malice.

Maeve felt her own cheeks heat with embarrassed color. Without a greeting, she quickly closed the door and returned on hasty feet to her own dressing room.

She prayed the hateful old thing would not mention the matter to Marianne LeClaire. In any case, it was too late now, and now Maeve Heron knew that the night was hers and that there was nothing left to fear.

The end of the fifth scene of Act IV, the occasion of Maeve's mad scene, had brought such loud applause that Henrietta Plum burst into tears of joy.

She heard the heart rending poignance of the last lines, "And of all Christian souls, I pray God. God be wi' you,'' then the great wave of applause rising and breaking and rising for the exit of Maeve Heron as Ophelia.

Under cover of the noise, Henrietta was free to cry out loudly, in the wings, "Bravo, my dear! Bravo!''

As Maeve came offstage, her golden wig disheveled for Ophelia's madness and dozens of small blossoms caught in the bright strands, Henrietta saw that her eyes were blazing with happiness. She took the slender figure in her arms, felt the nervous dew of Maeve's body through the thin white garment and urged, "Come with me now, and let us get you warm. You will take cold for certain!''

Maeve, so elated that she hardly seemed to hear, smiled widely as her fellow players in the wings spoke to her and wrung her hand in turn.

"Quiet!" the stage manager said sternly, but he could not help grinning at Maeve in silent congratulation. "Take her away, Henny!" he said with mock anguish to Henrietta Plum, who pulled at Maeve's arm to cajole her into the dressing room.

When they were closed in its warm shelter once more, Maeve leaned against the shut door with her head thrown back and her eyelids curtaining for an instant her bright eyes. Maeve laughed with delight. Then she opened her eyes and hurried to the chaise longue in sudden weariness. She lay down.

"Oh, Henny, Henny!" she said in a trembling voice. "I am so happy. No one has ever been so happy in all her days!"

"So am I, my dear, so am I," said Henrietta Plum. "I've never taken to an actress so much in all *my* days. You are a sweet child; you are very good. And tonight has proved that you are going to be up there with the finest." The old woman had taken up a clean towel and was blotting the moisture on Maeve's satiny face, gently removing the golden wig from her head.

Relieved, Maeve took out the confining pins and shook out her night-black hair.

"Mercy!" Henrietta was clucking like the fowl of her namesake. She applied the towel to Maeve's hair, rubbing it briskly to dry it out. "In a moment," she said, "you will have to stir yourself and get into a dressing gown; that shift is as wet as water."

Obediently Maeve rose and allowed Henrietta to remove the white gown and put her into a thick robe. Then she lay down gratefully again and said in a low voice slurred with exhaustion, "Thank you, thank you very much." She closed her eyes again.

"There, now," said Henrietta in a satisfied way, "you are all right for a while. You have a whole act before we must dress you again for the curtain."

Contentedly Henrietta Plum took from its hanger the elaborate third-act gown Maeve had worn for the play within a play—a delicate, glittering creation of lavender trimmed in gilt and crystal that made a lilac glory of Maeve's changeable eyes. "Properly, of course," Henrietta grumbled, "you should appear in your little white shift. But this will have to do; I will not have you take pneumonia wearing that damp gown. We will have to have a duplicate made," Henrietta suggested, smiling.

After Maeve had rested and was again arrayed in the elaborate lavender gown, her blond wig rearranged, Henrietta Plum declared, "Well, my dear, you know your cue by now."

Maeve did, by heart: amusingly, the line that would bid her to the wings to be ready for the curtain calls was Fortinbras' "Let us haste to hear it,/ And call the noblest to the audience."

William Morgan, with whom she had shared this small jest, was as delighted as she had been with its faint irony.

Maeve grinned. "The 'noblest,' " she said, "will be on time."

"Then I shall run out and watch a little of the last scene. I do love it!" Henrietta grinned. "Do you know I played Gertrude myself about a hundred years ago?"

"No! Where?"

"In a number of little English towns no one has ever heard of," Henrietta replied good-naturedly. "So, my dear, I shall see you anon."

Maeve smiled at Henrietta, giving one last glance in the mirror after the door was shut again, savoring the small silent moment before she would enter the stage once more.

Judiciously she opened the door a crack and heard the mellow voice of Fortinbras declaiming, " . . . call the noblest to the audience./ For me, with sorrow I embrace my fortune. . . ."

Moving quickly down the passage, Maeve imagined that the words of Fortinbras had a peculiar quality that she had not noticed during rehearsals. Was it uncertainty? That was strange, for not only was Fortinbras played by an actor of great poise and long standing, but this was the moment that all the cast welcomed—the last moment of the play.

Vaguely hearing Horatio's last line, ". . . lest more mischance,/On plots and errors, happen," and Fortinbras' magnificent closing speech, "Let four captains/Bear Hamlet, like a soldier, to the stage," Maeve found that she had timed it perfectly. She was in her appointed place and had time to take several deep breaths and adjust her sleeves before the drama's final words were delivered: "Go, bid the soldiers shoot."

The dead march sounded, and the soldiers bore away the bodies of Hamlet and the King, Gertrude and Laertes. A peal of ordnance caused the floor to vibrate, and hastily Maeve put her fingers in her ears.

She waited for the four "bodies" to rise from their litters. Harley Blaine leaped to the floor, quickly followed by Laertes and the King. But to the surprise of the others, Marianne LeClaire, the "dead" Gertrude, lay quite still on her pallet, extremely white. Maeve felt a chill of apprehension.

Harley Blaine, with a look of unease, cried out, "Marianne! Get up! It's time for the curtain. What's the matter—are you ill?"

Marianne LeClaire neither moved nor made an answer. Harley Blaine gave a muttered curse and moved toward her. The soldiers had set the pallet on the dusty backstage floor. "Marianne," Harley Blaine repeated more urgently. The theater's physician, Dr. McCormick, stepped forward and gently pushed Blaine aside. He had been summoned by Lester Wallack, who, as the King, was robed in a royal cloak and wore a grizzled beard and wig. Wallack stood by anxiously as Dr. McCormick bent to the splendid woman and put his ear to her breast. The doctor felt her pulse and placed a mirror before her mouth. Then he straightened, looking somber.

"Harley, she's dead," Dr. McCormick said softly.

"I knew it, I knew it!" They turned at the sound of the terrible shriek. "That woman's done it! That woman killed her!" Grace Macon, Marianne LeClaire's dresser, was pointing a shaking finger at Maeve Heron.

Maeve was so stunned by this attack, following on the heels of the doctor's incredible announcement, that she recoiled as if from a physical blow.

No one seemed to be able to take in the meaning of the screaming dresser's words, for all attention was riveted on the statuelike form of Marianne LeClaire.

Harley Blaine gave a cry and knelt by the body of his wife, repeating in a dazed fashion, "Marianne, Marianne?"

"I tell you," Grace Macon shrieked again, "*she* has done it! I saw her with the bottle!" And the woman began to sob; deep, tearing sobs that had an ugly sound in the momentary silence.

Insanely, all the while, the loud applause of the audience continued.

Lester Wallack shook his head as if to clear it and snapped, "I must get out there. Leave both curtains down," he ordered. "And shut that crazy woman up," he whispered to Henrietta Plum, who was standing slack-jawed with horror next to Maeve.

Henrietta nodded and went to Grace; taking her gently by the arm, Henrietta led the woman away.

Maeve and the other players, not knowing what else to do, stood awkwardly silent together as they heard the surprised audience murmur from behind the curtains. The appearance of the manager, not the cast, was the signal for some unusual announcement.

They heard the manager's bell-like voice rising over the descending murmur of the watchers:

"Ladies and gentlemen, I am sure you are puzzled at the absence of our magnificent cast; you are wondering why one old grizzled man"—polite laughter—"is taking up the space that should be given over to younger, more handsome men and lovely women . . . to fine artists who have brought you tonight's production of Shakespeare's *Hamlet*."

At first Maeve was surprised at Wallack's circumlocutions; always a man of a very few and exquisitely chosen words, he was wandering in his speech. Then it came to her: He was still suffering deeply from shock; also, he might be playing for time, trying to decide what to tell the audience. Maeve's admiration for the manager increased a thousandfold.

She herself felt anew the impact of the shock upon herself; her legs were trembling so she feared she would faint. Harley Blaine's sensitive glance read this, and he led her to one of the elaborate thronelike chairs upon the stage and sat her down.

After a minute pause they heard Wallack continuing. "I am here alone, ladies and gentlemen, to share with you some very grave news indeed." He paused again, and Maeve's heart thudded.

"Marianne LeClaire," she heard Wallack continuing with slow, painful effort, "is . . . dead."

The great collective gasp that went up from the listeners sounded, "Ohhhh," like a hoarse wind echoing in an empty cavern. It was one of the most terrible sounds Maeve Heron had ever heard, and hearing it, she knew a sudden grief for the dead woman. All her old anger at Marianne LeClaire evaporated as quickly as snow in the sun.

After the sighing had lessened, Lester Wallack resumed. "Miss LeClaire was apparently taken ill with great suddenness. Therefore, ladies and gentlemen, I have appeared alone to make this sad announcement. Remembering her beauty and her gifts, I can only say, in Shakespeare's words, 'She should have died hereafter.' "

There was a long hushed silence.

Lester Wallack said simply then, "Good night."

As he emerged again through the steel-gray velvet curtains, his face mushroom-pale with shock and wet with sickly perspiration, Maeve Heron heard the audience's leaving—a subdued murmur filled the theater as the people filed out.

"Why," cried Harley Blaine to Wallack, "did you tell them that? Couldn't you have said that she was ill, for the sake of God?" Blaine's voice had a touch of hysteria; it was almost broken.

"Harley, Harley," Wallack said reproachfully, putting a sympathetic hand on Blaine's broad shoulder, "what purpose would that have served? How do you think it would be received if I had lied about such a matter . . . and then the newspapers came out with the real story?"

"Newspapers!" Blaine repeated the word as if it were part of a foreign tongue with which he was unfamiliar. "But—"

"The police will have to be called, you know," Wallack said quietly. He turned to George Berkeley, the actor who played Laertes, and asked, "Has that been done?"

"Not yet," said Berkeley. "We were waiting for your advice."

Wallack's snapping eyes thanked the players for their loyalty, but he said tersely, "Thanks. Call them now. If a man is not at the corner, send Jesse to the station on Twelfth Street."

Berkeley nodded and moved away.

"Now," said Wallack, turning to the others like a general to his troops, "John and Avery, leave the . . . leave Miss LeClaire where she is. The police will require that, I suppose."

"Why are you calling the police?" Harley Blaine demanded, his generally controlled voice sounding thin.

"Harley." Wallack strode to the disheveled Blaine and

took him by the arm. "You are in no condition to talk of anything now. Go with Avery and John. There is some brandy in my dressing room."

Reluctantly Harley Blaine followed the manager's suggestion, moving off the stage with a stumbling gait.

"And cast," Wallack raised his voice, as if this were a rehearsal, "please go to your dressing rooms and stay there until the police arrive, would you? I'm sorry about this—sorry about the curtain calls"—a tight smile creased his white, wry face—"but you . . . you understand."

Suddenly the manager's own control seemed about to desert him; his shapely mouth, under the thick black mustache, trembled with strain. The cast obediently began to disperse in various ways.

Lester Wallack stared for a moment at the goblet from which Marianne LeClaire, as the character Gertrude, had drunk.

"And don't touch anything," he said briefly. He sat down alone in one of the chairs to await the Metropolitan Police.

Chapter 12

HENRIETTA PLUM was still with the distraught Grace, so it was Maeve herself who removed the blond wig of the ill-fated Ophelia in the welcome quiet of her dressing room. She hesitated over the fastenings of the elaborate gown; the police would be here soon, she reflected, and would want to question them all. She had best stay dressed for the moment.

Maeve sank down on the chair before her dressing mirror and looked at the face staring back at her—the green eyes were wide with consternation, and her makeup was thick and smudged from the clammy dew of her nervous sweat. Absently Maeve began to remove the makeup with cold cream and freshen herself with a damp towel and cologne.

What on earth, she reflected, had that mad woman meant by accusing her? In spite of the warmth of the little room, Maeve was overcome with a quick chill and shivered convulsively. She rose and took her dressing robe from her closet, wrapping it around herself over the elaborate costume.

She was in the midst of brewing tea when a soft knock called her to the door. William Morgan, in faultless evening dress, stepped into the room to take her hands in his. His tender face was unsmiling, but his melting eyes reassured her.

"William!" she cried. "Oh, William!"

Then she caught sight of the man behind him, a tall, stern-looking man in a dark, ill-fitting suit; he had light-gray eyes that were piercing and bright and ugly rust-colored hair.

"Miss Heron?" he addressed her in a rumbling voice.

"May I trouble you for a moment? I am Inspector Argis of the Metropolitan Police."

"'Come in," she replied nervously, standing aside to let the men enter. William Morgan followed the inspector.

"Major, er . . . Morgan," Argis began. "If you will excuse us. . . ."

"I'll remain, if you don't mind," Morgan said calmly.

"May I ask, in what . . . capacity?"

William Morgan looked at Maeve: "Miss Heron's fiancé," he replied quietly. To Morgan's relief, Maeve did not comment but carried it off with a cool half-smile at Argis.

"I see." Inspector Argis stared at them in turn with his sharp light-gray eyes. "Very well then. Shall we all sit down?"

He gestured Maeve and Morgan to seats; instead of choosing one of the straight chairs, Morgan sat close to Maeve on the chaise longue. Argis sat by the dressing table.

"This is all routine, Miss Heron," the inspector began, rubbing his chin with a freckled hand. "I have already ascertained from Mr. Wallack the . . . particulars."

The last word had a sinister ring; Maeve stirred nervously. William Morgan took her hand.

"But as I was on my way to you, I was accosted by a woman called Grace Macon, who made a most vehement statement—that she saw you in the property room handling the bottle from which Miss LeClaire's wine was poured in the last scene."

William Morgan made an impatient movement and opened his mouth as if to speak, when Maeve cried, "Of course I handled the flagon! I picked it up without thinking what it was; I was thinking of something else. I was just . . out having a breath of air and happened to pick the flagon up while I was in the prop room."

"A breath of air, Miss Heron, in the *property* room?" Argis' voice was heavy with sarcasm. "But why the property room?"

"Don't take that tone, Inspector," William Morgan snapped. "I heard the ridiculous accusation of this Macon woman. She is a fool. What do you mean by assuming this . . . accusatory tone?"

"I beg your pardon." Argis reluctantly altered his tone; now it was bland and neutral. He was keenly aware of

Morgan's position, of the friendship between his father, the Senator, and the commissioner of the Metropolitan Police. "We must follow every line of inquiry in a sudden death." To Maeve he said more gently, "Why the property room? It seems a strange choice."

"Not at all," Maeve answered coolly. "It is unheated . . or less heated . . . than the dressing rooms, and I was feeling the need of some . . . brisker air to relieve my opening-night nerves." She smiled at Argis. Slowly he smiled back.

Morgan rose from the chaise and looked down at Argis. "Miss Heron is very tired, as you can see, Inspector. It has been a horrible evening. Can you not continue your questions another time?"

"There are a few more questions, Major Morgan," Argis replied obdurately.

"I think they should be put in the presence of my attorney," Morgan insisted.

"Isn't it a little early for that, Major Morgan?" Argis' voice was heavy with meaning.

"I don't like your implication, Inspector," Morgan retorted quickly.

"Please, William," Maeve said softly, putting a hand on Morgan's black sleeve. "I will answer any questions the inspector puts; I have nothing to hide."

"I know that, my dear," William Morgan said in a tender voice, "but I will not have you badgered. I really think you had better wait until my lawyers are on hand."

" 'Badgered,' Major Morgan?" Argis repeated with irritation. "Under the circumstances, Miss Heron had better have an attorney present. I suggest you retain him as soon as possible. Please have him accompany Miss Heron to headquarters tomorrow morning at ten." Argis could not conceal his anger.

"Miss Heron," Morgan returned coldly, "will not vist headquarters, Inspector. You may send someone to her home if you so desire. I will give you the address."

"Very well." Argis was tight-lipped. He took a small notebook and a pencil from his pocket. Morgan glanced at Maeve and smiled. She nodded at William Morgan, and the latter gave Argis the address of Maeve's boardinghouse.

Involuntarily Argis' sandy brows raised when Morgan repeated the modest address. The inspector wrote it down, closed his notebook with a snap and replaced it with the pencil in the pocket of his shapeless suit. Wishing them an abrupt good-night, Argis strode from the room and shut the door with a soft slam.

William Morgan, his dark eyes full of concern, sat down again by Maeve and took both her hands in his. He raised them to his lips and, after turning them over, stared at them smilingly and kissed the palms.

"I hope you will forgive me," he said softly, "for saying that I was your fiancé without your permission. I had a very good reason for doing so, it seemed more . . . politic at this moment."

"You know best in this," she said submissively. Then she smiled widely and added, "Besides, you were only saying what is true."

"Maeve!" he cried. Unbelief was struggling with elation in his lean, handsome face. "Do you mean that you accept me? Can you mean it?"

She nodded. With an exclamation of joy, he knelt on the dusty floor before her and bent his head to kiss the hands on her lap. "Maeve, oh, my love," he whispered. "You will never regret it!" He looked up at her then with glowing eyes. "All this—horror, this foolish mistake—will all be cleared up by morning, you'll see. I'll take care of it all, my darling."

He rose and sat beside her. Taking her face in his hands, he kissed her for the first time on the mouth, and the kiss was the most magical thing she had ever known—demanding, sweet, passionate and tender all at once. She was shaken. His eyes were alight at her response, but he said, "You must be very tired. I'll leave you while you change; then I'll take you home . . . or wherever you want to go."

"I would rather be with you," she said softly. He took her in his strong arms and kissed her again, hungrily and long. The kiss took her breath, and she swayed in his arms.

He laughed with delight at his own helpless ardor and her quick answering feeling. "If I don't go now, I shall never leave." With one last adoring look at her, he closed the door.

Maeve sat down before the dressing mirror, amazed at her own lightning decision to accept him. It had happened in almost an instant, her warm certainty that she loved him beyond all other men. The deep excitement she knew at his touch, in his nearness, made her old feeling for Fingal Pearse seem like the yearning of a child. Grace Macon's wild accusation was probably the "misunderstanding" William judged it.

How sweet were his embraces, the kiss of his mouth! No man so sensitive, with his experience of women and the world—he was known in New York society, Henny said, as "quite a ladies' man"—could ever make love the mockery that Fingal Pearse had done. No, love with William could only be as magical as the caress of his mouth!

Maeve Heron went to meet the man she had promised to marry, trying to forget the terrible sight of Marianne LeClaire, lying so still in her queenly robes upon the pallet.

Three hours later Inspector Andreas Argis lay back wearily in his chair at headquarters and said to James Lock, his aide, "I think there's something funny about Blaine and that Heron woman, Jim."

James Lock's blue Irish gaze turned to the weary face of his chief. He thought for the hundredth time how strange it was to be commanded by a Greek; and a red-haired Greek at that! Andreas Argis had come up the hard way, he reflected, in a department full of Irishmen. It was almost unheard of for a man of Argis' ethnic origin to rise in the police. He had always puzzled and intrigued James Lock, but soon Argis had won his subordinate's deep respect, for Argis was a brilliant man with almost a mind-reading ability. Therefore, now when Argis said there was something "funny" about Blaine and the Heron woman, Lock was inclined to go along.

"How's that?" he asked.

"Well, I interrogated the whole lot—from the manager to the callboy. And from every one of them I got a kind of picture of Blaine and the girl: Wallack let slip that Blaine had got her employed at the theater; the callboy overheard Blaine and LeClaire quarreling about the girl. I interviewed the cook and the maid at the Blaine-LeClaire house, and both of them testified that Blaine and his wife fought like cats and dogs all the time.

"Most of all," Argis continued, "the fact that Heron was in the property room, where she had no business to be, interests me. As a matter of fact, one of them told me that Wallack absolutely forbids the actors to leave their dressing rooms before the curtain on opening night—a kind of superstition, or something, I suppose—and this was Heron's first big part. So it doesn't make sense somehow."

"And yet she is engaged to this Morgan, you said, the Senator's son?" Lock asked.

"Yes. On the face of it, that would destroy her motive; in other words, why kill a rival when you are no longer interested in the rival's husband? But this engagement could be a device."

"How do you figure that?"

"Why, to make us conclude exactly what we almost did! To destroy her motive for killing LeClaire!"

James Lock's snub-nosed face was alight with admiration. "You think of the damnedest things," he said, chuckling. "That would not have occurred to me in a million years."

Argis commented silently that this was the reason he himself was an inspector and Jim Lock still a lieutenant. "But the clincher, Jim," he continued, "was what the Macon woman overheard one day during rehearsals—LeClaire telling Blaine that she was going to ruin him and the Heron woman, that she was gathering evidence."

"I'd like to see that evidence."

"We will, soon enough. I'm seeing her investigator the first thing in the morning. We might learn some very interesting facts."

"And you think the propman's in the clear?" Lock asked.

"Well, not yet, of course, but it looks like it. He wasn't even there last night—his wife was giving birth—and he has no clear motive. His assistant could unwittingly have put the poison there himself. But Blaine, remember, had access to it on the stage."

"As did others," Lock interjected.

"Others," Argis said dismissively. "Blaine and Heron had the *motive*, Jim."

"Andreas," Lock said hesitantly, "do you think you might be jumping the gun?"

Argis looked at his subordinate from weary, reddened eyes and answered tersely, "No."

"There's going to be hell to pay, with Morgan involved," Lock commented.

"Maybe. He'll have the best lawyers money can buy. But I think they did it—Heron and Blaine." Argis spoke in that stubborn manner Lock knew too well. He almost pitied the

Heron woman and this fellow Blaine, with Andreas Argis set against them.

A newer immigrant than Lock, the Greek inspector felt a rage against the wealthy Morgan that was also, Lock knew, the rage of the have-not against the have.

"He wasn't there last night, you said." Lock spoke with wry amusement. "Do you realize that today is another day?"

"Too well." Argis' deep, rumbling voice was thick with exhaustion. "Let's go."

As they rose and Lock turned out the lights, he wondered if Argis' conviction of the actors' guilt would have been so strong were it not for the fact of William Morgan.

Relations between Senator Ransom Morgan and his son, William, had never been easy. Now, as he looked up from his gleaming desk in the library of the Morgan mansion, it seemed to the portly Senator that his son was about to tell him something unwelcome.

Ransom Morgan divined this from William's defensive, stubborn stance—the Senator thought, just as it had been that afternoon so long ago! The Senator's memory turned to the day that his son had first defied him with an especial vehemence, crying out, "I will not do it, Father. I will not do it if you kill me."

The issue, Ransom Morgan recalled, had been that of the hunt, and William Morgan, turning his sickened gaze from the bleeding pheasant in Ransom Morgan's hand, had refused to engage in the hunt. From that day the son and father had grown farther and farther apart. The years had not closed the gap.

Now, studying his son's lean face and feeling dark eyes, Ransom Morgan recalled himself to the business at hand, saying, "Yes, son? You wanted to see me?"

"Yes. May I pour you a glass of sherry?"

"Apparently you think I am going to need it," Ransom Morgan returned in a dry tone.

"You are," William Morgan said brusquely.

Without a reply, Ransom Morgan took from his son's hand the proffered goblet of Amontillado; for once its savor and bouquet were lost on the lusty old man. He sipped at the russet wine perfunctorily and rose from his desk chair.

"Father, perhaps you had better sit down."

"Good God, boy! What is it now? You are not a gambler; have you gotten a woman into difficulties?" The Senator's handsome face was full of consternation. The boy was always after some woman, he thought.

"Sit down, Father," William Morgan repeated in a low voice.

Ransom Morgan sank down into one of the silken armchairs flanking the hearth with its crackling fire and set his goblet down on the claw-footed table between the chairs.

William Morgan remained standing.

At last he said, "The woman I love . . . the woman I am going to marry . . . is in deep trouble, through no fault of hers or mine."

"Trouble!" the Senator ejaculated. "Alice? How could that be?"

William frowned and drew up the companion chair to the small table. He replied, "It is not Alice Van Renssalaer of whom I speak. She is a boring fool."

"What? I was given to understand—"

William Morgan drained his glass of sherry and set the goblet on the table. "No commitment was ever made, Father. There is nothing to reproach myself with. You have misunderstood if you thought otherwise. It's Mother's idea."

"Your mother . . . Mrs. Dady. . . ."

"Damn Mrs. Dady!" William slammed his fist upon the table, causing the fragile goblets to dance.

"Control yourself," Ransom Morgan ordered sternly. "Tell me at once what this is about! Who is this . . . woman in trouble?"

"Her name is Maeve Heron. She—"

"Maeve Heron! God above, boy! That actress accused of the LeClaire murder? You must be insane!" Ransom Morgan sprang to his feet, his florid look emphasized by the wine, the heat of the fire and his raging disapproval.

"Please, Father. You know what the doctor said." William Morgan had risen, too, and touched his father on the arm.

"The doctors can all go to the devil!" shouted Ransom Morgan. "You have lost your mind! Why, to think of bringing disgrace to our name in this manner—it is enough to drive me to distraction!"

The Senator strode rapidly about the room, running his hands through his thick white hair.

"Be reasonable, Father. As a lawyer yourself you know better than to condemn her out of hand."

"That is not the point." Ransom Morgan wheeled to face his son; the dark eyes that in his son were large and passionate were burning coals of rage above the Senator's mottled red cheeks. "The point is that you are going to marry this . . . nobody, this . . . murderess . . . and involve the Morgan family name in her notorious affairs!"

"I had hoped," said William Morgan, "to discuss this with you rationally. I have retained Whitney Farlow in her defense—"

"Whitney Farlow! Why, his fee must be *ruinous*!"

"That is my affair; the fee, after all, is being paid from my private funds that Grandfather left me. That is not a matter that needs to be discussed," William said repressively. "What does need to be discussed is the fact that I am going to marry Maeve Heron. If you do not receive her as a daughter in this house, then you need not receive me ever again. I will pack now and be gone before dinner."

"Then go and be damned to you!" Ransom Morgan shouted.

"Ransom. William." They turned at the sound of the soft voice. William Morgan's mother stood on the threshold of the library, her hands outstretched in appeal to them both.

"Stay out of this, Fanny," the Senator snapped.

"I'm sorry, Mother." William Morgan went to her and kissed her on the cheek. "I have no choice. She's the only woman for me."

The younger Morgan strode from the room, and hurrying after him, his mother saw him running up the curving stairs to the second floor.

"Ransom, how could you?" she cried and began to weep.

Awkwardly Ransom Morgan put a heavy arm about his wife's plump shoulders and said in a consoling way, "Don't worry, Mother. I'll see to that young woman myself."

"What on earth do you mean?"

"I mean that she is guilty of a crime and must be punished for it. And when she is convicted, William will be safe again."

Horrified, Fanny Morgan stared at her husband, smiling triumphantly below the portrait of Septimus Morgan, his eyes glittering in the light of the orange flames.

* * *

The skilled argument and strong influence of the famous attorney Whitney Farlow had made it possible for him to obtain for Maeve her temporary freedom under bail, and the large personal fortune of William Morgan had afforded it.

Therefore, this gray morning, as the courtroom arguments began, Maeve Heron reflected that she had a great deal to be thankful for. She turned from the defense table and sought the face of William Morgan. Yes, he was there! Maeve smiled at him, and her heart lifted.

She glanced down at the exquisite ring on the fourth finger of her left hand—it was a Brazilian aquamarine of the most brilliant blue-green and of stunning clarity, surrounded by twinkling blue-white diamonds. It was the one item of adornment she had clung to steadfastly, while following all of Farlow's other directions to the letter. Her hair was plainly dressed, and she was attired in a modest dark-blue skirt and jacket of fine but dull material; her ivory shirtwaist blouse was buttoned to her throat and tied with a narrow necktie of soft cherry red.

Maeve Heron altered the position of her chair a little so she might look again at William Morgan. He was gazing back at her with intensity, and she saw that his mouth was set sternly and that new lines of strain had formed between his brows and around his mouth. Nevertheless, he smiled at her and nodded with an almost jaunty air to reassure her.

She turned her head again, winking back the tears that were gathering. He had made the last few days so festive that there were long moments when she almost forgot the shadow of the accusation and the trial. William Morgan had moved into a nearby hotel and was on hand every morning to escort Maeve on shopping expeditions, to accompany her to Farlow's office and later to the theater, where, as Henrietta Plum said cynically, because of the scandal, the play was doing "land-office business."

Harley Blaine's bail had been provided by his own funds and those of Lester Wallack. Maeve glanced to her left, where Blaine sat with his own attorney. The actor's very mane of hair seemed subdued and drab in the rain-dimmed light; he rarely met Maeve Heron's eyes anymore. She felt a sharp compassion for Harley Blaine, noting his dull gaze fixed on her glittering ring. Well, there was no help for it.

Maeve looked again among the spectators beyond her,

finding Amelie in the second row. The beautiful mulatto smiled and nodded; she was smartly but modestly dressed in a lovely suit of ivory and cocoa brown, no doubt of her own creation. Maeve smiled warmly, thinking how glad she was that Amelie was with her now.

William had abetted the move, saying that it disturbed him for Maeve to be alone at night in her anxiety. Once again Maeve Heron's whole being warmed at the realization of his generosity; she had told him everything, the story of her residence at Hallie McDermott's and of her escape.

She recalled his look of pain and his words, almost Harley Blaine's, "What sacrilege, for you to live in such a place!"

Maeve was turning from her contemplation of Amelie when the sight of a tall, striking-looking man flickered on the edge of her vision. She half turned to encounter the penetrating stare of Fingal Pearse.

It had been said that Whitney Farlow of Boston had never lost a case. Now, as he rose from his chair at the table of the defense and sauntered toward the jury, addressing them in his elegant drawl, the spectators could see why this was so.

There was in Farlow's bearing such utter self-possession that he appeared to be only half attending the business at hand. But those who watched him closely could see the alertness in his bearing, the fine-drawn sensitivity that made him aware of the slightest nuance of feeling in judge and jury.

His stately bearing dazzled the jury, it was clear, against that body's will; his dark-gray suit with its faultless fit was set off by a lighter-gray shirt of a shade and fineness none of the jury had ever encountered; at Farlow's neck was a sculptured maroon cravat. His proud face below its noble head of silver hair might have been that of an ancient emperor carven on a cameo. He exuded probity.

"The defense," he said, and his mellow voice boomed to the ears of every listener, without ascending, without effort, "calls Grace Macon."

The dresser, scuttling forward to climb the stand, was far from prepossessing. She was attired in rusty black, and her small, crablike eyes peered out with malice from under the brim of her ugly black hat with its comically ascending single feather.

Whitney Farlow smiled at her warmly, as if she were a

young beauty, and said in a confidential, easing tone, "Ah! Miss Macon. Or surely it is *Mrs.* Macon."

Farlow's heavy jocosity disarmed the dresser. She simpered and bridled, replying, "Mrs. Macon," but the picture was so absurd that one of the younger jurors tittered.

The judge frowned repressively, and the young juror subsided.

"Well, Mrs. Macon, why don't you tell us again what you so helpfully told our fine Inspector Argis?"

The tone of his question utterly rattled Grace Macon.

"I thought you was *her* lawyer," Grace Macon remarked in a puzzled fashion, shooting a malicious glance at Maeve Heron. At this the tittering juror could no longer contain himself, and he laughed aloud.

The judge's gavel tapped, and he said sternly, "I will not warn the juror twice of his lack of decorum. And, counselor, the witness' point is well taken. I suggest you restrain your insidious comments."

"I beg the pardon of the court," Whitney Farlow answered coolly, half smiling in the direction of the jury. Annoyed, the judge saw that the jurymen were already under the spell of Farlow; his bizarre approach was fascinating them, as always.

"Mrs. Macon," Farlow said tenderly to the witness, "please repeat to us what you said to Inspector Argis."

With relish, Grace Macon began to repeat the statement. The statement was full of malice and contradiction, which Farlow skillfully pointed up. She concluded, "And that woman was just like the one that took my Alf away from me."

"Alf?" Farlow questioned softly.

"Me husband, in the old country."

"Ah! What a pity! And why don't you tell us what happened to that terrible woman who took your Alf, Mrs. Macon?"

The attorney's silky question was so sympathetic, so kindly that the foolish Grace Macon fell at once into the trap. She grinned unpleasantly.

"Had a accident, she did," Grace Macon blurted.

"An 'accident,' Mrs. Macon?" The inverted commas in Farlow's voice were so clear the most unsubtle of the listeners could hear them.

"Objection!" the prosecuting attorney was on his feet.

"This line of questioning is immaterial, irrelevant!"

"If Your Honor please, I intend to show its extreme relevance," Whitney Farlow said, unruffled.

"Very well, then, Mr. Farlow. Objection overruled. Proceed."

"Tell us about the 'accident,' Mrs. Macon," Farlow said in a wily tone to the now-uneasy dresser.

She was stubbornly silent.

Interested, the judge leaned forward and said, "The witness will answer the question."

"She was . . . scalded, she was," Grace Macon replied in an almost inaudible voice.

"Speak up, please," Farlow ordered briskly.

"I said she was scalded!"

"Ah? And how did that happen?"

"She got in the way of hot water from me teapot."

"Come now, Mrs. Macon," Whitney Farlow said, and his voice was no longer soft and silken. " 'Got in the way'? Surely she wasn't small enough to fit in the spout of your teapot!"

This was too much for the jury and most of the spectators. Even Maeve Heron and William Morgan had to smile, and the judge himself, while not actually smiling, relaxed his mouth into the simulation of one.

"Mr. Farlow!" he said, however, in a scandalized manner.

"You know what I mean!" shrieked Grace Macon.

"No, Mrs. Macon, I do not know what you mean. My acquaintance with domestic matters is not wide. You must tell me. The fact is that you threw a teapot full of scalding water at this young woman and disfigured her face for life, is that not so? And that your husband suggested you leave the country to avoid the vengeance of this poor young woman's brothers?"

"Yes, yes!" Grace Macon cried out.

"And I further state that you served a term in jail for your assault, Mrs. Macon."

"Yes, what of it?" The dresser's malicious face was twisted with hatred. "I'd do it again, I would and wish I could do it to that . . . hussy!" She pointed at Maeve Heron, who turned paper-white.

"You may step down, Mrs. Macon," Farlow said coldly. "I have no further questions. I hardly think we will be further aided by the testimony of a convicted felon, which is inadmissible in any court of law. Your Honor, I move that this witness be dismissed from further participation in this trial and that all her testimony be discounted and removed from evidence.''

"Granted."

Maeve, studying the jury, saw with a feeling of hope that they were looking back at her with new eyes.

As the court was recessing, Whitney Farlow said to her in a low voice, "I am sorry to have you put through that unpleasantness, but as you see, we have won a major victory."

Maeve nodded and smiled at him. "I am entirely in your hands," she said. Indeed, William Morgan had spoken to her in glowing terms of this famous man—Farlow, he said, won the respect of judges by his encyclopedic knowledge of the law, charmed juries with his brilliant tactics and had earned the respect of the world at large through his constant victories.

Nevertheless, Maeve's alternate strain and elation had left her feeling very weak, so it was with gratitude that she saw William Morgan approaching her, followed by the indignant Amelie. Blaine stared at them, then moved slowly away.

"My dear," said Morgan, "we will have time for a nice long luncheon. You look so pale; I think you can use a glass of wine. Are you all right?"

"I am always all right when you are here," Maeve whispered.

Morgan's lean, handsome face lit up; he took her arm.

"I think I will put the *voudon* on that old witch," Amelie said angrily. Maeve and William Morgan smiled.

Amelie leaned to Maeve and whispered in her ear, "Hallie sends you her love. She said she would serve you best by staying away."

Maeve was so touched she felt she was on the point of tears.

"Excuse us, Amelie," Morgan said quietly, "but I have something very important to take up with this lady."

"But of course, M. Morgan." Amelie gave him a satiric curtsy and joined the departing spectators.

Maeve asked Morgan, "What is this matter of such importance?"

"We'll discuss it at luncheon." Morgan's response was

solemn. He gazed down at her with his heart in his eyes.

Maeve wondered at his words; then, over his shoulder, she caught sight of the man she had all but forgotten in the rush of events. Fingal Pearse, the captain of the *Falcon*, was standing in a far corner of the emptying court, staring fixedly at her and William Morgan.

Maeve Heron knew the distant cold of a nameless apprehension.

Chapter 13

WHEN THEY emerged from the courthouse into the drizzly air, Maeve was thankful for the heartening red of her waterproof cloak from Stewart's, the snugness of her scalloped boots that she had bought at J. & J. Slater's. The subdued colors the wily Farlow insisted on for courtroom wear oppressed Maeve's spirits, especially in the gray November weather. She looked away from Blaine and his attorney, standing under the portico.

William helped her into the waiting carriage and said, "We will have the leisure to drive uptown to Delmonico's; I think you need a really good luncheon."

"You are so kind to me," she said softly, looking up at him as he settled beside her on the cushions. Maeve took Morgan's hand.

As always, a new light came into his melancholy eyes, and he pressed her small gloved hand tightly between his own, calling carelessly to the driver, "Delmonico's," not taking his dark look from her green one all the while.

"Maeve," Morgan began in a slow, gentle voice, "would you mind if I asked you something?"

"Anything," she said with simple trust, and he squeezed her hand.

"Who is the . . . man I saw you with that night, the one who was in the courtroom today?"

Maeve's heart thudded. The moment she had dreaded was soon to come. "His name is Fingal Pearse," she said, nervousness making her voice sound high and thin in her own ears.

William Morgan was silent—waiting, she was aware, for her to go on. When she said no more, he commented with tender reproach, "I have learned his name. But what is he to you?"

Morgan was staring straight ahead with an anxious expression. Maeve studied his fine profile in the gray glare of the rainy light, realizing all at once how dear he had become.

Silently she vowed, *But I shall tell him. Yes, I shall tell him.* For she was too proud, too much in love as well, to lie. *No matter what it costs me,* she reflected darkly, *I shall tell William Morgan the truth!* All the stubborn pride of Shane O'Neill, the wild independence of Floure, her mother, rose in Maeve Heron.

She raised her head, and still staring at William Morgan's cameolike profile, she said clearly, "William, I do not come to you . . . untouched."

William Morgan turned his stately head then and looked down at Maeve, exclaiming, "Why, my dear, if you are referring to your marriage . . . I hardly think—"

"I am not referring to my marriage, William." Maeve's green gaze was steady, holding his dark one. "My husband, Michael, was . . . unable to be a husband to me, you see. Fingal Pearse has been my lover."

As she said the last words, Maeve's heart was beating so strongly that she could hear it whirring in her ears, and it made her voice tremble and break.

She saw William Morgan turn quite pale. Without touching him, she sat still and waited.

At last he said in a queer, choked voice. "I see. Do you . . . love him?" It was as if he had to force the question out.

"No," said Maeve Heron. Then she repeated, "No, I do not," in a stronger voice. And with the saying of it, she knew deeply that it was true. She did not love Fingal Pearse. He haunted her, she had once been obsessed with him, as with a distant melody she could not quite hear, he had been a drumming in her blood that she felt always pounding, in spite of his cruelty, despite the strictures of her reason; but it was completely over, she knew now. It had ended when she first looked into William Morgan's eyes.

"If you wish to release yourself from our engagement,"

Maeve said in a steady voice, "I'll understand. It's over . . . but I had to tell you; there must be only truth between us."

She took a shallow breath and waited.

After what seemed a long moment, William Morgan bent his head; he took her gloved hands, which had formed themselves into small fists, and gently uncurled her fingers and kissed them one by one.

"Thank you for that. I admire you more than any woman I have ever known. To part from you would be my sentence, not my release. But I will never share you with another man, from this day forward. You must understand that."

Maeve looked up at him and saw that his dark eyes retained a hint of pain and anger and wounded pride; still, a gleam of admiration for her struggled with the other emotions. He had never looked so desirable. A strong new feeling overwhelmed her, and she cried out passionately, "Oh, William, I love you, I love you so very much."

"Maeve!" A jubilant wonder filled his voice, and she saw that his whole face was alight with it; Maeve was almost frightened of the power of his love. Her words had transformed him; careless of the passersby along the busy avenue who could see them clearly through the broad windows of the carriage, William Morgan took her in his arms and kissed her passionately, again and again.

"Maeve, Maeve," he said, when they had drawn apart, "marry me tomorrow!"

"Tomorrow!" she repeated, laughing softly. "But, William, we do not yet know—" She paused, reluctant to speak of the threat of her conviction.

"Don't speak of that!" he urged her. "We know all that we need to know—that we love each other. And now, more than ever, you need me, Maeve. You know you do."

She heard the truth in his pleading, smiling at his eagerness. *Yes, yes,* she thought, *I do need him now!* And he laughed triumphantly, seeing the dawning assent in her face.

"You will then, you will?" William Morgan's rapture touched her almost unbearably. She nodded. "I will arrange all the matters this afternoon," he said with quick excitement. "And we will have, at least, the weekend." Maeve smiled at the man who was like no other man she had ever known, the one human being who seemed to love her as Shane had done, or Thomas Rossar-Mescro.

And she walked by his side into the elegant haven of Delmonico's, her slender hopes rising.

Judge Patrick Monaghan gave a low curse; the cabby's spirited horse had overshot the entrance to the Union Club on Fifth Avenue and was almost at the door of the church.

"Hold hard, Your Honor," called the Irish teamster, chuckling, "we shall get you there all warm and dry." The rain was a downpour now, the judge noted with irritation.

The teamster spoke to the tractable horse, and the judge felt the carriage backing up slowly to the neat, columned entrance of the club.

"Thank you, my boy," the judge called out and handed the driver a bit of extra fare. Pulling down his hat and wrapping his rain cloak more securely about him, Judge Monaghan took three long strides across the narrow sidewalk and up the four short stairs to shelter. He could hear the Irish teamster calling out, "Thanks very much, Your Honor," and the spirited hooves of the horse, the rattle of the carriage as it moved down Fifth Avenue.

The neat black attendant at the door of the Union Club murmured a respectful greeting to the judge, taking his dripping cloak and hat. "A mighty bad night," the man said softly, and the judge replied heartily, "Damned if it isn't! How are you, Jebediah?"

The man grinned with pleasure at this special recognition from so prominent a man, and said, "Mighty fine, sir, mighty fine, thank you."

"Is the Senator here yet?"

"Yes, sir, he's in the smoking room. But I think they've already set you gentlemen a place in the dining room, so we're all ready for you."

Nodding amiably to the smiling Jebediah, Judge Patrick Monaghan proceeded to the smoking room. Senator Ransom Morgan was seated in a high-backed leather easy chair before the fire. When he sighted Monaghan, the Senator rose and greeted the judge in his booming, pompous fashion.

"Patrick, my boy! It's been a long time. Good of you to meet me like this."

"Not at all. You have the longer journey home. I appreciate your making the appointment in town. It's been a long day."

Ransom Morgan chuckled. The address of his mansion, on

the upper country border of Manhattan, at 201st Street, was one that seemed distant indeed to his city friends. The judge himself occupied a fine brownstone house not far from the Union Club.

"Sit down, sit down, Patrick," Ransom Morgan urged. "Have a little brandy."

Ransom Morgan gestured to the table at his elbow, where a silver tray contained a decanter and two glasses.

"Well," Monaghan rumbled, "the doctors say nay. . . ."

"But what do you say, Pat?"

"I say yea, Ransom. It hits the spot on a night like this."

The Senator poured one of the snifters half-full and handed it to the judge. Morgan noted that Monaghan's nose was surrounded by broken veins. The man was still a drinker, all right, the Senator reflected. So much the better! A man in the throes of drink was a beholden man.

He sat down again in the high-backed chair and waved the judge to the one opposite. "Sit down, Patrick! Sit down," Morgan said in a hearty fashion. "Ease yourself, man."

With a sigh of pleasure, Judge Patrick Monaghan lowered his portly body into the neighboring easy chair and took a generous swallow of brandy. At once, Ransom Morgan noted, the judge's broad face flushed redder, and his red-veined blue eyes glowed with an unhealthy glow.

"Well," said Morgan comfortably, "I suppose you followed the trail of that bastard Wirz. I'm glad they finally hung him."

The judge ignored the reference to the notorious commandant of the Confederate war prison at Andersonville. "Why have you sent for me, Ransom?" he asked bluntly.

Senator Ransom Morgan winced at the other's crudity. He had to restrain himself from blurting out, "Shanty Irish!" Instead, he smiled and commented with mock reproach, "Ah, Patrick, my friend, do not be so precipitate. Enjoy that excellent brandy, and then let us dine. We have the evening before us to discuss business." Ransom Morgan chuckled in his deceptively easy manner and added with mendacious concern, "Besides, my boy, that is the very matter the doctors charge you with . . . isn't it now? That bullheaded way of yours that brings on high blood pressure?"

Patrick Monaghan smiled back at the Senator in a shame-faced fashion. "Perhaps you are right, me boyo," he admitted, grinning. "But I was not born to the purple, as you were, you know. I'm a man of few words and quick action. Besides, you've aroused my curiosity, Ransom. What is this all about?"

The Senator recognized the failure of his small jest and answered bluntly, "I want you to tell me how to go about buying a jury."

Judge Patrick Monaghan's heavy hand tightened around the stem of his glass; it was arrested halfway to his lips. He stared at the Senator and then with great care placed his snifter on the round table between them.

"Ransom, I do not think I heard you right."

"You heard. I do not care to repeat it."

Patrick Monaghan swallowed uneasily and protested, "But you have engaged the best lawyer in America. He will get your son's fiancée off."

"I do not want her off, Patrick." Ransom Morgan leaned forward and put his large, manicured hand on the judge's knee.

"What's that?"

"I want the little bitch in jail . . . or better, I'd see her hanged." Ransom Morgan's declaration was made in a low, silken voice that chilled the other's blood.

"You cannot mean what you are saying."

"I mean it, Pat. And you will aid me."

"I?" The judge took up his glass and swallowed the rest of the brandy. His hand was trembling, Ransom Morgan saw, when the man put down his glass again. "And why should I aid you in this . . . villainy, Ransom?"

"I think you know that well enough."

Patrick Monaghan leaned back in his chair and closed his eyes; his florid face was muddy with shock. "You would not bring that up again, surely, after all these years? Not that."

Ransom Morgan smiled, and it was an unpleasant smile. "I would, Pat, like a shot, unless you help me."

"But what have you against the girl? She is a sightly wench and seems respectable enough."

"Respectable! Why, man, Blaine took her out of Hallie's place."

"I don't believe it." With shaking hands, Judge Patrick Monaghan took up the decanter and poured the snifter almost full. "I don't believe it."

"Believe it, Pat. I know. Do you think I am going to let my only son marry a whore?"

"But, Ransom, there are other ways. . . ." Monaghan's tone was querulous with pleading.

"There is no other way, Patrick. Are you going to help me, or must I produce those letters?"

"The letters!" Monaghan's red-veined blue eyes were wet, and he turned them doglike to Ransom. "You are the one who has them then. My God, and all these years I have been in an agony of wondering." He set his glass down and put his mottled face in his hands."

"Buck up now, Pat. Everything will be fine. All you have to do is tell me how to proceed. And of course, there will be a good bit in it for you."

At last the judge lifted his moist face from his hands and said in a defeated, listless voice, "I have no choice then. I will help you."

"Splendid!" Ransom Morgan boomed. "Shall we dine, then, Pat?"

The judge shook his head. "I don't have much appetite, after all." He straightened in his chair and said in a cold voice, "Here is what you will have to do—"

Ransom Morgan shifted his chair closer to that of His Honor Judge Patrick Monaghan.

Maeve Morgan opened green, drowsy eyes, feeling the sweet weight of her husband's dark head on her shoulder. He was sleeping deeply; she smiled at the sight of his smooth, relaxed face. Maeve kissed him above his heavy brow and examined him more closely, this man who had brought to her body its first ecstatic primal joy.

She was glad to see that the lines of strain that had etched his skin in the first days of the trial were for the time erased. He stirred in his sleep, smiling, burrowed nearer to her lace-covered breast.

Maeve studied the remarkable room with new wonder. She raised her eyes to the vaulted ceiling, painted in Gothic patterns of gilt and blue and scarlet; the stained glass window high in the magic altitudes let in the early-morning light. To her left a double leaded window, like that in an ancient castle, revealed a sweeping view of the broad river that William familiarly called the Hudson.

Very gently, so as not to disturb her husband, Maeve
Morgan removed her arm from under his head and eased herself from the royal blue coverlets that spanned the carven bed
with its intricate posters and headboard of Gothic design. She
slipped her feet into the satin slippers by the bed and rose to
wander ecstatically about the incredible room, giving a quick
glance now and then at the sleeping man on the bed.

As she looked at William, Maeve knew that she had never
felt such tenderness for any human being. He had done so
much! she thought. Bringing her to this magical place, giving
her such beautiful things. And then—last night! Her face
colored.

Maeve went softly to the great heavy chest against the wall
and opened one of its soundless double doors. The sight of the
furs and the garments hanging within filled Maeve with a
renewed sense of wonder.

She saw then that William had reached out his arm in his
sleep to encounter only the silken coverlets; a small frown
creased his handsome brow. Smiling, Maeve closed the door
of the chest and stole back to the bed; after sliding the
gleaming slippers from her feet, she got under the coverlets
again and kissed her husband's outstretched arm.

Maeve was pleased that William Morgan was still asleep,
though he smiled to feel her kiss, for she intuited his deep
weariness. He had done so much, she mused, since yesterday!

Lying back on the pillow, Maeve took William's hand and
gave herself up to the joy of remembering.

Events had moved with a dizzying rapidity since he had
made his impulsive proposal in the carriage. He had left her at
her boardinghouse that evening, after the court had ad-
journed, with the declaration that he had a great deal to do
and would call for her at noon the following day.

Maeve, with the excited Amelie, had made her own preparations. True to his word, William had appeared yesterday at
noon, so laden with parcels and boxes that he could barely
stagger up the stairs to her room.

Giggling wildly, Amelie had helped William with the parcels and boxes; the three unpacked them all, and Maeve and
Amelie cried out like children when they saw the contents.
There was a wonderful cloak of heavy lilac velvet, trimmed
with silvery furs, and a gown, muff and hat to match. Two
boxes held lingerie so frail that it seemed to Maeve no more

substantial than mist, in colors of ivory and lilac, flesh pink and creamy yellow and ice blue. Besides these, there were several day and evening dresses, each more wonderful than the one before.

When Morgan handed Maeve a velvet casket, she opened it and found herself speechless. Inside were the most exquisite jewels she had ever seen—a wonderful demi-parure, consisting of brooch and earrings, made of stamped gold set with emeralds, intricate hair ornaments of pearl, combs set with turquoise and coral, matching rings, bracelets and earrings of diamonds and aquamarines, amethysts and rubies, topaz and emeralds.

"It is like a tale from the *Arabian Nights*," Maeve said softly.

William smiled at her delight, saying, "Some of these pieces have been in my family for generations. Others"—he laughed—"were wrested from the sleepy clerks at Tiffany's this very morning. I bought your ring," he confessed, showing her the wedding circle of aquamarine and diamonds that matched her engagement ring, "the day I bought the other. I had hopes even then."

The tactful Amelie at that point left them alone, and William Morgan took Maeve in his arms and kissed her. She knew with his kiss a sweet magic that would erase forever the memory of Fingal Pearse. She brushed aside the image of his hard, penetrating eyes, swept along in the hurry and exhilaration of William Morgan's plans.

That day Maeve was to begin to know what later became so clear—the extraordinary gift of William Morgan to charm others, to enlist them in his impulsive, sometimes bizarre enthusiasms.

When Maeve's new clothes had been donned, while William strode impatiently in the hall and a large valise was packed with the things she would need for the next two days, William hurried her and Amelie to the lovely church a few blocks away where, William said, he had been taken as a child.

St. George's, he told them, had hidden runaway slaves in its underground passages, bravely defying the tradition of other churches that had remained aloof from the terrible plight of the fugitives. The rector, he added, was a close friend of his and had been persuaded to perform the hasty wedding.

At the end of the simple rite Maeve bade Amelie an affectionate good-bye. William, taking up their valises, said to Maeve, "Now, I have a surprise for you I hope you will like."

And he had bustled her into a carriage that drove them to a steamboat landing. "Where are we going?" she asked with smiling curosity.

"You'll see." He grinned and, to her embarrassment, kissed her in the full view of the passengers on deck.

The steamboat had taken them upriver to a place called Tarrytown, where they were met by a carriage driven by a grinning black in bright livery.

Morgan greeted the black amiably, and the man bowed low to Maeve, saying, "Welcome, Mrs. Morgan." To William he reported, "Mr. Spalding says I'd better take good care of you and your missus."

Maeve smiled at the good-natured driver and asked William, when they were seated in the carriage, "Who is Mr. Spalding?"

"Another friend of mine," Morgan answered. "His family owns the house where we will stay. They are in Europe now and I have *carte blanche* with the place. I thought it might be pleasanter than a hotel."

His casual reference to the house left Maeve totally unprepared for the imposing pile that greeted her eyes when they drove near: It was an absolute castle from a fairy tale.

"All it needs," Maeve said breathlessly, "is a moat and drawbridge."

"I can't imagine how they neglected that!" William Morgan laughed and whispered, "It is wonderfully vulgar and fanciful. I love the place."

The coachman accompanied them through the marble entrance hall, replete with antique motifs such as a vaulted ceiling and leaded windows, to a dramatic flight of curving stairs.

"Mr. Spaulding said put you in the State Bedroom." The man grinned, placing their luggage gently near the massive chest in the amazing Gothic bedchamber. And he was gone.

"Shall I leave you," William Morgan asked with considerate charm, "to . . . change and . . .?"

"No, do not leave me now." Maeve Morgan was amazed at the boldness of her own voice. She held out her velvet-clad arms to William Morgan.

"Maeve, Maeve." He seemed unable to say anything other

than her name, over and over. With incredible gentleness, William Morgan removed Maeve's fur hat from her heavy black hair and took the muff from her hands, tossing them onto a chair.

Then ever so slowly, with trembling hands, he began to remove her garments. Watching him, Maeve was again assailed with that emotion almost akin to fear, observing the power her beauty exercised upon this man who was kneeling now before her nakedness, holding her slender ankles in his hands and kissing her bare feet.

She submitted to his caresses, touching his dark head with her small hand. Maeve Morgan looked down on his upturned face, beseeching, and then observed him lower his face again to continue his ardent caressing of her snowy flesh. She felt his hot lips upon her, knew the stroking of his strong fingers, tracing the shape of her slender legs and then the slight, bewitching roundness of her hips and narrow waist, trembled as the hands reached, with William's upward rising, to her breasts.

He was standing now, holding her nearer and nearer, kissing her so deeply that she almost cried out for her breath and carrying her, soon, to the span of the great Gothic bed, as the early twilight crept through the leaded windows of the remarkable castle.

Then somehow in the dusk he had gone and swiftly returned, divested at last of his own garments. And Maeve gazed up at him, overcome with his beauty, which had been only half revealed to her before. William Morgan's muscular body was like that of a classical statue of an antique youth. His torso combined the broad-shouldered, narrow-waisted look of an athlete with the strong reediness of an ascetic.

Maeve felt the flutter of her heart. He stood above her, staring, and his dark gaze seemed to stroke her face and body with loving hands. Her whole self began to open slowly to him; it was like a sudden flood of sunlight to the eyes of one long pent in darkness. Maeve was stunned by the sensation—she, who had been shut and lonely for so long, obsessed with the cruel man who cared nothing for her at all! She was warmed and shaken by the presence of William Morgan in a complete, deep way that made her former longing seem like that of a dreaming adolescent.

She could not form a single word but knew that from her

eyes a great softness was shining to William Morgan, for Maeve in all her days had never felt so open or so sure. *This,* she thought with wonder, *this is the man I have always loved!*

He was silent, but his look told her what no words of his could have expressed. She saw his dark head lowering to the center of her body and, with an ecstasy of unbelief, felt then the rhythmic beginning of a caress so poignant that at first her still-unknowing body took it for pain. But then the sensation became a tiny point of burning light within her that narrowed and narrowed to a minuscule point of pleasure so acute that she could not keep from crying out. She heard her own cry with a kind of wonder, as if the sound had issued from another throat than hers. The little, oval burning light became a joyousness unknown to her; it widened, like circles of fire on fiery water, until the waves of piercing delight were lapping first her loins and then her legs, rising upward in shuddering rings to wash her belly and her breasts.

Abandoned to the storm of shuddering wonder, Maeve cried out and cried again, thinking wildly, *I can bear no more! If there is more of pleasure, I will die.* But he was not done, and she discovered with their closer converse that there could be more. She had not died! For then she felt another kind of new delight, which he took with her together. Where there had been a throbbing hollowness, she had been filled. Their bodies danced, and where the broken light began to darken, fires were lit to narrowness again, which thinned and widened ever more, this time with even more stunning power, into a wide and wheeling fire of broken light. And plummeting, Maeve deeply drowned, feeling then somewhere above her the distant impact of the world's exploding and her abundant husband's own triumphant cry.

Watching William Morgan stirring now, Maeve Morgan came again into his arms with the hungry gladness of a wanderer returning home.

"And so," Maeve said to her husband, "I saw you that very first day we landed in America."

William Morgan tightened his hold on her narrow waist. They were sitting on a brocade loveseat in the Spaldings' magnificent art gallery, enjoying the cozy sound of the crackling flames in the huge marble cave that served as a fireplace. The weather that afternoon was wet and wild and had cut short their outing on the grounds of the estate.

But it was a matter of indifference to William, he told Maeve, as long as they were together. He gloried now in their aloneness. He leaned his head lightly against her fragrant hair, inhaling its scent with excruciating pleasure, a delicate, elusive scent that seemed to have his wife's own fairy air.

"It was fortunate," he said now softly, smiling, "that I did not see you that day."

"Now why is that?" she asked in a teasing voice.

His fingers pressed her slenderness again. "Because, my love, on that solemn and terrible occasion I am certain that if I'd seen you, I would have broken step, or dropped my sword, or done something equally disastrous." William Morgan laughed, and his laughter had a free and infectious sound. "I'll never forget the effect you had on me when I saw you as Phebe." He quoted softly, " 'Who ever loved that loved not at first sight?' "

I, thought Maeve, and burrowed into his side like a helpless animal hiding. *I learned to love this wonderful man.* Her gesture affected William Morgan deeply; he held her tight, kissing the top of her head, unable to find words for a long moment.

From nowhere to Maeve Morgan sounded a line from her first speech to Silvius, and before she was aware of it, she had whispered it aloud: "Thou tell'st me there is murder in mine eye. . . ."

She felt her husband stiffen. Gently he drew away from her, still supporting her lightly with his encircling arm and looked at her with consternation. "Maeve, why did you think of that just now?"

Maeve loosed herself from his grasp and rose to move to a small octagonal table where jewel-colored decanters of wine and fragile glasses were set. "Forgive me," she said, "I cannot get it out of my mind."

"The trial." His knowing answer was so melancholy that she regretted having spoken. She nodded.

"Of course you cannot," he said in an understanding way. "Nor can I. I fear that the distraction of this place has not been great enough—I had hoped to put it all out of your mind, for a few days at least." He smiled. "Pour us each a glass of strega, darling, and let us see if the witch's spell will cast these dark things out."

Obediently she took up a cut-glass flagon with its contents of golden green and poured them each a small glass. Bearing the little glass to William Morgan, Maeve sat down beside him again.

"Those who drink this together, you know," he said, "will love each other forever."

She could not help smiling at his boyish look; they touched their glasses and drank.

His lean face sobered in a moment, and he set down his glass. "Let us talk of it then," he urged her. "Perhaps it will relieve us both."

Maeve turned her goblet in her fingers, enjoying the new-leaf color of the liqueur that was tinged with orange by the light of the fire. "The testimony of her servants was very damning," she said at last in a flat voice that made her husband stir uneasily.

"But I think the major victory is won," he insisted. "The discrediting of Grace Macon has done irreparable damage to the prosecution's case."

Maeve was grateful for his netural tone. It was as if he knew that this objective appraisal of the case would comfort her the most. She was aware that for a man of his passionate nature, such blandness was hard won, and she took his hand.

"The investigator will be there tomorrow," she remarked, and a small shudder ran over her delicate frame. William Morgan could no longer keep up his pretense of calm, and he moved closer and took her in his arms.

"There is nothing he can say that could convince them of your guilt." Maeve heard the uncertainty creep into his words.

"Everything will come out," she said fearfully. "My living at . . . Hallie McDermott's . . . and maybe even the thing that drove us from Ireland."

"Oh, my dear, that is most unlikely. And if necessary, Miss—Hallie McDermott can testify that you were not—" He stopped, embarrassed.

"Oh, my God, my God!" she cried out and began to weep. "What kind of witness would she be—the . . . madam of a house? Oh, William, what have I brought upon you?"

He took the goblet from her hands and set it on the table before them. Holding her close, William Morgan began to kiss her face and hair.

At last he said passionately, "You have brought me the greatest good fortune of my life. As for everything coming out—yes, it will. It will come out that you have been brave and good and enterprising, that you have suffered terrible things and risen above them. And it will come out that you are the wife of William Morgan, a man who believes in you with all his heart."

Maeve looked up at him, her tearstained face lightening. He was heartened by her look of dawning hope.

"Yes," he repeated, "the wife of William Morgan. The jury cannot help taking that into account. It is not only a private pledge, but a public statement of my belief in your innocence." She nodded, looking brighter at every moment.

"You'll see; come now." He spoke as if she were a child. "Dry your eyes, and let's find out if they will give us some dinner."

Maeve laughed at his mock humility; the Spalding servants loved him and fairly hovered to do his bidding. As they left the gallery for the small dining room, it occurred to William Morgan that perhaps he had been a fool to alienate his powerful father, and he began to search in his mind for a remedy.

Chapter 14

"IT IS unprecedented," Whitney Farlow concluded angrily. "I have never had any great respect for Monaghan, but now he seems either on the verge of mental decay or under some undue influence."

Farlow's stolid associate, Harold Boerum, merely nodded, but it was obvious that he had missed no detail of Farlow's report. They were in the latter's luxurious office, distinguished from other such rooms by its Persian carpets and elegant eighteenth-century furnishings.

No two men could have been more unlike: Farlow was finely turned, slender, impatient and fastidious; Boerum's Dutch heritage lent him a kind of bland heaviness, a look of sleepy strength which in fact masked a razor-brilliant mind and an encyclopedic knowledge of the law even vaster than Whitney Farlow's. It was the private jest of the staff of Farlow and Boerum that one need not consult books when Harold Boerum was on the premises.

Always slow to comment, Boerum now digested the comments of Whitney Farlow and said at last, "I heard something most interesting this afternoon—that Senator Morgan was instrumental in having the other charges against Monaghan repressed."

"Morgan," Farlow said softly, a brightness coming into his glance. "It fits, Harold; it fits. He could only disapprove of his son's marriage. But my God, what a way to eliminate an unwanted relative!"

Harold Boerum had never adjusted to his associate's rather
sinister humor, and his full mouth tightened.

"This transcript," he said, picking up a sheet from
Farlow's desk and studying the proceedings of the trial in the
clerk's flowing hand. "This is particularly disgraceful:
Miller's badgering of Lester Wallack, your objection and the
immediate overruling of it by Monaghan." Boerum shook his
head. "Even he was never this prejudicial before."

"That's not the worst, Harold. Read on, read on," Farlow
muttered in a sullen fashion.

Boerum took up the transcript and read farther; there was
no sound for a time in the quiet room.

At last Boerum looked up from the close-written sheets and
said to Farlow, "You are right, Whit. I've never seen
anything like this. The testimony of that investigator and his
insinuations against your client are based entirely on hear-
say."

"Of course! But if it were only a case of personality
problems—Monaghan and I have always been at daggers'
points—I would not even consider the matter. But this is
flouting the law. I am considering moving for a mistrial."

"You must be tired, Whit," Boerum remarked in a tone of
reproach. "Monaghan will deny your motion, of course. You
know full well that we would have to take another course."

Farlow sighed. "You're right. And whether Maeve Morgan
is fit to endure the delay is uncertain; she looks whiter and
thinner by the day. I'll tell you something, Harold, that I have
never said before in all my time at law: I am . . . I am actually
afraid."

"I've never seen you like this before." Even the stolid
Boerum was ruffled. "Afraid?"

"Of the outcome of this trial."

"Nonsense, Whit! You are merely tired. I have told you
time and again you cannot overwork yourself the way you
do." Farlow made a sound that might have been agreement.

"I wish," said Boerum, "that you would go home and
think no more of it tonight. There is an avenue I might ex-
plore myself."

"What avenue?" Farlow cried impatiently. "You know
quite well that I wish to be informed of any idea you might
have that relates to this case!"

Boerum regretted having spoken; Farlow's disturbance was

great, and his associate judged that he was in a nervous state indeed.

"It is only half formed as yet, and I do not wish to present it to you yet," Boerum said nevertheless in his stubborn way. "You say the Morgan woman is reacting to the pressure?"

"If you were in court, where you should be, you would know," Farlow snapped.

Harold Boerum gave Farlow a worried look; the attack was so irrational that it was obvious Whitney Farlow was in an unsteady state. He had dismissed Boerum's offers of aid early in the case, insisting that Boerum pursue his own cases at hand.

Farlow put his lean hands over his eyes. "Yes, Harold, I am tired. You are right. No client of mine, I must say, has ever affected me so strongly as Maeve Morgan. There is something about the woman, something so . . . vulnerable and yet courageous."

Boerum nodded with understanding. "Would you like me to come tomorrow?" he asked gently. "I can assign a few things to Marsh."

"No." Farlow shook his head. "No, thank you, Harold. I fear the effect on the jury would be adverse. It would appear that we were dealing from a weakened position, bringing out more reserves, as it were."

"Very well."

"I only pray," Farlow added, "that imprisonment will be the worst penalty she receives."

"Whit, this is not like you. The jury—"

"The jury is the very factor that disturbs me the most. I feel that they are no longer . . . with me, as they were at the beginning."

"The jury," Boerum repeated thoughtfully. "The jury."

Farlow glanced at him sharply. "Do you think it is a repetition of that railroad matter, Harold?"

"Anything is possible," Boerum replied in his slow voice. "It is worth looking into."

For the first time that evening Whitney Farlow seemed to be himself again. He smiled at Boerum and said buoyantly, "I think I will, Harold. I think I will."

William Morgan's attempts toward reconciliation with his father had been in vain, and his interviews with Judge Charles Patrick Dady and others in the political world of New York had given him no satisfaction. He was stunned at the cynicism of those he met. The general consensus was that, after all, "Whitney Farlow had never lost a case."

But William, who had studied law, was almost as sensitive as Farlow himself to the atmosphere of growing conviction of Maeve's guilt, and William Morgan lay wide-eyed in the nights and watched his wife in her uneasy sleep. He was possessed of a fear so terrible these latter days that it walked with him as a constant companion.

Yet for Maeve's sake he assumed an air of undying optimism, hiding from her his weary consternation and blessing the chance of his long leave and her leave from the play that gave them so many sweet hours together.

William Morgan was aware that she, too, fell under the shadow of fear, but he found her assuming for him the same courageous mask he had put on for her. In the early evenings before they dined, they would stroll the few blocks down Fifth Avenue from their hotel to walk around Washington Square in the early dark.

Thirty years ago, William told Maeve, the elegant square had been first a potters' field and then a parade ground for soldiers. Now there stood the imposing Gothic pile of New York University, standing since 1837, and a charming residential area with rows of high-stooped houses distinguished by handsome white doorways.

But this evening toward the latter part of November, a cold and driving rain that had the sound of sleet kept Maeve and William within doors. He noted her restlessness and suggested, "Why don't we dine downstairs? Let's dress for dinner, so we will feel festive."

Dressing for dinner was a task he was not fond of, but William Morgan was well aware that Maeve would be distracted by the pleasure of choosing a gown and wearing the glittering jewels he had given her.

She assented—to his tender amusement, she appeared to be doing so to please him—and summoned Amelie from her adjoining room to help.

William Morgan treasured these moments, which he was allowed to witness, when Maeve emerged from her dressing room with a frail wrapper over her petticoats and chemise and with Amelie stood before the chest, examining and discussing gowns. A gown was chosen—a garment of shining blue-green that reminded William Morgan of sunlit Italian water—and slipped with care over Maeve's black hair.

When Amelie had dressed her hair to her satisfaction and Maeve had clasped about her white neck an exquisite necklace of emeralds and aquamarines, setting its matched eardrops in her pierced ears, she rose. Smiling, she turned and whirled for William's approval.

"Beautiful," he judged softly and, taking her hand, said, "Let us go down, then, to dine."

They noted that the dining room was sparsely populated this evening, surprisingly so for a night so wet and chill, and that the waiters were possessed of a bright-eyed tension, constantly glancing toward the lobby of the hotel.

"I wonder what ails them," Maeve said, sipping her coffee at the end of the meal.

"I can't imagine." William's voice was lazy and relaxed; in the peaceful room, sharing the delight of Maeve's company, he had all but forgotten for the moment the thing that haunted them. He took a sip of brandy and studied the circling smoke from his thin cigar, his glance always returning to the lovely picture opposite.

But suddenly the sound of a multitude of voices and the rattle of carriages broke in upon their peace. "Good Lord," Morgan said, "it sounds like a riot!"

He rose from their table and strode to the French window. On Fifth Avenue he saw an immense crowd beginning to gather, despite the rain. A nervous member of the Metropolitan Police was attempting to bring order.

"Stay here," he said to Maeve. "I'll go to the lobby and see what it's all about."

Uneasily Maeve waited for his return. But the expression on his face, as she watched him approaching her again, told her there was no cause for alarm. With a half-smile, he resumed his place, saying, "It's the reception for General Grant. I had forgotten."

Maeve Morgan studied her husband. There was more in his casual statement than appeared on the surface. It was as if he were saying to her. "That world is dead for me now; nothing occupies my mind but you."

And yet she wondered if there were not regret in him; had it not been for her, he would have been among the number receiving the famous general who, it was said, won the war for the Northern States. Maeve thought she saw a sad look in William Morgan's eyes.

But he added in apparent indifference, "The manager said they had not expected so many." He smiled at Maeve. Then a sudden idea seemed to occur to him. "My parents will no doubt be here. I think this may be a splendid opportunity for them to make your acquaintance."

"Oh, William!" He saw the discomfiture on her lovely face.

"Come, my darling. We are in our own hotel, on our own ground as it were. If we should decide to return to our rooms, we can do so at any time. I am bound and determined," he said with a stubborn inflection, "for them to know you and acknowledge you as my wife. And when they see how wonderful you are. . . ." He smiled at her.

"Very well." There was nothing, she thought, that she would not do for him—he was so good to her.

"Let us find a place in the lobby and make you comfortable." He made a quick gesture for the bill, a gesture Maeve always enjoyed watching, for it expressed so perfectly his good-natured ease—the ease of one born to order and command without imperiousness, but with the sure expectation of being served and obeyed. Maeve had seen that waiters, like almost all others, reacted to her husband with willing warmth.

The bill quickly settled, William rose and pulled out Maeve's chair so that she might rise without difficulty.

Together they walked toward the lobby, which was milling now with spendidly dressed, excited people: imposing men in blue uniforms; women in wide-skirted evening attire.

"Ah!" William said in a low voice to Maeve. "Look. They must be waiting now for the appearance of the general. You see those two? They are two of our most famous soldiers—Winfield Scott and Ambrose Burnside." William nodded to a passing officer.

Then, in the milling crowds at the entrance to the hotel, Maeve discerned a familiar figure, the plump matron with the rather kindly, foolish face whom she had seen that evening with William and the priest and Mrs. Dady. "Your mother," she said to William in a low voice. Behind the woman was a man in evening dress, a man of some distinction with a white mane of hair, whose face seemed a travesty of William

Morgan's in its broad redness and smug expression.

"And my father." Something in William's tone made
Maeve glance at him with quick uneasiness. She saw anger in
his handsome face struggling with an attempted smile.

"Come, my darling." He urged her forward. As the crowd
surged inward, William Morgan's father and mother were
borne toward Maeve and William. In a moment they were
face to face.

"Mother," said William Morgan. "Father. May I present
my wife?"

William Morgan's mother stared at Maeve for an instant,
dumbfounded; his father turned redder. Then the plump
woman gave Maeve Morgan a tentative smile and held out her
hand. "My dear," she said, appearing to move forward as if
she would take the younger woman in her arms.

"Fanny!" Ransom Morgan's pompous voice cut through
the babble of the crowd about them. He took his wife's arm
firmly and drew her to his side.

With a cold nod at Maeve and William, Ransom Morgan
urged his wife onward through the crowded assembly, giving
not a glance backward. But she, crying, "William," looked
back in a beseeching fashion.

Soon they were lost in the multitude pressing toward the
great ballroom of the Fifth Avenue Hotel.

William Morgan's face was white with anger. Maeve saw
his jaws clench as he stared after the retreating figures of his
mother and father. Through a mist of tears, Maeve was aware
of an increase in volume among the voices of the people in the
street and the shouting of men trying to restore order in the
crowd.

General Grant was apparently approaching.

"Let's get you out of this," William said firmly. "I don't
want you to be among so many people. It is not safe."

And pushing ahead, he forced a path for them toward the
stairs, where now several hundred people were descending.

With constant exclamations of "Excuse me!" and "Pardon
me" and "Make way, please," William Morgan cleared a way
for Maeve to ascend. She was relieved now to be escaping the
crowd, for below she thought she heard a woman scream and
a man shout angrily. Maeve drew a deep breath of relief when
they reached the haven of their rooms.

Amelie, she saw, was peering from their sitting-room window into the street below. "*Mon Dieu!*" she cried. "I have never seen so many people. Do look."

Maeve and William joined her and looked down into the rain. There were hundreds of people jamming Fifth Avenue, cheering and waving, as the carriage of General Ulysses S. Grant approached the entrance of the Fifth Avenue Hotel.

The crowd closed in. "They will crush him to death!" Amelie said nervously.

"No, no." William Morgan's voice was soothing. "See? The soldiers and the police are making way."

"Is that the general?" Maeve asked, distracted from the unpleasant scene enacted a few moments before by this new spectacle.

"Yes."

"He is not much to look at," Amelie blurted. "So short and fat, with that ugly beard like a dog's."

Then she put her narrow hand to her mouth and looked at William Morgan. "Oh, I am sorry."

But she saw that William Morgan was smiling. Maeve thought, *Amelie, indeed, is right. He is not an imposing man, for all his fame.* She had seen a picture of the other famous general, Robert Lee, and had remarked to William that he was the epitome of a soldier, saying that General Lee reminded her of William himself.

"He is not," William said now in a teasing voice, "as handsome as Maeve's hero, General Lee." Maeve blushed.

"Or General Beauregard," said Amelie pertly.

William and Maeve could not help laughing at her impudence, but Maeve, feeling that Amelie had gone a little far, asked William, "Who are those with him, the gentleman in the fur and the other officer?"

"William Astor and General Hooker," Morgan replied. "Well, well, and there is Mrs. Dady." Mrs. Dady! Maeve peered down and saw, before the raised umbrella hid her from sight, the austere matron being handed down from her carriage.

"I wonder what she's doing in all this," William murmured.

"Mrs. Dady, the—" Amelie stopped abruptly.

"Amelie," Maeve said, "would you excuse us?"

Amelie glanced at Maeve's tense face and said apologetically, "Oh, please pardon me. I had come to your window because the view. . . ." Her voice trailed off and she left the chamber with embarrassed promptitude.

When they were alone, William Morgan took Maeve in his arms. "My beloved," he said, and in the simple words she recognized his sadness and apology.

"Your father . . ." she began.

"Please, Maeve, never mention him to me again."

In his face Maeve Morgan saw a determination she had never marked before. She nodded, and for a moment they were silent.

Then he said in a choked voice, "If he cannot recognize you as my wife, he need never recognize me as his son."

"But, William. . . ."

"Maeve, don't say any more." The authoritative note in his voice arrested her. She stood in submissive quiet, resting her head on his chest.

On the edges of her vision, Maeve Morgan saw a bright light and heard a crackling and booming.

"What is that?"

"Fireworks, probably," said William Morgan. "A firework display for General Grant."

Now they heard the loud music of a band.

William led Maeve to a sofa.

As they sat down, he said softly, "My darling, when the trial is over, I thought we might go away."

"Yes?"

There is an assignment in New Orleans, in the South, with the army of occupation, where I might take command. How would you feel about that?"

"Why, I don't know. It would be . . . an adventure, perhaps." She smiled at him, and his wide smile answered hers.

"Then I shall apply. I think it would be a good idea."

"Yes," she assented with forced brightness. "So do I. When the trial is ended."

Over both of them still lay the broading shadow of fear. *If,* Maeve Morgan reflected coldly, *only they believe me.*

"My dear," said Mrs. Charles Patrick Dady to Julia Dent Grant, "I cannot thank you enough for asking me to be one of your ladies-in-waiting."

The indomitable Mrs. Dady was entertaining the hero's

wife at tea in her imposing drawing room. She considered Mrs. Grant a most prepossessing, ladylike woman.

"And your gown," she effused. "was in exquisite taste."

The general's wife made a polite sound of thanks, for the flow of Mrs. Dady's words gave her little opportunity to speak protractedly.

"I am through," Mrs. Dady said dramatically, "with Fanny Morgan."

Mrs. Grant raised her brows interrogatively. "Why, my dear Mrs. Dady!"

"I have learned that she actually made overtures to that . . . woman. Only the good sense of her husband, I am sure, prevented Fanny's inviting the creature to your husband's reception!"

"My husband," said Mrs. Grant quietly, "speaks very highly of young Major Morgan. And perhaps the girl is . . . innocent, Mrs. Dady."

"Innocent, my dear Mrs. Grant! Good heavens!" Mrs. Dady stared at Julia Dent Grant in amazement. "Why, I should imagine this will be the end of Major Morgan's Army career."

Mrs. Grant was discreetly silent. Her husband had declared to her privately that a good soldier was a good soldier, whatever his indiscretions.

Nettled and afire with curiosity, Mrs. Charles Patrick Dady asked her distinguished visitor if she would care for another cup of tea. And suddenly Mrs. Dady wondered if there were anything to the rumor that the general drank. He was by his own admission, a "backwoodsman" to whom everything was new. Mrs. Dady would never forget his frank declaration of boredom at *Fra Diavolo* the week before.

She concluded forgivingly that the general did not understand New York society; that would excuse his defense of young Major Morgan. Mrs. Dady was glad that it was all settled in her own mind.

In court that afternoon Colonel David Hunter, in mufti, had come to witness the trial of Harley Blaine and Maeve Morgan. As Major William Morgan's commanding officer he had come to know and respect the boy, he told his aide, in the presence of General John Frémont.

The general had drawled, "Nevertheless, David, the young

man is a social embarrassment to the Morgans, you know.
Perhaps the New Orleans assignment . . . where it doesn't
matter. . . ."

"Doesn't matter?"

Frémont shrugged. "Among the Rebs, after all. And New
Orleans is very far away indeed."

The colonel frowned but forbore to answer his superior
sharply. "He is a very good officer, sir," said Hunter.

Frémont commented, "I would deprive him of his commission if there were any way. His indiscretion has been unbecoming, most unbecoming."

"Indiscretion, sir? Marriage?"

Frémont looked offended at his subordinate's tone of sarcasm. "Marriage to such a woman. He has destroyed all his
chances at promotion, you know."

"But General Grant, sir, will hear nothing against him." At
once Colonel David Hunter saw that he had gone too far.
General Frémont had risen in a huff and left the room.

Now, as Hunter studied Maeve Morgan at the table of the
defense, he thought, *Damn them all, I will support the boy in
every way I can. He does,* Hunter concluded wryly, *have the
support of Ulysses S. Grant! And that is no small matter.*

"The defense calls Lester Wallack."

The announcement was received by the spectators with
great excitement. Lester Wallack, that famous employer and
friend of Maeve Morgan and Harley Blaine . . . called again!

Maeve Morgan's pale face took on new color above the
somber dark green of her gown. If anyone could help them,
she thought, it was Lester Wallack. But to her surprise,
Harley Blaine's tawny cheeks assumed a muddy color, and he
slumped in his chair, unable to look toward the witness box.

Hushed and breathless, the spectators watched the im-
pressive manager take the stand. The fawn color of his well-
tailored suit made him look more massive than ever.

Lester Wallack's face, Maeve noted with puzzlement, was
grim; he seemed to be holding himself in tight check. He
glanced at her and smiled a little, but kept his eyes from
Harley Blaine. What did it mean? she marveled.

"Your Honor," said Whitney Farlow, "this witness has
already been sworn in for previous testimony; may I proceed
directly to examination?"

Judge Patrick Monaghan nodded, his flushed face revealing a peculiar dismay.

"Will you tell me, Mr. Wallack, what you revealed in a sworn affadavit in my offices this morning?" There was another collective, indrawn breath from the watchers. What did Farlow have up his sleeve now?

"Yes," Lester Wallack replied, and his voice was heavy with reluctance. "I cannot any longer, in good conscience, keep silent. I believe I witnessed the murder of Marianne LeClaire by Harley Blaine."

For an infinitesimal moment the courtroom sat in stunned silence. Then there arose a clamor and roar of surprise; journalists were scribbling madly in their notebooks, and a woman's jubilant cry could be heard, rising above the other voices. It was Henrietta Plum's, Maeve realized dimly in her shock. She could barely believe what she had heard.

Harley Blaine gave a low groan, but he kept his proud head high. It was with a mighty effort, Maeve knew, that he kept from crying out. She turned and sought William in the crowd. On his face she could see a blend of total disbelief and the glow of hope.

She turned back to the scene before them.

"As I have testified," Wallack resumed, in a tight voice that Maeve barely recognized, "I played the role of King Claudius in the play *Hamlet* in which Mr. Blaine enacted the title role. In the last scene of the play, the dueling scene, the King places a pearl in a goblet, thinking to poison Hamlet. But through a concatenation of circumstances, Queen Gertrude, enacted by Miss LeClaire, is poisoned instead. The dramatic line accompanying this action by the King goes as follows: 'Stay; give me a drink. Hamlet, this pearl is thine;/Here's to thy health.' "

Even in their shock and in the solemn moment, the spectators could not resist a thrill at hearing the voice of Lester Wallack suddenly assume its dramatic force. Actorlike, he had slipped for the moment into the role of Claudius and for that moment was the King.

"Hamlet's line," Wallack resumed in the same sad tone as before, "goes, 'I'll play this bout first; set it by awhile.' And the action suited to that line in the play is a wave of the hand and a resumption of Hamlet's mock duel with Laertes. But it came to me last night that on the night of the . . . murder of Marianne LeClaire, Harley Blaine did not use his customary gesture. On that night, instead, he did something that seemed to me, later, very strange: He picked up the goblet and passed one of his hands over it.

"In the tension of opening night," Wallack went on, "and in the necessity of playing my own role and at the same time, as director, keeping an eye on the progress of the production, I had no time to consider this tentative change . . . or lapse, as I considered it might be. Harley Blaine is a gifted impulsive artist who sometimes made last-minute changes in his stage business. I thought at the time, if I thought of it at all in the events that followed, that it must be that.

"However, as I lay awake last night. . . ." Lester Wallack paused, and he put a massive hand to his eyes. Then he lowered his hand, raised his head and continued in a broken voice, "As I lay awake last night, I realized that this was the only opportunity for poison to be introduced into the goblet from which Miss LeClaire was bound to drink. And that—" Wallack's powerful voice trembled and broke again.

He cleared his throat and spoke once more. "I realized that even though Harley Blaine is . . . my friend, I could not conspire . . . with murder in his behalf."

At last Harley Blaine met the flashing eyes of Lester Wallack, and he rose from his chair, crying out, "Yes! Yes! I did it then, and all the world must know! I poisoned Marianne LeClaire. And Maeve Heron—Maeve Morgan had no part in it at all! I will swear to that, before you and before God!"

Pandemonium broke loose in the court. There was an exodus of journalists, shouting to the others to make way; Henrietta Plum and Amelie were weeping with delight. William Morgan bowed his head into his hands; his own face was wet with tears of relief.

Maeve Morgan's wild, elated emotion of thanksgiving was struggling with a feeling of deep sadness when she looked at Harley Blaine. In the roar of voices, he turned to her and said with a terrible clarity, "I did it all for you."

Her green gaze, as she stared at him, was full of soft compassion. "I'm sorry, Harley," she said.

Judge Patrick Monaghan, his scarlet face the picture of indignation, banged his gavel again and again, crying out, "Order! Order in the court! We will have order, or the court will be cleared at once! Bailiff, arrest all those who continue to make this disturbance!''

As if by magic the great hall grew quiet, and Maeve Morgan heard dimly, in the loud beating of her heart and the increasing weakness of her limbs, the judge's instructions to the jury, saw the officer approaching Harley Blaine.

When it was over, she felt almost too weak to rise. Then William was beside her, Henrietta Plum and Amelie surrounding them, clutching at her, laughing and weeping, journalists questioning her and William in loud voices.

Through her tears she recognized the faces of Colonel Hunter and his aide, heard the elegant voice of Whitney Farlow say to William, ''Well, I have won this time by default,'' then the consoling utterances of Farlow to Blaine's attorney.

She watched for a moment as Harley Blaine was being led away to another room and relaxed against William Morgan as he urged her out of the courtroom toward the corridor.

Slowly, in the massed crowd leaving the court, William led Maeve Morgan toward the door and freedom.

She prayed her trembling limbs would support her; William looked down at her with concern. For a very brief instant he loosed her and let Henrietta and Amelie walk beside her; he was for that instant ahead. From Maeve's left, appearing as if from nowhere, suddenly there was Fingal Pearse.

She looked up at him in dismay, and Amelie made an angry sound.

With lightning quickness, Pearse leaned to her and said in a low voice, ''We are not through with each other, Maeve, marriage or no marriage. We will never be through with each other.''

Then he joined the milling mass, and somehow William Morgan was back beside her, smiling, smiling down at her in jubilation, holding her close to his side.

But even in her triumphant joy Maeve Morgan could not forget the threatening sound of the words of Fingal Pearse, the captain of the *Falcon*.

Part IV

HARBOR

Chapter 15

IN THE fleeting seven months of her residence in the great Eastern city, Maeve Heron had been but dimly aware of the devastation lying south of the untouched richness of New York. The war had been for her a distant tale of horror that had no firm reality. The side on which William Morgan fought had been the side of "right," bringing Amelie and her people from bondage.

But by the winter of 1867 Maeve Morgan was to learn more. The questions that had been so clear before were becoming increasingly complex. For the first time in her life she belonged to the ranks of the conquerors, and this was an unsettling thing. She could not forget the green, magical land of the O'Neills, under the heel of one tyrant after another. Now her husband, William Morgan, wore the uniform of those who had looted and pillaged this new country of soft-tongued, resentful people who recalled Maeve's own.

Almost five years had passed since New Orleans had fallen to federal troops, and when Admiral Farragut had sailed in, the impassioned residents had made a bonfire of their properties rather than give them to the conquerors. But the scars remained; the city that in the 1850s had been so prosperous and gay was now a shadow of itself. Like a splendid woman in worn finery, Maeve Morgan thought.

And yet New Orleans' varied wonders that remained caught at Maeve Morgan's fancy—the slowly increasing commerce of the wharves that, stilled by war, was beginning to revive again; the winding, mysterious little streets and lace of iron-work on the once-white houses; most of all, the soft Louisianian voices mingling with French and Spanish and German tongues. Here and there Maeve caught the brogues of those who lived in the "Irish channel" and the strange patois of the Cajuns, a dialect that her limited French could not encompass.

This February afternoon, marveling at the mildness of the winter air, Maeve walked slowly with Amelie past Jackson Square, the French Quarter's heart. Glancing at the handsome bronze statue beyond the railings, she asked, "Who is that man?"

"He was the city's savior, Andrew Jackson," Amelie replied with absent irony, studying the dilapidated fountain and the thin grass.

"But look there," Maeve said, puzzled. "It is written 'The Union Must, and Shall Be Preserved.' "

"The butcher Butler had it written there," Amelie replied angrily, and Maeve fell into embarrassed silence. William had told her with disapproval of the occupation by General Benjamin Butler, a cruel man whose treatment of the conquered women had even caused a furor as far as England, where his actions were remarked upon in Parliament.

Butler had decreed, William admitted bitterly, that Southern women who showed disrespect to the invaders be treated as women of the streets plying their trade.

As they turned into Chartres Street, Amelie touched Maeve's arm and smiled sadly, saying, "It is none of your fault."

Maeve's eyes filled with quick tears. Poor Amelie, she reflected, was still unable to comprehend the changes in her beloved city.

"Oh, Maeve, oh, Maeve," she said now, "you cannot know how beautiful this was before the war—all sunlight and whiteness and voices calling."

The haunting phrases stabbed at Maeve; in this last year she had grown even closer to Amelie. The other officers' wives, though courteous enough, could not forget the trial and Harley Blaine, and to the Southern women she passed on the streets and encountered in the stores, she was the wife of a man who wore the hated blue of the invader. Maeve had learned not to mind so much when they pointedly stood aside for her to pass. Yet her loneliness was deep and abiding, despite the tenderness of William Morgan.

"Oh, Amelie, will I ever . . . belong again?" she asked.

"Someday, when your husband takes you back home . . ." Amelie replied.

"And will you come?"

"Let us not speak of things so far away." Amelie was evasive. "Come, now," she added brightly, "you have much to be thankful for. We both have; we go in lovely dresses while these other women look like scarecrows."

Maeve smiled at the other's practicality. But for her, that very circumstance was a cause at times of peculiar pain, for the hatred of the conquered women, she knew, was heated a hundred times over by their envy. She, Maeve Morgan, the wife of an invader, went about in lovely garments, where they themselves wore patched and stained dresses, dresses that had been in vogue perhaps five years before.

And sensitively Maeve Morgan had taken to dressing in more unobtrusive clothes when going abroad by daylight. Only among the other officers' wives, at evening parties and dining at Galatoire's, did she feel easy in her gleaming clothes.

"That is very dear of you," said William Morgan, holding her tightly in his arms. He himself had come to wear a look of sad distaste. "I am not, I think," he said to Maeve, "a very good soldier."

She comprehended the source of his unease at once; he had visited New Orleans, he told her, before the war and had been charmed wholly by the variegated place. To see it like this, Maeve thought, saddened him almost as much as it saddened Amelie.

She sighed. "What is the matter?" Amelie asked a little impatiently.

"Nothing," Maeve replied softly. "I was . . . thinking of William."

Amelie was silent for a moment; then she said boldly, "You were thinking, too, of the life in New York. Is it not so?"

Maeve wondered at her friend's perception. Yes, always she thought of New York and the theater without even knowing she did. The life that had begun with such a blaze of brilliance flaring out with such cruel suddenness.

They were approaching a shabby pink house on Chartres Street. It was here that Juliette Thibault, the former owner of

Amelie, kept her dressmaking establishment and lived in the cramped quarters above.

Before the war, Amelie told Maeve, Mlle. Thibault had had an elegant shop on Royal Street and occupied the whole of the Chartres Street house, with its three iron-laced upper stories. Maeve at first had felt it a kindness to patronize Mlle. Thibault, but she soon learned that the *couturiere* could create clothes of a Parisian elegance. William encouraged her, therefore, to buy more of her things from Mlle. Thibault rather than send to New York.

"The days of Butler are gone," he commented, smiling. "I would like to see the people prospering again, and perhaps your patronage will bring the other women."

Maeve realized that this was so, for the other officers' wives, even Colonel Hunter's wife, envied Maeve her delicate beauty and her flair for dress that so enhanced it. Thus it was that she had become a regular patron of Mlle. Juliette Thibault.

It has been said that a Parisian shopgirl possesses the gift of dressing like a duchess on a sou. Mlle. Juliette Thibault shared this talent with her lowlier sisters, and in spite of the sharp thinness of her face that gave her the look of a ferret, Juliette Thibault even now had a certain chic.

This February afternoon, on an upper floor of the house, Juliette's married sister, Claire Roget, regarded her with envy.

"I do not know how you keep your admirable figure, Juliette, and at your age." The younger Mme. Roget's own proportions were of an unenviable richness.

"By eating almost nothing since 1862," Juliette Thibault replied sharply, "so that I might have the money to make myself dresses and to keep this business. And my age, dear Claire, is not so venerable as that."

Rebuffed, Claire Roget took another bite of the filled pastry that Juliette could now afford to serve with coffee, and sought another subject of discussion. "You have clients this afternoon?" she queried, noting that her sister's sharp black eyes kept darting to the clock on the broken mantel.

"The young Mme. Morgan," Juliette said, nodding. She smiled and added, "Her husband is apparently most generous to Mme. Morgan. Ah! What a *tournure* she has! What a style."

"Ah, *that* one!" Claire Roget exclaimed around a mouthful of pastry. Swallowing, she resumed in a more articulate manner, "She has a look very *spirituelle* for a murderess."

Annoyed, for Maeve Morgan was her best client, Juliette Thibault retorted, "She was cleared of all charges in that regard."

"All the same . . ." Claire insisted.

Juliette Thibault thought sourly that her sister's designation of *spirituelle* was Gallic-bourgeois for "much too thin," a look she envied with all her heart.

"Mme. Morgan is very kind and the most beautiful woman in New Orleans," Juliette said decisively. "She has a waist like a willow wand; why, it is no more than seventeen inches, Claire."

Spitefully Juliette let her gaze wander to her sister's cowlike middle.

"Well!" Claire Roget's look of offense deepened. "I suppose that one must deal with everyone these days, even the Yankees. But I see no need, Juliette, for you to be so . . . forthcoming with the woman. We are, after all, Confederates, however things were before the war."

The people of New Orleans had not been ardent secessionists, Juliette was well aware. It was only with the coming of the invaders that their passionate feelings had been aroused.

She sniffed. "I, for one, have a living to make. And so, may I remind you, has Georges." Claire Roget looked pained at this reference to her husband, whose café was flourishing far less than the dressmaking business of her sister. It was Juliette's frank contention that Georges was not "nice enough" to the Yankees, and the Army and its families sought more congenial places.

Juliette's Gallic practicality was aroused.

"But even the Yankee women, I have heard, do not accept her. Or would not, were it not that her husband is so highly thought of by this Colonel Hunter and even by that drunken pig Grant. It is said that there is something . . . not quite natural about her relationship with the slave Amelie."

The dressmaker laughed. "Amelie is no longer a slave, my sister. And besides, that is arrant nonsense; I know the girl in and out, God knows I *should*! She belonged to me for all those years. And Amelie is absolutely besotted about men."

"All the same . . ." Claire Roget persisted with that phrase that so maddened her brighter, more generous sister.

"Well, Yankees or no, Claire, I am putting money in the bank again, and I have pastries to serve my guests."

The shot went home, for Claire was so parsimonious a hostess that she served only the most sour wine and coffee unaccompanied by comestibles.

Juliette's portly sister stiffened. She rose. "Well, I had best leave you to your work," she said coldly. "But when I think of the days before the war . . . the establishment on Royal Street. *Mon Dieu*, Juliette, you had a dozen seamstresses! And now you have to do it all alone. Why, this Morgan woman's very husband might have been the one to fire your establishment!"

"He never reached New Orleans," Juliette replied blandly. "It is of no use, Claire, to think of the old days. The new days are enough for me to manage."

Claire Roget kissed her sister perfunctorily, and when Juliette Thibault descended with her at the ring of Maeve Morgan, she stared hard at the white-faced Yankee woman.

If I were as rich as that, Claire Roget thought with bitterness and envy, *I would not go about in such gloomy-looking colors.*

Claire did not deign to glance at Amelie but brushed past her and hurried out the door.

For nearly two hundred years, William had told Maeve, New Orleans had always celebrated Carnival—the Carnelevamen, putting away of meat for Lent, marked by the final fling of Mardi Gras. In the days before the war there had been Carnival from Twelfth Night until Fat Tuesday. There had been hardly an evening without a ball, an opera or the theater, and there had been two public balls a week, with ladies admitted free. The private balls were given by the old Creole families—demure affairs that made the public balls even gayer by comparison.

Carnival had been suspended for the bitter years of the war. Barely having enough food to stay alive, the natives could hardly have afforded the expensive entertainments and costumes of the olden days, even had they had the heart for celebration.

"Mlle. Thibault," Maeve said excitedly to William one afternoon, "says this will be the first Mardi Gras since the war."

He smiled at her childlike enthusiasm but said, "I'm afraid if you celebrate, you will have to celebrate alone. I am on duty that night."

She exclaimed with disappointment. "But why? Surely on a night like that. . . ."

"It is on a night like that that we are most needed. After last July no one knows how things might turn out."

Maeve recalled the horrors of the previous July, when a race riot had broken out and two hundred people were killed or wounded. She shivered to remember the far sounds of screaming and shouting, the explosions of guns, the terror with which she had waited for William to return.

"I see. In that case, then, I will not have a costume made. I will stay here." She tried to keep her voice steady, but a trace of disappointment tinged her words.

William took her in his arms, saying, "Nonsense. At least go to the opera with the Hunters. You should not be cheated of all celebration. I have already cheated you of so much."

His own bitterness was so open that Maeve looked up, surprised, at his gentle face. New lines of strain had formed themselves upon his brow and about his mouth during these last months. She was alive to his constant agony—the agony of a man who must perform duties he hated. For the harsh measures of Radical Reconstruction were still being enforced, despite the long battle of President Johnson with the Radicals in Congress. Yet William continued to accept the situation.

"My dear," she asked again, for what seemed the hundredth time, "why can't you resign your commission? Why can't we go back to New York, where we both belong? At least," she amended wryly, "to a certain extent."

Her question, and the cynical tone of her last comment, seemed to bring William Morgan new pain. "I have told you repeatedly, my darling, that I have a duty to perform. And I wish you would not speak in that hard way . . . it is something you never used to do."

"I never used to feel imprisoned!" she cried. "Not even . . . not even at Hallie McDermott's. At least there I had work to do. Here I am utterly idle. Jinjy and Maria and Amelie do everything. All I am left with is to dress myself and go to the opera or the play among all those snobbish women of the

garrison or stiff old Creoles, who fairly spit at me! To look
and look and look upon the stage and never walk upon it!''

She stopped, appalled at her own outburst, the culmination
of a year of discontent and loneliness.

"Maeve, Maeve," William Morgan said, stricken. He
loosed his hold upon her and walked with laggard steps to the
sofa, where he sank down. He lowered his head and put his
hands over his face.

At last he said in a cold voice, "You have been feeling this
all this time, without telling me. I knew that I was a fool to
think that . . . I was enough."

She was horrified at the pain she had caused him. She
hurried to his side and, kneeling on the bright carpet before
the sofa, touched his bent head gently. "Oh, William, forgive
me. I didn't mean it. Truly I didn't. You are enough, you
are." But her words carried no conviction for William
Morgan.

He looked up with a melancholy smile. "At least, my
dear," he said, "go to the opera on the night of Mardi Gras."

"Yes, yes, I will."

But it was not the thought of the opera that brought a sudden gleam to the green, discontented eyes of Maeve Morgan.
She had another plan.

The tall man in the costume of a pirate and black wig
peered through the eyeholes of his large mask at the woman in
green with flaming hair. She stood boldly alone at the edge of
the crowd, the bright mask that matched her eighteenth-
century gown almost concealing her small face.

The pirate made his way among the shouting revelers
toward the woman. If she was a cocotte, he thought, she was
certainly one of the highest order, for there was in her
demeanor a look of good blood that had, no doubt,
discouraged more than one. The pirate saw a man approach
the woman in green and address her. Her posture remained as
proud and aloof as ever—the pirate could not see the expression of her face—as though the man had not spoken or indeed existed at all.

The hard mouth of the man in the pirate's clothes creased
into a dry smile. So that was the way she was playing, he
mused. What was she anyway? The puzzle teased at him. Certainly not one of the high-nosed Creole daughters, not unac-

companied in this milling crowd of drunken lunatics, and not with that flaming hair! That, however, could be a wig, the pirate judged.

He moved nearer to her, standing a little apart with apparent indifference to her presence. She was staring at the floats that were passing now on St. Charles Street—rather crude floats, this year, the pirate thought, for New Orleans was not yet a city of riches—containing elaborately costumed passengers, with painted faces.

The Rex parade, by far the largest and most ostentatious, had taken place that afternoon, and this was the much more decorous parade of Comus. After the long drinking of the day, there was a feeling of surfeit, but no one about the pirate and the woman in green would have admitted to such a thing. A jubilant couple near the woman commented rather tipsily on the passing parade.

"Why Comus?" the woman asked her companion.

He replied loudly over the din, "The Demon Actors of Milton's *Paradise Lost*," and he laughed. "There's Satan on the second float, see?"

The man in the pirate's clothes fancied that the woman in green had stiffened to attention at the mention of "Demon Actors," and a wild suspicion overtook him. He strode toward the slender woman in the green dress with its elaborate wide skirt. She looked like a woman of Versailles, he thought with a hot stab of excitement and hoped that her morals would be as free.

At his approach she stood quite still, staring up at him through the openings of her bright-green mask. It concealed her entire face, with its lower part of green lace, like a tiny skirt, extending to her chin.

"Mademoiselle," said the man in the pirate's clothes and bowed, for the others had moved on and a space had cleared about the woman in green. When she did not reply, the pirate said whimsically, "Señorita? Fräulein?"

Something that might have been amusement flickered through the lace of her lower mask. She made no reply.

"Madame," said the pirate in a tone of mock desperation, "will you not speak to me, or have I been too bold?"

But the woman in green still made no reply, nor did she lift her mask, which was usually a sign from the women of the streets that they were willing to bestow their favors.

Undaunted, the tall man in the black wig and the clothes of
a pirate bowed again, crooking his arm. The woman in green,
to his amazement, moved toward him, took his arm and
walked with him in the direction of the St. Charles Hotel,
where one of the public balls was being given.

"Would you condescend to accompany me to a public
ball?" The pirate's question, though on the surface gallant,
had an undertone of irony that did not escape the woman at
his side.

Indeed, a woman, unaccompanied, who went off with a
stranger, would hardly be the kind who attended a private
ball.

Maeve Morgan began to regret her impulsive action. Fingal
Pearse, she reflected, had not changed at all. Nevertheless,
she would go along with the charade. She wondered how long
it would take him to recognize her.

The man in the pirate's clothes led her to a long refreshment
table at the farther end of the ballroom and provided her with
a glass of champagne. She nodded her thanks, still not
speaking, and the pirate studied her with interest.

Even in the brighter light, her face was fully disguised by
the satin mask. But her slender white neck had something in
its lines that rang a bell of recall in the stranger. What was it?
he puzzled. Then he caught sight of the sparkling necklace and
commented, "You are a brave lady to wear such jewels when
you are unprotected. Men have been killed for less, and a
woman like you. . . ."

Maeve Morgan was chilled at the implication. What a fool
she had been! The fiery impulse that drove her to excuse herself to the Hunters, on the grounds of a headache, steal home
and array herself in the extravagant costume and go forth into
the wildly celebrating crowds had faded now to regret. She
caught sight of two enlisted men she knew, dancing with their
wives, and prayed they would not know her.

The pirate followed the direction of her turning head, and
the faint suspicion he had entertained before grew stronger.
"Shall we dance?" When she nodded in assent, he took from
her the half-filled goblet of champagne and set it on the table
beside his own.

He guided her lightly onto the floor that was whirling with
dancers. And when the man in pirate's clothes breathed from

the woman's nearness a faint, elusive scent he knew so well, Fingal Pearse could name her. For the scent recalled a May afternoon, the feel of her satiny body and the lilac shadows of his chamber in the dying sun.

Fingal Pearse felt his quick desire run like the heat of wine through his every vein; his loins were beating with it, and his awakening flesh yearned toward the slender creature so close to him. But he kept his trembling voice light as he asked with brutal suddenness, "So you have tired of your domesticity, Maeve Morgan?"

He felt her body go rigid in his grasp but admired the self-possession with which she replied, "Your costume is most appropriate, Captain Pearse."

"Then you knew me before I knew you." He held her more closely, whirling her again in the rhythm of the waltz. "I am shamed. There are things between us that should make it hard for me to forget. I want to atone for a certain afternoon."

He looked down into her glowing eyes, gazing back at him through the satin mask, and felt in her the slightest relaxation of her proud and upright body. His hard hand moved down a trifle from her minute waist, feeling the bewitching swell of her hip. She was, he realized, bare of the bones and wires and horsehair implements that made most women's bodies, clothed, so graceless to the fingers.

With an almost imperceptible motion she moved closer to him an instant in the dance, and Fingal Pearse knew a hot feeling of triumphant lust. She would be his, by God, tonight, he vowed, and as for Morgan. . . .

"Where is the upright Major Morgan this evening?" he asked coarsely. "Is he allowing you this holiday?"

She drew back and did not answer.

"Maeve, it has taken me a good while to find you. I do not intend, this time, to let you escape until I show you *real* love."

Now he felt in Maeve Morgan a fearful withdrawing and wondered if he had gone too far.

In a feeble effort to distract him, she asked evasively, "What has brought you to New Orleans, Captain Pearse? I am not foolish enough to believe that you have come only for me."

"I *have* come for you, as a matter of fact. But," he added, laughing, "a man must make his way in this world. And I do have other interests."

"Yes?"

"I am now the captain of a showboat on the Mississippi River. Does that not have a fictional and dramatic ring that would capture the likes of you?" He laughed again and said temptingly, "A showboat, Maeve. Where dramas are performed. Dramas needing actresses of your beauty and gifts."

Looking into her eyes again, Fingal Pearse saw a brighter glow in their greenness, a brightness akin to lust at the sound of his words.

Then, in a low voice that pretended indifference, she answered, "I have given all that up. All that is behind me."

"Maeve, do you know how you sound when you say such things? As if you were saying, 'My life is all behind me.' "

Fingal Pearse's encircling hand knew the sudden limpness of her body, as if her whole self acknowledged the dark truth of his declaration. And when in the whirling waltz the lace attachment to her mask for a moment displaced, he saw a deeper color dyeing the neither part of her soft cheeks.

He was overpowered with a new surge of desire and said tightly, "I will have you again, Maeve Morgan, I swear it," and he drew her protesting body closer to him in the dance.

But out of the corner of his eye he saw in another part of the vast ballroom a small disturbance. A black soldier in the hated blue of the occupation was facing a drunken man in the costume of a toreador.

The white man's face was congested with anger, the black soldier laughing.

"There is going to be trouble," said Fingal Pearse bluntly. "Come, come with me now."

Puzzled, Maeve moved swiftly after Fingal Pearse. There was the sound of a scuffle, a woman screamed, and with an angry roar resembling that of beasts aroused, six men began to move in around the white man and the black soldier. Then the six were twelve, and the twelve were twenty.

"Hurry," said Fingal Pearse, leading Maeve from the ballroom into the lobby of the hotel. "Let us go upstairs."

She stopped and asked hesitantly, "Upstairs?"

"My rooms are there," he said impatiently. "It will be safer."

But she stood stubbornly at the bottom of the long staircase, staring back at him. Fingal Pearse could see in Maeve Morgan's stance the memory of that other afternoon, the af-

ternoon when he had taken her to luncheon in the hotel in
New York where he had rooms upstairs.

"I will find a carriage and go home," she said.

The uproar from the ballroom had increased, and now the
lobby was filling with frightened women and tense-faced men,
women and men in bright and varied costume, their masks
stripped away or hanging awry.

"Come with me, I say!" Fingal Pearse took Maeve Morgan
by the arm and began to lead her forcibly up the stairs.

At that moment a detachment of federal officers and men
burst into the St. Charles lobby. At their head was Major
William Morgan.

He caught sight of the man and woman on the stairs and
paused abruptly. Then, with a terse order to his men, he broke
from them and came in four long strides to the stairs.

Fingal Pearse realized at once that William Morgan knew
his wife.

"Take your hands off her, Captain Pearse," Morgan said
in a cold voice.

Pearse glanced at Maeve. Because she was still masked, her
expression was invisible, but her body slumped into a posture
of defeat. She drew the mask from her face.

"Put that back on!" William Morgan snapped. Maeve,
who had never heard him speak so, obeyed, remaining quiet
still in her shock.

"So we meet again, Major Morgan." Fingal Pearse strolled
slowly and with arrogance down the stairs until he stood a
head above the dark man in the blue uniform.

William Morgan's hand went to his pistol, and Fingal
Pearse drew from his scarlet-sashed waist a wicked-looking
little dagger that had been masquerading as a toy.

"I can cut you to ribbons, Major Morgan, before you
shoot," Pearse said coolly. William Morgan raised the gun
and cocked it; it was aimed at Fingal Pearse's heart.

Maeve cried out to Morgan, "William! William, no!"

William Morgan raised his dark, tortured eyes for a split
second to his wife's face, and in that second of time Fingal
Pearse struck out, as swiftly as a striking snake, with his
narrow dagger.

The point of the dagger went deep into William Morgan's
arm; he grunted with surprise and pain and discharged the
pistol. A bullet lodged in Fingal Pearse's side.

Crying out her husband's name, Maeve Morgan ran down
the stairs and came to him, reaching out. With a deft motion
she tore away one of the heavy panels of her wide overskirt
and wound the fabric tightly around William Morgan's
bleeding arm.

Fingal Pearse, though in an agony of pain, made no sound.
Swaying dizzily, he watched Maeve's ministrations with bitter
eyes and then staggered to the hotel desk to ascertain the
whereabouts of a doctor.

Morgan's lieutenant came running from the ballroom,
followed by three other men. "What is it, sir?" he called. He
and the other three held drawn pistols in their hands.

"Nothing, Hogan. An insect bite. Is everything under control in there?" He nodded toward the ballroom, still
discharging its crowd of weeping women and grim-faced men.
One of them cursed the soldiers as he passed, and Lieutenant
Hogan made a hasty forward movement.

"Never mind, Hogan," William Morgan said, raising his
uninjured arm.

"But, sir, who knifed you? Shall we take him?"

"Not yet," said William Morgan. He drew Hogan aside
and said something in a low voice into his lieutenant's ear.

Hogan nodded, shooting a sharp glance at the departing
Pearse. "I've heard of him before, sir. Of all the bare-
faced—" The young lieutenant stopped, with an embarrassed
side look at Maeve.

She realized with a hot-and-cold rush of relief that Hogan
had not recognized her at all.

"I have a feeling," said William Morgan to his subordinate, "that I will be handling this matter personally."

Maeve turned cold. There was a deadly resolution in her
husband's voice she had never heard before. She had an
uneasy feeling that the two men would meet again and that
one of them would not walk away from that encounter.

In sick confusion, she moved away with William Morgan.
She was torn between her new admiration for her husband
and the burning, unwelcome chaos of emotions that Fingal
Pearse's touch had aroused once more.

Yet as they left the hotel in wretched silence, Maeve
Morgan was thinking sadly that Fingal Pearse at first had not
even known her, whereas the loving and familiar eyes of
William Morgan had pierced her disguise at once.

Chapter 16

WILLIAM MORGAN maintained a stony silence as the carriage bore them toward their house on Royal Street. He stared from the window with unseeing eyes, half turned from her, at the straggling revelers. The sound of their drunken merriment, the brightness of their raiment, contrasted grotesquely with the faces of William Morgan and Maeve.

At last she blurted, "You must get to a doctor."

He turned then and looked at her as if she were someone he had just met and was uncertain of liking. His unfathomable dark gaze lingered on the high-piled flaming red hair of the wig, descended to her pale face and the swanlike neck. When he saw the necklace, his mouth twisted into a mocking half-smile.

He made no reference to her appearance—his eyes, she thought coldly, had been reference enough—but suddenly she hated the gaudy costume and the flaming hair, feeling like one of the women in Hallie McDermott's, not the mischievous, almost unsexed spirit that had driven her into the night.

William answered curtly, "I must report to the garrison. There is a doctor there."

Deeply pained at his tone and feeling obscurely betrayed that he was leaving her now, Maeve bit her lip to keep from crying. To hide her face, she stared from the other window, and they rode the rest of the distance in frozen silence.

When they reached the white house with its lacelike balustrades of black wrought metal, William descended and handed Maeve down from the carriage. "Wait for me," he ordered the driver. To Maeve he said a blunt good-night and waited until he had seen her enter the house and heard the greeting of Amelie, who had opened the shadowy door to her.

Maeve heard the carriage drive away and, ignoring the comments of the astonished Amelie, ran up the stairs to the chamber she shared with William.

A bright fire was burning in the hearth, for the evening had turned chilly. Snatching the elaborate wig from her head, Maeve threw in the fire, gagging at the bitter odor of burning hair. It was horrible, yet she had to see it utterly consumed, for the false hair had become a tawdry symbol of her own mad recklessness, and she could not bear to look upon it again. Holding her breath so that she might inhale less of the dreadful odor, Maeve unclasped the fastenings of the green costume. How ugly and bedraggled it looked now, with its torn panel and the dirt stains around the bottom incurred from her uncaring entrance into the carriage. Maeve threw the dress on a chair, leaving the necklace around her white neck.

It was all over, she reflected darkly. William had looked at her, not with hatred—she could have borne that—but with a disinterested face in which there had been no love. And all because of one foolish escapade! She began to cry, with loud tearing sobs, so loudly that she did not hear the footsteps in the upper hall. There was a soft knock at the door; that, too, she must not have heard at first, for now it had the sound of repetition. The knock was growing louder.

"Who is it?" Maeve called in a trembling voice.

"Amelie."

I cannot face her now! Maeve thought desperately. She crept to the door and said, "I'm sorry, I am tired. I'm going to bed."

"Please, Maeve." Amelie's persistent cry reached her. "Let me in. There is something wrong."

Resigned, Maeve unlocked the door and stood aside for Amelie to enter.

Amelie closed the door and peered at Maeve. "What is it?" she asked softly, taking Maeve's hand. Then, sniffing the odor from the fire, she exclaimed, *"Mon Dieu!"* and made a grotesque face.

For the first time in hours, Maeve Morgan smiled. "It is the wig."

"I thought as much," Amelie said, grinning, and went to the narrow French window nearest the hearth. She opened it, saying, "I will have to burn some incense here, or M. Morgan will spend the night in another room."

Turning, Amelie caught Maeve's woebegone expression and colored deeply, her pale *café au lait* skin almost russet with embarrassment.

"It doesn't matter. He will probably do that anyway."

"Maeve." Amelia came to her, urging her to sit down on the four-poster bed. "You look exhausted. What is wrong, my friend? What has happened? You went out, I think, alone, to celebrate the Mardi Gras."

Maeve nodded miserably.

"And Captain Fingal Pearse has come to town," Amelie remarked wisely. Maeve regretted for a moment that she had ever confided in Amelie about Fingal Pearse and marveled at the spy system which enabled servants to know everything before it reached the ears of their employers.

"You knew that!" she exclaimed. "You did not tell me."

Amelie smiled. "I wish you had never learned. M. Morgan loves you with all his heart; this Pearse man"—Amelie shrugged one of the eloquent Gallic shrugs that had become so familiar to Maeve—"has the evil in him."

Maeve pondered the phrase. Perhaps it was true; perhaps Fingal Pearse did have the "evil in him." Yet she could not help recalling his hard leanness and the power of his strange cold eyes. And unbidden, the vivid and disturbing memory of the afternoon in May came to her.

"What happened?" Amelie repeated.

Sighing, Maeve told her all of it.

Amelie shook her head and made a little clucking sound of disapproval. "Oh, my, oh, my." But seeing Maeve's haunted face, she said consolingly, "Never mind. M. Morgan will come around. Here, I think you need this." She poured a glass of brandy and gave it to Maeve.

Looking at it with distaste, Maeve nevertheless drank it up obediently. The liqueur left a burning path down her throat, yet in a moment or two she began to feel calmer, and she reflected sadly that she understood now about Shane. There was a magic in it, indeed, this perilous liquid.

"He is like my man, Jean-Paul, this Pearse." Amelie sat down in a small slipper chair by the bed. "Ah, Maeve, I fear you are like me. You are one of those who listens to a far bird crying and goes to capture it. And it always flies away. My man Jean-Paul was like that, too. It is unfortunate,'' she concluded sourly, "that he listened to a number of distant birds, and none of them was me."

Maeve did not smile, for she heard the pain below the surface of the bitter Gallic humor. She reached out and touched Amelie's hand with grateful affection.

"Maeve, do not throw William Morgan away," Amelie pleaded. She studied her friend's face but was unable to read the emotions upon it. "Go to sleep now," Amelie said gently. "You are so very tired. It will come right in the morning. You'll see."

"Thank you, Amelie." Maeve's words were thick with weariness and the effect of the unaccustomed brandy.

When Amelie had gone, Maeve rose from the bed, almost staggering with exhaustion, and completed her undressing. She washed and scented herself with the elusive perfume that William so loved and brushed out her tangled black hair.

Wearing a tissuelike night garment of narcissus color, at last Maeve lay down, waiting for the sound of William's return. But soon her tired eyelids could not support their own weight, and she began to drowse, hearing the words of Amelie, "You are one who listens to a far bird crying."

And for a magic interval outside of time, Maeve Morgan was Maeve Rossar-Mescro again, riding the hills of Tullaghoe and seeing, beside the secret pool, the shadow of the wings of an unknown bird.

Was it true? she asked herself sleepily, half awake, half dreaming. Was she one of those who listened always for the distant sound and was destined to know no peace in the here and now?

In the confusing manner of dreams, time became unreadable again, and Maeve Heron was standing on the decks of the *Falcon*, riding the roll of the seas and hearing the sad cries of the wheeling gulls that followed.

And in her dream there were the images of her husband, William Morgan; and Thomas Rossar-Mescro and Michael and Shane; and the golden man called Fingal Pearse. At the sight of Pearse Maeve knew again, half dreaming, the same wild heat of her senses' confusion that she had known awake.

She clung to the memory of Amelie's last words, "All will come right, you'll see."

Yet another voice sounded, "It is all there, far away, the peace and magic; here and now are only pain and restlessness." And much later in her half drowse Maeve Morgan thought she heard a man's footsteps approach and pause and then recede down the corridor.

All did not come right, however, in the morning or in the mornings and evenings that followed throughout the languorous half summer that was the Southern spring. William Morgan, without an explanation, moved his belongings from the chamber that he had shared with Maeve and occupied a small guest room on the floor above.

Maeve could not comprehend the turn of events. She had believed, as Amelie said, that William would "come around." And when he did not, Maeve sank into a numb withdrawal, from which, as the weeks passed, she found herself powerless to emerge.

But the garrison women, at least, had no new sins to reproach her with, for her identity had remained hidden from Lieutenant Hogan and the other man of her acquaintance who had been at the St. Charles on that fateful night.

Fingal Pearse, to her relief, had not reappeared. She learned that the showboat had sailed upriver for the summer and would not return to the port of New Orleans until the fall. Maeve drew a deep breath of gratitude. With Pearse away, she felt, she was somehow safe for the time being.

And the spring that seemed so empty to Maeve in her loneliness was an eventful one for the states of the conquered but rebellious South.

In March, over President Johnson's veto, the First Reconstruction Act was passed by Congress, establishing martial law in five Southern military districts. The rebelling states were to be readmitted to the Union after they called constitutional conventions elected by both black and white.

March had nearly ended without the Southern States calling such conventions, and an angry Congress passed a supplementary Reconstruction Act that required federal military commanders to set up procedures for registering voters.

And the violent hatred of the Southerners, never far from

their volatile surfaces, flared into new insurrection. At the end of March a newspaper up in Tennessee published the first report of a mysterious new secret organization called the Ku Klux Klan, an "Invisible Empire of the South." The Klan had been organized, it was said, to support white supremacy and oppose Radical Reconstruction.

Something in the sound of it reminded Maeve of the distant Fenians. Stories had reached her ears of terrible outrages perpetrated on white Southern women, and she read with sympathy of the angry men who rode in the night to avenge themselves upon the lawless blacks aroused by those called the carpetbaggers and scalawags.

From the beginning Maeve had looked on those newcomers with distaste; they were rabble-rousers of the worst order, vulgar and unmannerly and illiterate. William had remarked that he himself was ashamed to be associated with such people, albeit by indirection.

It was on a mild afternoon in April, as she was preparing rather listlessly to depart for a musicale at Mrs. Hunter's house, that Maeve heard another mysterious name.

She was passing through the lower hall when she heard the murmuring voices of Amelie and Jinjy from the parlor. They had announced their intention of hanging fresh curtains there while Maeve was out.

The secretive quality of Jinjy's tone caused Maeve to stop and listen, although she disliked doing so.

Nonetheless, she found herself unable to pass. She stilled the rustling of her wide silken skirts and frankly listened.

"Georges Roget," Jinjy was murmuring. "Mlle. Thibault was furious! She said to Mme. Roget that her husband was doing harm enough to his café without joining the Knights."

"The Knights?" It was Amelie's more precise inflection.

"The Knights of the White Camellia. They are like that . . . Klan thing in Tennessee. My uncle was very frightened. He said they will kill all black men who misbehave."

"I think perhaps we should tell M. the Major Morgan," Amelie declared. "Or at least Mme. Maeve."

"Oh, no! Oh, no!" Jinjy's stage whisper held terror. "If you tell them, I will say I don't know what you are talking about. I don't want those people after me!" And suddenly there was a loud crash.

"Jinjy, Jinjy!" Maeve heard Amelie cry. "Are you all right?"

Maeve cleared her throat and went into the parlor. The elfin Jinjy, woolly hair like a black cap upon her small head, was picking herself up from the floor. An overturned chair was beside her.

The two women looked at Maeve with disconcerted faces. They were obviously wondering, Maeve thought, how much she had heard. She felt a quick stab of hurt; there had been a time, she reflected, when she and Amelie had been so close. Amelie had always told her everything. But now somehow they had become black and white, Southerner and alien, despite the fact that Maeve's own husband had helped make Amelie free. She was puzzled at this contradiction.

However, Maeve put the thought from her mind and went to Jinjy with concern. "Are you sure you're all right?" she asked the impish Jinjy.

"Oh, yes, ma'am," Jinjy answered eagerly and giggled. Amelie's face had closed; it was smooth as an egg and totally unreadable. She smiled politely at Maeve.

The distant politeness of the smile pained Maeve even more, but she said to Jinjy in a gentle way, "All right. Be careful." And returning Amelie's smile, she left the house.

Entering the house of Colonel and Alice Hunter, Maeve Morgan reflected that she had left one alienation only to face another. Alice Hunter had always been warm and kind, but the other women were not so generous.

Maeve returned the greeting of the Hunters' amiable maid and glanced nervously at her image in the gilt-framed hall mirror; it was almost six and a half feet in height and gave her back a clear view of her whole self.

In an attempt to brighten her own spirits, Maeve had asked Amelie to arrange her black hair in a new French coiffure. The hair was drawn back from the ears and swept to the left behind, terminating in front in one startling ringlet a yard long. Five elaborate curls bubbled over her forehead. The arrangement had seemed chic and interesting at home, but now Maeve feared that it was too dramatic and noted that its starkness emphasized the new thinness of her face.

Her cheekbones were very prominent, and her face was so

pale! Maeve pinched her cheeks to restore some of their color. She was thankful for the flattering shade of her velvet mousquetaire hat of lavender-pink, with its scarf of darker ribbon and rosette of ombré feathers. Fastidiously she had removed its edging of pink flowers. The other hats, she knew, would already be summery even in April, but Maeve had clung stubbornly to the metropolitan style of wearing velvet until May, hating the look of light straw in April.

She dreaded the other women's avid curiosity about her strained looks and hoped her lovely dress would distract them. It was lavender-pink to match the hat and was fashioned of shot silk, bowed in darker velvet, and flaunted a moderate but impudent little bustle, a style that had not generally reached Louisiana.

Rousing herself from her moody thoughts, Maeve hurried into Alice Hunter's drawing room.

Mrs. Hunter, wearing a simple but elegant gown of gleaming blue-gray that pleasantly enhanced her coppery hair and soft blue eyes, came forward with outstretched hand to meet Maeve.

"My dear," she said warmly, "how lovely you look." But then she peered at Maeve more closely with her kind, near-sighted eyes and murmured in a lower voice, "But you have grown thinner. Are you all right?"

The benign concern of Alice Hunter, so different from the inquisitiveness of the others, nearly overcame Maeve, and she felt quick tears gathering in her eyes. But she winked them back and answered courteously, "I am just a little . . . tired, that's all." She smiled at Alice Hunter.

Her hostess moved to the tea table and indicated the spread of bright fruits and cakes there. "Sit down, Maeve, and let Mary serve you something. I think you know all these ladies," she added with an encompassing smile at the others.

"Yes." Maeve nodded, forcing a smile for Esperanza Hogan, the Italian wife of Lieutenant Hogan, who returned her greeting coldly, staring at Maeve with her little black eyes like raisins in her plump face, nodded to the haughty New England wife of Captain Holder and to others with whom her acquaintance was slight.

She realized in that moment, when the women looked at her with an envy approaching hatred, that she looked far too fashionable. It was bad enough that William's private income enabled her to wear next year's dress; it was her boldness in adapting the hat to her own style that ignited the hottest flame of resentment.

Maeve sat down reluctantly in the empty chair next to Esperanza Hogan, who disliked her most of all, and heard the woman ask with mock anxiety, "I hope you are well, Mrs. Morgan?"

Maeve, aware that the woman's spiteful inquiry referred to her new thinness—Amelie had had to alter the waist of the gown she was wearing—answered strongly, "Very well indeed, Mrs. Hogan. And it is *obvious* that you are!" The last comment was accompanied by a friendly smile and, with perfect timing, her green glance dropped to Mrs. Hogan's broad middle.

Maeve added, "I love your dress. I almost bought it myself when I saw it at Stewart's back in . . . when was it? . . . 1866. But that shade of lavender is so difficult for us dark women—we have to be so careful of looking sallow." Very quickly then, Maeve turned her glance away.

Mrs. Hogan was now the color of a ripe plum, fairly bursting with contained indignation.

Maeve hated herself for the cheap device, yet could not prevent a feeling of bitter triumph.

But she noticed that Alice Hunter was staring at her with bewilderment and reproach. Maeve had never concerned herself with petty matters in this fashion.

Stricken with shame, Maeve sought to atone for her actions by hastily plunging into conversation with Alice Hunter—the only one among the women, Maeve reflected, who seemed to have any wider interests at all. "There are such exciting things going on back in New York," Maeve blurted, attempting brightness, "with the Equal Rights Convention called for May and the women so active. Doesn't it make you a little homesick, Mrs. Hunter?"

Miserably Maeve realized that she had made another gaffe. The stony face of Mrs. Holder grew even more somber, and Alice Hunter, seeming even more puzzled at Maeve's lack of tact, answered gently, "Ah, I am always homesick, Mrs. Morgan, as are most of us."

"I imagine," said Mrs. Holder in an acid voice, "that Mrs. Morgan is more homesick than most of us—for the theater and all that."

Maeve realized sickly that Mrs. Holder looked on her as little better than a woman of the streets because she had acted on the stage. But she made her voice steady as she replied, "We have a very good choice of plays here in New Orleans, so the deprivation is not so great as that. And the wonderful opera!"

"I don't think that is what Mrs. Holder meant," said Esperanza Hogan in a purring voice. "You must have led such an . . . exciting life as an actress, Mrs. Morgan."

The memory of the murder and the sensational trial was instantly green in every listener's mind. And that, Maeve thought, glancing at Mrs. Hogan's triumphant smile, was exactly what the fat bitch had in mind.

The kindhearted Alice Hunter stepped into the breach. "There are excitements enough here for me," she said in a rush, with a little uneasy laugh, "what with these White Knights or whatever they are. I am more worried about David than I was during the war, I do believe."

Mrs. Hunter bit her lip. She herself had made a very tactless comment, she realized too late. It was as if Maeve's earlier unease were communicating itself to all the women. Mrs. Hunter glanced at the gold watch pinned to her bosom. "I do wonder what is keeping Mme. Costello," she said nervously. "She promised to come to sing for us at three."

There was another uncomfortable little silence, and then plump Mrs. Hogan said abruptly in her harsh voice, "My husband thinks we should just hang all these Rebs and get it over with."

"Mrs. Hogan!" Alice Hunter gasped. Captain Holder's wife shot a look of disapproval at the younger woman, and the other women sat in appalled silence.

All of a sudden Maeve Morgan could bear no more. The malice of Mrs. Holder and the petty carping of Mrs. Hogan—the bitterness of the women toward her—were overwhelming. Maeve felt that she would scream and run around the room breaking things if she did not relieve her feelings. Hardly knowing what she did, Maeve cried out, "And he, an Irishman, your husband? A man whose people have been ground under the heels of the English and the landlords and the Danes . . . a man from our tortured country made a statement like that? Don't you realize, you fat fool, that *we* are the English here and the Southerners are the Irishmen?

And the Knights are only trying to protect themselves and their women and children, just as the Fenians—"

The other women were staring at her openmouthed. Maeve halted her impassioned speech, for she had nearly given away a secret that she had kept for these few years that seemed so long. She could feel her heart hammering, and she trembled in every limb.

"Are you acquainted with the . . . Fenians, Mrs. Morgan?" Mrs. Holder asked after a moment. Maeve turned to her and almost recoiled at the dislike in her plain face.

"I think," Alice Hunter intervened, her soft face flushed with dismay and her voice shaking, "that perhaps we should not discuss this any further." She looked at Maeve, and there were tears in her kind eyes.

Without another word, Maeve rose, putting her hand to her flowerlike mouth to hide its grimace of pain. She hurried from the room and, closing the door softly behind her, heard Alice Hunter say in her forgiving way, "I do not think that she is well," and Esperanza Hogan's rough voice crying, "The woman is a traitor . . . a traitor!"

In the corridor she managed to control her face and say a hasty good-bye to the surprised maid. But when she reached the street, the torrent of Maeve's weeping broke forth. She fumbled in her little silken reticule for a handkerchief; under its inadequate shelter, she felt the salt flood of tears on her cheeks.

The full realization of what she had done came to her. *Dear God,* she thought, *Alice Hunter will tell her husband and her husband will tell William. And then . . what will I say to him?*

With this grim question echoing in her mind, Maeve Morgan found her stumbling way back to the white house on Royal Street.

An hour later, as she was lying glumly on her bed, Maeve heard a light tap on the door and Amelie's inquiring voice.

"Come in," Maeve called listlessly, staring out the French window.

When she looked up, Amelie was standing at the foot of the bed, her graceful hands on her hips, glaring at Maeve. "Maeve Morgan, you are a fool," she said.

Maeve, almost speechless with shock, stared at Amelie. Then indignantly she cried, "How dare you take that tone with me? What on earth do you mean by talking to me like that?"

Amelie smiled her ironic Gallic smile and sat down on the slipper chair next to the bed. "I ran into the Hunters' cook at the market just now," said Amelie.

"I see." Maeve stared back defiantly at Amelie. "And what is that to you? Am I to report to you on all my actions?"

"I say you are a fool because Major Morgan's anger will be very great. And there is only one way you can appease him."

Maeve sat up in the bed. "What are you talking about?"

"Maeve, Maeve! Did you learn *nothing* at Hallie McDermott's? Have I not told you time and again that all men are the same under their trousers? And your body, to Major Morgan, is a better betwitchment than *voudon*!"

Maeve flushed crimson.

"And I know that he has not been to your bed."

"What right have you to mention such things?" Maeve demanded. "How could you possibly know about our . . . private concerns?"

Amelie shook her head and said, as if Maeve were a child, "Do you think that the guest room cleans itself? Every morning Jinjy makes the bed that the major occupies in that room."

Maeve looked away and said in a low voice, "What can *I* do?"

"If a man does not come to your bed, you go to *his*," Amelie advised bluntly. "You know quite well that he would not be able to resist you."

Maeve heard the truth in Amelie's words. Indeed, William's desire for her had sometimes been almost frightening; she recalled her first awed realization of her body's power over her husband.

"Come now," said Amelie, "get up, and let us get you prettily arrayed for dinner. You must be so enticing that his anger will fly away like a bird on the wind." Amelie's grin glittered in her pretty face. "We have prepared the dinner he likes the very best. And now I shall prepare *you*. The rest you must accomplish. Come now."

Amelie went to the great chest and withdrew the beautiful blue-green gown of watered silk that was one of William Morgan's favorites.

"That is much too elaborate for an evening at home," Maeve protested.

"This is a very special evening." Amelie was firm. "This gown shows off your bosom to a niceness . . . and makes your skin look very white and your eyes very wonderful."

Maeve was forced to agree that the dress was one of the most becoming she owned.

"And now for your face and hair." Amelie led her to the dressing table and began to brush her night-colored hair until it fairly glimmered; with skilled hands, Amelie wound it into a heavy chignon and dressed it simply on the forehead. It was a look Maeve knew, that William especially liked. "Ah! You are so pale. Have you rouge?"

"Of course not," Maeve said indignantly. Only women of the streets wore such a thing offstage.

"But yes, you do," Amelie insisted. "Do you not still have your makeup box from the theater?"

"Oh, yes, of course. In the chest."

Amelie brought the box and took out the rouge. Lightly she applied it to Maeve's cheeks; her application of it was so natural that Maeve looked at her own face in surprise.

Carefully Amelie lifted the rustling gown over Maeve's smooth head and fastened it. Maeve placed in her pierced earlobes her intricate eardrops of aquamarine and emerald but chose no other ornament. Then she put her frail scent on her neck and arms and ears and in the hollow of her throat.

"There!" Amelie said, surveying Maeve with complacent eyes. "You look very lovely. Now, my friend, you can deal with the anger of Major Morgan."

Chapter 17

MAEVE MORGAN lay wakeful, listening to the night sounds of the house. She heard the tall clock in the downstairs hall strike eleven and pondered the hours just past.

Amelie's mischievous plan had come very near to success. From William's tense entrance into the house, quite late for dinner, until his sudden exit from the parlor, Maeve had felt him warming to her with something of the old loving look in his eyes.

She was aware that he knew what had happened at the Hunters'; its shadow lay on his tight face and in the grim set of his mouth. But to her surprise he had said nothing of the matter, prevented at first by the presence of the servants.

Maeve noted that he drank more wine at dinner than was his custom; when, at its end, they had gone into the parlor, and he said sternly, "Maeve, there's something I want to discuss with you," she had answered gently, "You look very tired. Can we not talk of it tomorrow?"

He had hesitated, then sat down on the sofa without further speech to listen to her play the piano.

She had chosen some of the more lyrical nocturnes of Chopin and felt in him a subtle relaxation. Once he had strolled to the instrument and lightly, hesitantly touched her gleaming hair. But when she looked up, he had left the room.

Now, an hour later, Maeve lay in an attitude of expectation, wearing a tissuelike nightdress of pale lilac, her hair streaming over her shoulders. She had seen his dark glance lingering on her soft white bosom, dazzling over the blue-green color of her gown, pausing on her rose-petal mouth.

She recalled Amelie's bold directive: "If a man does not come to your bed, you go to his." And she shuddered with fear at the idea of such a thing. What if—Maeve's limbs turned icy under the thin coverlet and the floating drift of her gown—what if he were . . . cold to her? She would die of humiliation; she, the proud Maeve Heron, whose self had exercised such magic on the senses of Michael Rathmullan and Harley Blaine, on the impervious Fingal Pearse and on William himself.

I cannot do it, Maeve concluded. *I will not. Let him come to me!* Yet she knew she had been wrong. She had hurt him so deeply, first wounding his very manhood and now attacking everything in which he believed.

And her starved senses, too, demanded surcease. Maeve recalled vividly his slender beauty, the tender fire of his mouth and the bewildered ecstasy she had known below his caress.

Now she knew a sudden, tingling warmth over all her body and freed herself of the coverlet. She rose and lit a candle, its fresh wick waiting whitely in a brass holder on the small table by the bed. Moving softly to the pier glass, Maeve Morgan held the candle high and let its yellow light show her the image of her face and body.

By the taper's flicker, she saw the glittering wealth of her hair; between its dark wings her face was glowing with excitement, her cheeks roseate and her green eyes alight. Over the lilac gown they had a peculiar value in contrast with the blackness of her hair and brows, the pallid rosiness of her face and the darker rose of her full mouth with its brief, impudent upper lip.

Lowering the taper a little and feeling an obscure, heated shame, Maeve let the light reveal her body through its filmy veil; she studied the curving shadow of her breasts, the darker hollows of her flesh so clearly revealed by the fabric. She gloried in the sensation of her own naked skin under the drift of gown.

Maeve returned the candle to the little table and, bending, blew out is flame. Then, with a swiftly beating heart, she took from the slipper chair the floating peignoir that matched the gown and wrapped it around her, sliding her bare feet into the satin mules, with their cloud-soft collars of marabou, and stole to the door.

Opening it soundlessly, she listened for a moment. All was silent in the house; only the deep-throated ticking of the tall clock in the hall below broke the stillness. Maeve took a deep breath and closed the door to her chamber. Keeping to the carpeted portion of the corridor, for her flapping mules made a little thump, she crept to the stairs and stole upward.

At the door of the guest room Maeve again paused, with her heart pounding loudly, so loudly that she had a wild fancy it would be heard in the quiet of the night; her breath was coming in short, shallow gasps. She put her soft hand on the doorknob and turned it.

The room was filled with moonlight, and by its pale illumination she saw her husband sit up, startled, and stare at her with his dark eyes. Maeve's nervous senses leaped at the sight of his bare dark chest, the narrow, hard-muscled nakedness of his torso where the coverlet had fallen away.

Astonished, he cried out her name softly.

Coming toward him without a word, she threw off the drifting peignoir and then lowered over her shoulders the loose gown. Standing before him boldly, she let the lilac nightdress float like a great flower to the carpet and revealed to him her nude white body with its rose-tipped, night-shadowed pallor.

"Maeve!" he cried out again, and his cry seemed a tortured, strangled sound in the stillness of the lonely chamber. He threw back the covers and rose, coming slowly toward her. Maeve saw now that he was naked, too.

With one stride he was near her, holding her with a steely grip in his binding arms, kissing her face and neck and breasts and hair with wild abandon, murmuring inchoate things as his eager flesh responded to her pulsing closeness.

She inhaled the clean musk of his skin, her soft lips parting under his devouring kiss and moved closer, stroking his dark head and firm neck and trembling face with her hands; the prickle of his heavy mustache, chafing her tender upper lip, filled her with an alien excitement. She could feel herself trembling wholly throughout her bare body, and a profound, hot pulsing deep inside her became so overpowering and sweet that she groaned under William's caress.

As if she were another woman, Maeve Morgan, hynotized,

felt herself acting in abandoned wildness; she ground her body against his and heard from him a different sound, the yearning, almost animal sound of a man in the throes of a terrible desire. He seemed unable to take his mouth from hers, powerless to draw back his seeking flesh from her satin nakedness.

Still clinging to his body, Maeve began, with seductive, excruciating slowness, to slide down to her knees, hearing him cry out anew at the silken friction of her skin. Kneeling, she clasped him closer to her and began to bestow a multitude of nibbling kisses upon his hard, concave belly. William's legs were shuddering so he could scarcely stand. She felt his shaking, as if he were battling a mighty wind; she started leisurely to give him an astonishing caress, and she intuited that his center was a great volcano—with immense convulsions it would erupt, rending him almost asunder.

Suddenly she knew neither him nor herself, only this wild and urging desire, and this not-knowing, William's strangeness enhanced a thousandfold the bladed sharpness of the need that stabbed her now; her skin burned like fever. He was so beautiful he made her weak.

Then his trembling strong arms were lifting her, lifting her to his clinging kiss again, lifting her body into his arms, carrying her to the bed, his shaky mouth bending to caress again and again the cloudlike, smooth softness of her upper arms and breasts.

Carefully he put her down and lowered himself to lie beside her, taking her in his urgent arms again, kissing her with long, starved kisses that seemed never to cease, and the caresses became for her the far-glowing flames of an ever-rising, unreal fire that theatened to devour her. She no longer had a face or name, nor had the man beside her, who had become in this wild, dancing converse a demon and a god of bursting pleasure, an instrument of burning, long, impossible delight.

Dimly in her frenzy Maeve heard her own voice cry out, and then his deeper, heavier cries, torn from their bodies by the shattering wonder of their meeting, and waves of indescribable pleasure, such as she had never thought to know, drowned her shuddering core, pounding at her like the waves of a stormy sea attacking the sand, rising to an unbearable height, then breaking, breaking, slackening to disappear, leaving a sunlit feeling within her that was utter peace.

When they had returned to sense, and Maeve felt his sweet weight, his sobbing breath hot upon her neck and his strong fingers tangled in her hair, Maeve Morgan somehow knew that all, from that night onward, would be well.

They would not be apart again, she thought with rapture. No, even when the showboat returned to New Orleans in the fall, they would be safe together.

Darkly then she wondered why she had thought of safety, thought of the showboat at all, and burrowed into William Morgan's shoulder, seeking haven.

The following afternoon, at William's direction, Maeve asked Amelie to have his things removed back to the large chamber on the second floor. Amelie, grinning broadly, complied, and once again the third-floor room reverted to its status of guest chamber.

By the time that summer came Maeve Morgan had almost forgotten their separation of the spring, and the humid, oppressive season that was so threatening to her delicate skin and cruel to her cool-loving temper changed its face entire. Her fully aroused senses somehow bloomed more fully in the lazy heat; Maeve knew a physical aching when William moved out of her arms.

Emerging from the white house only in the mornings and evenings during the summer's height, Maeve spent many a blazing afternoon in unusual languor. She would lie in her shaded chamber, listening to the musical cries of the street sellers, advertising their wares of cantaloupes, their skill at scissor grinding; or the cinnamon-colored voices of Jinjy and Amelie could be heard singing the Cajun airs that had become so familiar—"Salangadou," "Pauv' Piti' Mamselle Zizi," those songs with such a haunting and sensous sound. With the sweet monomania of the March-born, she dreamed of William Morgan.

And the former wonders of the ancient port city were restored for a moment in these small and magical ways to Maeve.

She noted that the lines of strain had gone from around William's mouth, and his sunburned face looked smoother. The events in Washington of which he sometimes spoke and which she read of seemed unreal to Maeve—Congress had given the military commanders of the South the power to determine who was eligible to vote; a constitutional convention in New York had rejected the vote for women. And a rising playwright named Augustin Daly presented the melodrama *Under the Gaslight* to New York audiences.

Maeve, in her summer languor and renewed enchantment in William's presence, heard all this as if it were the far-off buzzing of insects. And if William Morgan knew a grim concern with the national events that so inflamed the Southerners, he returned each evening to the shadowy house with a feeling of delighted comfort.

Sweating and weary, he would enter to the sound of ice tinkling in thin glasses and the ripple of Maeve's piano. The canny Amelie, born to the land where the summer was an enemy to be kept at bay, cooled the house by creating darkness; the curtains were always drawn during the heat of the day. And the sight of Maeve, William declared, in her frail dresses the color of flowers and leaves, of sky and water, soothed him almost as much as the chilled drinks in the tinkling glasses. Summer covers had been placed on all the furniture, in smooth, light fabrics pleasant to the body, replacing the sticky velvet and velours of the originals.

Thus, the long summer passed with relative ease for Maeve and William. It was not until an evening toward the middle of September that Maeve Morgan felt a stir of change within, and the face with which she greeted William was almost that of another woman.

He had always enjoyed her changing faces, and this night, as he sniffed the somewhat cooler air, he found that Maeve's eyes, for months so languorous and heavy-lidded, looked bright and wide again. William knew how she loved the autumn, saw that she marked its approaching now by wearing a gown the remarkable blue of northern asters.

He said as much and was rewarded by her admiration. "I marvel that a man can be so aware of such things," she said softly, kissing him tenderly.

He held her for a long moment, his chin upon her hair, and then said teasingly, "I have a surprise for you."

"A surprise?" She pulled away and looked up into his face with the enthusiasm of a child. "Oh, what is it, what is it?"

He laughed and pulled her to him again. "The showboat has returned."

She heard the news with a mingling of pleasure and unease;

surely William knew that Fingal Pearse was its captain. She could not forget, even now, the grimness with which he had told Hogan that night in the St. Charles that he would handle the matter of Fingal Pearse.

Surprised at her silence, for she had spoken often of how much she had longed to visit it, William Morgan stepped back a little, loosing his hold upon her and raised her face with a gentle hand. "What's this?" he queried. "You were so sorry to miss it last spring."

"Oh, I'm very glad to hear the news," she answered hastily "It's just that I didn't expect it . . . so soon."

She was relieved that he seemed to accept her feeble reply, and he went on, "Hunter has decided that the city will not fall to the Confederacy if we absent ourselves for an evening. We thought we would make up a party—the Hunters and ourselves, the Holders and a few others."

"And the Hogans?"

"Oh, yes, I suppose they will be included," William responded carelessly. "Would you like to attend?"

"Of course, I would love it!" Maeve made her response bright, thinking that the party would not be much to her liking. And if they encountered the captain of the *Falcon*—but she thrust the thought from her. She did not want to disappoint William with an inadequate response, and indeed, she did not wish to spoil her own pleasure in the long-deferred outing.

On the evening they chose, Maeve's misgivings seemed unfounded. Even the women she so disliked, with the exception of Alice Hunter, seemed to have put aside for the evening their malice. Glorying in the crispness of the air, Maeve was gratified when the stiff New Englander, Mrs. Holder, condescended to admire Maeve's ensemble of velvet, the color of an American Beauty rose, with its trim of jet and black braid.

To compensate for the brightness of the gown, Maeve wore no jewels at all, except for two simple drops of jet in her pierced earlobes, and the plainest of black hats over her glistening, plainly dressed hair.

Aside from the merest civilities, Maeve avoided any conversation with the admiring Lieutenant Hogan and Captain Holder, for she was loath to arouse any jealousy in their less attractive wives. It was only with William and the friendly secure Hunters that she could let herself be jocose and free.

It was a pleasant, stimulating coolness that greeted the party as it ascended the ramp to the showboat. The crisper air had touched Maeve's cheeks with a natural glow, and her green eyes danced with anticipation when she heard the music of the band and saw the multitudinous lamps reflecting themselves upon the dark water.

William was looking upon her fondly, and she knew a sudden surge of indescribable well-being and happiness, that feeling that the servants of Tullaghoe had called fey, adding soberly, "Beware, such joy is too good to be true."

Maeve Morgan then experienced with full force the meaning of that somber caution, for coming toward them now, dressed in the fine black suit and ruffled shirt of the river gambler, was Captain Fingal Pearse.

After their magical reunion on that April night William Morgan had forgiven Maeve everything—her innocent escapade on the night of Mardi Gras, even her ill-considered pronouncements in the home of Colonel and Mrs. Hunter. So certain was he of her now, after the exquisite intimacies and growing closeness of the dreamlike summer, that William Morgan almost welcomed the sight of Fingal Pearse.

His anger acted like the stimulus of champagne. He felt almost giddy with the challenge of the coming encounter. And he fervently hoped that David Hunter's suspicions were well founded.

None of the women of the party knew that their officer-husbands had arranged the outing for purposes other than social.

A week before, on the day when William invited Maeve to the showboat performance, David Hunter had called a meeting of his staff. The activities of the Knights of the White Camellia, he said, had been increasing at an alarming rate. And it was strongly rumored that Captain Fingal Pearse had had a hand in the organizing of the local outlaws. A further rumor had it that, upon Pearse's return to New Orleans in the autumn, he was planning to lead the Knights in even greater mischief.

"And it is my belief," said Hunter, "that Pearse's primary cohorts are employed upon the riverboat. It might be interesting," he added, smiling, "to visit the showboat with our wives, for an evening's performance, to look into the setup there."

So it had been arranged. At this moment, as Pearse came toward them, smiling his hard smile, William Morgan's maleness stirred. How he longed to knock the arrogant bastard down, to take his throat between his own hands and choke the life out! But that, unfortunately, was not in accord with Colonel Hunter's plan. So William Morgan made his face bland when Pearse greeted Hunter, saying ironically, "Good evening, Colonel. How interesting to see you in mufti at our little performance! I hope you will find everything of interest."

There was a hint of insolent mockery in the words that renewed Morgan's desire to knock the captain down. "Major Morgan," Pearse said then. "Mrs. Morgan, welcome."

William glanced sidelong at Maeve and was overjoyed that her lovely face revealed only cold distaste, for she did not speak at all, only nodding with the barest civility.

"But do go in," Pearse said to the party in the same tone of maddening mockery, "the drama is about to begin. Not that," he added in a tone of familiarity to Maeve, "the play will come up to the standards of Mrs. Morgan."

William Morgan seethed, both at the intimacy of the words and at the reminder that Maeve Morgan, unlike the more respectable women of the party, had acted on the stage. But with superhuman effort William Morgan retained his poise and, touching Maeve's arm lightly, said, "Let us go in then, my darling."

When they entered the theater, the women exclaimed with delighted surprise. The playhouse had been designed after the plan of the famous Blackstone Theater of Chicago and was lavishly furnished.

"Why, it is huge!" Maeve cried, her eyes sparkling.

"I believe it has a seating capacity of about fourteen hundred," William responded. "We have seats in the dress circle."

"The dress circle!" Maeve repeated with a kind of laughing wonder. William nodded, and gestured toward the section containing hundreds of cushioned armchairs upholstered in purple velvet.

"It is amazing," Maeve commented, looking about the

auditorium. Hundreds of gas jets and innumerable mirrors made the white walls gleam. The band was now playing an almost satirical air that characterized the comical melodrama they were to see.

When the curtains rose, Maeve exclaimed softly to observe the elaborate drop curtains and intricate set pieces that the playhouse boasted. "Good heavens!" she whispered to William. "Wallack's itself would not be ashamed of this scenery!"

He smiled and took her hand, delighting in her delight.

She soon was lost in the play. True, as the sarcastic Fingal Pearse had stated, the play did not come up to her standards—it was the melodrama *The Fireman's Flame*, featuring a villainess of such deep-dyed evil and a heroine of contrasting goodness so good that Maeve laughed merrily at its absurdity. But to her joy the players were treating the drama in a tongue-in-cheek fashion that was well suited to the sophisticated New Orleans audience.

Maeve knew an almost physical yearning to assume the garish purple gown of the dark villainess, Vesta Violet, and to mouth her wonderfully silly lines. "Ah," cried Vesta, fluttering her feather fan, "I will never forget those wonderful days in Baden-Baden"; then aside, she hissed, "Little do they know I am wanted by the police in Walla Walla."

So total was her enjoyment that Maeve barely noticed when at one point William excused himself and that on his return Colonel Hunter, then Captain Holder and the lieutenant were repeatedly going in and out.

When at last good triumphed over evil and the wicked but lovely villainess, Vesta Violet, was bodily tossed into the wings, disposing of her for good and all, Maeve was lost in contemplation of the technical side of the exit. She hoped for the sake of the actress who played Vesta that aides both prompt and strong were waiting in the wings. And for an instant her longing to be back onstage was well-nigh unendurable.

She felt William's thoughtful stare and arranged her features into a more neutral pattern, smiling and applauding. He seemed to have read her thoughts but said only, "I am so glad you enjoyed it. They are planning to go on to Galatoire's." He lowered his voice. "Will you plead a headache to please me?"

Maeve looked at him, puzzled, but the hint of mischief in his dark, magnetic eyes gave her a clue, and she murmured, "Of course."

While William made their excuses and the party waited for carriages, one ostensibly to take the Morgans home, William's manner became abstracted; he stepped aside, and Maeve thought she heard his commanding officer mutter something like, ". . . a good many guns, more than necessary. No, we'll wait. They may lead us to the others."

It sounded very mysterious, but Maeve was too curious about William's odd request to pay much heed. When they bade good-night to the others, her husband, with a jubilant face, handed her into another carriage. But instead of giving their home address, he said to the driver, "The market!"

Maeve turned to him, grinning. "What is all this?" She had made several excursions by day to the famous French market, which was now regaining some of its former liveliness, but they had never been there together.

William kissed her hand, grinning back. "Hunter's wife is nice enough, but I have had a sufficiency of women like hawks and pigeons—I craved an hour alone with a wilder bird . . . a bird of paradise!" He turned her white hand over and lingeringly kissed the palm.

She was assailed by a variety of emotions. First, her delighted laughter rang out when he spoke of hawks and pigeons. Hogan's wife was so like those fat, cooing city birds, and the wife of Captain Holder did indeed have the look of a bird of prey. But her quick laughter was soon stifled in a feeling of hot excitement when he kissed her palm. How aware she was of his physical presence! It was a constant enchantment.

But now, paradoxically, he was acting like a boy, chattering to her of the delights of New Orleans. The perpetual changes in his personality, over the substructure of strength and loyalty, fascinated her more every day they were together.

She expressed surprise at all the activity at the late hour.

"Ah," he said, smiling, "New Orleans has finally awakened from its bitter sleep, and now it wants to turn every night into day!" Maeve was swiftly becoming infected by his sense of adventure.

They were driving now near the wharves, and she could smell the many and varied smells of the wonderful port—spicy foods and rotting wood, river smells, odors of crayfish and shrimp, spices and sawdust and rum, and even flower-filled gardens, for the mild air of New Orleans allowed the blooms to grow far beyond the season when they were dying farther north.

"Some of these people look like those of Marseilles," William said, gazing from the carriage window.

"What are they like, the people of Marseilles?"

"Oh, dark and lusty, full of juice! I will take you there, my darling, someday soon. I will take you everywhere!"

And with fresh jubilation he kissed her on the mouth, in the sight of all the night wanderers. She gloried in his carefree air tonight.

As he had predicted, some of the market stalls were still open for business, and when William sniffed the air and cried, "Stop! Stop!" to the grinning driver, Maeve laughed aloud. He paid the black lavishly and handed Maeve down to the busy street.

The jambalaya man, stirring his pot, brightened at the sound of William's colloquial French. He measured out two bowls of the steaming mixture and handed them spoons. They ate the rich conglomeration standing on the street, like two peasants, Maeve thought with delight. It was delicious.

She laughed again, between spoonfuls. "Imagine the famous actress Maeve Heron and the darling of New York society eating jambalaya in the open!"

"It is the only way to live," he retorted. "And conduct most unbecoming to an officer."

Then his dancing eyes caught sight of a black turbaned woman, calling her wares, carrying a napkin-covered basket. *"Calas tout chaud! Calas tout chaud!"* she cried.

William called out to her, holding up two strong, lean fingers. They were rice cakes, Maeve discovered, and perfectly mouth-watering. How much she had missed in her previous visits!

"And now we shall dine," William said a little more quietly, squeezing her arm against his body.

"Dine!" she repeated, laughing. "I *have* dined."

"Ah! You have not dined yet; I will get you in training for Paris!"

And he led her up the busy street. "It is not far," he said.

But again his eye was caught by another vendor. It was a

grizzled black woman with a basket of flowers. When William
and Maeve paused before her, the woman inquired eagerly, in
a peculiar blend of French and what Maeve had learned to
recognize as gombo, "Some lovely carnations for the lady?
Roses?"

"Roses," William Morgan said firmly, for in the bland
autumn air of Louisiana, there were roses left. He indicated
the freshest, a bright magenta color that exactly matched
Maeve's ensemble. He chose three with his own hands,
examining them carefully for thorns, and to Maeve's
bewilderment, after paying the woman, turned a little away
from her and made an odd, swift, furtive motion toward his
pocket.

When he held the three roses out to Maeve, their stems were
banded together by a remarkable ring. She exclaimed with
delight, holding the ring-banded roses closer to examine the
beautiful gem.

It was a ring consisting of three gleaming stones—a pure
blue-green aquamarine, a lovely amethyst and a perfect
emerald. She slipped the ring from the stems and put it on her
finger.

"William!" she cried. "It is wonderful!"

"Now," he said softly, so that the flower woman could not
hear, "whatever color your eyes turn, you will have a gem to
match them!"

He was gazing down into her eyes with adoration and with
quickening desire. And as they strolled along in the direction
of the restaurant he had chosen for them, he said to her,
"When I first saw you on the stage, your eyes were as blue as
the sky; then later, in the restaurant, you were wearing green,
and so were they. Tonight they are almost purple! I was
thinking of all that when I had the ring made for you. After
all, it has been so long since I have given you a real present."

She nestled close to him, warmed as always by his cleverness and his generosity, loving him most for that sensitive wit
that placed him above all other men. "You are too good, too
kind to be true."

"I hope not," he retorted. "Perhaps, later this evening,
there will be an opportunity for me to appear more . . .
real."

She blushed, but her pulses quickened at his seductive comment.

He then led her up a flight of stairs to a small, plain room, candlelit, full of delicious odors. A special dinner was waiting for them. As she drank the delicate wine he had ordered, Maeve wondered, suddenly, what Hunter had meant; then she shrugged inwardly, reflecting vaguely that the men's grim military business was none of her own. She was too happy to consider it now.

However, as the autumn advanced, Maeve Morgan began to notice an increasing absence in her husband's manner. He had grown more reticent about the operations of the garrison, and more often than not, he returned home far later than had been his wont. He seemed hollow-eyed with exhaustion and tight with strain, yet when she questioned him, he replied evasively, making references to the "shakeup in Washington."

Maeve was quite aware that the events of several months before were much on William's mind. Secretary of War Stanton, who opposed President Johnson's more humane concept of Reconstruction, had been suspended from the Cabinet, and William's friend, General Grant, had been named as his replacement. Meanwhile, William had explained to her, Congress was seeking grounds to impeach Johnson. And should that occur, it was William's opinion that Ulysses S. Grant stood a powerful chance of being elected President.

She had pondered then, in the late summer, the effect of this on their lives. William and his commander, David Hunter, were both favorites of the general's; perhaps William, who had been trained in the law, was considering a political career.

If that were so, she concluded sadly, she herself could be nothing but a hindrance to him as a wife, considering the sensational events of the murder and the trial and her own shadowy background before that well-publicized event.

And yet, Maeve thought, William had never expressed a strong interest in a political appointment. He considered Washington a provincial, uninteresting city. Surely the faint possibility of Grant's becoming President could not make him so grim and preoccupied. Maeve was sure that the cause was far more immediate and connected it in her mind with the Knights.

They had been, William said, very quiescent these last

weeks—almost frighteningly so. And he remarked that he feared the quiet was the lull before the outbreak of a storm of new violence.

Nevertheless, even in his preoccupation, William Morgan was more tender and considerate than usual with Maeve, and she responded gratefully. She forbore to question him further and tried to put the matter out of her mind.

October was a very rainy month and was marked with chill air uncharacteristic of the mild Indian summers of Louisiana. For several days the light was a muddy, depressing gray; Maeve directed Amelie to brighten the house with whatever autumn blossoms could be found. The furniture, divested of its summer covers in September, now wore the warmth-producing fabrics of velvet and velours once more. But Maeve, in defiance of convention, had had the sofas and chairs recovered in remarkable colors that New Orleans was unaccustomed to.

In place of the somber plum color, she had had the upholstery redone in rich shades of russet and peacock green. William, who was usually so alert to his surroundings, had hardly noticed. But when she pointed out the changes, he had responded with warm approval.

Like most of the March-born, Maeve was awake to the needs and feelings of others to an extraordinary degree; she was possessed of a passion to emphasize and move in harmony with all that was pleasant in the world about her.

Thus, during these days of oppressive chill, Maeve put aside all of her clothes that were sober in color and took to wearing bright shades of orange-russet, blue-green, gold and scarlet.

This afternoon, as she made her way toward the house of Juliette Thibault, she was dressed in a trim skirt and jacket of crimson, trimmed with plain black braid; a black mousquetaire hat of felt, with a narrow band of scarlet about the crown, was set pertly on her smoothly arranged hair.

She had dismissed the carriage a few blocks away from Juliette Thibault's so that she might enjoy the exercise of a brief walk in the chill air, the air that reminded her most of New York's.

But she was soon to regret having done so, for she came face to face with a trio of shabby Creoles, also on foot. No doubt, Maeve reflected somberly, they could no longer afford to keep a carriage and even found it a hardship to hire a public one. Modestly she cast her eyes down and tried not to hear the low-voiced remark of the woman: "There is another of them, Raoul, one of the Yankees' wives."

The answer of the woman's companion was indistinguishable, but unable to resist, Maeve looked up, and her eyes caught those of the woman's. She was young and delicate and could have been pretty were it not for the careworn thinness of her well-shaped face and the rusty black of her garments. The eyes were dark and deep, and they stared at Maeve with a melancholy hatred that was wholly disconcerting.

Then from nowhere appeared four drunken men; two of them were black, and two white, and they flaunted the new vulgarity of their clothes like strutting cocks. One of them laughed loudly and nodded toward Maeve; her blood turned cold.

But one of his companions frowned and, shaking his head, said something in a quiet voice. Maeve thought she comprehended the words "officer's wife."

The laughing man turned his eyes away from Maeve and lit upon the three Creoles. The young woman with the tired face was accompanied by two men, one apparently her brother, for his resemblance to her was strong, and the other perhaps her husband, for the latter had sharply contrasting fair hair and blue eyes; his demeanor to the woman was one of tender protectiveness.

Out of the corner of her eye, Maeve saw the four vulgarly dressed men approach the Creoles. She was too far away to hear, but it seemed one of the drunken men made a remark to the young woman that turned her male companions rigid with anger.

The blond man made a hasty movement toward the inside pocket of his shabby coat, but the dark young man cried out sharply, "Raoul!"—Maeve heard this with clarity—"No!"

And again she felt a coldness throughout her body. She knew that Southern men not only had been disenfranchised but nominally, at least, went unarmed. To show the laughing, drunken men a gun would be to sign one's death warrant. She watched the blond man undergoing a torturous struggle between his caution and his righteous ire. But the young woman put her thin hand on his arm and spoke to him softly. The angry young blond man stood still for an instant, his shoulders slumping in defeat. Then, as if unable to contain himself longer, he raised his fist and shouted at the drunken men, "You are safe now, you low bastards! But we are not done, you will see! We are not done yet!"

Threateningly the four began to move toward the blond man, but the dark man and the thin dark woman urged him quickly away.

Maeve was trembling with indignation. As she made her way to the house of Juliette Thibault, she raged inwardly, *My own husband belongs to the Union that makes such outrages possible!* William had said that the dark days of the notorious Butler were gone, yet again and again Maeve Morgan had seen the blue-clad soldiers wink at such incidents as the one she had just seen. *No wonder the Knights had been formed!* Maeve thought angrily. She had hardly believed it when Amelie had told her that the scalawags and carpetbaggers egged the freed blacks on, plying them with liquor and playing on their dazzled, freedom-elated senses.

"I wish I were a man!" Maeve Morgan said aloud. She realized she was standing on Juliette Thibault's very doorstep, and the dressmaker, who had opened to her, was staring in mystification.

"Why, Mme. Morgan!" Juliette exclaimed. "You are trembling. Come in at once."

Embarrassed, Maeve followed Juliette Thibault up the narrow stairs and into her snug parlor, hardly listening as the Frenchwoman chattered to her, bustling about to make Maeve comfortable and offer her a steaming cup of the strong coffee New Orleans was so famous for.

"You know what they say." The sense of Juliette Thibault's words penetrated Maeve at last. "Black as night, hot as hell and strong as the devil."

Puzzled, Maeve tried to make out the meaning. Of course! She was talking about the coffee. "I know," she stammered a reply. "I have always enjoyed the coffee very much."

"But sit down, my dear lady. You look quite pale. Did . . . something happen out there?"

Maeve hesitated; then she poured out to Juliette Thibault the story of what she had seen.

When she noticed the worried expression on the little dressmaker's face, Maeve remembered at once the con-versation of Jinjy and Amelie, so many months ago, the conversation of implying that Mlle. Thibault's brother-in-law, Georges Roget, was a member of the Knights. Maeve was conscience-stricken. The poor woman, she reflected, had worries enough in this regard without her adding to them!

So hastily she entered into a discussion of the dresses she had come about, trying to ignore the look of anxiety on the dressmaker's face.

In the middle of their conference, Mlle. Thibault was abruptly summoned downstairs by the ringing of her bell. Maeve caught the names "Raoul and Madeleine Deplis" and then "Georges." It was the penetrating voice of Juliette Thibault's sister, Claire Roget.

Maeve crept to the door which the dressmaker had left ajar and heard her say sharply, "Be quiet. Mme. Morgan is here."

Claire Roget's lowered voice was still quite distinguishable to Maeve. ". . . Canal Street . . . the wharves . . . where the showboat is anchored. Help me stop him, Juliette. They plan to meet at midnight."

Again Juliette Thibault's strictures for quiet were heard, and her reply was too low to be made out. Maeve moved back to her chair at the sound of the closing door and the approaching steps. As she bade the dressmaker farewell, noting with compassion the tautness of her face, Maeve Morgan was possessed of a wild notion, the same ardent fire that had sent her into the night, dressed as a lad, so long ago in Tyrone.

Chapter 18

MAEVE MORGAN hardly knew what was in the bottom of her mind when she had heard the plea of Claire Roget or what madness overtook her when she was alone in her own room.

But somehow the ugly incident in Chartres Street had taken her once again into the past. She knew only that when she had looked into the sorrowing eyes of Madeleine Deplis—for she had a strong feeling about the identity of the couple mentioned by Mme. Roget—she had seen her own eyes of long ago. Maeve Morgan in that moment had looked into the desolate eyes of Maeve Heron on the day of Shane O'Neill's burial: the Maeve rejected by her uncle, Arthur O'Neill, betrayed by Michael Rathmullan, the Maeve who stood alone on the deck of the windswept *Falcon* and watched his body given to the sea. And the lonely Maeve in the Gypsy's clothes who stood one spring afternoon on the steps of a brothel, seeking admittance; the defiant woman who had dressed herself as a lady of the court of Versailles and fled into the teeming night of Mardi Gras.

Maeve crept to the great chest against the wall that held her luxurious dresses and searched among their voluminous folds for a small locked chest. Finding it, she withdrew it from the tall press and unlocked it. Inside lay the scarlet dress and shawl of Narilla, Maeve's Gypsy relative, a little dagger and, in a silken pouch, a pair of golden earrings.

Yearning over these pathetic pieces of finery—why had she kept them so long?—Maeve suddenly cried out, "Thomas, oh, Thomas!" and began to weep. How long had it been since she had given a thought to her beloved great-grandfather, Thomas, the Romany. Did he still live? she wondered. With a feeling of desolate guilt, she removed the shawl and gown and found, below the breeches and shirt and cap of a boy, the heavy white sweater she had been given on the *Falcon* and a small pistol.

Kneeling before the open chest, Maeve Morgan knew where her madness would take her that night, as it had taken her into the mist of Tullaghoe. Insane as it seemed at this moment, she must go with them tonight, go with the men who would drive away the vulgar oppressors of people like Madeleine and Raoul Duplis, the kinsmen in spirit of the Gypsies who ran from the hornies and people driven from their lands by the world's Adares.

Catching sight of herself in the tall pier glass, Maeve saw that her head was high and her eyes glowed with the light of the fanatic. She laughed aloud.

"What a liar I am!" she said. It was not only for the sake of "oppressed people" that she itched to ride again in the night—it was for the sake of herself, she concluded with frank shame, and for the sake of that dark, driving thing that made her, as Amelie had said, one of those who listened to the song of a distant bird.

And it was madness, Maeve thought, utter madness—what had she been thinking of? To aid those who were, in the last analysis, the enemies of her beloved husband.

Maeve Morgan shook her head in disbelief, almost dizzy with the realization of the wrong she had been about to commit. Resolutely she folded the boy's shirt and trousers, replacing them with the large-billed cap in the chest. She locked the chest and hid it away. *Tomorrow*, she promised herself, *tomorrow I will dispose of those things for good and all.*

Weak with relief, Maeve began to remove her street clothes and looked into the press to choose a gown for dinner. The wind had risen, and she could hear a heavy rain drumming against the windows. Tonight of all nights was the time to wear a dress of warm joyousness, she decided, and took from its hanger a delicious gown of golden orange. It was the color of the flesh of a nectarine, and Maeve felt more cheerful already.

She rang for Amelie to help her with her hair, noticing that the unusual color gave her eyes almost a tone of hazel. Her white skin, against the brightness, gleamed like a candle flame.

When William returned, chill and wet, his face lit up at the sight of her but soon reverted to its former lines of anxiety and strain.

"What is it?" she asked softly.

"I must go out again," he answered evasively. "I just came home for a quick dinner—can you manage it, my dear?—and the sight of your sweet face."

Pouring him a glass of brandy, she said, "I will see to dinner at once. It is . . . something . . . serious tonight, is it not?"

He nodded. After a brief hesitation he declared in a low voice, "I should not tell you really." He glanced about as if to make certain they were alone. Then he said, "It is the Knights, Maeve. We are going to wipe them out tonight. Completely."

The words chilled her blood. "Dear God!" She felt her hands turn to ice.

"I had to tell you, you see," William whispered and took her white face between his long, slender hands. "For if anything happens to me—"

"Don't say that! Please!" She turned her soft face and kissed his hands, first one and then the other. "I would . . . die if anything happened to you."

"If anything happens to me," he continued, "I want you to know how much I . . . have loved and adored you, always. And to know that you will be . . . all right, for I have made my will in your favor long ago."

"Oh, William!" She bowed her head and began to weep. Not only was she in utter terror for his safety, but now she had the added guilt of her own treachery to face. Dear God, to think what she had almost done!

Reading her stricken look as concern for him, William Morgan was touched almost to the point of tears. "Maeve, Maeve," he said gently and kissed her for a long, breathless moment.

Then, raising his head and trying to smile at her, he said, "You wouldn't send a man out hungry now, would you? Go, go, darling, and speak to Amelie. I must not linger."

Reluctantly she left him, glancing back once at his slender figure in its coat and trousers of trim dark blue that emphasized his lean grace; he was sitting in an attitude of high tension, staring into the flickering fire.

Throughout the hasty dinner Maeve forced herself to chatter of inconsequential matters in an attempt to distract him from the night that lay ahead.

But at last, when he had quickly downed a cup of steaming coffee and stood tall and straight before her for a farewell kiss, Maeve bit her lip to keep from crying out. How dear and good and kind he was—how she had come to need him!

He kissed her hard; she felt a serpent of longing uncoil deep within her. But he wrenched himself away, put on his broad hat and strode from the room without a backward look.

When finally Maeve sought the solace of sleep, her last strange waking thought formed itself: *If only I were a man and could go with him!*

It seemed only moments before Maeve was fairly jerked from her uneasy sleep by a sharp tapping on the door. Her first idea was that they had come to tell her William was dead. Weakness washed over her limbs, and for an instant she was powerless to move.

The knock was repeated more loudly. Galvanized into sudden motion, Maeve threw back the covers and rose, stumbling, from the wide bed to rush to the door.

She opened to the sleepy Amelie, blinking in the corridor.

"Something has happened to him!" Maeve cried.

"No, no, *ma chérie*," Amelie said quickly, pushing Maeve back into the chamber. "Something very strange is going on, however. Mlle. Juliette Thibault is downstairs in the parlor."

"Mlle. Thibault!" Maeve was dumbfounded. "Here?" She looked at the clock. "At this hour?" It was nearly three.

"Something is very wrong indeed," said Amelie with a sober face. "She is almost hysterical. I have never seen a lady of such chic come out almost in deshabille."

Even in her anxiousness, Maeve could not prevent a little smile at this description of the Frenchwoman's unspeakable solecism.

"I will come down," she said firmly. "Tell her I will be downstairs in a moment."

"She says to hurry, please," Amelie said, closing the door.

Maeve snatched up a peignoir and put it on. After slipping her chilled feet into velvet mules, she hurried from the room and down the stairs to the parlor.

Juliette Thibault stood shivering before the small fire, which apparently had just been lit by Amelie. The dressmaker's gray-threaded dark hair was falling about her face; she looked, Maeve thought, like a witch fleeing from her accusers, and the younger woman was flooded with compassion.

"Mlle. Thibault! You are so wet! You must be frozen. Amelie!" Maeve called out. The curious Amelie was lingering at the door. "Please get some brandy at once for Mlle. Thibault."

Nodding, Amelie entered the parlor and went to the sideboard to decant a generous glass of the liqueur, which she brought to the shivering little woman.

"Thank you so much." The dressmaker drank the brandy almost at a gulp, and gasping, said, "Oh, madame, I must speak with you at once. And alone."

Maeve hesitated for a split second, glancing at Amelie. Then she said, a little reproachfully, "Amelie is my friend and must be allowed to remain. Whatever you say will not go beyond this room."

Looking at Amelie again, Maeve saw her raise her pretty head in delighted pride.

Juliette Thibault slumped into a chair, still holding the empty glass, and said in a despairing voice. "Very well then, I must put my trust in both of you. For the situation is desperate." She looked up then and absently placed the empty goblet on a little marble table at her elbow.

"What is it?" cried Maeve, coming to the distracted woman to kneel beside her and put a gentle hand on her bony shoulder.

"My brother-in-law, George Roget," the dressmaker blurted, "and the Captain Pearse are now outside this house, awaiting permission to enter. They are wounded, and both could die."

"Enter!" Maeve was so stunned that she remained kneeling by Mlle. Thibault's chair. At last she rose and went to the sofa, where she sat down abruptly. "Enter this house?" she cried out with disbelief. "Mlle. Thibault, my husband is an officer of the United States Army. Have you taken leave of your senses?"

"No, no, my dear lady, don't you see?" Excitedly Mlle. Thibault got to her feet and came to Maeve to kneel down like a supplicant before her. "It is the plan least mad of all—no one, no one would ever look for members of . . . the Knights in the cellar of Major Morgan!"

"But . . . but why," Maeve stammered, "why do you dare to approach me with this?"

"Oh, madame, I beg you, there is so little time! Because"—the dressmaker controlled her voice with effort—"because the Captain Pearse believes you will help him. And Georges. Because the Captain Pearse says he is an old friend of yours. And you have the compassion . . . the understanding. . . ."

Juliette Thibault's beseeching words trailed away. She stared up at Maeve like a begging animal. "Oh, please, madame, please. All it means is a few hours of shelter for them. No one need ever know—your husband need never know! If they are exposed to the elements, with their wounds, they will surely die."

"But why can't they go . . . elsewhere?" Maeve asked desperately.

"The Yank—the federal officers will find them anywhere else!" cried Juliette Thibault. "They could go no farther, and this seemed the only possible haven."

"Your house. . . ."

"My house and the café have been watched all the afternoon and evening by the Ya—the federal officers. It was only through the most perilous ruse that I was given word, and even now I fear they may be watching."

"But if these men are seen coming into my husband's house, he could be shot as a traitor!" Maeve threw off Juliette Thibault's desperate hands and began to move nervously about the room.

"Oh, madame, I pray you, do not delay longer! Only let them stay in your cellar until dark tomorrow night!"

"Tomorrow night. Mother of God!" Maeve almost shouted. "Do you think I would risk my husband—"

"Do you want your friend to die?" Juliette Thibault asked shrewdly. "And my poor sister's husband?"

Maeve stared at her, wondering what Fingal Pearse had told her. She realized, of course, that she did not want either man to die—Pearse had brought her pain, had wounded her own husband, yet Maeve did not wish him dead. And more, she sympathized with poor Mme. Roget. She was reeling with confusion.

But no, she did not want them to die!

"But they will need a doctor. . . ."

Juliette Thibault, hearing in the tentative words a form of surrender, said quickly, "I will take care of them. I have tended such men before, during the war."

"Very well, then. But we will give you no further aid. You cannot expect Amelie . . . or anyone else in this house, to aid you further. I am going upstairs now, and I am going to bed. Amelie will unfasten the door to the cellar. I wish to know no more of this."

And trembling, Maeve left the room, hearing the cries of Juliette Thibault pursuing her, "Oh, madame, thank you, thank you!"

Maeve wanted only to reach the haven of her room.

Then she heard Amelie's crisp direction, "Enough. Now we must hurry."

When she reached her own room again, Maeve Morgan shut the door and hurried to the hearth. The fire was dying, and she felt chilled to the bone. She poked at the embers and placed more wood and paper on the fire, heartened to see it leap up bright again.

Straightening, she stood still for a tortured moment and whispered aloud, "Dear heaven, what have I done? What have I done now?"

She drew her fragile peignoir more closely about her and sat down before the fire, wondering what it was within herself that drove her to these mad, disloyal actions, when she was everything to William Morgan?

It had not, she reflected, been like this when she was on the stage. The stimulus of that had made her twice the person she was now, paradoxically making her more of a woman, not the confused half spirit she had become in this alien place, restless and angry in her idleness.

Someday, she thought, *someday I shall be upon the stage again. And then everything will come right!* In the midst of her self-absorption, the freezing realization of William's mortal danger touched her with its dreadful hands. She had been thinking only of herself, when her husband might be lying dead, out in the chill night, in the driving rain!

And there were enemy fugitives under his very roof.

Overcome with confusion and despair, Maeve Morgan put her head between her hands. She did not know how long she sat slumped in that defensive attitude before, with a cry of thanksgiving, she heard William Morgan's familiar step upon the stairs.

William Morgan, warmed by Maeve's joyous welcome and the knowledge that the troops had done their utmost toward success, was indifferent to the fact that he had had so little sleep.

It was with a feeling of stubborn optimism that he entered the office of his commander, Colonel Hunter, ready to outline for his superior another plan for taking Fingal Pearse.

Therefore, he was not prepared for the coldness of Hunter's greeting. "What it is, sir?" William Morgan asked at once.

"Sit down, Will." There was a forbidding terseness in Hunter's order, and William Morgan obeyed with some unease.

"Will, something has come to my attention, something so . . . outrageous and unbelievable that I. . . . Well, it is this. I have been advised that Pearse and Roget were allegedly seen entering the cellar of your house."

"Why, why . . . that is laughable," William Morgan protested.

"I could not agree more."

"Why, I was at home late last night and this morning, and—"

"But you were not in every room of the house, of course," Hunter remarked.

"Certainly not. But good God, David—"

Hunter pushed back his chair and rose, striding restlessly about the room. "Will, I need not repeat to you my opinion of you. Your courage and probity have always been known to me. Hell, I was *there*. I spoke to Private English after that business in Virginia, near the Rapidan. He told me there were only eight of you—Collins was dead by then—and you gave them your hard tack and lived on melted snow. I know all about you, Will," Hunter concluded earnestly.

"But there are others who cannot be so sure," William Morgan added quietly.

"Just so." Hunter nodded, his face somber. "And some kind of investigation will have to be made. You know that. But I will make it personally."

"Thanks, David." Morgan rubbed his eyes and then asked, "Who was it who saw them allegedly enter?"

"Hogan." *Hogan!* William Morgan exclaimed silently. Why was there always something about Hogan? He always looked at Maeve with such admiring eyes, while his plump little wife smoldered, William mused.

"Hogan," he repeated.

"Yes. You recall when he and the sergeant took off after the escapees. To do Hogan credit, he testified that when he saw the men enter your house, he thought at the time he had been mistaken about the identity, putting it down to some sort of undercover plan."

"That is very farfetched," said William Morgan, coloring with vexation.

"Hogan means well to you and your wife apparently," Hunter commented a little dryly, and Morgan studied him, again feeling his earlier unease.

"Well, there is no point in postponing it, David," he said firmly. "Shall we go now?"

"Very well. I don't like it, you know, Will. I would vouch for you sight unseen. But what must be must be."

William Morgan nodded, his weary face taut, and followed his commander from the office.

"I don't like it, Roget." Fingal Pearse's deep voice, speaking its unaccented French, reached Georges Roget from a shadowy corner of the cellar.

"What is that, my friend?" Roget shifted his aching body with a small groan, trying to make out the face of Fingal Pearse.

"I don't like staying here all day," Pearse replied softly. "The Yankees could swoop down on us at any moment. It's just a feeling, Georges."

Roget reflected that Pearse was Irish, after all, and the people from that strange country seemed to see things before they happened. Impatient with his own fanciful notion, nevertheless, Roget asked, "What do you think we should do?" Pearse was a good man, in spite of his peculiarities, a tough man who had seen the Knights through a good many tight places. When Pearse spoke, Roget listened.

"I think," said Fingal Pearse, "that boldness is our only hope. I feel we should make the break now by daylight. There will be more watchers in the evening."

"But . . . but it is mad!" Georges Roget declared. "In the broad daylight we will walk into their hands!"

"Not if we are two drunken chimney sweeps," Pearse retorted, and Roget could hear the smile in his tone. "We can take the back streets to the canal. We will go separately because they are looking for two men. When you get to the wharves, look for a little shrimping boat, called the *Jamba*. It should be about the fourth one down. Tell them my name, and wait for me there. They will aid you. Then, when it is dark, they will take us to a steamboat traveling to the north. We will stay there for a while, until this all dies down."

Roget shook his grizzled head with wonder. Fingal Pearse seemed to know half the world, and that half apparently was ready to do his bidding at any moment!

He heard Pearse moving about now in the dimness. "Ah!" The triumphant cry reached Georges Roget. "These brooms and poles will do very well indeed."

He heard Pearse chuckle. "Evidently the former occupants of this house were too penurious to hire the public sweeps; their servants did it for them."

Roget, whose wife, Claire, pursued a similar policy, flushed in the darkness.

"Here." He could make out Fingal Pearse now, in the narrow daylight from the grating. Pearse's face, smeared with soot, his golden hair covered by a battered hat, was almost unrecognizable. "Now you, my friend," said Pearse. His voice, thought Roget, sounded as jubilant as a schoolboy's in a plot of mischief.

Surely the Irish are mad, thought Georges Roget, but he followed the other's directions, rubbing his own face with the dirt and making other adjustments in his costume according to Pearse's instructions.

"Now let us see," said Fingal Pearse softly, creeping to the narrow grating. From this angle he could just make out the quiet street behind the Morgan house. "Courage, Georges," he said then, touching the other man on the shoulder, for Roget was shaking with terror.

"I really think this is the only way. To leave in darkness, by stealth, would give us more surely away than to walk by day as sweeps. New Orleans is full of such ne'er-do-wells and derelicts. You know that well."

Roget took a deep breath to quell his rising nausea and nodded, unable to speak. Pearse gave his shoulder a reassuring pat.

"Now, Georges," he whispered, "when I squeeze your arm, get out of this at once. Get out onto the street as fast as you can, then head toward Canal. Hide your face with your pole and broom as much as possible. Act quite drunk; sing if you must, but not so loud that you will be arrested for disturbing the peace! And wait for me on the *Jamba*."

After a breathless instant Georges Roget felt the urgent pressure of Fingal Pearse's hand, heard him say, "*Now!*" and then in blind, animal fear found himself scrambling upward from the cellar and onto the empty back street. With a gulping breath of relief, Roget knew that for the moment all was well. And he began to stagger toward Canal.

The hour was very early, but Maeve had risen to see her husband off to the garrison. A sleepy Amelie had prepared the coffee and hustled another servant into assembling a hasty breakfast.

Maeve, seated opposite William in the dining room, raised her coffee cup with a trembling hand.

"You needn't have risen so early," he said in a tender voice that made her shrink with guilt. "Why, my dear, you are so tired that you are trembling. You look very pale as well. You had better go back to bed as soon as possible."

Maeve could hardly bear his concern with the knowledge of the men hiding in the cellar below them. "I'll be all right," she murmured, avoiding his eyes.

A sudden shriek from Amelie startled them both. "No! That is quite unnecessary. There is quite enough wood right here!"

William Morgan raised his brows. "What ails Amelie this morning?" Generally she was the soul of propriety, going about her housekeeping tasks with quiet competence, rarely raising her voice even to the intractable imp Jinjy.

"I . . . I don't know," Maeve answered with unease. "I shall go and see."

"Don't trouble when you are so tired," William said easily.

But Maeve had already risen and was halfway out of the room.

In the kitchen she faced Amelie, whispering angrily, "What do you mean by crying out like that? Major Morgan wondered what the matter was."

Amelie raised ironic brows. "I was only telling Jinjy," she said with heavy emphasis, "that it was not necessary to go to the cellar for wood, that there is plenty here."

Maeve was overcome with a cold sickness in her stomach pit. She swallowed. "I see." She attempted a smile. Without further comment, she returned to the dining room.

"Well?" William was smiling, his dark eyes deep-shadowed with his weariness. "Is everything all right?"

"Oh, yes, yes," Maeve answered hastily. "Amelie has . . . a headache, that is all. She has promised to be more quiet."

William Morgan finished his breakfast and took a last appreciative sip of the coffee. He sighed. "Well, I must go."

After rising with him, Maeve circled the table and came into his arms. "Until later," he said lightly, kissing her hair. She clung to him, and he stepped backward, gazing down at her.

"What is it, darling?" he asked. "Are you feeling unwell?"

"No, oh, no!" she replied with a peculiar quaver in her voice. "I am just so . . . relieved that . . . you are all right."

"Go to bed," he said gently, giving her a little pat. "I will see you this evening."

And he had quickly gone. With heavy feet, Maeve climbed the stairs to her chamber, seeking a return to sleep without success, haunted by the specter of William's own enemies she was harboring below.

Abandoning the idea of sleep, late in the morning Maeve rose and dressed herself in a gown the blue-green of a peacock to lift her own spirits. The rain had gone, but the hazy, anemic sunlight was almost more oppressive than the driving rain. Maeve settled herself in the parlor with a book, trying to thrust from her consciousness the image of the men below, counting each hour that struck as one less to endure until the dark. For with the dark they would go.

Then, she resolved, she would never do another wrong to

William Morgan. All of it would be forgotten!

It was barely noon when she heard the sound of approaching horses; nervously she got up from her chair, letting the forgotten volume fall with a thump to the green carpet, and hurried to the window. Drawing the rich curtains aside, Maeve saw two men in blue uniforms dismounting from their steeds. A small coffee-colored boy was tying the horses to the hitching post. The men were Colonel David Hunter and William Morgan.

It was not a social call, Maeve Morgan knew too well, not at this early hour and without the colonel's wife. And she knew why they had come. The white hand that held the curtain began to tremble with such force that the velvet fabric wavered in her hold; Maeve grasped the curtain, fighting a giddiness that threatened to fell her.

Well, she must not give in now. Dropping the curtain, Maeve turned from the window and moved out of the parlor toward the entrance door.

When Amelie opened to the two men and William caught sight of her face, Maeve knew with a sinking heart that he was reading her very thoughts. But he said only, "We are sorry to break in upon you at this hour."

Frightened at his formal tone, Maeve forced a smile and said, "Come in. You are welcome, Colonel Hunter. Shall we go into the parlor?"

David Hunter's expression was embarrassed, Maeve noted; however, he answered her courteously and followed into the pleasant firelit room. "How nice this is," he murmured.

"Thank you." Maeve dug her nails into her palms to let the little pain distract her from the awful giddy whirling of her head. "Please sit down," she managed to say calmly, "and let Amelie get you something. Would you like some coffee, or perhaps some wine . . . or perhaps we could give you luncheon?"

William Morgan held up his slender hand, unsmiling. "Nothing for me, thank you."

Colonel David Hunter shook his head as well. Then his sharp blue gaze turned to the carpet. Maeve, following the line of his glance saw with dismay that the book still lay facedown where it had fallen. Flushing, she stooped and retrieved the book.

"I . . . I must have dropped it," she said foolishly. "I am

not accustomed to visitors at his hour, I suppose, and. . . ." Her voice trailed off uncertainly as she observed the uncomfortable look exchanged by her husband and Colonel Hunter. She saw that the men were still on their feet.

After ringing for Amelie, Maeve sat down on the sofa and said desperately, "Please sit down. Do not let me keep you standing." She felt as if her voice were emerging in an hysterical soprano.

But David Hunter kept to his feet and said in a low, hesitant voice, "Mrs. Morgan, I am afraid I am not here to pay a social call." Her heart thudding, Maeve waited for him to continue.

"I have already told Will that, last night, one of my men advised me that he saw Fingal Pearse and Georges Roget enter this house."

Maeve drew a shallow breath and replied in a trembling voice, "But that . . . that is impossible, Colonel Hunter."

For the first time David Hunter smiled the friendly smile Maeve Morgan knew. "I think so, too, Mrs. Morgan. But certain circumstances make it advisable for the premises to be searched. I'm sorry. I have tried to make this as . . . decent as possible by undertaking the search myself."

Maeve's terror was so great by then that she could not trust herself to speak. She merely nodded her head once, trying to smile. Her palms were slick with sweat. She clasped them in her silken lap.

Amelie entered, and Maeve said weakly, "Never mind, thank you. The colonel does not desire refreshment." Amelie gave her a frightened look and withdrew.

Realizing now that her voice had not completely failed her, Maeve said to Hunter, "That is very kind of you."

"Shall we . . . proceed then, Will? You can show me the way. I suppose we can start with the attic if there is one."

Maeve was unconscious of what she said next. When the men had left the room, she sat rigidly on the sofa, listening to their firm steps echo on the stairs and grow more distant as they took the following flight to the attic at the top of the tall white house. She had no idea how much time had elapsed before she heard their returning feet, then their entry into the kitchen, William's calm voice directing Amelie to light them to the cellar, Amelie's desperate attempt to excuse herself from the task, her usually low voice high, almost shrieking as she protested that the cellar was not fit to be seen.

But Maeve heard William's firm order overriding Amelie and, with a sinking heart, heard the men descending. She feared her heart would stop its beating.

But a few moments later, when William and Hunter reentered the parlor, she was thunderstruck to see the expression on their faces—a mixture of puzzlement and relief. And she heard David Hunter saying, "My apologies, Mrs. Morgan, Will. There was no one there, Mrs. Morgan."

Her heart gave such a frightful leap that she feared it would fairly break. No one there! She saw William's gaze upon her, heard him telling Colonel Hunter that he would return to the garrison a little later. And Hunter was gone, and William Morgan had returned to the parlor.

He stood in the doorway, studying Maeve an instant. Then he shut the door and asked in a cold, dead voice, "But they were there before, weren't they, Maeve? Roget and your lover, Fingal Pearse?"

Chapter 19

MAEVE STARED back at him, speechless, fumbling for a reply.

"It's no good, Maeve," William Morgan said in a hard tone she had never heard from him before. "Your face gives you away. When David Hunter said there was no one in the cellar, your mouth almost fell open."

She shrank from the coldness of his address; the brutal phrases seemed to be emerging from the lips of another man, a man who was not the loving and protective William Morgan.

But a mocking little voice within her cried out, *What did you expect? He has given you nothing but love and goodness, and you have repaid him by sheltering his enemies, deceiving him once more. And for Fingal Pearse! Of all people, Fingal Pearse, whose dagger has penetrated his flesh!*

And as William came toward her, his face congested with rage, she gasped involuntarily and moved back into the symbolic shelter of the bright cushions.

"Don't worry," he said with contempt. "I have never struck a woman in my life and have no intention of doing so now. But if you were a man, I would put a bullet through your head."

Maeve felt the dread faintness assault her again. Her senses swam. But she dug her nails into the palms of her hands and began to know the return of a kind of desolate courage.

"They were there," she admitted in a voice she barely recognized as her own, it was so flat and high.

William Morgan sat down in an armchair opposite the sofa.

In an instant all his overpowering ire seemed to have deserted him. He asked her with a despairing, strangled intonation, "Why, Maeve? Why? Are you . . . still in love with that scoundrel, Fingal Pearse?"

She hesitated only a second before she cried out, "Of course I am not in love with Fingal Pearse! I never have been!"

"Haven't you?" William Morgan asked skeptically, the anger returning to inflame his question. That brief hesitation, Maeve reflected, had confirmed for him the truth that he believed.

"I acted in simple humanity," she protested. "I could not let . . . them die."

"You could not let *him* die," William Morgan retorted. "You have destroyed everything between us, Maeve, everything."

She had never heard such desolation in a human voice.

"You have hidden my enemies," he added bitterly. "You have committed treason."

"No one else knows!" she cried. "You are safe."

"*I* know," he replied quietly. "And every time I look at you I will always wonder what mischief you are planning next. My God, Maeve, it is like living with a loaded pistol pointed at my heart!"

She rose, feeling a terrible calm. "You need not worry," she said, surprised to hear her own steadiness. "I will leave your house today."

"Where will you go?" he asked dully. "Back to New York?"

"No. No, not yet."

"Where then?"

"They need actors on the showboat," she said simply.

A look of ironic sadness crossed Morgan's face. "Of course. I should have known. You will ultimately go to him. But you will not, I fancy, find him there now. He is a fugitive. And so will you be. Is this the kind of life you choose?"

"I wish I could make you understand. I am not going to Fingal Pearse. I am going back to the world I know."

He made a dismissive motion with his hand. It was impossible, she knew, to convince him. "You will not be in want," he said coldly. "Let me know where you are, and I shall provide for you."

"I want nothing more from you, William. You have done too much for me already." Her voice broke suddenly, and he looked at her with an air of unwilling hope, but she saw the hope die almost as soon as it appeared.

"Good-bye then, Maeve," he said at last and, after rising, left the parlor. She heard the hoofbeats of his horse die away in the quiet afternoon.

And slowly Maeve Morgan went to find Amelie.

Maeve Morgan moved with resolute grace up the ramp of the showboat *Sally Barton*, her blue-green umbrella sheltering her from the misting rain of the late afternoon. Amelie stood on the wharf below, guarding the two small trunks which had just been left there by the hired drayman.

The *Sally Barton* was bustling with its preperformance impetus. Maeve felt a rhythm of quickening and knew at once that she had found a kind of home. She pictured the sleepy players, who doubtless did not rise until noon, having their luncheons now in the manner of those whose hours were forever out of step with the common world's.

Her coming now was not the wistful entry of Maeve Heron into the port of New York or the beggarly arrival at Wallack's Theater, where at first she had assisted the wardrobe mistress and thrilled to move across the stage in a silent part. She was the actress Maeve Heron once more, who had dazzled audiences as the shepherdess Phebe and won such wild applause in her single first night as Ophelia. In her little carryall now Maeve carried the treasured reviews, for there had been glowing ones, despite the untimely death of Marianne LeClaire.

Now she approached one of the hands, who was polishing the brass rail of the *Sally Barton* to an even greater luster, and asked calmly, "Could you please tell me where to find the theater manager?"

The deck hand ceased his activity and stared at Maeve with puzzled, admiring eyes. She did not look like his idea of an actress, with her hair untouched by dye and her complexion so fresh and pure. "His office is there, ma'am," the man said, pointing with a weathered hand at a mahogany door nearby.

"Thank you," she said warmly, smiling, and the deck hand ducked his head in shyness.

"You have been so kind," Maeve added. "Could you tell

me his name and if he is in his office now?''

''Mr. Leitzel,'' the man replied, his old eyes bright with admiration, ''and he is.''

Thanking the man again, Maeve went boldly to the door and tapped upon it. She heard a growling command to enter.

Mr. Leitzel was an unpleasant-looking man smoking an evil-smelling cigar. He did not raise his eyes when Maeve entered but continued to scribble on a pad of paper. ''What is it?'' he demanded.

''Do you need an actress?'' Maeve queried bluntly, letting her voice out to its full power. If Mr. Leitzel was a man who did not waste time, then indeed, she would not waste it either.

The man's grizzled head snapped up from his work and he stared at the beautiful woman standing in the door. He was a man of middle age with a greasy face of a peculiar red-brown color and indeterminate brown hair worn rather long, swept back from his bumpy forehead. He had a thin, ungenerous mouth and mean little porcine eyes. ''You don't waste any time,'' he remarked in that grating tone in which he had bidden her enter.

''I have no time to waste,'' she retorted but softened her reply with a bright smile.

''What are your qualifications?'' Leitzel asked more quietly.

She reached into her reticule and without fumbling or hesitation produced the clippings from the New York newspapers. She handed them to him without speaking.

Leitzel scanned the clippings and raised his shaggy brows. ''Well,'' he said simply, chewing on his nasty cigar. Then he looked up again and studied her from head to foot. ''What have you been doing all these years?''

''I was married,'' she said briefly.

''*Was?*''

''I have left my husband,'' she answered curtly. ''I wish to return to the stage.''

''Wait a minute,'' Leitzel said, recognition dawning. ''You're the . . . the lady Fingal said was married to Morgan.''

''Yes.''

''Fingal's not here now, you know,'' Leitzel said cautiously. ''He'll be . . . away for a while.''

''I did not imagine that he would be,'' Maeve said dryly.

Leitzel stared at her with suspicion but said only, ''I can't have irate husbands cluttering up my boat, you know."

Maeve knew a warm elation. "I am hired then," she said.

"Yes. But have you left your husband for good?"

"For good," Maeve assured him. "And you are hiring me right now?"

"You come with the highest recommendations of the captain."

There was a teasing familiarity in the man's voice that fired Maeve's anger, but she controlled it sternly. "Fine," she said calmly, "thank you."

"Don't mention it." And Leitzel set forth the terms. They were very generous, and Maeve's heart lifted with her relief and excitement. "Where are your things?"

"My . . . my attendant is waiting on the wharf now."

"Your attendant, is it? So we will have to find room for milady's maid?"

Maeve started to correct his impression of Amelie's title but concluded that it would be fruitless. Instead, she answered briefly, "Yes."

To her surprise Leitzel chuckled. "Very well, your highness. You can handle repertory?" he asked abruptly.

"Quite well."

Leitzel nodded and rose, striding heavily to the door. He opened it and yelled, "Barnaby!" The weathered hand who had directed Maeve to Leitzel's office came hurrying. "Bring this wo . . . this lady's trunks aboard. And show her the empty cabin in the actor's wing."

Maeve waited for the hand and Amelie to ascend. When Amelie reached her, Maeve took her hand and said, smiling, "It will be all right, Amelie. Everything is going to be all right!"

Not even pausing to hear Amelie's happy exclamation, the woman who was now Maeve Heron hurried down the deck, in the wake of the laden Barnaby, to their new home.

In the rushing whirl of the days and weeks that came after, Maeve was to come to know the real meaning of the form "repertory," which she had so casually remarked that she had mastered.

A repertory actress was required to act a half dozen varied parts on different evenings with dizzying sequence, and Maeve Heron was cast one evening as the wide-eyed heroine in a golden wig—for the heroines of the simple melodramas so popular along the Mississippi were invariably fair, just as the villainesses were as surely dark—and the next night, Maeve appeared with her own night-black hair, but heavily made-up and comically bedizened, in a role of broad wickedness.

Leitzel saw with satisfaction that Fingal Pearse had made no error. Maeve Heron was a magnificient actress, far too good for the parts that she was playing. And this pleased the canny Leitzel even more. For Maeve Heron's salary, generous as it was, was less than she could have commanded in New York. And Fingal Pearse would have something to say about that when he returned, Leitzel thought. *If* he returned.

For Maeve Heron, the passing time had brought a new content that was almost happiness. It was heaven to smell the greasepaint again, to walk in the hot glamor of the great stage lights, before the magnificent scenery that was equal to Wallack's, to don the varied costumes and to live the varied characters she portrayed.

She had almost stopped waking in the night, reaching out for the hand of William Morgan. Now, as the spring came, he seemed only a distant vision, a memory of gentle loveliness that was another life, a life that she was done with.

This afternoon, she stood with Amelie on the deck of the *Sally Barton*. In the manner of the free-and-easy players, Maeve was carelessly dressed in an old lavender gown of comfortable looseness, glorying in the feel of the wind in her disheveled hair.

"*Mon Dieu!*" Amelie exclaimed after an interval of silence. "I will be glad to be off this old brown river!"

Maeve did not reply at once, for she had come to love the broad brown waters, come to know with a kind of affection the towns and cities on the *Sally Barton*'s route—the high, emerald-green banks of Natchez, with its white, ruined splendor and almost junglelike vegetation; the great bustling port of Memphis, slowly coming back to life; and, to the northwest, the metropolitan life of St. Louis on the border of the Northern state, Illinois.

Days on the showboat had a carefree quality that lifted Maeve's spirits as nothing had ever done. She loved the free afternoons when the boat had docked at the larger cities. She and Amelie spent pleasant hours in the stores, but Maeve did not spend much.

For she was guarding her store of money for the day when there would be enough to establish herself again in New York.

And the generosity of William Morgan had made possible a wardrobe that needed little augmenting, even if she had come away with only half her possessions. She had left the Morgan family jewels, taking only the things that William had bought for her alone, disregarding Amelie's cynical disapproval.

Now Maeve admitted silently that Amelie had a point, at least about the river—the brown waters had taken on a turbulence that made her a bit uneasy. She had heard the actors talking of past floods. Looking down over the railing, she watched the driftwood of the river rush by in the water's eddies and whirls. A rising wind whipped at her blue-black hair, and a vagrant tress tangled in the long curled lashes of her left eye. She brushed the lock impatiently away.

"What are you doing without a hat?" Amelie asked with sudden sternness. "Your face will get burned and chapped in this wind."

"There is not much sun," Maeve answered absently, though indeed, the rising wind was ungentle on her pallid face. And she knew with amused certainty that Amelie would cream and bleach her face and hands tonight and smear her with buttermilk as soon as they were back to the cabin.

Maeve sighed, assailed by a feeling of deep loneliness. The other players on the boat avoided her; she had a feeling that it had something do with Fingal Pearse and that the rumor of her friendship with him set her somewhat apart. Early on she had asked Amelie what the other servants said about her, but Amelie had been evasive.

"Do they say that . . . Captain Pearse and I . . . ?" Maeve had begun an awkward question.

"No, nothing like that," Amelie had reassured her. "But it would be just as well," she added in a dry way. "At least it would keep the gentlemen in their places."

Wryly Maeve had been forced to agree that at least the news of her imagined relationship had ensured her privacy.

The *Sally Barton* was drawing in now to the landing of a little town between Mississippi and Tennessee named, Maeve remembered vaguely, something like Greenville.

It was not an interesting landing, so she barely looked at the shore when the *Sally Barton* plowed ahead. She heard in a dim way the sound of landing—the gangplank creaking and jerking over the side of the boat, seeming to fly into place as the steamer bumped an old wooden dock.

"Well," Maeve said lazily to Amelie, yawning, "a town

like this means *East Lynne* tonight.''

"And if Lady Isabel is full of freckles, she will be a pretty sight,'' Amelie remarked sourly. "Ah, these awful little places!'' she added with the scorn of the metropolite.

"Do you miss it so, Amelie?'' Maeve asked with shamed compassion. "I have been so selfishly involved with my own work that I have hardly listened when you spoke of your discontent.''

"Oh, Maeve, I am grateful to be with you!'' Amelie cried, taking the other's hand. "You have been so good and kind to me always; you have taken such care of me. It is just that . . . sometimes I do long for the city sounds and places.''

"We will have them again, I promise you.'' Maeve smiled reassuringly at Amelie. "But come, you are right—I will look like a guinea egg if we don't get in out of this light.''

And she was about to turn from the rail when the sight of a familiar figure on the ramp below caught her attention. Maeve gave a low cry of amazement.

"What is it?'' Amelie asked at once.

Without replying, Maeve Heron pointed with her white finger at the tall man ascending the ramp of the *Sally Barton*. He moved with an air of command, the misty half sunlight glimmering on his morning-colored hair. And in his hard, unburned face his ice-blue eyes were startling. It was Fingal Pearse.

Maeve stood at the rail, still staring, putting a nervous hand to her tangled hair. She saw then that Amelie had moved on along the deck in the direction of their cabin.

The man had reached the deck now and, smiling widely, bowed to Maeve. "Mme. Morgan,'' he said in that ironic voice that even now was able to make gooseflesh rise on her arms. "This is a pleasant surprise indeed. I want to thank you for your former hospitality.''

In a moment all of Maeve Heron's frustrated anger, long repressed, overtook her, and hardly knowing what she did, she rushed against the body of Fingal Pearse, crying out and pummeling at him with her small fists, "How dare you, you cold-blooded bastard! You have ruined my life, you have treated me like . . . like a fallen woman! Now you dare to stand there and thank me for my hospitality!''

"Maeve, Maeve Heron! Control yourself.'' Fingal Pearse grabbed at her arms and held her with a viselike grip around her fragile wrists.

She struggled in his relentless hold for a moment, then, realizing that the contest was so unequal as to be absurd, went limp. Fingal Pearse laughed softly, looking down at her, and whispered, "Little rebel spitfire!"

In a rush of remembering, she knew them as the very words he had used to her in that little cabin on the *Falcon*, the night he had stolen to her by the light of the flickering lanterns.

And a new, strange desire for him, tumultuous within her as the river tides she had come to know as home, roiled in her body. Helpless, she submitted to his urgent kiss and the feel of his demanding hands around her soft waist, careless of the staring deckhands and the coarse presence of Leitzel, who stood at the door of his office, chuckling.

The sound of the manager's vulgar mirth, however, brought Maeve Heron to her senses. She pulled herself away from the brutal grasp of the tall, blond man and slapped him with all her strength.

Then, overcome with weeping, Maeve Heron ran to the shelter of her cabin.

Fingal Pearse stared after her, smiling a crooked smile.

Leitzel's loud laughter greeted him. "Well, me boyo!" the manager said teasingly in a clumsy imitation of an Irish brogue. "The lady is a handful now, isn't she?"

An expression of blandness shuttered Pearse's swarthy face. "How goes it, Leitzel?" he asked in a not-too-friendly tone.

The manager's coarse face darkened with resentment. "You are still the Prince of the River, I see," he retorted.

"More than ever, Leitzel. Let's go into your room, my friend. We have a great deal to discuss."

When they were inside the manager's office and the door was closed against intrusion, Leitzel asked, "It's over then? Your problem in New Orleans?"

"For the nonce," Pearse replied in a careless fashion that maddened his hearer. The devil was afraid of nothing, Leitzel reflected, and nothing seemed to down him! "They had to dismiss the charges against me for lack of evidence. And the federal commander," Pearse concluded dryly, "seemed strangely reluctant to involve the Morgans. It seems that William Morgan is his fair-haired boy, not to speak of Ulysses S. Grant's. And yet, would you believe it, Major Morgan has resigned his commission."

Leitzel lit one of his evil-smelling cigars and questioned,

"And gone back North? I sincerely hope he will not show up here."

Pearse shrugged, increasing Leitzel's irritation; the manager remarked, nettled, "You don't seem to be disturbed by the thought."

"I can handle that . . . society boy."

"You seem to really hate him, Pearse. What more do you want? You have taken his wife—"

"Nobody," said Fingal Pearse lightly, "takes Maeve Heron. The lady belongs to herself alone." Leitzel was surprised at the note of yearning in the voice of the callous Pearse. "And you have hired her," he said, smiling at the manager.

"Yes. She is a magnificent actress."

"At what salary?" Leitzel named it, and Pearse snapped, "Double it."

"What? But, Pearse—"

"Double it."

"I take it, then, that you are in command of the *Sally Barton* again." Leitzel's reply was heavy with sarcasm.

"I own half the tub, you know."

But why have you really come back, Pearse? You had committed yourself for no more than a year."

"That, Leitzel, is my business," said Fingal Pearse, and he abruptly left the office, with the curious manager staring after him. A man with the reputation of Fingal Pearse, he judged, had not returned for the sake of a mere woman.

Maeve Heron's cabin, adjoining Amelie's, was near the *Sally Barton*'s stern and the perpetual wash of the giant paddle; the familiar sound had always lulled Maeve into sleep.

But this spring midnight she lay in wakefulness, listening to the sounds of the river and the rain. The advent of Fingal Pearse had shattered her hard-won calm to the extent that even her performance had been affected.

When, as Lady Isabel, she had shivered in the snowy park, hearing her comical cue—"Will you stay on here?"—Maeve Heron had known for an instant that dread blackness of mind, the actor's nightmare, when there was no memory at all. She had recovered, however, just in time, seeing for that instant the terror of the actor staring into her eyes.

Maeve stirred restlessly in her narrow bunk bed; something in the night, with its wild wetness and the neat confines of the cabin, recalled the night four years ago on the *Falcon*, the night that Fingal Pearse had entered her space, bringing with him such a tumult of emotion.

Abandoning sleep, she rose now from the bunk bed and donned a thick blue wrapper, for the air of the cabin was chilled with lateness and the strong wind that intruded from the deck below the door.

She wandered to the dresser and began to brush her long hair with nervous, rhythmic strokes. "This is not the *Falcon*," she said aloud, meeting her own green gaze in the glass. No! And she was not the unawakened child who had fallen under the spell of the captain of the *Falcon*! And been ravished, not loved by him, she thought savagely.

All that was done, Maeve resolved, beginning to be soothed by the silken rasp of the brush upon her hair. And she would never repeat again the lapse of this afternoon. Finally, when her arm began to tire, she put down the brush, feeling sleep start to steal across her limbs.

She was removing the wrapper from her shoulders when she heard a familiar footstep on the deck outside. The footsteps slowed and paused before her door. When she heard the expected knocking, Maeve hesitated, the wrapper sliding down her arms.

Then she slipped the garment around herself again and stole to the door, listening.

"Maeve."

It was Fingal Pearse.

"Go away, Captain Pearse," she replied clearly and coldly with her face against the doorframe.

"I have something to tell you."

"Tell me in the morning." Triumphantly she listened again and heard nothing but the wind and an uncomfortable shifting of feet. She could picture his dismay and smiled.

But then the knocking sounded once more, less soft, and she frowned.

"You must let me talk to you," Pearse said. "It is about Thomas. Thomas Rossar-Mescro."

Thomas! Her heart leaped and fluttered. Thomas.

At once she unlocked the door and stood aside for Fingal Pearse to enter.

To her surprise, he looked almost chastened, and his face was somber. His customary mocking smile was absent, and the coldness of his peculiar winter-colored eyes seemed warmed by some sorrowful knowledge.

Fingal Pearse did not touch her but remained standing by the door as she hastily closed it against the rain-filled wind. He was hatless, and his golden hair was dark with moisture.

"I have something to tell you," he said, and again Maeve knew a kind of soft surprise at the gentleness of his voice.

"It is about Thomas?" she asked with anxiety.

"Thomas is dead," said Fingal Pearse flatly, staring down at her with his strange light eyes.

"Dead." Numbly and with disbelief Maeve repeated the brief, terrible word. How hard it sounded, how final! she thought, and a searing pain attacked her throat and breast, a lump of unshed tears that coiled like a cold fist within her. "Dead," she whispered, and she moved to the bunk bed to sink down upon its narrow softness.

Fingal Pearse still stood in his former position, but his eyes followed her movements. His face was full of pity.

"How . . . how did you learn?" she asked then, her voice trembling.

Pearse took a wrinkled letter from his damp black coat. "It is all here," he said. He moved then, for the first time, to bring her the letter.

She took it, saying, "Thank you. I . . . I will not read it now." And she put the letter on the table by her bed. "It was . . . kind of you to bring me the news," Maeve added. "Particularly after this afternoon."

Fingal Pearse's mouth relaxed into a little ironic smile. Then he grew solemn again. "I knew this afternoon," he admitted, "but I could not bring myself to tell you then. It did not," he continued, the smile returning faintly, "seem the proper time."

Maeve Heron looked up at the tall man whose pale eyes so strangely mingled the coldness of the Vikings with the softer colors of the Gael. She reflected on what Andres had said so long ago of Fingal Pearse—"Thomas trusts him."

And the silent repetition of the old Gypsy's name brought the tears at last to the surface of her eyes. She felt them slipping down her cheeks, in a slow, soundless weeping that was more affecting to the man before her than the wildest sounds of grief.

Fingal Pearse sat down in the straight chair on the other side of the bunk bed and reached over to stroke Maeve's hair.

She was surprised at his gentleness, the almost brotherly feel of his hand.

With her trembling back to him, Maeve Heron could still see his hair, almost silver about his ears, below the dark, peaked cap he used to wear on the *Falcon*. In the glare of day at sea, she recalled, his pallid hair had gleamed like the sun of early spring in Tullaghoe. And his eyes, the light blue of the morning sky in winter, had seemed at once piercing and gentle, demanding and cool and wise.

She turned now to contemplate him, and his gaze was upon her; its coolness washed away her body's grief, as it had done so long ago after the death of Michael Rathmullan, even as the eyes' power filled her veins with the blue-white heat of a greater fire.

Maeve glanced at his seated form; its splendor still had the ability to shake her deeply. He was still so slender, yet the apparent strength of his limbs was undiminished, and he sat as a gladiator rested, ready at any moment to rise, combat-ready.

Maeve, in a quick flood of remembrance, lived again that night in her cabin on the *Falcon*; she saw in the dim light of the passageway the shadow of a tall, lean man, reached under her pillow for the little dagger Narilla had given her.

Feigning sleep, Maeve saw again under lowered lids the tall man draw near, felt his strong, long-fingered hand upon her head. And she remembered the melting of her limbs under his touch. Now, as then, she heard the words "madness and blindness and astonishment of heart."

Then she recalled his hands bruising her naked breasts and her body's freezing; his contemptuous words: "Your virtue is safe with me." But her virtue hadn't been safe with him, Maeve thought sadly, for after that there had been that afternoon in his hotel in New York, when she had anticipated so much but had received so little. He had taken her like a beast, Maeve thought angrily.

Yet warring with those memories and the image of her humiliation this afternoon were his latest kindness and the softness with which he contemplated her across the narrow width of the little bed.

"You are a very complicated lady," Fingal Pearse remarked, smiling at her.

She was chilled at the accuracy of his perceptions. It was almost as if he could read her mind.

"What do you mean?" she asked evasively.

"You are sure of only one thing, Maeve Heron," he replied. "You are sure only of the woman who walks upon the stage."

Maeve pondered this. Yet, feeling that his mental power over her was taking on the strength of his physical power, she answered with a question: "Why do you say that?"

"Because no man will ever be sure of you," Fingal Pearse declared. "Your emotions are wild as the wind, Maeve Heron, and as changeable. Not Morgan or Blaine, or any man, could ever know any peace with you at all. And it is that very quality that has brought me after you, all these years, from the night on the *Falcon* to the city of New York and the port of New Orleans." His smile was mocking again, but it seemed this time he mocked himself. "And now to this treacherous river."

She wondered at his declaration. He had not even touched her, yet his words seemed to stroke her like hot, hungry hands.

"I want to marry you, Maeve Heron. I want you to divorce William Morgan and marry me."

She stared. Then she commented, smiling, "I cannot believe my ears. Is this the man who said he could never marry anyone, not even me?"

"Mock at me, if you want. I deserve it. Yes, it is the very man."

"Once," she said gently, "I would have wept with delight, Fingal Pearse, to hear such words from you. But now"—her voice was a little sad—"it is not like that at all."

"I know," he said. He rose and looked down at her with all the force of his light eyes. "But I will not give you up, Maeve Heron. I am determined that no other man will have you. I will win you yet. Remember what I say. But I will not annoy you again until you come to me with an answer."

With one light touch upon her hair, Fingal Pearse left the cabin.

Maeve lay wakeful again for a long hour, listening to the driving rain against the open deck of the *Sally Barton*.

Chapter 20

WHEN THE next morning dawned, the crew of the *Sally Barton* surveyed the swollen river with thankfulness. The rain had ended sometime during the night, and the pallid sun revealed small increase in the height of the swirling water. The threat of flood, for the time being, had been averted.

But in the days that followed, Maeve Heron paid scant attention to the river. For the news of Thomas' death and Fingal Pearse's astonishing proposal had plunged her into an unhappy state blended of guilt and confusion. She knew a profound remorse for the years that had intervened since her last sight of the old Gypsy, years in which her own concerns had so overwhelmed her that she had never even tried to communicate with the old man. There had been months, indeed, when she had not even given him a thought.

And she had judged she was done with the maddening man named Fingal Pearse! Now he was a presence constantly intruding upon her peace. True, he had been as good as his word and after that late night had not approached her again in an intimate fashion or spoken again of his desires. Yet always, when he passed her on the decks or casually walked through the auditorium during a rehearsal, Maeve felt he was watching, waiting.

Almost a month passed in that peculiar manner, and this afternoon in early May, as Maeve stood with Amelie in the shade of the upper deck, watching the *Sally Barton* approach the Memphis port, she wore a face of such discomfort that Amelie remarked upon it.

"What is it?" asked Amelie. "You must stop this lingering on the death of your great-grandfather. He was so very old; he would have died," Amelie said in her practical Gallic way, "whether you were with him or not."

"I know," Maeve admitted. "It is . . . not only that." She had not yet told Amelie of Fingal Pearse's declaration.

"It is something about the handsome Captain Pearse, I doubt not," said Amelie shrewdly.

Maeve looked away, pretending to interest herself in the teeming wharves of the city they were approaching.

"Come now," Amelie said teasingly. "It is so, is it not?"

Maeve sighed. It was impossible to keep a secret long from Amelie. With an amused resignation, therefore, she told Amelie of what had happened that evening in her cabin.

"He is a man of enormous beauty," Amelie remarked frankly. "There, he is down there now."

Following the direction of her friend's dark glance, Maeve looked down toward the bow of the *Sally Barton*, where the lean figure of Fingal Pearse could be seen, towering over the men around him, calling commands as the boat entered with thumping grace into the slip.

"Yes." Maeve nodded. "Yes, I suppose he is." And she looked with new eyes on his slender power, the hair ruffled in the slight breeze, her hungry senses touched in spite of her by his physical splendor.

He did, she reflected, understand her as no man had ever done, even the all-forgiving William Morgan. Why then did she hesitate to accept him? Was it because she deeply knew that he would bind her, restrict her as William Morgan would never have deigned to do—that Fingal Pearse had the power to persuade her through her senses into a half-unwilling state of bondage, that she would awake from it with regret when it was too late . . . or because he took her like a . . . Hun?

These questions whirled in Maeve's brain as she observed Fingal Pearse on the deck below. But soon an interesting tableau distracted her from her musing. A quiet, elegantly dressed stranger who had been waiting on the wharf came eagerly up the lowered gangplank of the *Sally Barton* to greet the captain. He must have very important business, Maeve judged, for he seemed to be hardly able to wait until the plank was down.

She saw the stranger conversing earnestly with Fingal

Pearse, and then Pearse with an impassive face replied. It was impossible from that distance for Maeve to hear what they were saying; she could only watch their moving lips, their words drowned in the babel of the wharves.

But then she saw the stranger glance up, and he caught sight of her. With an angry face he said something more to Fingal Pearse, who took him by the arm. The stranger shook off Pearse's detaining grasp and stormed up the gangplank to the main deck. Surprisingly Fingal Pearse did not try to detain the man further.

Something in his demeanor told Maeve that the man was from New York, and she felt a strange excitement. The elegance of his suit and the careful cravat, the gleaming rightness of his hat and a certain unmistakable air of confidence spoke of a metropolis. Yet there was a faint air of raffishness that also hinted of the theater to Maeve's sensitive eyes.

Hardly knowing why, she moved away from the rail and toward the stairs leading to the lower decks. But the stranger had already reached her level, and he swept off his shining hat with a gallant gesture, smiling at her.

"Are you Miss Heron?" he called, walking quickly toward her, the breeze of the harbor disarranging his carefully combed white hair. His face was pleasant, with regular features, yet there was the kind of shrewdness in his glance that bespoke the man of business.

"I am," she said with the urban caution she had never abandoned.

Apparently her manner amused him, for something in it was so like his own. The man smiled broadly and said, "I am a representative of Daly's Theater in New York. I would like to talk with you."

With pleased surprise, she responded to the man's friendly smile and said, "Will you come into my cabin? We can talk there."

There was that in his manner that made such an invitation seem very natural to Maeve, and indeed, his matter-of-fact reception of it reassured her.

"I am Benjamin Leonard," the man said easily when they had reached Maeve's cabin. "I saw your performance in Greenville not long ago. And I'd like," he added bluntly, "to see you on a New York stage again. You were wonderful as Ophelia."

Maeve was overcome with gratitude, both for his warm praise and for the professional, nonjudgmental way in which he spoke. Nothing in his tone referred to the notoriety of the trial, or indeed of anything outside the world of her skills.

She murmured her thanks and said, "Please, won't you sit down?" He sat down casually on her little bunk bed and tossed his splendid hat on the table.

"I have written Mr. Daly about you," he said, "and he would like very much to audition you."

Maeve was at a momentary loss for words. Misinterpreting her silence, Benjamin Leonard queried, "Is there some obstacle to such a plan? How do you feel about this?"

"I am delighted," she answered frankly. "It is just that . . . your proposal has been so very sudden." She smiled. "I suppose I have become accustomed to the more leisurely pace of the South."

Benjamin Leonard laughed. "Forgive me for being so abrupt. I am used to stating my business quickly and settling it with dispatch." He rose from the bunk bed and picked up his hat. He reached into his neat breast pocket to draw forth a small white card.

"I will be at this address for several days. I hope that you will send word to me as soon as you have had a chance to think it over. Mr. Daly has authorized me to provide you with all expenses and to arrange your transportation to New York."

Dazzled, Maeve took the card from him.

"There is just one thing that puzzles me, Miss Heron."

"And what is that?"

"The captain," said Leonard, "this Captain Pearse . . . he told me that you were no longer on board. It was most mysterious. But my hardheadedness"—he laughed—"won out, as it happened."

He touched his hat to her and said, "I hope you will send word to me very soon." With that he was gone.

Maeve moved to the door and watched him walk down the upper deck and disappear down the stairs.

"So that is it," she said aloud. "That is what made me hesitate to answer." The determination of Fingal Pearse to bind her to him, even at the expense of all she valued, had made him lie to Benjamin Leonard. She felt a surge of anger, followed by a nameless apprehension that shadowed her new triumph.

Maeve Heron had often seen, in the plots of the dramas they performed, grotesque and uneasy parallels to her own tumultuous life.

In the perennial melodrama *East Lynne*, as the orphaned Lady Isabel, Maeve felt herself akin to the unfortunate woman left penniless when her titled father died, humiliated and mistreated in her uncle's home, saved by her marriage to the young hero. The villainous Francis Levinson, who persuaded Lady Isabel through deceitful means to run away from her husband, was identitifed with Fingal Pearse in Maeve's imagination, just as the upright, handsome Archibald Carlyle reminded her of William Morgan.

She mentioned this to Amelie. The latter had shrugged, uncomprehending, and remarked, "I can hardly see you in real life as a repentant figure."

Maeve could not help laughing at Amelie's clear-sighted skepticism, but the light blow struck at her deeply, for there were many nights and days of late when she had known a wistful yearning for the days with William Morgan.

There were other dramas, too, in which Maeve found a double significance; the cynical plays of Molière that Leitzel, with a stroke of daring, presented at the landings of the larger cities, were full of references to Maeve's own life.

This evening as Amelie prepared her for the part of Elmire in *Tartuffe*, the great French dramatist's comedy of morals, Maeve stared at herself in the glass. Her face was doll-like in its heavy makeup, her eyes exaggerated to wideness by paint and pencil, her powdered hair in a tall *fontage* with six ascending layers of curls, thrust with jeweled pins.

She touched the one long, narrow curl that fell over her creamy shoulder. The elaborate costume was one that Maeve took generally for granted, but she hated it tonight, for there was a look of garishness that recalled her ill-fated costume of the Mardi Gras. That she had then worn the trappings of a cynical era only increased, tonight, her sense of irony and sadness.

Now more than ever the character of Tartuffe presented itself to Maeve as Fingal Pearse, with his rascally speech, "I know the art of pacifying scruples. . . . There is a science, madam, that instructs us how to enlarge the limits of our conscience according to our various occasions. . . ." In contrast she remembered William Morgan, with his ever-giving love that had permitted everything to her, almost to the limit of treason to his country! On the other hand, the arrogant desire of Fingal Pearse threatened somehow to bind her. She could not forgive his attempt to avert the meeting with Daly's representative.

"Oh, Amelie, Amelie," Maeve cried in a melancholy voice that ill accorded with the lacquered frivolity of her gown and hair. "I have been such a fool."

Amelie's pretty face, the color of *café au lait*, looked back at the seventeenth-century lady in the glass. "What do you mean, *amie*?"

"I have ruined my life," Maeve replied brokenly.

"O-la-la!" Amelie scoffed in a cheerful fashion. "You are a silly woman. You have been approached by one of the most famous theaters in America; we will go to New York, and you will be famous and very happy."

The woman in the high curled wig with its glitter of jeweled pins looked up from the mirror into the mirrored eyes of Amelie. "I have done such wrongs to William Morgan. . . ."

"And yet?" Amelie asked teasingly, hearing the ambiguity in Maeve's tone. "And yet the spell of the Captain Pearse is not quite broken, is that not true?"

Maeve nodded. "What will happen, Amelie?"

"What is meant to happen," the other replied in her fatalistic manner, a reply that had never satisfied the strong-willed, self-driving Maeve. "But come now, it is almost time," Amelie urged her.

Through the half-open door of the dressing room Maeve could hear the rustle of the wide gowns of Mariane and Madame Pernelle; all of them were to enter together, with their servants, in the first scene of the opening.

Maeve hurried from the dressing room, turning sideways so that she might exit without injury to her voluminous gown.

Hearing Madame Pernelle's "Come, come, Flipotte, and let me get away," Elmire pronounced her first words in a high, silvery voice: "You hurry so, I hardly can attend you."

And Maeve Heron had no further memory of anything beyond the light concerns of the faithless lady of fashion Elmire.

But in the fourth act of the play Maeve found herself oddly distracted from the business at hand. She had glimpsed over the golden mist of the footlights a man in the second row of velvet chairs who seemed extremely familiar. His shadowed face had a peculiar expression, alternately smiling and sad.

Long-developed training enabled Maeve to deliver her lines, at the same time hearing—as if she were two women at once—the sense of the words to herself:

> Ah! How your love enacts the tyrant's role,
> And throws my mind into a strange confusion!
> With what fierce sway it rules a conquered heart,
> And violently will have its wishes granted!
> What! Is there no escape from your pursuit?
> No respite even?—not a breathing space?

As she continued the speech, Maeve heard, in those insincere protestations of Elmire, her own unease over the brooding pursuit of Fingal Pearse.

She was able to see now that the man in the second row was attending closely to all that was being enacted on the stage.

The scene that most disturbed her was to come near the end of the play, for it contained a speech by Orgon, Elmire's husband, that echoed to Maeve her own perfidy to William Morgan:

> Strange things indeed, for my own eyes to witness;
> You see how I'm requited for my kindness,
> I zealously receive a wretched beggar . . .
> Load him with benefactions every day . . .
> And he meanwhile . . . tries with black treason. . . .

Maeve, as Elmire, had no lines in the scene, and was required to stand with enameled poise throughout the bitter speech. Maeve's eyes for an instant roamed beyond the golden lights, and she made out, at last, the features of the quiet man. He was William Morgan.

So unreal was the sight of William Morgan that Maeve hardly credited his presence in the wings. As the other players hurried past, the women's voluminous dresses brushing against them, Maeve and William Morgan stood silent, staring at each other.

Neither seemed able to find words; Maeve was aware only

of the tall breadth of him before her, his handsome face sober
with wonder to look upon her.

At last she said, "Come, William, come to my cabin," for
she was vaguely aware of the staring eyes about them. Almost
blindly he followed as she went out onto the deck, not pausing
in her dressing room to remove her extravagant clothes, to exchange them for something more suitable. When they reached
the upper deck and were alone in the confines of her small
cabin, he closed the door with a gentle motion.

Again they stood facing each other, studying each other's
features. His, she saw, had a look of settled sadness that
touched her as nothing had ever done before. Suddenly he
moved toward her and took her hurtingly in his arms to kiss
her as if he could never bear to let her go again.

Having released her for a moment, William leaned back a
little to look down at her. It seemed his starving gaze could
not be sufficiently fed, for his dark eyes devoured endlessly
her painted eyes and reddened mouth, as if the dark eyes were
entering her with their avid scrutiny.

He could say only her name, over and over; his slender
hand cupped her satiny chin as once more he drew her close
and took her mouth.

She was overtaken with the shock of his sudden appearance; she trembled so that William, with his arm still
holding her, led her to the bed. He knelt down before her to
take her hands and kiss them repeatedly; then he laid his
ruffled head upon the lap of her voluminous gown, and she
touched his hair with a soft motion. His nearness burned.

William raised his head from her lap and looked up at her
face. And although he smiled with his old sweetness, she
could see, in the grim lines of his lean jaw and the darkness
below his melting eyes, the agonies he had suffered. He
slipped easily from his kneeling posture in a moment and sat
on the floor beside her, leaning his long length against the
little table. She could not take her eyes away from his face.

"I could no longer stay away," he said in a tired but joyful
voice. "No matter what you . . . no matter what has happened," he amended with quick grace. "I have resigned my
commission. And I have been," he added wryly, "wandering
aimlessly, trying to screw my 'courage to the sticking-place' to
approach you."

Maeve remembered then the first night he had called for her at Wallack's theater in New York. He had used the line from Shakespeare on that occasion, too.

"You have found it in your heart to forgive what I have done?" she asked in disbelief.

"All that is over," he replied soberly. "I have come to ask you to begin again with me."

"I have been offered," she said hesitantly, "an audition at Daly's Theater."

He gazed at her and said softly, "I understand. But there is no reason we cannot be together all the same."

Looking down upon him, Maeve began to know a molten burning that her body had not known before with him, even in the transports of their passion. And something in herself, profound and strong as the currents of the river where the boat rolled now, flowed warmly as she looked into the eyes of William Morgan.

"How is this possible?" she asked. "You heard the speech of Orgon in the play," she continued sadly. "I have been as treacherous to you, you who gave me everything."

He moved close to her again and, after kneeling by her, put his arms around her waist to draw her to him once more for a long, demanding kiss. "I told you," he repeated breathlessly, "all that is over and done with. Come back to me, Maeve. Come back. I cannot bear it without you. There is no hope, no light, no joyousness anywhere without you near me."

She was almost unbearably moved by his urgent declaration, and the expression in her eyes seemed to invite him, for he rose and sat beside her, enfolding her with his arms. She laid her head against him, suddenly knowing the wonder of an ancient comfort she had all but forgotten.

Maeve felt the vibrating rumble of his deep voice against her cheek as he told her of the time of their separation. A look of pain was on his lean face. Groaning, he leaned toward her again and took her face between his hard hands.

"Oh, Maeve, Maeve, do not send me away now! I have dreamed of this for so long, I've been so afraid. . . ."

"Afraid?"

"That you might not consent to come back to me." She felt a faint moisture on his cheek where it touched hers. She stroked the little place below his ear and felt the hectic racing of his pulse. Maeve kissed the pulsing spot.

"Will you?" he pressed her. "Will you come with me now?"

Before she could reply, they heard the heavy steps outside the door and drew apart a little at the harsh sound of a fist striking wood.

"Who would that be?" William asked, standing.

"I cannot imagine, at this late hour," she replied uneasily.

"Shall I answer?"

"Yes." She nodded and watched him moving to the door. When he opened it, Fingal Pearse was standing on the threshold.

"Major Morgan," Pearse said to William with ironic ceremony.

A look of cold anger froze Morgan's face, and he retorted, "What is it, Pearse? What do you mean by coming to my wife's cabin at this hour?"

Fingal Pearse laughed, and his laughter had an unpleasant sound. "Why, Major Morgan, I have been here many times before."

Maeve's indignant exclamation was drowned in Morgan's cry of terrible anger; he leaped upon Fingal Pearse to take the fair man's sunburned throat between his fingers.

Pearse twisted out of Morgan's grasp, kicking out at the dark man with his agile foot. But William Morgan stepped gracefully aside, and his right fist smashed into Pearse's jaw as he moved again toward the surprised captain.

"Come, then, Morgan," Pearse grunted, breathing in great gasps, "come out onto the deck."

"With pleasure," Morgan replied and stepped onto the deck after Fingal Pearse.

Almost numb with fear, Maeve rose from the bed and moved on unsteady feet after them, standing transfixed at the door of the cabin, unable to take her horrified gaze from the sight of the grim contest before her.

She stifled a scream, her hand against her heart, when she saw William Morgan's footing slip; the fist of Fingal Pearse cracked again William Morgan's jaw, and he fell with a crash down the short flight of stairs heading to the second deck. Maeve cried out and ran to the railing.

Below, she saw the crumpled form of William Morgan; he looked utterly lifeless. A small crowd had gathered on the main deck now and was staring up at the tableau on the second deck.

Maeve's head swam so she feared she would tumble over the railing onto the deck below to lie by William Morgan. But stubbornly she grasped the rail so tightly that her fingers ached, and peered down upon the sprawled form of her husband, unable to move from where she stood, sobbing loudly now with deep sobs that seemed to rend her whole being.

She heard a burly hand shouting to Leitzel, "It's all right, sir, the captain's in control." But in a split second William Morgan was stirring and had leaped to his feet again to tackle Fingal Pearse about the body, to bring him down on the deck.

Pearse's face was swollen with William Morgan's blows, but he never ceased to struggle in the other's grasp. Morgan knelt above him, delivering stunning blow upon blow to the captain's bleeding face.

Maeve hid her face for a moment in her shaking hands, hearing the renewed shouts of Leitzel and the massive deckhand. The stairs vibrated with the latter's heavy tread as he ran up them to the second deck.

With lightning swiftness Fingal Pearse was in command again; pushing at William Morgan with almost superhuman strength born of mighty rage, the blond man had risen to a kneeling position, throwing Morgan over backward.

"Stay away, Charley!" Pearse shouted, gasping for breath, at the burly hand. "Stay out of this, or I'll give you as good as I'm giving this bastard."

Indecisive, the massive deckhand paused on the stairs, and now Maeve could hear Leitzel's coarse call. "Leave them alone, Charley! I think the captain's been waiting for this for a long time."

Maeve saw Fingal Pearse's grim smile in the moonlight; it was as if he had spoken his own violent agreement with the manager's words. The half-smile chilled Maeve Morgan's blood, and she drew a shallow breath, waiting to see what the dreadful encounter would bring.

She winced at the sound of Pearse's blows upon the face and body of William Morgan; she knew she would never forget that horrible sound—like a wooden mallet pounding a great ripe melon until it smashed into pulpy slivers.

She felt a rising nausea; the whole night seemed to swim,

Patricia Cloud

and the ghastly vision of the two men struggling in the moonlight, like gods of night and day with their dark and golden hair, became misty before her.

I will not faint, Maeve cried out silently. *I will not faint*.

For now she must not take her eyes from the battle; she knew it was a contest to the death. Pearse, she was certain, would have concealed about him the knife he habitually bore. And likely William Morgan carried his Army pistol.

A contest to the death! her mind repeated sickly. One of the men below, both men she had loved, would die. The dark, gentle man who was William Morgan or the incorrigible golden son of Vikings who was Fingal Pearse.

The dark realization flooded Maeve's fear-weakened body like a dread wave of the sea, and she saw Fingal Pearse battering the face of William Morgan. Images of past days flashed now before her inner sight—images of Captain Fingal Pearse and Major William Morgan.

Horrified then, she saw Pearse reach into his belt, and the moonlight glinted on something of silvery metal. The dagger! Maeve screamed then, a piercing scream that must have rattled Fingal Pearse. For the briefest portion of an instant, he was caught off guard, and William Morgan, pressing his advantage, made a quick, desperate motion with his arms, a scissorslike chop that knocked the dagger from Pearse's hold.

Cursing, Pearse tried to retrieve his weapon, but Morgan staggered up and brought down his booted foot with great force on Fingal Pearse's reaching hand.

Pearse cried out like a maddened bull, and Morgan, having snatched up the dagger, faced Pearse now in the moonlight. They were crouching like two fierce warring animals, facing each other on the narrow deck, waiting.

"Have you had enough?" Maeve heard William Morgan cry out to Fingal Pearse.

"Not until you die, Morgan." The breathless reply of Fingal Pearse struck at Maeve like a cold blast of wind, and she began to shake throughout her slender body.

Pearse began to move toward William Morgan, and Maeve could see now that Morgan had no desire to kill the other man, for he moved in feints and darts and with bobbing steps, like a dancer, from the advancing captain's path.

"Don't come any nearer, Pearse!"

Fingal Pearse, unheeding, moved on toward William

Morgan, who was standing with his back to the rail. Morgan threw the dagger over the railing.

The struggle between the two men began anew, and as they wrestled with each other, they moved out of Maeve's line of vision. She was so frozen with terror that her feet would not move. Now, in desperate ignorance, she could only hear the battle on the deck below her, only surmise at the identity of the body that made a quick, terrible splash on the swirling water.

Maeve heard the shouts of the crew, heard someone bellow, "Heave to! Heave to!" But it was too late to divert the *Sally Barton*. As she leaned limply now against the rail, Maeve's ears were assailed by the men's cry of horror, catching the words "The wheel! The paddle-wheel's got him!"

She realized then that the fallen man had been struck by the inexorable paddle and gone completely under. Her legs at last gave way, and she found herself kneeling on the deck.

Slowly, ever so slowly then, there came the sound of a man's stumbling feet ascending the stairway. First there emerged the disheveled head and the bruised face, then the weary body of the man she had so long awaited, in her uncertainty and yearning. There was no uncertainty now as she watched him coming toward her.

Leitzel was behind him. The manager said meaningly, "There has been an accident . . . a bad one. Now leave the *Sally Barton*, and let us hear no more of it."

EPILOGUE

FEW COULD turn their eyes away from the woman on the landing.

Let them look then, she thought with amused defiance. And she paused a deliberate instant, her gray-gloved hand at rest along the gilded banister.

Her lights and shadows fairly took the breath; the inky hair drawn back into a heavy coronet had a hint of midnight blue, enhancing milk-glass skin so fine it seemed virtually poreless. And her vivid gown annoyed the women in its mocking simplicity, deepening the blackness of her hair, making her neck and bosom glow like silk before a candle flame.

The men in evening dress staring upward from the lobby knew only that she was beautiful, but she aroused the envious curiosity of many women. With all her striking looks, there was nothing vulgar in the woman on the stairs; she bore herself with dignity. And in that era of bows and flounces, when fashionable ladies' ruffles were innumerable in shot silks, Watteau stripes and plaids and their intricate hair was massed with flowers, the gown of the woman on the stairs reproved even as it bowed to the prevailing mode. It looked like next year's dress, and that was unforgivable.

The color of an American Beauty rose, the gown was a thin velvet; the skirt, drawn tightly back about the narrow waist and sweetly swelling hips, cascaded into a few soft ruffles that echoed the graceful petals of the rose itself. The short train swirled like a small fiery wave on the dark-green carpet, as if the carpet were a great leaf for the flower of the woman. Her only ornament was an emerald pendant set in misty filigree worn on an almost invisble chain about her long white neck.

She was unclassifiable. The woman wondered if any of them would recognize her now; memories had grown dim in the festive whirl of 1870 New York. There was a murmur among the women, who saw in her a quality alien to themselves. The repressed mischief of the green, slanting eyes, the lips' defiant tilt, not quite smiling, marked her as more than an idle lady of fashion.

The little drama was enacted for only a moment; suddenly through the crowded lobby a very tall man in faultless evening dress strode forward, smiling up at the vivid woman on the stairs.

Her sculptured face with its high cheekbones, which had been almost expressionless, relaxed in an answering smile, and she came with quick grace down the green-carpeted stairs to meet the newcomer. The man tossed his cloak to an attendant, held out his hand for the identifying ticket, without taking his eyes from the woman's. He bent and kissed her gloved hand. Then he offered her his arm, and they proceeded to the dining room.

The space was wide and glittering, where lights played upon a central fountain whose murmur mingled with the discreet bubble of low voices, the chiming collision of silver and fragile china. The diners in the restaurant reacted much the same as the observers in the lobby.

An obsequious waiter seated the tall pair at a small table beside one of the narrow windows shut against the autumn chill; they were screened by tall plants in great carven tubs.

Both the woman and the man, for all their elegance, had an uncomfortable air. They were not cozy; it was as if they had brought into the gaslit room the scent of the October wind, a wind of distant places that stirred the dark trees beyond the long panes.

The man spoke to the hovering waiter in the tone of a man accustomed to ordering; when the waiter withdrew, the man whispered something to the bright-gowned woman. She threw back her head and laughed in a free, unfeminine manner. The eloquent eyes of her companion were quickly tender. He gazed at the woman's gloves, which she was now removing, and an envious diner near them caugh the phrase "a rainy garden."

The waiter wheeled in a bottle of wine nested in a silver bucket; there was a popping cork, a foaming, a reverent decanting. And as the man and woman raised their glasses, the neighboring diner heard him say, above the murmur of the fountain, "And there was lightning in my blood." It was declaimed like the line of a poem. The vivid woman, listening, sat for an instant of enchanted stillness, her glass arrested halfway to her lips. She seemed to be remembering.

Maeve recalled that other night five years ago when she had dined in this very room with Fingal Pearse and felt the intense, dark gaze of William Morgan. Now she smiled at her husband and asked, "Did you tell them your decision?"

"Yes. I rejected their proposal. I want to be free to travel with you this next year. And have you come to your decision?"

"I have," she answered, smiling. "After the long confusion, I have come to a new kind of uncertainty. So I leave my life to you."

The man looked at her with adoring eyes and said, "I give it back to you, Maeve. You belong where I saw you tonight. And now that Father's dead and I am in control, it's possible to form your own company if you wish. I want you to go on with it."

Maeve bowed her shining head. "All this for me, who have wronged you so."

"I would wrong the world if I took you from your gift. Besides"—he laughed—"I'd be very bored with an ordinary wife. As it is, I can go to sleep with Juliet and breakfast with Lady Macbeth."

She looked up then, with the fire of enduring passion in her Gypsy eyes. "I love you," she whispered. "How I love you, William Morgan."